W9-BTF-462

ALTERNATE GENERALS II

BAEN BOOKS by HARRY TURTLEDOVE

Alternate Generals (editor)
Alternate Generals II (editor)
The Case of the Toxic Spell Dump
Thessalonica
Down in the Bottomlands (with L. Sprague de Camp)

The War Between the Provinces series:
Sentry Peak
Marching Through Peachtree
Advance and Retreat (forthcoming)

The Fox novels:
Wisdom of the Fox
Tale of the Fox

ALTERNATE GENERALS II

Edited by
HARRY TURTLEDOVE

ALTERNATE GENERALS II

A Baen Books Original

Baen Publishing Enterprises
P.O. Box 1403
Riverdale, NY 10471
www.baen.com

ISBN: 0-7434-3528-1

Cover art by Dru Blair

First printing, July 2002

Library of Congress Cataloging-in-Publication Data

Alternate generals II / ed. by Harry Turtledove
p. cm.
ISBN 0-7434-3528-1
1. War stories, American. 2. Generals—Fiction I. Title: Alternate generals two. II. Title: Alternate generals 2. III. Turtledove, Harry.

PS648.W34 A79 2002
813'.0108358—dc21

2002018604

Distributed by Simon & Schuster
1230 Avenue of the Americas
New York, NY 10020

Production by Windhaven Press, Auburn, NH
Printed in the United States of America

10 9 8 7 6 5 4 3 2 1

TABLE OF CONTENTS

ALTERNATE GENERALS II

American Mandate

James Fiscus

September 1918. World War I nears its end in Europe, and the Ottoman Empire offers to surrender to the United States. The British, eager to keep the French out of Constantinople and the Straits, urge President Wilson to accept. A month later, a small American force steams into the Golden Horn. At the Versailles Conference, America accepts a League of Nations Mandate over Constantinople and other parts of Turkey. General of the Armies John Pershing commands American forces.

Smedley Butler stood on the upper walk of the Galata Tower, the streets of Constantinople's European district winding down the low hill to the Golden Horn and the Bosporus below him. The iron railing was hot from the late August sun. He stared east across the dark blue water of the Bosporus to the shore of Anatolia. Smoke rose from Üscüdar, the shattered Asian suburbs of the imperial city, where Dwight Eisenhower and his company had died as

Turkish Nationalists drove American troops from Asiatic Turkey. He looked south over the narrow flow of the Golden Horn to Stamboul, the ancient center of Constantinople. The minarets and domes of Süleyman's great mosque were bright in the early afternoon sun, as were the slender towers of the other great mosques of the Ottoman sultans.

"Will the Nationalists move more men across, General?" The young marine second lieutenant commanding the observation post shifted nervously.

"No need to. Mustafa Kemal already has an army behind us. Besides, we have the Governor General's yacht to help."

The *U.S.S. Arizona* rode at anchor half a mile off the Golden Horn, her twelve 14-inch guns aiming beyond Butler to the Thracian Plain and the Nationalist army infesting the city. Aft of her rear turret, an awning blazed white in the afternoon sun, shading Governor General Albert B. Fall's reception for the allied ambassadors. Smedley handed the binoculars to the lieutenant and turned to enter the ancient stone tower. Butler's movements revealed a wiry toughness earned from three decades' campaigning as a marine.

Explosions slapped behind him. He spun around as another explosion banged across the water. A white fountain spouted from the far side of the *Arizona*. Smoke, gray turning black, billowed over the ship. Shock froze Butler for an instant.

"Call Army headquarters. Order Colonel Patton to full alert."

Butler was breathing heavily from his charge down the interior steps of the tower as he jumped into the rear seat of his open staff car. "Customs dock."

Smedley's aide and Army liaison, Major Shaw, asked, "General, what's happened?" Shaw's gaunt face showed his concern.

Butler gripped the top of the door as the car bounced down

the cobbled street. “Explosions on *Arizona*. Can’t tell if the Navy blew themselves up or if the Turks are attacking.” The blast of the car’s horn forced a way through the crowd of European and Turkish pedestrians. The third and fourth stories of the stone and wooden houses loomed over the Rolls Royce as it slid around a sharp corner onto Istiklal Street. The driver swerved, just missing a small red trolley car, and accelerated toward the water.

The explosion twisted the deck of *Arizona* from under John Pershing, hurling him against the aft turret. He dropped to one knee but refused to fall further. A cloud of oily smoke swept across the battleship’s fantail. Pershing pulled out a handkerchief and tied it over his nose and mouth. “Damn little good this will do.”

“General Pershing, sir, are you hurt?”

The concerned face of an ensign hovered above the general. “I don’t think so, son.” Pershing stood slowly, testing his balance, feeling his sixty years. He coughed deeply, trying to clear the smoke from his lungs, but only drawing in more. “How is the ship?” He reached to straighten his hat and found it missing.

“Don’t know, sir. Captain Hahn and Admiral Kessler were both forward showing some pasha around. With the general’s permission, I must get to my station.”

“Go.” The ship jerked and listed heavily to starboard. Civilians attending the reception shoved past Pershing to the railing. Pershing saw an Army major who commanded the governor general’s honor guard. “Reynolds, organize the evacuation here. The Navy is busy trying to save the ship.”

“Sir.”

Pershing scanned the deck for Governor General Fall’s shock of white hair, seeing him far aft, surrounded by a small cordon of aides. As he neared Fall, Pershing called, “Is your launch near, Governor?”

Fall ignored Pershing, helping an American oilman

toward a rope ladder recently tied to a stanchion. He turned to Pershing. "Best hurry, General."

Pershing heard a woman's scream of "Sally," and turned. An American woman bent to help a girl of about five, who sat on the deck holding her leg and crying. Blood stained the hem of the child's yellow dress. An older girl in a matching outfit clung to the woman, her eyes wide with fear.

Pershing shoved his way back to the small group, and knelt by the youngest girl. "Here, let me see." Pershing gently examined the girl's leg, which had a slight cut. Emptiness gripped him, as he realized the girl was only a year or two older than Mary Margaret and that the older girl was near Helen or Anne's age, when all had burned to death before the war. He glanced up at the woman, filled by memories of Frankie, dead in the same fire. He forced himself to concentrate on the present, glad that his touch seemed to comfort the girl. "I don't think it's serious, Madam."

The woman looked down, fear fading as she recognized Pershing. "General, is the ship sinking?"

"Not till you're safe." Pershing spotted Reynolds. "Get these people to the launch, Major."

A rumbling explosion—felt through the deck more than heard—shook the massive battleship. Pershing stumbled as *Arizona* listed further. At the fantail, he helped a wounded sailor climb over the rail, and felt the man slip from his hands into the arms of sailors on a local caique. He glanced at his hands, seeing the blood and blackened skin that had peeled from the sailor's arms. Pershing wiped his hands on his uniform, trying to ignore the charred-lamb stench of burned human flesh.

"General Pershing." A Navy lieutenant, his white uniform covered in grime, saluted. "Sir, the fire's near the forward magazine."

"Can you flood it?"

"No water pressure. Please abandon ship, General."

Pershing fought his instinct to stay, to help the wounded,

knowing his command was ashore. "I'm sorry, Lieutenant." Pershing turned to the stern and climbed down into the steam launch, crowding onto a deck packed with sailors and a few civilians. Fall and the oil tycoon stood on the far side of the launch.

The boat dropped away from the battleship on the fast current, moving out of the heavy smoke from burning bunker oil. Pershing yelled to the boatswain at the wheel, "Get us around to the bow so we can see the damage."

The launch sliced through the calm water toward the dreadnought's bow. The *Arizona*'s port side appeared undamaged, but the ship's heavy list stabbed her 14-inch guns upward, twelve great barrels silhouetted against the sky. The launch rounded the sharp bow.

The foredeck of *Arizona* vanished in a ball of flame that billowed above the tall masts. Pershing saw—or imagined, for he was never sure—both forward turrets lift upward before crashing back through the main deck. The shock of the explosion smashed into Pershing, knocking him into the crowd of sailors. Sound roared over him. He raised his arms in protection against falling debris.

The dreadnought shuddered and rolled. Her tall basketweave masts dipped into the Bosporus, her guns jutting upward. The screams of crewmen flung into the sea rose above the death rattle within the armored hull. The ship vanished beneath the roiling surface. Oil carried fire across the blue water.

Old Glory and Butler's red flag with his single brigadier's star snapped in the wind as Smedley leapt from his still-moving car. A growing throng of Turks and Europeans crowded the small plaza, voices raised in half a dozen languages Butler recognized, and a dozen he didn't. Black smoke rose from the burning oil marking *Arizona*'s grave. Smedley stared in shock at the flock of small boats circling, seeking survivors. "It only took me ten minutes to get here. Battleships shouldn't die that quickly."

A marine sergeant, a stocky, powerful man with gray hair and a face lined from decades of campaigning, saluted sharply. "The swabbies say Turks floated a mine to her on the current, but nobody knows, General."

"Where's Pershing, Sergeant Cooper?" Butler always felt rapport with Cooper, a relic of the old Marine Corps whom he remembered from the march on Peking and the Panama Battalion.

"With the Governor General, I hope, sir. His launch is picking up survivors."

Butler glanced around the long, narrow promenade, only a few feet above the swiftly moving Bosporus. Four- and five-story stone and brick buildings, mainly occupied by European or local Greek-owned businesses, crowded the waterfront in a jumble of pastels and stonework. Behind them, buildings climbed the low hill to the medieval gray stones of the Galata Tower with its layer-cake crown of balconies. The crowd grew rapidly, and Butler's hand brushed his holstered .45 at the thought of yet another riot sweeping the city.

Smedley relaxed slightly as two trucks loaded with marines bounced to a stop. "Good timing," Butler said. "Major Shaw, keep the promenade clear, but go easy. The city could go up like a ton of dynamite. Don't light the match."

"I understand, sir." Shaw saluted.

"Sergeant, where's your phone?"

Cooper pointed to a low wooden shack. "Inside, General."

Butler stepped into the small guard post, his boots clicking on the plank floor. He cranked the handle on the phone.

"Headquarters, Lieutenant Zack."

"General Butler here. Is the garrison on alert?"

"No, sir. Not without Colonel Patton's orders. I'm trying to reach him, sir."

"Where is Colonel Patton?"

"Not quite sure, sir. He's playing a polo match against the wogs, General, over in Stamboul." The answer came with obvious reluctance. "Civilizing them, he said."

Smedley Butler took off his broad-brimmed campaign hat for a moment and wiped sweat from his forehead with his sleeve, brushing his dark hair back, using the gesture to bring his temper under control. "Full alert. Now. Send the Army to reinforce the perimeter."

"Yes, sir."

"Marine riot squads into the streets. If the residents of Stamboul see this as a signal to attack foreigners, the sultan's police won't stop them. Send every vehicle you can spare to move the wounded to hospital."

"Yes, sir, General."

"Damn Patton!" Butler said in a harsh whisper as he walked from the building. "Aristocratic bastard should be on duty, not playing polo. No wonder the Turks ambushed him in Armenia."

"We finally have some ambulances, sir." Sergeant Cooper saluted. "And the governor general's launch just landed."

Butler glanced at the flock of aides circling Fall as he walked away from his launch. The governor general's shock of white hair was like a flag in the center of the crowd. His voice, loud as always, carried his New Mexico drawl across the plaza.

Butler pushed through the gaggle of sycophants around the governor general. "Governor Fall, was General Pershing injured?"

"Nigger Jack's playing nurse . . ." Recognizing Butler, Fall sputtered to silence, then continued, his voice petulant. His bronzed face, white hair and drooping mustache made him look like a carnival pitchman. His blue eyes were narrow and cold. "Pershing is still on my launch. Bring him to me, General Butler."

Pershing's normally immaculate uniform was covered in soot and dirt. He helped a sailor, whose right leg twisted hideously at the knee, stagger to the dock. Butler took the sailor's other arm and the two generals eased the man to a stretcher.

"Glad you made it ashore, General. We were afraid you'd been caught in the explosion."

"There were children aboard. I could not abandon them to a fire." Pershing's voice broke slightly as he talked.

"I understand, sir," Smedley said.

"General Pershing, we must talk. Now." Albert Fall's drawl cut through the cries of the wounded. He indicated the tall, chunky oilman he had escorted from the sinking *Arizona*. "You have not met Mister Walters. He landed from the *Princess Matoika* yesterday to sign a new concession with the sultan's government. We must stop the Nationalists, General. They refuse to honor the sultan's agreements."

"Mister Walters, you will excuse us, sir, as this conversation may involve military matters," Pershing said.

Fall started to object, then followed Pershing and Butler into the nearby guard shack. "General Pershing, the Army has allowed Mustafa Kemal and his followers to become an irritation. Get rid of this bandit."

"Mustafa Kemal and the Turkish Nationalists have just driven a hundred and fifty thousand Greek troops from Anatolia. He has twenty thousand of his men at our backs in European Turkey." John Pershing's tone made his contempt for Fall clear. "We have twenty-five hundred troops holding our perimeter and General Butler's fifteen hundred marines holding the city. If we stay in Constantinople and the Turks attack, we die, Governor. We must evacuate."

"I give you orders, General. You do not order me," Fall nearly shouted.

"I advised President Wilson to reject this mandate. He did not. With Wilson gone, President Harding refuses to send more troops, and yet you block a diplomatic solution with Mustafa Kemal. The American Mandate is over, Governor."

"I am not here to surrender American interests to a wog," Fall said, his New Mexico drawl thicker as his voice rose again. He pulled out a cigar and lit it, not offering one to Pershing or Butler.

"You don't defend American interests, Governor. You defend American companies," Butler said. "You ordered the sultan to revoke European oil concessions and give them to Americans. There is a price for that. The French signed a treaty with Kemal last year. The British are about to. You have isolated us from European help to defend your racket."

"We do not need Europe, General Butler. You didn't run from the Niggers in Haiti. Why do you run from the Turks?" Fall puffed a cloud of cigar smoke into the air.

Butler spun and walked to the far side of the room so as not to strike the politician. Fall's voice rose behind him, "General Pershing, remove this man from his command."

"No, Governor, I shall not."

As Fall stalked from the guard shack, Butler stepped back to Pershing. "My apology for losing my temper, sir."

"None needed, General Butler." A smile softened Pershing's expression for an instant. "You have, I hope, informed your father and the Naval Affairs Committee he chairs of developments here?"

"Yes, sir. I am told Harding still loves the man. Mister Fall raised much money for the party."

"Money is power, General, but I too have contacted friends in Washington." Pershing coughed heavily, clearing the tightness from his lungs. "I will not have my men die in this city to save Albert Fall and his cronies a few dollars."

The evening sun burnished the calm surface of the Golden Horn and sparkled from the forest of minarets rising above the Ottoman capital. Jazz flowed from the Pera Palas hotel behind Butler. His fresh uniform and the lack of his .45 increased the peaceful feel of the night, but he knew the feeling was false. Butler turned his back on the city and watched Sergeant Cooper cross the veranda. They exchanged salutes.

"How's the city?"

"Five men beaten by a mob over in Stamboul, but not seriously hurt. Antiriot squads showed up and the Turks ran."

"It won't be that easy stopping the Turkish army," Butler said, wishing again that America had never accepted the Turkish surrender and been drawn into the politics of colonies and oil.

"General Butler, I talked to a Turk who was in the sultan's navy during the war. He saw torpedo tracks in the water."

"Where was he?"

"On a caique off *Arizona*'s starboard side."

"Could it be a translation error?"

"No, sir. He worked for the British Embassy before the war. Speaks English good enough."

"I want to meet him tomorrow, Sergeant." Butler returned Cooper's salute, and walked slowly into the Pera Palas, tucking his hat under one arm, and passing through paneled hallways to the bar. The room blazed with electric lights.

Straight and trim in a clean uniform, Pershing stared out a window at the brief twilight. Lieutenant Zack stood with several American and British officers a few feet from Pershing.

Zack saluted Butler, who repressed a smile. "I respect your salute, Lieutenant, but I'm uncovered. You've only seen me under arms, when I keep my hat on indoors as you Army boys do all the time."

"I forgot, sir."

"That's all right, Lieutenant." Butler moved on to Pershing. "General Pershing . . ."

Pershing held up one hand. "Georgie Patton was killed this afternoon, General."

"How, sir?" Butler felt the shock of the news twist his gut.

"He was playing polo. Shot from the crowd by a sniper. Fifth man this week. As usual, no one was caught."

Pershing took two Scotches from a passing waiter and handed one to Butler. "The surgeon said he was killed by a ball from an old musket. Something left over from the days of the Janissaries. Georgie might have liked that." He raised his glass. "Colonel Patton!" He drank deeply.

Butler echoed Pershing's toast, thinking at the same time that not much had been lost with Patton, except a commander who wasted his men in battle. Butler was certain that if Patton hadn't been wounded in Armenia he'd have stayed in command and played Custer. Never would have fought his way back to Trabzon the way Bradley did. Pershing's voice yanked Butler from his thoughts.

"General Butler, your news?"

"Yes, sir. We found a man who saw torpedo tracks before *Arizona* exploded."

"Nonsense." A rear admiral Butler recognized as one of the governor general's toadies moved closer. "The Turks don't have a submarine and we'd have seen a surface ship. He saw a school of fish."

"The Turks captured a French boat during the War that we have not recovered. Several German boats are still missing in the Mediterranean." Pershing's voice rose in anger. "You are not doing your job if you don't know that, Admiral Simon. Now that you have replaced Admiral Kessler as chief of my naval forces, you will correct your inattention. General Butler's suggestion is credible."

"Even if the Turks had a submarine, they couldn't run it. And if they could get it away from the dock, they couldn't hit all of Asia with a torpedo." Fall stood in the center of his darkly paneled office, puffing clouds of smoke from his cigar.

"The Turks couldn't stop the British at Gallipoli, either, but Mustafa Kemal did. And he couldn't drive the Greek Army into the sea." Pershing's anger flared at the politician. "Look across the Bosporus to Anatolia. You'll see Mustafa Kemal's army, not King Constantine's."

"The British destroyed themselves at Gallipoli, and the Greeks are little but wogs living in ruins their fathers left them. American civilians will evacuate on the *Princess Matoika,* along with your wounded. After they steam, you shall defeat the Turks," Fall said. "We will not surrender our concessions."

Pershing coughed heavily, waiting for his breath to return before talking. "That liner will carry five thousand men, women, and children. She can not leave the Golden Horn if the Turks have a submarine waiting."

"The *Matoika* will do as I order, and so shall you, General," Fall said. He turned his back on both generals, dismissing them.

Butler and Pershing stalked down the hall in the Palazzo Corpi, their footsteps echoing in unison through the old American Embassy building. "I'd like to know how much that bastard skimmed from the oil concessions," Butler snapped.

"At least as much as Gulbenkian, according to a cable from Washington," Pershing said.

"Mister Five Percent and his American twin."

"Except that Fall took the money under the table," Pershing said, thinking, Charlie Dawes is a wonder at finance, and that's what it took to get that information. Always good to have the right man in the right place.

Marine guards snapped salutes as the two generals walked quickly down the wide steps set in the building's classical façade. Pershing led the way back toward the Pera Palas. He stood a moment listening to the clear notes of a Dixieland pianist.

"Find that submarine and destroy it, General."

Late morning, and the summer's heat was already building. A pack of wild, raw-boned dogs lazed in the narrow street. Some snapped over scraps of food tossed by passing Turks. Butler and Cooper, both dressed as merchant seamen, instinctively avoided the pack's spoor.

"I suppose the dogs keep the rats under control," Smedley said to Cooper in a near whisper. Butler knew that the two marines stood out, but hoped to draw less attention on foot than in his car. The anger of the city was directed at the American military. Civilians had been relatively safe.

The three- and four-story buildings, their upper floors overhanging the street, dimmed the afternoon sun. The brightly painted houses often had irregular shapes, built to match the turns of the street as it wound up the hill. The Turkish women who came to the Para Palas or the other European buildings north of the Golden Horn often dressed as Europeans. Here in Stamboul, long skirts, headscarves, and thin veils covered most of the women. Some of the men still wore turbans and baggy pants and jackets instead of the fez and European suits.

The street opened into the tree-filled plaza around the mosque of Ahmed I. Six minarets stabbed gracefully into the sky around the massive structure. Ranks of small domes rose as if to support a great central dome. The two marines moved quickly past the low arches surrounding a courtyard attached to the main building, passing the Egyptian and Roman obelisks that had once decorated the Byzantine Hippodrome.

Butler and Cooper skirted a marine antiriot squad that watched the vendors in an open market. The two marines entered a side street that led them away from the gray domes of the Sultanahmed and wound their way through a new pack of curs. The dogs refused to move for mere pedestrians. The street widened at an intersection. A dozen dogs stared at each other in the middle of the plaza, teeth bared and hackles raised, protecting the territories of rival packs. Other dogs slept in the shade.

"There's Süleyman," Cooper said, indicating a tall, powerfully built Turk who waited in a coffee shop across the intersection. The Turk's black suit and dark fez gave him the look of a merchant or bureaucrat. Süleyman stood as the two marines joined him.

"Süleyman, this is General Butler."

"Efendim." The Turk bowed slightly, his voice carrying respect without subservience. "Brave men died when your ship sank, Efendi. May God show them mercy."

The marines accepted cups of strong, sweet coffee from a waiter. "Süleyman Efendi," Butler said, "you saw torpedo wakes?"

"Evet, Efendi. Three or four." Süleyman indicated several Turkish men standing across the street. "The waiter is my cousin, but it is better if we talk in the back where we are not watched." He wiped coffee from his thick, black mustache, and stood, moving his six-foot frame with the ease of an athlete as he led Butler to the rear of the building. Cooper stayed in the coffee shop, watching the street.

The carcass of a recently butchered goat hung by the back door, the metallic scent of its blood filling the small storeroom in which Butler and Süleyman talked.

"Süleyman, why do you help us?"

"From the time Sultan Mehmet captured Constantinople until this day, my family served the Osmanli. If I betray the sultan, I betray my family."

"But you help foreigners?"

"You support the sultan. Mustafa Kemal does not."

Looking at the man, and judging him, Butler decided to trust the Turk. "Can you find where the Nationalists keep the submarine?"

Süleyman smiled. "Efendi, I do not need to find it. Near Bursa a cove shelters the submarine."

"Can we send in ships?"

"Mines would sink your ships before they reached the cove, Efendi."

"How close can we land?"

"A march of one hour. I will guide you."

"Tonight, then."

"Allaha ismarladik," Süleyman said, ducking through a rear door.

Butler rejoined Cooper, already selecting his raiding force from the marines he'd brought from France. He finished his coffee, which was now cold.

"We still have men across the street watching close, sir," Cooper said.

Five Turks dressed in European suits stood arguing, but always with one man watching the coffeehouse. A crowd followed the gestures of the men as they pointed to the coffeehouse. One man stepped forward and pointed at Butler and Cooper, shouting, "Amerikalilar!"

The dog packs, roused by the crowd, stirred.

"The mob will catch us before we make the guard post, sir," Cooper said.

"Stay here." Butler ducked into the storeroom and returned with the goat carcass. He dropped an American five-dollar gold piece on the table. "That should buy a new goat. Back to Sultanahmed. Straight through the dog packs. Go."

Cooper shoved several Turks aside, clearing the way for Butler. A tall man grabbed Butler. Smedley slammed the dead goat into the Turk's face. A few steps carried the marines into the intersection. Dogs snarled and scurried aside. Butler turned and hurled the goat back into the center of the square. It landed between the packs as several men started to follow the marines. Dogs from each pack pounced on the meat. Instantly, curs poured from the shadows, filling the street with fifty or sixty fighting dogs. The men fled into a shop door. The din of snarling and barking drowned the shouts of the Turkish mob, trapped on the far side of the canine sea.

John Pershing and one aide crossed the veranda of the Pera Palas. Pershing glanced at the distant Golden Horn, seeing the bright lights of the liner *Princess Matoika*, knowing the ship was already packed with wounded soldiers and marines. He walked quickly through the hotel's garden to a closed limousine.

Pershing and his aide climbed into the back seat. The general's orderly, Frank Lanckton, sat behind the wheel, a Turkish officer in the front seat beside him.

The Turk glanced back at Pershing. "The Ghazi waits."

Pershing nodded, tapped Lanckton on the shoulder, and said softly, "All right, Sergeant, let's get where we're going." The general leaned back in the seat. Fighting the Germans had been easy, he thought, backed by the power of an America enraged to war. The enemy was clear, the mission direct. In Turkey, Pershing's men died one or two at a time in ambushes and probing attacks on his lines, as the Nationalists sought to free their nation. Pershing could not view them as his enemy. Feeling the tightness in his chest left by the heavy smoke, Pershing coughed deeply. He leaned back and closed his eyes as Lanckton swung the car slowly into the empty street and drove toward the docks.

Butler crouched just over the crest of a low hill, feeling rather than seeing the marine scouts around him in the darkness. His attack force had steamed from Constantinople two nights before in an old Turkish ferry, and crept along the European coast of the Sea of Marmara for a day. Nearing the Dardanelles, the marines transferred to a fast Navy patrol boat and dashed east for the Kemalist submarine base near Bursa, landing at night and marching across a headland.

Below him, light seeped from warehouses facing a long dock, illuminating mounds of supplies. A door opened and a flood of light revealed the low conning tower of a submarine. Inland, a dozen huts were crowded together. The camp's perimeter remained in darkness. Smedley shifted his weight, and the Thompson gun slung on his shoulder slipped. He grabbed the submachine gun before it could bang against the tree.

Marine skirmishers edged down the hill. Butler studied the base several more minutes, trying to pick out its defenses, then ducked back across the crest and dropped to kneel beside Cooper and Süleyman. The three squads of Butler's attack force were spread along the hill. Two men in each squad carried packs of explosives.

"BARs are dug in to cover our withdrawal, sir," Cooper said.

"Good." Butler turned to their Turkish guide. "Süleyman, stay here with the gunners."

"Efendim? Hayir. I fight beside you." He held up his Thompson.

"Are you tired of Stamboul, Süleyman, to risk your life?"

"Dawn will find us back in the city, inshalla."

Butler nodded in the darkness, his nerves tightening as he waited. After what seemed hours, he heard a whisper of sound and a Marine private dropped beside him.

"Barbed fence halfway between the base of the hill and the huts. Fifty yards of cleared ground between the fence and guard posts at the edge of the camp. Bunkers every one hundred yards. Turks had pickets out at the base of the hill. They don't now."

"Move out, Sergeant. Let's sink that sub."

Ten miles north of Constantinople, John Pershing's launch bumped against a low seawall set between a European-style mansion and the Bosporus. He stepped from the rocking boat onto the landing of the compact, classically styled summer home of a merchant or diplomat from Pera. The front door of the building opened as the engine died. A man's voice, speaking in French, said, "General Pershing, welcome to Anatolia. May we find peace tonight."

Not waiting for his aide, Pershing stepped into the light streaming from the building and answered in the same language, "Thank you, Kemal Pasha. Between us, we shall."

Pershing followed Mustafa Kemal down the entrance hall into a large drawing room. The Turkish leader was a slight man, wearing a gray military tunic and jodhpurs. Unlike his photographs, the Turk's rectangular face was clean-shaven. His steel-gray eyes studied the American as Mustafa Kemal shook hands with Pershing. "I am sorry Governor Fall would not meet with me."

"I come in his place, and with the authority of the United States Government," Pershing said, continuing to speak in French. "Marshal Kemal, please accept my congratulations on your victory over the Greek army."

"I asked the Turkish people to fight for every rock in our country, and they did. We fight now to make the nation modern, to take our place again in the world."

"Meeting you, Kemal Pasha, I know you will accomplish your goal," Pershing said, keeping his gaze on the Turkish leader, feeling the power of the other man's personality. But you won't do it easily if America decides to fight, he thought.

Every sound in the night screamed for Butler's attention. Metal clanged on the dock, followed by an easy call in Turkish and laughter at someone's clumsiness. The weight of spare drum magazines tugged at his equipment belt as Smedley worked his way down the hill.

He concentrated on placing each step, testing gently for firm footing before adding his full weight. Gravel rattled in the darkness as his men moved down the gradual slope, and he silently cursed their carelessness. The skirmishers directed the attackers to breaks they'd cut in the few strands of barbed wire circling the base.

Thirty yards from the first buildings, flame stabbed into the night. A machine gun spat tracers, dashes of light crawling toward Smedley, then whipping past him. Four marines spun backward into darkness.

Smedley fired the Thompson in bursts toward the source of the tracers. He pulled down on the forward grip to keep the gun from climbing. His shells chugged out with a deep roar. The line of marines fired and screamed curses as they ran into the machine-gun fire. Men died and fell.

Butler leapt a low ditch, Süleyman beside him. Both fired into the machine-gun team as they landed. A rifle butt whipped out of the darkness. Butler fired, letting the Thompson rise, spewing shells across the soldier's body.

A Mauser jabbed from an open door. Süleyman fired. The enemy rifleman staggered back as shells slammed into him. Butler sprinted between a series of low sheds, closer to his target with each dash.

He paused in the shelter of the last building as a dozen men, including one of the sappers, caught up with him. A long, narrow dock separated them from the sub, and Smedley saw figures moving behind piles of supplies.

Butler whipped off his campaign hat and held the Thompson at his side. He ran into the open, gesturing wildly behind himself, Süleyman at his side.

A figure on the submarine called, "Kiminiz?"

Süleyman called back in Turkish.

Half a dozen men separated from the shadows ahead of Butler. One shouted, "Dur! Dur!"

Smedley fired, holding the Thompson's barrel down but letting it sweep from right to left across the group. Men fell or spun into the darkness clutching wounds. As the last round spat from Butler's Thompson, an officer in a long gray coat stepped into view.

Butler dropped the submachine gun, feeling the sling's pull on his shoulder, and clawed at his .45. The officer's pistol snapped up and Smedley dove aside. A bullet tugged at his sleeve. Smedley fired as his pistol rose, the upward recoil of the automatic sending his second round into the Turk's gut. Beside him, Süleyman screamed as a Mauser shell slapped into his chest. A burst of Thompson rounds swept Süleyman's killer from the dock.

Smedley ducked behind a stack of cargo and changed drum magazines on his Thompson. He pointed to three marines. "Hold here if the Turks attack."

Butler leapt for the sub, landing heavily on the foredeck. He scrambled up a ladder to the conning tower, firing at a figure in an open hatch, but missing. Smedley reached for the closing hatch. The metal slipped from his fingers as it clanged shut.

"Here, sir!"

Butler dropped back to the foredeck as a marine fired into an open torpedo-loading hatch. Smedley grabbed the hatch cover and nodded to the marine, who pulled a timer and hurled an explosive pack into the depths of the sub. Butler slammed the hatch closed. "Get off! Now!"

The marines jumped to the dock as a deep explosion shook the submarine. Roiling bubbles of air erupted from the ruptured hull. The flash of tracers stabbed toward Smedley again, and he heard the rattle of a German-made machine gun from the warehouses.

The slow thud of Thompsons echoed from the buildings. The Maxim stopped firing. Cooper's voice called from across the dock, "We got this lot, but more are coming."

A marine private stared at the body of a fallen Thompson gunner, who had taken a burst of machine-gun fire in his head. "God, it took off Roland's head."

"Steady, Warren, steady. Carry him out, son."

Butler hoisted Süleyman's body and dashed for the buildings, followed by the surviving marines with the other dead and wounded. At the warehouses, he dodged around a shattered Maxim gun and three dead Turks before letting two of Cooper's men take Süleyman's body.

"The camp is clear, General," Cooper reported. "About twenty dead wogs. The rest took a shine. Judging from the lights, a convoy's coming up the main road, sir."

"All right, back to the boat. Fast." Butler felt sweat, or Süleyman's blood, on the back of his neck.

✧ ✧ ✧

Mustafa Kemal walked to a sideboard and picked up a crystal decanter. "Raki, General?" Kemal poured two glasses and handed one to Pershing.

Pershing sipped, the anise-flavored liquor sweeping all other taste from his mouth.

"In the field, I denied myself the pleasure of raki, but we are here as friends." Mustafa Kemal drank again. "General Pershing, give the American people the thanks of my nation. Your occupation saved us from the British and the French."

Pershing saw the trap, and smiled. "I believe our presence has helped the Turkish people."

"Your charitable organizations spared the people of Istanbul much suffering and saved many refugees from starvation. Let us forget your attempt to invade Eastern Anatolia. I am sure you wish to as well."

"We have much to discuss."

"No, General Pershing, we discuss only how you leave Turkey: as an enemy driven from our land or as a friend who leaves in peace."

"If you try to drive us out, we'll have a million men here in six months."

"We sank your dreadnought, General. We will sink your fleet as it tries to rescue you, or give you aid."

"Not with the same submarine, Kemal Pasha. We just sank it," Pershing said. If, he thought, Butler is on schedule. "Constantinople remains under the protection of our navy."

"That gives you the guns of your cruisers and destroyers. It does not give you more troops." Mustafa Kemal smiled. "We drove out the Greeks, and will drive you out as well. If your troops stack their arms and board your ships, we shall let you go."

"That would be surrender. Demand surrender and dishonor, and you will call down the wrath of America," Pershing said. "But I do not want to see your men, or my men, die needlessly."

"Our peoples can remain friends." Mustafa Kemal sipped his raki. "If we can find honor for both of us. Will Governor Fall agree?"

"Fall I can deal with, Kemal Pasha. Can you assure me that your army will not attack as we withdraw—with our arms?"

"I guarantee my army. I can not guarantee the people of the city."

The sleek patrol boat carrying Butler and his attack force bumped against *Princess Matoika.* Smedley knelt beside a wounded marine, adjusting the rough bandage on the man's shattered leg. "They've got a full surgery aboard the *Matoika,* and you'll be in top shape by the time you steam into New York." Butler stood aside as sailors slid the man onto a litter that was quickly hoisted up the liner's white flank.

Butler stared at the row of eight blanket-covered bodies on the small fantail. To Butler's surprise, the captain of the patrol boat had found a red-and-white Ottoman flag, which now covered Süleyman's body. "Eight dead, Sergeant Cooper, and another twelve wounded. That's a high price."

"Yes, sir."

"It will be higher if the Turkish army attacks."

Butler climbed a ladder to the small conning tower, seeking a better view. The Golden Horn flowed west to east, pouring into the Bosporus and dividing the peninsula on which Stamboul, ancient Constantinople, sat from its northern suburbs. The Galata Bridge, the first of two bridges over the waterway, crossed the Horn near its mouth. Smedley scanned Seraglio Point and the mosques of the ancient city. Turks crowded the shore of the Golden Horn, held from the southern end of the bridge by a cordon of troops.

Further east, through the arch of the Galata Bridge, Butler saw the Upper Bridge, also defended by a line of troops confronting a growing crowd. "I think the Turks smell blood. Ours."

Butler slid down the ladder to the deck. Gripping his Thompson, Smedley jumped from the boat to the Galata dock before the waiting sailors had secured the lines. Major Shaw saluted sharply. "Welcome back, General. Did you sink the bastard?"

"Not enough water to sink her, but that hull won't float again." Butler took in a long line of American civilians waiting for passage to the *Matoika.* Most were minor officials of the mandate government, though he recognized a cluster of American oilmen and their families. An American destroyer was tied to the seawall; the ship's high, knife-edged bow swept back a quarter of the destroyer's length before dropping sharply to a low main deck running aft. "How do we stand, Major?"

"General Pershing ordered withdrawal from Stamboul to the bridgeheads last night. No sign of the Turkish army, sir. Our lines swing north from the Horn and around Galata to the Bosporus north of the Dolmabahce Palace."

"We're still protecting the sultan, then."

"Not really, sir. He's gone back to the Topkapi."

"Good. The sultans haven't lived in Stamboul for fifty years. What's the old fool up to?"

"Praying before the Relics of the Prophet, or something."

"Where's Pershing?"

"The Pera Palas."

Refusing to yield to his fatigue, John Pershing stood beside his desk as Albert Fall stormed into the office, followed by an Army lieutenant.

"General Pershing, this man damned well ordered me into your presence," Fall said, his Western drawl thickening as his voice rose to a shout.

"My apologies for the offense, Governor Fall. I sent the lieutenant to ensure your safety. And your arrival." Pershing turned to a man standing near a window overlooking the imperial city. "Governor, this is Mister Palmer of the Department of State. He arrived this morning on the destroyer *Fanning*."

"I saw it dock. I'm glad the Navy sent us another ship to help whip the Turks."

"Not quite." Palmer handed an envelope to Fall. "As you will see, Governor, the State Department and the Senate are investigating the oil concessions the sultan assigned to American firms. There's strong evidence you accepted a rather large bribe, Mister Fall."

"Bunk."

"Perhaps, but the Secretary of State finds the charges substantial enough to order you back to Washington. You are suspended from your office."

"You don't have the authority!" Fall ripped open the envelope and stood staring at the official stationery, his mouth opening and closing silently.

"General Pershing." Palmer handed a second envelope to Pershing. "The secretary has appointed you interim governor general, until a new civilian governor is named or until Governor Fall returns to his post. Mister Fall, the *Fanning* will have refueled by noon, at which time we steam for America. With your permission, General Pershing, I'd like your lieutenant to help me pack Mister Fall's official papers."

"Have a safe voyage, gentlemen." Pershing waited till the door closed before calling for his orderly. "Sergeant Lanckton, they should give Charlie Dawes the Nobel Prize for engineering that bit of work. Maybe make him vice president. Hell, make him president."

Butler, the Thompson still slung over his shoulder, stepped aside as Fall and his escort left Pershing's office. He frowned, then returned a salute from the general's orderly. "Is the general free?"

"Yes, sir. Governor Pershing said to show you right in, General," Lanckton said.

Butler heard the change of title, and smiled. "Where's Fall?"

Lanckton grinned. "Mister Fall is recalled."

Butler entered Pershing's office, and saluted. "Congratulations, Governor."

"Frank stole the pleasure of telling you, I see," Pershing said, then listened to Butler's report of his mission. "Well done. We are a little stronger with that submarine dead. As I'm sure you saw, we have withdrawn from Stamboul."

"Yes, sir."

"A night ago, I met with Mustafa Kemal."

Butler nearly gasped in his surprise. "Sir!"

"The Ghazi realizes that we only came to help the Turkish people until they were ready to assume the burden of self-government." Glancing at a wall map showing the encircling Turkish forces, Pershing added, smiling, "We agreed that they are ready for that burden."

"And the politics at home?"

"Secretary Hughes wants us out of Turkey, and with the help your father's given in Congress, Hughes brought along his cabinet colleagues at the War and Navy Departments. Only Fall delayed matters, and he is now gone. The cable arrived this morning with President Harding's orders to withdraw from Turkey, if we can do so without fighting the Nationalist Army and stirring up a full war."

"I'm gone two days, and the world changes," Smedley said, smiling. "The *Princess Matoika* can't carry all the Americans in the city."

"The charities and missionaries are staying, as are most of the smaller businessmen," Pershing said. "The *Henderson* brought your marines and can carry them home. I've commandeered the two American merchantmen in port for the Army."

"When do we leave?"

"The *Matoika* steams in the morning. We start loading troops as soon as she clears the Golden Horn."

"I hear the sultan's at the Topkapi?"

"He's an old man seeing the end of a dynasty that's ruled this city for five hundred years," Pershing said. "I don't know what he'll do."

"Will the Nationalist Army nip our heels when we pull out?"

"Mustafa Kemal Pasha gave his word that his army will not attack, and I believe him. He wants good relations with America."

"But he doesn't control Stamboul."

"Not until his forces enter the city, and he won't do that till we leave."

"We can blow the bridges, General. The walk around the Golden Horn is too far for a mob. Both freighters are in the war harbor. I'd like to move them past the bridges to the Bosporus seawall before we load."

"One moves tonight," Pershing said. "Unfortunately, the second is repairing hull plates damaged when it hit a piling. It'll be ready to steam on time, but only if we load her in place. We can't blow the bridges till the freighter is clear."

Butler stalked the end of the Galata Bridge, his boots thudding with each step. For the first time since he'd been in Constantinople, the bridge was empty, no longer packed by the peoples of Europe and Asia who normally streamed between Stamboul and Galata. The restaurants and shops built under the bridge were empty. The caiques and other boats usually tied to the bridge had been forced away, though many hovered on the flanks, ready to swoop toward the marines, as were the flocks of gulls circling the docks.

Nearly a hundred of Butler's men crouched behind a makeshift barricade of cargo bales. Most held bolt-action Springfield rifles. Every fifth man pointed a Thompson at the crowd milling across the plaza formed by a wide intersection. Three teams with Browning Automatic Rifles used their BARs to stiffen the defenses. East of the Galata

Bridge, another marine unit held the Upper Bridge across the Horn.

The mob of several thousand Turks stirred, occasionally pushing toward the marine line. Many in the mob held rifles. At the Galata end of the wide bridge, two belt-fed Browning machine guns waited to sweep death into the mob if the marines retreated.

"General Butler, a wog's coming."

Butler watched a Turk in a dark suit and fez walk slowly toward the marines. He held a white flag high over his head. "Efendim!"

Butler recognized the man as an advisor to the sultan and waved him through the marine line. "Halim Pasha, may I order a car for you?"

"No, Butler Efendi, I come with a letter for you, or General Pershing. From the sultan."

Smedley opened the letter, written in English on stationery carrying the curling Arabic script of the sultan's seal:

> *Sir, Considering my life in danger in Istanbul, I take refuge with the American Government and request my transfer as soon as possible from Istanbul to another place.*
>
> *Mehmet Vahideddin, Caliph of the Muslims*

"That's the end of the Ottoman Empire, then," Butler said, remembering the warmth of Süleyman's blood, shed to save the dynasty. "Where is the sultan?"

"In the Topkapi. At the Baghdad Pavilion. His family is safely at the Dolmabahce. Will you come?"

"Give me a moment." Butler walked across the bridge to the forward communications post. "Get General Pershing."

"Yes, sir."

Sergeant Cooper saluted. "Little action coming, sir?"

"Oh, yes, Sergeant, of that I'm certain. I want twenty-five men ready to move out as soon as I talk to Pershing. Thompsons and Springfields."

"Sir, General Pershing on the line."

"General," Smedley spoke over the static of the jury-rigged landline, "the sultan has asked for refuge. He's trapped at the Topkapi. His family is at the Dolmabahce Palace."

"We've withdrawn south of the palace. I'll send a patrol boat for the sultan's people. Bring him out safely, General Butler. We will not abandon a man who was our friend."

Butler ordered a BAR mounted over the cab of a truck and had the side rails of the bed strengthened with planks. He directed Halim Pasha into the cab before crowding into the back of the truck with his men.

"Major Shaw, hold the bridge as long as you can, but if the crowd threatens to take your position, withdraw and sink this bridge as soon as the freighter exits the inner harbor."

Shaw saluted. "Good luck, sir."

Marines opened a gap in the barricade. Bouncing over the cobblestones and threatening to fling men from the bed at every jolt, the truck shot straight at the crowd. Several men pushed a wagon into the street, clearly hoping to block the Americans. Butler tapped the BAR gunner on the shoulder.

A burst from the BAR slammed into the wagon, scattering the men pushing it. The truck skidded around the wagon and tore along the waterfront toward Seraglio Point, quickly passing the red bricks of the Orient Express railroad station and bouncing across the tracks before angling inland and up the hill toward the palace.

The marines dropped to the ground and spread out. Leaving a squad to guard the trucks, Butler and Halim Pasha led the rest uphill through low hedges and scattered trees that offered little cover. Nearer the gray walls of the Topkapi the trees spread a wide canopy overhead. Two guards in Turkish army uniforms held a post at the stone wall of the ancient palace.

Halim Pasha called in Turkish, and the guards answered,

lowering their Mausers and stepping aside. "These men are loyal to the sultan. They say Nationalist troops have occupied the second court of the palace and have started moving into the third court. The sultan's men hold the fourth, just inside this gate."

"Will they fight beside us?" Butler asked.

"The Kemalists are guarding the palace, not looting it," Halim answered. "The sultan has ordered his men to not fire. Turks will not fight Turks today."

Leaving several marines at the gate, Butler led his men through the gate into the palace grounds. The marines spread to the right, slipping off the path through a garden thick with trees and bushes. Ahead, Smedley saw a large, octagonal building. Gray-and-cream marble formed wide arches on the ground floor supporting a main floor with high, arched windows whose white frames held stained glass mosaics. The main floor blended with a terrace running for ten or fifteen yards to a smaller version of the large kiosk and on to the main buildings of the palace.

"The Baghdad Kiosk," Halim said, "built after Murad IV captured that city. The smaller is the Revan . . ."

Butler ignored Halim's nervous chatter. The garden opened to his right. A dozen Turkish soldiers sat around a dry fountain smoking and talking, Mausers resting against the center pedestal. A smaller group stood, rifles ready, glancing toward the closed windows of two-story buildings forming a wall at the front of the garden. A soldier shouted, and rifles snapped toward the Marines. Butler's finger tightened on the trigger of his Thompson.

"Hayir! Hayir! No!" Halim shouted. He spoke rapidly in Turkish, and the soldiers slowly lowered their rifles.

"Tell them to set down their rifles. Now."

Responding to Halim's shouts, and the steady muzzles of the submachine guns, the Turks set their rifles carefully on the grass.

"Down, flat on the ground, hands behind their backs."

The Turks followed Halim's orders. Marines hauled the Mausers back to the trees.

"Sergeant Cooper, hold here in the trees. Thompsons cover the wogs by the fountain. Springfields cover those windows. Anybody see a head pop out, put a round into the wall about a foot away from them. If they fire back, kill the bastards."

Halim turned at a question called from the balcony. He answered a tall Turkish officer, and said to Butler, "The commander of the guard. Come."

Halim led the marines across the garden to a door in the base of the Baghdad Kiosk, and quickly upstairs to the main level. Moving into the central room, the marines stared in wonder at the intricate inlays of ivory, tortoise shell, and mother of pearl on the window frames and doors and at the blue and gray tiles forming mosaics of flowering vines and geometric patterns.

Butler gestured, and marines dashed to the far doors, ready to duck through on command. Halim moved ahead of Butler, saying over his shoulder, "The sultan is here."

Smedley cursed under his breath and followed, Thompson ready.

Halim paused, one hand on a marble railing. Twenty yards away, a small platform jutted out from the terrace, shaded by a rectangular bronze baldachin set high on four bronze pillars. A slight man wearing a dark European-style uniform stood looking across the city to the Mosque of Süleyman and the Golden Horn.

Halim approached, bowing and talking in Turkish. Mehmet VI turned slowly, and spoke to Butler as Halim translated. "I came to see my city for the final time. Dolmabahce is beautiful, but I could not feel the past from that modern place." He stepped down to the terrace, and turned again to look over the city, speaking in a voice Butler could scarcely hear as Halim translated:

> "The spider is the curtain-holder in the Palace of the Caesars."

The sultan walked toward the Revan Kiosk, saying, "Mehmet the Conqueror recited that poem while standing in the ruins of a Roman palace that sat here. Now, it applies to us."

Butler paused to study the Golden Horn. The Upper Bridge had just closed behind the American freighter as the Galata Bridge opened to free the ship. A ball of flame erupted from several of the pontoons supporting the Upper Bridge, which slowly settled into the water. The mob looked like a black amoeba swarming around the marine line at the Stamboul end of the Galata Bridge. Butler knew he was nearly out of time.

The sultan and several aides stayed in the center of the group as they hurried past a shallow pool to stairs leading down to the garden. Butler and the marines herded the sultan's party out of the palace grounds and began working through the formal gardens outside the wall. Across the mouth of the Golden Horn, Butler saw American ships loading at the waterfront of the Bosporus.

The thud of Thompson guns and the pop of Springfields echoed up the hill. Butler waved his leading squad forward, and called softly to Cooper, "Hold here." Smedley followed the first squad, dodging from hedge to hedge. Rifles snapped again, followed by the Thompsons and the heavier thud of a BAR.

Nearing the truck, Butler saw his guards crouching behind cover, firing at several dozen Turkish police and soldiers. Butler and the marines with him followed a shallow gully downhill in a wide arc.

Butler's team broke from cover on the attackers' flank. Fingers of the mob drifted back and forth in the rail yard below them, slowly edging uphill in support of the group firing on the marines. The Springfields of Butler's group picked off half of the attacking Turks in their first volley.

"At 'em, boys," Smedley shouted, leaping to his feet and charging across the hillside. The remaining Turks broke, fleeing downhill. Men with Springfields dropped to cover and picked off any of the crowd who moved toward them.

Butler ordered the riflemen to fix their long bayonets to the Springfields and circle the truck. The Thompson gunners stood in the truck's bed, and the BAR team again prepared to fire over the cab.

Butler turned to the sultan and spoke as Halim translated. "Your Majesty, I need you and your men to sit in the center of the truck. You will be safer." Mehmet nodded, and accepted help from two marines as he climbed aboard the truck, followed by his party. Halim climbed into the cab beside Cooper, who drove.

"All right, we go through the crowd to the bridge. Bayonets circle the truck, but stay close. Thompson gunners, stand ready to fire over the men on the ground. Aim for the cobblestones in front of the mob. You'll take the first ranks down with ricochets. Seeing the wounded flop around will slow up the rest."

Butler jumped onto the running board next to Cooper. "Slow ahead, Sergeant."

The crowd parted reluctantly before the line of bayonets and the threatening muzzles of the BAR and Thompsons. The truck moved as if it were a boat parting a sea of people. A shot slammed into the side of the truck, slashing splinters into a marine's face and spinning him into the sultan.

"On the roof."

A Springfield fired once and a figure fell from the crenellated brick tower at the end of the railroad terminal. The crowd pulled back as Butler's party passed the station. The plaza stretching to the Galata Bridge was empty, except for a dozen bodies. But the mob was thick in the streets feeding toward the bridge, like tributary rivers pouring toward the sea. The truck neared the bridge, blocking the marines manning the barricade from firing. The mob flooded toward Butler's men.

"Thompsons!" Butler shouted.

The bursts of gunfire shattered against the cobbles, sending shards of stone and bullets like a scythe into the mob, which shuddered and fell back. Rocks landed amongst the marines on the ground, and a man dropped, clutching his head. Butler handed his Thompson to Cooper and jumped to the ground. He grabbed the fallen Springfield as two marines hoisted the wounded man into the back of the truck.

Major Shaw ran up as the unwounded marines leapt from the truck. "Glad you made it, General. Where's the sultan?"

Butler nodded to the vehicle accelerating toward Galata. Rifle fire thunked into the bails of cargo and the crowd surged forward. "Charges ready?"

"Yes, sir."

"Pull back, Major."

The marines dropped back in groups, moving, covering their fellows, moving again. Butler stayed with the last team, thrusting his bayonet into an Ottoman policeman who climbed the barrier. Rounds fired from behind him dropped more of the mob, and Smedley was halfway across the wide bridge. Shots from the crowd smashed one of the elegant street lamps lining the bridge, sending fragments of its crescent moon knifing into a marine, who staggered on to safety.

As Smedley crossed the far end of the bridge, the heavy water-cooled Brownings swept death toward Stamboul. The crowd dissolved an instant before explosions slapped across the water, flame and smoke rising from the center of the bridge.

John Pershing stood on the deck of the cruiser *Galveston*, watching the sun set behind the city, turning the water of the Horn golden again. A small group of Turkish officers stood on the Galata dock, a Turkish flag flying from a car behind them. Pershing saluted. "Fire a twenty-one-gun salute for the new republic, Captain, and for Mustafa Kemal."

✧ ✧ ✧

My thanks to Vince Kohler for suggesting the story and to Chris Bunch for kicking me until I finished it.

Southern Strategy

Michael F. Flynn

The day is cruel hot, and the asphalt road shimmers in the distance, as if molten. The car has become an oven. Sweat beads and drips on forehead; clothing sags and clings. Stevenson has turned the wing window to blow air on his face as he drives, but it helps only a little, and brings with it the cloying scents of honeysuckle and marigold and rich, black loam. Telephone poles snap by. He swings around a flatbed piled high with cotton bales and pulled by a battered old John Deere. The driver is white and does not look especially happy.

Stevenson pulls a handkerchief from his pants pocket and mops his face. Cypress shrouded with Spanish moss crowds in on both sides, encroaching on the road, growing up even through the soft asphalt, so that he seems to be driving through an all-devouring jungle. Then the foliage opens out unexpectedly, revealing mean little farmsteads with tumbledown shanties and battered old trucks up on blocks. Some properties are overgrown with briars and brambles where darkie sharecroppers have been cleared off the year before. Good land, but the owner is terrified of selling and the neighbors even more terrified of squatting.

Later, Stevenson comes to a checkpoint, and the reason why the neighbors run scared. The land here has been cleared, too; but more expertly, to provide a killing field. Three cars wait while the soldier inspects their papers. Somewhere hidden from the road a machine gun nest guards the sentry. The soldier makes a tempting target and looks as if he knows it. The machine gun will do him little good if circumstances ever call upon it. Stevenson tries to put the lad at ease by smiling a little when it comes his turn, though perhaps it is the tired, middle-aged look that causes the young man to untense.

"Papieren," he says. No *bitte*, but he is no more unfriendly than any Hun demanding an American's travel permit. By its very nature, the act constitutes an offense. Stevenson tries not to show it, but his eyes may narrow just a little. This is America, after all, even if only Alabama.

The sentry studies the travel papers, his lips moving slowly. Sweat pours from under his coal-scuttle helmet. He's probably thinking about the water cooler in the guard shack, or a beer later in the barracks. Stevenson glances in his rearview mirror and sees no cars behind him on the long, black road.

Finally the sentry makes a decision. Perhaps it is thirst. Perhaps it is, with no more cars to stop, a desire for a bit of diversion. He waves Stevenson over to a small apron tamped down in the earth beside the road. "Fahr hin!" And when Stevenson hesitates, adds more peremptorily, "Dort drüben."

Stevenson sighs. There is no point pretending incomprehension. Everyone knows *gehen* and *kommen* and *papieren*. And *Halt, oder ich schieße*! And if you don't understand, the Germans don't care anyway. Things are not much better in the French zone; and some of the Triple Monarchy troops—the Serbs, especially—could be downright nasty. Even the English follow the German lead. Perhaps they still nurture resentment from the Great War, over American troops that never came.

Stevenson parks the car by the guardhouse and follows the sentry inside the small, wooden shelter. An officer sits at a desk there reading some papers. In a photograph on the wall behind him, young Frederick William poses with his new English *Kaiserin*, Elizabeth Wettin-Windsor, the niece of the British king, who bears the wistful look of all dynastic brides. The sentry raps on the doorjamb. "Wir Besuch haben, Herr Leutnant," he says with some humor. "Es gibt der Mann auf den Morgensbericht." Stevenson pretends not to understand, but neither is he surprised to be expected: the penalties of a public life.

The officer sits up and stares with cool eyes, but Stevenson senses curiosity or indifference rather than hostility. "Sit down, senator," the man says at last, indicating a rickety wooden chair. "This will take not long if you cooperate."

"For a few minutes in the shade," Stevenson answers more dryly than he feels, "I may be tempted to drag this out, lieutenant . . ." He scans the officer's name-tag. " . . . Lieutenant Goldberg."

It is a thin joke and Goldberg gives it a thin smile in return. "You are no more unhappy than I am, here *in diesem Land ohne Kultur*." He gauges Stevenson's wry grimace and his smile broadens as he makes a notation. Stevenson is annoyed with himself for letting his knowledge of German show. Kept secret, it might have proven useful later.

"So, what brings you to Alabama, so far from your Illinois?" A pen, one of the new ball-point kind, is poised over a tattered notebook.

Stevenson judges the question *pro forma* and tries his cover story. "I'm here to meet privately with some Party officials, in the hope of putting an end to the Situation."

The Situation is what everyone calls it, trying to

downplay its significance, trying to talk around the subject as if it does not really exist. It isn't an occupation; just . . . a situation. Some of Stevenson's circle even pretend that League troops are in the South by invitation—as if President Black has had any choice in the matter.

"And you have by yourself come? A man of your importance? Your father was a vice president, not so?"

"My grandfather—for Grover Cleveland, a long time ago. I'm sure you know how delicate our domestic political situation is, lieutenant. My associates and I thought it best if we kept my little trip off the record."

Goldberg shrugs off the widening rift between northern and southern Democrats. Domestic politics means less to him than the intolerable heat or the lack of a first-rate symphony; or of even a decent beer. "And these people you plan to meet with . . . None of them are the *franc-tireurs*, of course. No one from your Klan, or from the SCLC, or from the terrorist band led by 'Tricky Dick'."

It is a polite invitation to a demurral. They both know that Stevenson would be a fool to contact any of the guerrilla groups operating in the League-occupied zone. What no one knows, least of all Stevenson himself, is how big a fool he can be. The sweat is a sheen on his face, but he checks a move toward his handkerchief. To mop his brow might imply nervousness at the direction of the questioning. "No," he says. "Just local Party officials."

Goldberg grunts his amusement, perfectly aware that the one does not preclude the other. "Their names?" he asks, but his attention is now only partly on Stevenson. A battered pickup truck with local plates approaches the checkpoint, and the sentry, judging the senator no threat to his lieutenant, leaves the guard shack to deal with it.

Stevenson tries ignorance. "I don't know who will be there. It's all been arranged very quietly by the governor's office. We will meet in—"

"Selma," Goldberg says. "You are to meet with Sparkman and his people in Selma." Stevenson shrugs, as if to say that if Goldberg already has all the answers from the *Morgensbericht*, then he need not detain Stevenson for questioning.

A commotion outside distracts him. A slurred drawl—half drink, half belligerence—shouts something about "nigger-lovin' Aryans" and "get yo' ass outta 'Bama." The lieutenant frowns and rises from his seat. When he steps to the door of the guard shack his holster is already unbuttoned. "Macht er Mühe, Soldat?"

"He's drunk," Stevenson says sotto voce. "Moonshine. That's always trouble." The lieutenant nods without turning. If he was not a careful man before his draft, a few months of occupation duty have made him one.

"An' a god-damn kike officer, too," the same voice says. Stevenson hears another voice, a woman's, urging caution. He looks around the guard shack thinking how little the barnwood walls would slow a bullet. He moves his chair away from the desk, ready to throw himself on the floor if something happens.

But Goldberg describes in graphic terms what drunk drivers can do to their families and calls upon the man's duty to protect his wife and infant son. The man curses, but Goldberg persists and Stevenson is astonished when the redneck actually steps out of his truck and allows his wife to slide behind the steering wheel. He mutters something about "women drivers," but gets into the passenger seat and his wife, with a grateful nod to the lieutenant, drives him away.

"Honor and duty," Goldberg says when he returns to the shack with an over-and-under shotgun in his hand. "These Southern men understand little of civilized behavior, but that much will reach them." He notices that his holster is still unsnapped and refastens it.

"You handled that well," Stevenson says.

Goldberg places the shotgun in a barrel full of confiscated weapons labeled *Beschlagsnahmen*. He pours himself a drink of water from the cooler; then, in afterthought, another for Stevenson. "You thought 'The Hun' would wave weapons and shout and bring on a shooting." He sits at his desk, pulls out a tag and writes on it. Then he takes the tag to the barrel and fastens it to the shotgun trigger guard, and puts the carbon in a small card box atop the nearby filing cabinet. Stevenson thinks about the Hun obsession with record-keeping more than about their reputation for ruthlessness.

The lieutenant speaks casually while he arranges the card box. "Tell me, Herr Senator . . . What is *your* opinion of 'niggers' and 'kikes'?"

It is the first time that the cool detachment has cracked. Stevenson chooses his next words with care. "I'm a northern Democrat, not a southern one. You must know my record." He gestures toward the reports on the desk. German thoroughness is a commonplace. "No decent man can approve of 'racial clearing.' "

"Yet your party cannot hope the White House to retain without the votes of your southern Democrats. And so, you must embrace 'under the sheets.' Only, these sheets have hoods on them." Goldberg's lips condense into a thin line. "Have you ever opened a mass grave, senator? Have you ever smelled the rotting bodies of people slain for no other reason but who they were? Such a thing could never happen in France or England or Germany."

Stung, Stevenson hangs his head. Argument would be futile and there is too much truth in the lieutenant's charge. Yet revulsion against the lynchings had been growing, even in the South; and Black—himself an Alabaman and former Klansman—had denounced them in his radio addresses. Stevenson sometimes wonders whether the race war would have happened at all had the League of Nations not meddled.

But he does not argue the point. He is not here to convince one Imperial lieutenant that the sight of foreign paratroops dropping on American cities had turned retail murder into wholesale atrocity. Stevenson isn't sure himself. The "clearings" might have happened anyway. It is vain to argue what might have been.

The Stonewall is not a very palatial hotel. Selma is not a very palatial town. Nothing in the south, in Stevenson's estimation, quite measures up to Chicago. He unpacks his bag, tests the spring of the mattress—it is lumpy—then opens the window. The muggy breeze bears the ashy odor of old wood fires, carried over from the charred ruins of Darktown. He sees the jumble of burnt timber frames over on the other side of the tracks. They look like charcoal lines sketched against the sky, like one of those new "modern" paintings. Standing by the open window, Stevenson fans himself three times with a copy of the local newspaper. He pauses, then fans himself again, this time with his left hand.

Turning away, he settles into the desk chair and waits for the pounding of his heart to slow. Sweat glistens on his broad forehead and he fans himself, this time in earnest. His eyes light on the dresser top and notice the opened Bible. He rises and glances at the text marked by a business card. *Vengeance is mine, sayeth the Lord.* The card announces the finest haircuts in Selma.

When he has regained a measure of calm, Stevenson descends to the lobby, where a boy chats idly with the girl behind the desk. He looks to be perhaps seventeen or eighteen. His hair is greased and swept back in the new style favored by the youngsters and he wears his pants low on his hips. They look as if they will slide off at any moment. Stevenson resists the impulse to order the pants pulled up. Instead, he takes him aside and gives him a cartwheel and a name. The boy grins. "Rootie-tootie," he says and walks off with a sassy, hip-rolling gait. Stevenson wonders what the younger generation is coming to. Then he shrugs and sets out for a walk.

The heat beats upon him. Cicadas chicker like boys running sticks across every picket fence in the world. The sound swells and crests and diminishes in waves, but it never entirely dies away. It is not the best weather for a stroll. Eggs would fry on the sidewalks. The locals know this and stay indoors. Stevenson fancies his progress marked from behind every shaded parlor window he passes. The heat pours up from the pavement through the soles of his shoes.

Stepping inside the barber shop at last is like entering a cave. As his eyes grow slowly adjusted to the dimmer light, he sees a row of older men seated along the wall. They bear the attitude of those whose conversation has but lately fallen silent. The barber stands with his implements poised over a customer's head. Stevenson's words congest in his throat and he must cough to loosen them. "A bottle of hair tonic," he says, putting as much rural Illinois into his twang as he is able, and pulls another cartwheel from his pocket. "The kind Fosdick uses." He fights the urge to mop his brow. His fedora remains firmly in place. He holds the silver dollar so that Walking Liberty is upright from the barber's point of view.

That worthy glances at the coin and regards Stevenson a moment longer. Then he puts his clippers down and takes a bottle of tonic off his shelf. He gives it to Stevenson, but says, "Keep the dollar, boy. I won't take another man's liberty." The Greek chorus breaks silence in a mutter of affirmations.

When he returns to the hotel lobby, Stevenson finds the errand boy waiting. The lad hands him a bottle of bourbon. "Here you go, mistuh," he says with a conspiratorial leer. Stevenson takes the bottle and stares at it stupidly, until he remembers that anyone might have seen him send the boy on an errand and the bottle will explain things nicely. "Thank you," he says, handing him a nickel tip. "It's my favorite brand." In truth, he does not recognize the label. It might be more hair tonic for all he knows.

Settled once more in his room, he places the bourbon

on the sideboard and lies down on the bed to rest. He wonders if he should signal at the window again, but decides not to press matters. All that remains now is to wait.

It is not a long wait. When Stevenson answers the knock, Governor Sparkman steps past him and heads directly for the liquor bottle, where he pours himself three fingers of bourbon, neat. Only after he has gotten himself outside two of those fingers does he turn and face the senator from Illinois. "How was the drive down, Adlai?"

Stevenson sits on the bed. "Tolerable, John. It was a US Highway all the way; as straight as God and local politics would allow." Sparkman's lips twitch—the US Highways were paved with more pork than asphalt—then he introduces his two companions.

Tallulah Bankhead, in her late forties, is niece and granddaughter of U.S. Senators and daughter of the late Speaker of the House. She has recently left the stage to take up her family's political mantle. Rumor has it that Sparkman is grooming her to be the next governor. (Stevenson doubts an actor can be a governor, but the Democrats could run a yellow dog in this state and still win.) He turns expectant eyes on the third member of the delegation.

He is an intense man in his early thirties, with broad lips that press close together in a look of permanent disapproval. Dark-haired and dark-complexioned, he appears brooding. Sparkman names him George Corley Wallace, state attorney general. His grip is firm but brief. "No trouble with the Hun?" he asks as he, too, seeks liquid solace. Bankhead, like Stevenson, has taken no drink, but she sits in the desk chair and eyes Stevenson with frank interest.

Stevenson tells Wallace that he has had no trouble and the young attorney general grunts. "You were lucky then.

Some local fellow says the Hun out the US Highway threatened to blow his baby's head off this afternoon."

Stevenson's eyebrows rise. "Red pickup truck about five years old? I saw that. The boy was likkered up and the gendarme talked him into letting his wife drive him home. That's all. Probably saved them all from a bad accident."

Wallace frowns. "That's not the way he tells it."

Sparkman, standing by the window, interrupts. "Look at them out there, goose-stepping down the street like they God-damn own it." He finishes the last finger, looks at the glass as if its emptiness were an affront before he sets it down carefully. "Tastes like hair tonic," he says. "Okay, Adlai, what's the word from the central committee?"

Stevenson considers how to present things. Southern pride is a touchy thing and though he has been rehearsing his little speech all the way down from Peoria, he knows it will not play well. "Hugo isn't standing for reelection," he says bluntly.

Sparkman is unsurprised. "Yeah, I figgered that. The Situation's not his fault—the God-damned League shoved it down his throat—but the people will never forgive him."

"The same goes for the veep—"

" 'Cept who cares what that sumbitch wants?" Sparkman snorts. "Ol' Hugo was a-gonna shitcan Curley anyway. How many vice presidents you know who serve time in jail?"

It's a rhetorical question. "What I mean," Stevenson presses on, "is that no one connected with the administration has a Chinaman's chance. We need an outsider if we're going to run a respectable campaign."

Sparkman stands a little taller. "Any names in that hat, Adlai?" His tone suggests he has a name in mind, but Stevenson quashes that thought right away.

"Party can't run a Southern man this time, John. Especially not the governor of Alabama—"

Sparkman swells like a banty rooster. "Now, hold on there—"

"—because folks up north blame *all* of you for the

Situation. They way you treated the coloreds—the lynchings and all—that's what brought the League in."

Sparkman strikes the dresser with the flat of his hand. "Adlai, that was just white trash troublemakers, not the quality folks. Not the Sparkmans or the Bankheads." His glance touches his attorney general, but he does not include the Wallaces among the quality. If Wallace notices, he gives no sign. "Most folks down here," Sparkman insists, "they might not care to associate with the coloreds, but they never wanted to see them hung or burned out. Live and let live—"

"Separate," says Wallace, "but equal."

Stevenson doesn't think separate can ever be equal. One or the other would get shortchanged, and he doesn't think it would be the whites. The point is moot now, anyway. "That doesn't matter, John," he tells them. "Up north, John Q. Citizen isn't making any distinctions between the trash and the quality. The city machines don't think they can deliver for a Southern ticket, and you and I both know Boss Daley can deliver votes if he has to dig up the graveyard with his own two hands and drag the corpses into the polling booth. No, it's time the party put a northern man up."

"Party hasn't put up a northern man since Franklin," Tallulah points out. "And there was less there than met the eye. He sure enough brought the Glorious Twenties to a roaring halt."

Stevenson shrugs. "That was just bad luck, the market crashing when it did. After eight good years with McAdoo, Franklin expected the good times to—"

"Then he was naive," snaps Sparkman. "It cost us the White House and it let that . . . that *engineer,* Hoover, take credit for the recovery."

It was only natural that people looking to rebuild America after the Great Panic should look to the man who had helped rebuild Europe after the Great War. But there is no point in picking over ancient history. "The point is, John," Stevenson says, "we don't plan to dig up Franklin and nominate him again. The Great Panic is all in the past, but this business down here—The Situation—that's happening *right now*. Even if the League troops went home tomorrow, folks would still remember it was the South brought it on us come election time."

Sparkman's irritation shows in the pinch of his face. "Who, then?" the governor snaps. "You?" A speculative glint in Sparkman's eye and he cocks his head. "You and me," he says more thoughtfully. "Illinois and Alabama. A balanced ticket. It might work."

Stevenson recoils in horror. "I'm only a simple senator from the Midwest." And besides—although he does not voice the thought—as little as Stevenson relishes the role of president, he relishes the role of sacrificial lamb even less.

"Well, not that prancing popinjay from Massachussetts!" Wallace says in a belligerent growl. "Not that son of a goose-stepping Kaiser-kisser!"

"No, not 'Little Joe,' either." Stevenson shudders at the thought of what might happen if presidents were chosen on their good looks and breezy self-assurance. "He's just the glove," he tells them. "His daddy's the hand, and none of us want *him* controlling the government. No, we've been talking up the junior senator from Missouri."

Sparkman shows surprise. "Truman? He's a Prendergast man. Why not just hand Big Jim the keys to Fort Knox? Besides, Missouri's a Southern state, too."

"No, John. I've worked with Harry in the Senate. Sure, he got his start with the Machine, but he's the only one of that crowd who ever *lost* money in office. And Missouri is a *border state.*" He lets Sparkman think that over.

The governor is not happy, but he sees the point. "All right, we can pretend he's a Southern man and you-all can pretend he's northern. Maybe we squeeze out a few more votes that way." He runs his hand through his hair. "Republicans make up their minds yet?"

Stevenson shakes his head. "Still split between Taft and

Warren. We may be able to exploit that. Divide the Republican vote the way Wilson did." Privately, Stevenson doubts they can pull it off. A solid run by a northern Democrat is all he asks for; something that will separate the Party from the clearings in the public mind. Afterwards . . . He thinks he can work with Earl Warren; but a congenial, cooperative term will only solidify the GOP's hold on the executive office, so he might as well butt heads with Taft for four years.

The four of them talk the pros and cons of Truman versus Warren or Taft. Sparkman promises to sound out the other Southern governors; but if the northern machines won't back a Southern man, he knows as well as Stevenson that they have no choice.

Wallace lingers after the other two leave and eyes Stevenson's bald pate. "You don't look like a man with much need of hair tonic," he says without preamble.

Stevenson hesitates, then closes the door, shutting the two of them in together. "So, you're the leader of—"

But Wallace holds up a hand. "I ain't leader of nothing. But maybe I know someone who knows someone. You wanted a meeting. This is it."

Stevenson takes a breath and walks to the other side of the room, where he leans against the dresser. He must reach deep down inside himself to pull the words out. "There has to be an accommodation," he tells the man who knows someone, "before it rips the Party in half."

Wallace grunts and crosses his arms. "Well, it's about time you-all got on board . . ."

"I beg your pardon?"

" . . . and we got some recognition for what we've done!"

The response startles Stevenson. The replies he had ready do not cover this comment. Again, he searches for words, but can do no better than to throw the same ones back. "Recognition? For what you've done?"

"Who's been fighting the Hun and his lickspittle, so-called

'allies' this past year—by ourselves? Generations of Southern men have bled and died so this land could be free. At King's Mountain, Yorktown, New Orleans, Pittsburgh Landing, Atlanta . . . We won't sit by idle while those Prussian pigs pollute it with every goose step they take. Even a Yankee should see that—if he can take his eye off the almighty dollar long enough."

"You have," Stevenson observes dryly, "an endearing way with words."

"But what do we hear from New York and Boston and Chicago? Silence, that's what. Where are the Northern boys now that our holy ground has been violated?"

"You need men," Stevenson guesses. The Germans must have cut deep into the nightriders' manpower.

Wallace juts his chin forward. "And guns."

"And what else?"

"And explosives!"

"And what else?"

"Some word of thanks from the rest of you sons of bitches!"

"Thanks? Thanks!" Some things Stevenson cannot swallow. "If it hadn't been for the clearings, none of this would be happening!"

Wallace is impervious to accusation. "Don't hand me that. Sure, there were some lynchings and things. Don't get me wrong—I never approved. A mob gets its dander up and they're likely to up and lynch the wrong nigra. That's not the American way."

"And lynching the right one is?"

"For murder or rape? Maybe not 'right,' but not the same kind of 'wrong,' either. But, like I said, I never approved. We would've worked things out. The coloreds and us, we been living side by side down here for a couple hundred years. We get along—as long as everybody knows his place. But then outside agitators come along and give folks uppity notions, fill them up with dreams their abilities can never achieve—so that they lash out like frustrated children and have to be spanked."

"I'd call what happened more than a spanking, Mr. Wallace."

Wallace says nothing for a moment. His eyes smolder; then he looks away. "Things . . . got out of hand."

"Just a little."

"The boys went crazy when the Huns landed. Pure loco. I couldn't stop them. No one could. No one planned what happened. No one meant for it."

"No one with responsibility, you mean, but I suspect there were plenty of your 'rednecks' just itching for the chance. When you use a mob, Wallace, it's a fine question who leads whom on the leash."

Wallace glares at him.

"Folks up north want the League out, too," Stevenson continues, "but we can't stand with you while the clearings go on."

"That's over with. The boys ain't killin' niggers any more. They're killing collaborators."

"Who happen to be mostly Negroes. Maybe there is a difference, but it doesn't look that way up north. It has to stop, Wallace, or you'll never get the support you need."

"Why? You Yankees too yellow to go toe-to-toe with the Huns?" Wallace taunts.

"With what? Potbellied men and gas-station jockeys toting shotguns and squirrel rifles? Against the army that sacked Tokyo?"

Wallace might play loose with the truth, but he knew it when he heard it. His next words are heavy with defeat. "Wilson should never have shrunk the Army. We would've had a first-class military of our own, not just a few regiments chasing bandits and renegades out west, afraid to fight because of some treaty, some 'scrap of paper.' Then we could've taken on the Hun."

A Great Peace to follow the Great War, Wilson had proclaimed in ordering the reduction in forces—starting, of course, with the Negro regiments he so despised—and going on to grant independence to the Philippines and Puerto Rico—and barring the "golden door" against "little brown brother."

The League will enforce the Peace from now on, Wilson had proclaimed. Stevenson had been only nineteen, but he remembered it clearly. Seen with the idealism—and self-interest—of youth, Wilson's demilitarization had seemed bold and courageous.

In hindsight, Wilson seemed less wise. To keep American boys out of the meatgrinder of the Western Front was one thing. Boys who had trained with wooden rifles? Folly! It would have taken two years to build an American Expeditionary Force around the few professional regiments. And the Western Front ate regiments for breakfast. No, Wilson had been right about that.

Staying neutral had let him play peacemaker to the exhausted participants, to referee the Treaty of Silver Spring, to midwife his brainchild, the League of Nations. Yet, it is Wilson's League that now humiliates the United States, citing the very Article 10 upon which Lodge's Republicans had based their opposition. Mandatory member intervention in domestic disturbances.

"No," Stevenson tells Wallace with heavy finality. "Our citizen militias cannot fight trained professionals. We must rely on persuasion, not the rifle and grenade; and for that we need Party unity; and for that, we need these killings to stop. You 'know people who know people'? Pass the word."

"So white men must lay down their arms while the SCLC commandos creep through the hills and bayous, and strike with impunity under German protection?"

There is no audience to impress with fine words of defiance. Wallace must be speaking from the heart. His regrets about the mob running out of control might even be sincere. "I want both sides to lay down their arms," Stevenson tells him, "and stand together against the occupation."

Wallace's eyes go wide, then he laughs. "King would never agree. Why would he go against his protectors?"

"He may have his reasons. But he needs a word from . . . the friends of your friends. We have to stop this before it goes too far."

Wallace's lips seem to thicken and a distant look comes over him. "It may already have," he says sadly. And indeed, the old world of the '30s and the '40s, of cheap, servile labor, are probably gone past recalling. No matter how the Situation plays itself out, things will never again be as they were before. Thus do reactionaries, fighting to preserve a half-mythic past, create in the process a new world order.

Wallace rises and makes to leave; but at the door he turns. "You know, Stevenson," he says, "I never much cared for the nigger. All that smilin' and shuckin' and jivin' . . . Nothin' there a man could respect. But that King, he showed they could stand up like men, and I got to respect that. If you ever see that murdering son of a bitch, you tell him I said that."

Stevenson goes all bland. "When would I ever see King?"

The two of them lock eyes for a moment and Stevenson senses the pressure inside the other man. Wallace is a boiler, building a head of steam. Then the Alabaman laughs. "When he wants to see you." And then Stevenson is alone once more.

That evening, in the hotel's restaurant, talk runs high. A German soldier has raped a woman—or so the bar talk has it. The honor of the South has been tarnished once again. If they had let it go at that—if they had spoken of liberty and independence and national honor; if they had spoken only of sovereignty betrayed—he might have stomached it. But—

" . . . snooty Europeans . . ."

" . . . bringin' them niggers back to Darktown . . ."

" . . . forced busing . . ."

" . . . cold-blooded guerilla killers livin' right over the tracks from us . . ."

" . . . goose-steppers can't be everywhere, and the minute they turn their back . . ."

" . . . ain't enough bayonets in the world . . ."

" . . . that Southern Colored Liberation Corps ain't turned over their guns like they was supposed to, so why should we . . ."

Stevenson hunches over his steak. It is overdone and salty. The vegetables are boiled to a mush. No one in the South knows how to cook. He wants to tell them that they are blaming the wrong people. It wasn't the coloreds that brought in the League, not King and his SCLC; but they, themselves, and the bloody savagery they had wrought on their neighbors.

But he says nothing. If the people around him despise the coloreds and hate the Germans, they do not exactly love Yankees, either. This is a land that treasures its grudges.

Northern governors, chafing over Black's inaction, had been quietly planning the dispatch of State troops to escort those colored children into that Little Rock high school—and had they done so all hell would have broken loose, maybe even a second War Between the States. A Republican president, Stevenson is sure, would have done exactly that—using Federal troops. President Black had at least seen the folly of throwing a match into a tinderbox.

Well, the match had been thrown—by the sanctimonious Europeans—and all hell had broken loose anyhow; and if the South has lost its sovereignty, the North had lost its chance to stand up for a principle. There comes a time when circumspection sails almighty close to acquiescence; when, as Burke observed, forebearance ceases to be a virtue.

We should have spoken up, he thinks as he signs the meal to his room. Is Party unity worth this? Yet, without the Solid South, the Democrats will never win the White House. Truman is doomed, but he must run a credible campaign if the Party is to be taken seriously in '56. That means northern and southern wings closing ranks. If the party splits, men of quality like Sparkman will lose all influence and restraint over men like Wallace. And even men like Wallace would give way to those who made no fine distinction between lynching the right or wrong Negro.

That night the dull thump of an explosion shakes the windows of the hotel. It wakes him and he lies in bed unable to sleep, listening to the rattle of distant gunfire that follows.

The next morning the Germans revoke all travel permits. Stevenson drives out with the locals to look and returns shaken to his hotel room, where he pours himself the last of the bourbon, and stares into it without drinking.

A crater in the highway and burnt and scattered flinders are all that remain of the guard shack. Telephone poles have been toppled and charred like so much kindling. Gasoline fires burn hotter than Hell itself. Of Lieutenant Goldberg and the young sentry, nothing but greasy ashes remain. Stevenson stares out the hotel room window at the blackened remains of Darktown and, for a moment, he imagines the sweetish odor of crackling flesh carried on the hot summer breeze. It is overpowering, as if millions have been incinerated.

The alcohol, when he throws it back over his throat, does nothing to soothe the roiling in his belly.

Now the Germans will retaliate in their usual ham-fisted manner and the American people would have their noses rubbed once more in the consequences of a fourth-rate military. (No more dangerous than Roumania, had been Hindenburg's famous sneer.) They would have one more reason never to vote Democrat again.

Sparkman is not so inept. He knows the Party's interests lie in making the Situation go away as quickly and as quietly as possible. Wallace can call it Kaiser-kissing if he wishes, but there comes a time to turn the other cheek and negotiate a solution. Even Wallace, intemperate as he is, must know better. The attack on the guard post doesn't quite make sense yet. Somthing is missing.

Stevenson senses that not all the pieces are yet in play.

Late that afternoon, helicopters settle on the town and disgorge elite storm troops, who fan out into every neighborhood of the city. If the locals think the Wehrmacht hard to deal with, they find these newcomers in their Prussian-blue uniforms impossible. Hardened veterans of the Philippine campaign, they have dealt with tougher resistance than anything the "good ol' boys" of Selma can muster. Men who have fought with Japanese fanatics in Pacific jungles will not flinch from potbellied white men in overalls. They arrest one man from every block, apparently at random, and bring them to a compound just outside the city limits. In the barroom of the hotel, Stevenson now hears fear mixed with the feckless bravado.

" . . . done arrested the mayor and the chief . . ."

" . . . hope they got that damn county assessor, too . . ."

" . . . bunch'a innercent townfolk . . ."

" . . . just a bluff . . ."

" . . . half a mind to get out my varmint rifle and . . ."

" . . . barbaric, that's what it is . . ."

The bartender, a swarthy, heavy-jowled man of Stevenson's age, listens and shakes his head. He and Stevenson lock gazes for a moment and trade rueful grins. Thus do rabbits discuss the wolf. "Martyrs stiffen a cause," the barman tells him. "If the Germans execute the hostages, they'll be sowing dragon's teeth."

Stevenson grants that German antiterrorism doctrine is every bit as barbaric as the terrorism itself. Yet, it is no more than poetic justice on the people who invented "racial clearing." Just what were those "innercent townfolk" doing in the months before the Situation? Lynching their neighbors; burning down their churches. Digging mass graves—and filling them up.

Just before nightfall, the German commander arrives. Provost-general Erwin Rommel is a veteran of both the Bolshevik War and the Pacific War and has a reputation as a just man. This is bad news for Selma, since justice of any sort would wipe it off the face of the Earth. Stevenson catches a glimpse of the general as he rides down the street behind the bullet-proofed windows of his staff car. Peaked cap, Eisenkreuz dangling from a blue ribbon around his neck, a look on his face of infinite distance and pain. A father about to spank an errant child.

Stevenson remembers the cultured, intelligent lieutenant Goldberg and wishes Rommel silent success. If the random hostages do not include last night's terrorists, they surely include those of other nights. An eye for an eye.

But the food lies heavy and undigested in Stevenson's belly. He can hear Wallace in his mind. Is it not important to lynch the "right" rednecks?

Stevenson is preparing for bed when a gentle tapping at his door freezes him. He scowls, begs a moment's grace, and puts his shirt back on, pulling his suspenders up as he reaches for the knob.

A bellboy stands without—rumpled gray uniform with a button missing, pillbox cap set slightly askew. "What is it?" he asks the young man.

"The package you ordered."

Stevenson has ordered no package, but sees the note affixed to the plain brown wrapper. Follow me. Make no sign. He looks again at the boy, wondering who has sent him. Too light-complexioned for the SCLC, but he might work for Tricky Dick. Unless there are other factions. . . . Stevenson places the package (sans note) on the dresser and follows the bellhop.

Dusk has slid quietly into night, but has brought with it no relief from the heat as bricks and asphalt slowly release the energy they have absorbed during the day. The bellhop leads him to a darkened alley cluttered with debris and trash cans, damp with fetid pools, rank with the stench of garbage and honeysuckle. A shape steps forward from the darkness and Stevenson recoils when he sees a well-muscled Negro man, broad in the shoulders, two hundred pounds and none of it fat. His head is shaved. A scar puckers one cheek and an implacable steel gleams in his eyes. Stevenson recognizes John Calvin King, "generalissimo" of the Southern Colored Liberation Corps.

"I saw by the newspaper," King says sardonically, "that you wanted to see me." His hands wave not a newspaper but an over-and-under shotgun. Stevenson notices a twist of wire on the trigger guard.

The bellboy slouches in the mouth of the alley smoking a cigarette, but he turns long enough to send a smirk in Stevenson's direction. "Ever hear of a white boy," King's voice says, "passin' fo' black?" When Stevenson turns a puzzled look on the guerilla leader, he explains. "Linc, there, he has seven white great-grandparents. Now, what do you call a boy like that?" He does not wait for Stevenson to answer. "A 'nigger,' is what. Same as if seven was black and only one was white. Shows the power of black blood."

Stevenson studies the bellhop and, now that King has pointed it out, he can see the slightly thicker lips, the slightly broader nose, the slightly duskier complexion. King, watching, lets him make up his mind before adding slyly, " 'Less I'm lyin'. There are some white folks who fight for justice."

King is playing with him, but Stevenson uses the opening. "Maybe more of us than you know."

"Doubt that, Stevenson. I sure didn't see many of you down here during the clearings."

Stevenson wipes his mouth with the back of his hand. "People up north," he says, "are predisposed to look favorably on your cause—"

"He talks purty," says the bellhop, but King waves him silent. "Go on."

"They don't like what's been done to your people. The burnings, the beatings and lynchings—they elicited a great deal of sympathy up north. They would like to help. . . ."

"But . . ." suggests King. "There's a 'but' in there somewhere."

"But they won't help you break up the United States—and that's what will happen if you keep up these vengeance strikes of yours. You have a grievance—God knows, you have a grievance—but they don't like the way the League butted in when you asked them for help."

"Who should I have asked?" King says bitterly. "Governor Sparkman? President Black? The good folks up north, who 'sympathized' with our 'plight' but never lifted one damn finger to help? If good does nothing, evil triumphs. And what was done to us was not a 'grievance'; it was not a 'plight.' It was evil! Not even some likkered-up mob losing its head because some pasty-fleshed white woman kicked up her heels for some po'-ass black boy and changed her mind next mornin'. This was deliberate, planned murder on a scale the world has never seen—carried out while officials and the 'quality folks' wrung their hands, or looked the other way, or even helped when they thought no one knew. Say what you will about the Kaiser's troops, or the Triple Monarchy, or the British Empire and the rest, but when we called on them, they came."

"Not for you," Stevenson tells him. "They're jealous of our prosperity—because we never got sucked into their wars—so they wanted to take the USA down a peg or two."

He is rewarded by a huge, black shrug. "I know that. But if a man helps get the boot off my neck, who am I to question his motives?"

"I never walked in your shoes," Stevenson admits, "but we've got to think toward the future. The longer the Situation goes on, the harder it will be to bring us back together as one nation."

"Never was one nation," King says. "Not for us."

"But it can be. Don't you see? It's what we work toward. If we lose the faith that it can be, we lose hope. And if we lose hope, we lose everything—all the good works that might yet come—and the future will be nothing but ambush and bushwhack and hate and separation, world without end."

For a moment, King seems captured by the image, as if he has had a dream of all God's children, black and white, lying dead side by side, equal at last. "If not the League," he asks suspiciously, "then who?"

"Us."

King's eyes widen. "The Democrats?"

"Why stick with the Republicans? What have they ever done for the Negro?"

The guerilla leader affects innocence. "Give us our freedom?" he suggests.

"That was nearly a hundred years ago. Today, they're lapdogs for Big Business and don't care about Negroes one way or the other."

"Maybe so," King allows, "but that puts 'em up a notch, don't it. 'Cause in case you haven't noticed, the Democrats down here do care about us. One way. Or is it the other?" He smiles at Stevenson's discomfiture. "What you up to, Stevenson? You got a strategy?"

"A deal," he says. "If northern Democrats take your side against the rednecks, our Southern wing could bolt . . ."

A cynical smile splits a black face. "So you need our votes because you'd lose theirs? Good Lord above, Stevenson! Can't you take a stand just because it's right? That's the acid test. Isn't governing a nation more important than winning an election?"

Stevenson flushes. "We can't govern if we don't win;

and if you help us win, then we'd owe you. But we can't help unless you break with the League and stop the vengeance strikes."

"Self-defense isn't murder."

"Retribution isn't self-defense."

King shows teeth. "Massacre don't look so good from the other end of the gun barrel, does it?"

"You lose the moral high ground when you stoop to the level of your oppressors."

"The high ground . . . ? The high ground . . . ?" King's laughter is bitter. "Shit, we already got all the 'low' ground: six feet of it, twenty thousand times over. We should stand by all meek and humble and 'yassah, boss' while they shoot us down, rape our women, burn our churches, just so other white folks can admire how Christian we are for 'turnin' the other cheek'? My mama named me for a preacher, but that don't make me one. Can you name one place in the world where 'turn the other cheek' won the day? Russia? India? China? Anywhere? No. The League wants us to trust them to keep order, but someday the League will go home. I'd rather trust my right to bear arms." King flourishes the shotgun he is holding and Stevenson takes an involuntary step backward.

"Sometimes," King says, now more to himself than to Stevenson, "I think I was born for this. That I was destined from all time to be the protector and savior of my people; to lead them into the Promised Land. Even if things had fallen out differently—no Great War, no League, no President Robinson winking while hooded nightriders rode out in the daylight—I would still find myself waging this struggle."

"But maybe with words instead of weapons."

King shrugs. "I just keep on keepin' on. If we don't stand up now, when can we? If we accept mass murder, against what injustice can we later rail? No! Never again! My destiny drives me. Here I stand; I can do nothing else."

"That's Martin Luther."

King gives him a look. "I know that, 'professor.' Just like I know you were born to be a trimmer. Always looking for the compromise. Always splitting the difference. Well, Stevenson, how do you split the difference between me and Georgie Wallace?"

"He wants to fight the Germans, not you. He's trying to control the mob."

King grunts. "A man rides a tiger, it's the tiger decides which way to run. So, how 'bout we compromise. They only kills half as many of us next year."

"Is it so terrible to bury the hatchet and search for common ground?"

"Long as the ground ain't quicksand—and the hatchet ain't buried in my head. Long as folks don't have to abandon their principles to come together. But principles don't matter to your sort, do they? Lord Jesus, I think I'd rather deal with ol' Georgie. I might not like where he stands, but at least he stands somewhere."

"That's funny," says Stevenson. "He said much the same thing about you."

King saddens Stevenson in an indefinable way. This might have been an educated man, had history treated him more kindly. Stevenson is not well read, himself; he finishes perhaps two books a year, not like Truman who consumes them weekly by the dozen. Yet he knows native intelligence when he sees it. "You'll be killed, eventually. If the nightriders don't get you, the Germans will. They came to restore order, not to help you wreak vengeance."

"They will take my gun," King prophesies, "when they pry it from my cold, dead fingers."

Stevenson shivers from a sudden vision. A shot. A body topples on a distant balcony. Cities burn in retribution. "Is it worth being killed?"

King stares as if from a distant height. "If a man hasn't discovered something he can die for, he isn't fit to live. The measure of a man is not where he stands when things are easy—fine words and sentiments flow smoothly when they cost nothing—but what measures a man is where he stands in tribulation. Has there ever been a Savior that the mob failed to crucify?"

"Predestination," Stevenson answered. "You're taking your namesake too seriously."

King gives him a quizzical look. "It bothers you. Why?"

A shake of the head. "I don't know, but I think, in another milieu, you might have achieved greatness."

"So might we all, Stevenson. You, me, Georgie, Sparkman. Our natures form us, but the world molds us. And so, instead of greatness, I lead a life that is 'nasty, brutish, and short'."

"First Calvin; now Hobbes. You're better read than you let on." Stevenson genuinely likes this man, or at least the man he might have been, but he can see now that he has come on a fool's errand. Jackson must have misread the signals. Now he can only hope that Jackson's guarantee is enough to let him leave this alley. "One word of advice. . . ." He waits until King shows by the tilt of his head that he will listen. "Don't let the Germans know you steal your arms from their checkpoints."

King turns the shotgun over in his hand and runs a hand down its barrel. "Now don't you go carrying tales to the Germans if you can't back them up," he says at last. "Words without facts are just words."

"Did you attack the—"

"And don't ask questions you don't want to hear the answer to." He pauses a moment as he studies Stevenson's face. Then he relents. "But maybe we hear about a raid, you know what I'm saying; and we duck in while others are . . . occupied . . . and take what we can. It pleases me to arm myself with weapons the League has taken from our oppressors."

"Who warned you about the raid?" Stevenson is certain the raid was Wallace's work; but he is equally certain Wallace would never have tipped King.

Expecting evasion, he is surprised when King answers. "Tricky Dick."

"You've seen him?"

"Him? No, nobody's ever seen that sly ol' fox. He sent a message, though. Told us you'd ask about him, too; and told us to tell you it was him."

Later, back in his hotel room, a shaken Stevenson seeks liquid relief and finds that King has a mordant sense of humor. Opening the package King's minion had given him, he finds the inevitable bottle of bourbon.

It is Old Crow.

The two storm troopers bang on his door early in the morning, but they allow him to shower and dress before escorting him to the Hauptquartier. The other men hanging about the hotel stare at Stevenson as he is marched past. It is the first clue the locals have that he might be someone important. The bartender is just opening up. When he sees Stevenson, he raises both hands, with two fingers spread in a V to signal encouragement.

A vigorous man in his early sixties, Rommel questions Stevenson about the incident at the checkpoint and how Lt. Goldberg handled the drunken redneck in the pickup truck. The interrogation is persistent, but polite. America is not a conquered province and a federal senator is no small thing to toy with. Rommel represents the League of Nations, not the Kaiser. He wears the green-and-white armband on his sleeve with the crossed olive branches. Officially, there are limits to what he can do to Stevenson.

Unofficially, of course, there are always tragic accidents.

Nervous in front of the iron-gray tactician, Stevenson pulls a pack of Luckies from his coat pocket, but Rommel curtly refuses him permission to light up. Stevenson is so startled that Rommel unbuttons enough to explain.

"I have sworn off the tobacco," he says. "It is—how do you say it?—a 'movement' in Europe. Perhaps you have heard? An Austrian painter—a crusader against vivisection and animal abuse—leads the campaign. I hear him speak once at a rally in Nuremberg, where they lit a bonfire and everyone threw into the flames their cigarettes. As a painter, the man was mediocre; but as a speaker, he is spellbinding. According to him, even the smoke of others is harmful; and so, there is no smoking in my presence."

Stevenson tucks his pack away. He doesn't think an anti-tobacco attitude will serve Rommel well in the South, but the general has not come here to endear himself.

He has not come here at all, Stevenson suddenly realizes with ice in his heart. He was lured here, by the bombing. But lured by whom? And for what purpose?

Rommel has detected his abrupt stiffening. "Yes? There is something else?"

Stevenson wonders where his duty lies—as a Democrat, as an American, as a human being. Here is a man who tramples on the liberties of American citizens, who arrests without warrant, who executes without trial. And yet, the people he has come to chastise have deserved what he gives them. Indeed, the avowed League policy of "rebuilding a multiethnic society" is more than they deserve. When Rommel presses him, he says only, "You may be in danger here."

The general is interested, but not surprised. Over the years, he has been in a number of unsafe places: Minsk, Bataan, Okinawa; as a young man in his twenties, in the shell-churned abattoir of the Western Front. Very little can frighten him.

And what does Stevenson have to frighten him with? A sudden, icy feeling in the gut that everything up to now has been a setup for something yet to come. The incident at the checkpoint; the meetings with Sparkman, with Wallace, with King; the rumors, the car bomb, Rommel's arrival. But to whose advantage? There is a devious mind at work. Wallace? He lacks the subtle touch. King? Rommel has come to protect King's people—but Rommel has come also to disarm them.

In the end, Stevenson mouths platitudes about safety and the breakdown of civil order.

Rommel's smile is a wolf's smile. "It is to remedy this breakdown of your civil order that I am come."

A growing noise outside the building forestalls any reply—which is good, because Stevenson has none. Only that the League is gasoline thrown on smoldering embers; that the United States could have handled things, given time. The trends had been good; lynchings had been on the decline. If only Black had been more assertive, and less defensive of "states' rights." If only the northern machines had leaned harder on their southern colleagues. If only Wilson had not made casual bigotry so fashionable with his praise for *Birth of a Nation.*

If only. Stevenson sighs.

People outside begin hooting. Looking out the window, he sees a bus escorted by a company of soldiers. There is a banner on the side of the bus: WE SERVE NEITHER KING NOR KAISER. If it is meant to reassure the whites of Selma, it fails. People hurl catcalls at the bus. They shake their fists. Some stones are thrown, but when the soldiers cock their rifles and level them at the crowd, the locals disperse, muttering. They know the Germans will fire if pushed. Stevenson sees the darkies through the windows of the bus, eyes white and wide as saucers. They are unarmed and they know it. The unwelcoming crowd is supposed to be disarmed too, but no one can believe that.

Rommel has joined him by the window. "Brave men," Stevenson tells him.

"They are soldiers doing their duty."

Stevenson watches the bus out of sight. "I wasn't thinking of the soldiers." When they turn away, Stevenson asks bleakly, "What's the point, general? Too much blood has been spilled for them to live in their old neighborhoods again. Neither side can pretend the clearings never happened."

Rommel shrugs. "I am only following orders. The World

Court mandated this busing. So long as my troops are here, your rednecks dare not make trouble."

"But your troops can't stay forever. Once they're gone, those people will go for each other's throats."

Rommel purses his lips, disliking the futility of his mission. "There is too much history here," he answers. "We do what we can, while we can. Yet, somehow, there must be a final solution to the redneck problem."

"What?" Stevenson asks sardonically. "Kill them all?"

Rommel makes no reply for a moment and Stevenson's heart freezes as, once again, the wind brings the odors of dead fires from the ruins of Darktown. Then the general shakes his head—though with how much reluctance Stevenson dares not guess.

Outside his hotel, a woman stops him with a hand on his sleeve. He sees red-rimmed eyes, makeup hastily applied, hair not quite in place. "They say you're an important man," she says. "A senator from up north."

Stevenson inclines his head. He does not deny it.

"You can tell them they're making a mistake, making a terrible mistake. They'll listen to an important man like you. Tell them they've made a mistake." Her voice grieves; her eyes plead.

Stevenson lays his hand over hers. "Tell who? What mistake?"

"My husband!" the distraught woman says. "They've taken my husband to the camp."

He understands now, and nods. "It's their policy," he says, "when any of their soldiers are killed by terrorists."

"But Leroy had nothin' to do with that! He's a good man, a decent man. God-fearing. He never had no truck with the coloreds—they kept to their side of town and we kept to ours—but he never wished them no harm."

Over her shoulder and down at the end of the street, across the railroad tracks, stand the cold embers of Darktown. The distant sound of hammers and saws echoes in the still, muggy air. Rebuilding—with hope or fatalism? "He wasn't one of the mob?" Stevenson says harshly. "Not one of those who fired those houses over there and shot the people who tried to run out of the blazing buildings?"

The woman backs away from him. "No, he never. Even if some of the coloreds was helpin' out the SCLC like folks said, they was only a few. Most coloreds are good folks. Leroy, he said they should just arrest the trouble-makers and leave the good ones alone. The night they— The night they— The night the fire broke out, he stood by the parlor window, cussin' and sayin' how they'd bring the Huns in for sure."

"But he didn't do anything to stop them."

She flinches at the accusation in his voice, but snaps in desperation. "What did you want him to do? One man? They'd call him a 'kraut-kisser' and a 'nigger-lover' and maybe burn our home down, too. But he never burned nobody, never shot nobody, never rode out at night."

No, Stevenson thinks sadly, he only stood by while others did. He understands, finally, the message in Revelation. Ye runneth neither hot nor cold, but lukewarm. Therefore, I spew ye forth from my mouth. The devil gets his due, but those who will not choose sides get nothing but contempt. He remembers King's words about how men are measured.

Yet, such a sentiment might itself be too easy. When standing up means to risk everything—wife, home, life itself—how many would sit by in quiet impotence? The Northern bosses loathe the barbarism in the South. Their graft is impartial; green is the only color that matters. But in the end they had held Party unity more dear, so who is Adlai Stevenson to judge Leroy? He looks over his shoulder to the German HQ and thinks how evil may be done even in a good cause, and not only by Erwin Rommel. Stevenson knows he ought to do something for Leroy, if only because the poor son of a bitch is the closest thing to a liberal the town has.

★ ★ ★

Stevenson counts himself wise for promising nothing, but he needs most of the Old Crow before he can accept the truth. There is no time to call Daley for instructions; and the phones would be tapped in any case. Stevenson sits at the desk in his room and scrawls a note on the hotel's stationery, informing Rommel about Wallace and King. "Rigorous questioning" at the barbershop will reveal Wallace's whereabouts, he writes. King is hiding in Selma's Darktown, but might be lured out to meet with Rommel, who is a nominal ally.

Rommel, with a German's obsession for legal literalism, will try to arrest King for theft of contraband and King, just as certainly, will resist. Wallace, his head stuffed with Southern irredentism, will never surrender either. But by making clear to them the common enemy, Stevenson might yet engineer the alliance he seeks. Martyrs do wonders for unity; the brotherhood of death can weld hostile factions together.

He calls the front desk and has a runner sent up. When the boy knocks—it is the same wavy-haired, swivel-hipped lad he used before—Stevenson hands him another cartwheel and a sealed envelope. He tells him the message is a plea to release some innocent hostages and that he should take it to Rommel immediately. The boy runs for the stairwell. Stevenson closes the door behind him and returns to the bottle of Old Crow.

Everybody does it, he tells himself.

All's fair, he tells himself.

Wallace and King are both bushwacking killers, he tells himself.

It's for the greater good, he tells himself.

It will unite the factions, he tells himself.

Finally, he can stand the sound of his own voice no longer. And besides, the bottle is empty. So he walks with careful, deliberate steps down to the lobby, where he enters the barroom and orders another bourbon.

"You look like you've had enough," the bartender reproves him. He has jowls like a basset hound, darkened now by five o'clock shadow. His dark eyes flash under lowered brows.

Stevenson surveys an empty room. The bar has not so much business that the man can afford to turn customers away. Stevenson says so, and loudly; so the bartender shrugs and pours the drink. Stevenson suspects it is watered.

His hand shaking, Stevenson lifts the glass to his lips; but the sudden roar of trucks past the window causes him to jerk and the glass drops and rolls across the bar top, leaving a glistening pool of liquor in its wake. Stevenson turns in time to see a troop truck turn the corner in the direction of the barbershop. Elite storm troopers in Prussian blue face each other ramrod straight on two benches in the back. They look neither left nor right and might have been cast from steel.

When Stevenson turns his back to the sight, the bartender has replaced the spilled drink. "I'd hold on to this one tight, if I were you," he advises.

Stevenson's mind is a haze. "Why?"

The bartender nods in the direction the troop truck has gone. "Shooting should start . . . about now."

As if awaiting that very cue, the distant pop of rifles comes faintly through the window. Stevenson squints at the bartender. A thought lurks in the back of his mind, but it will not come clear. Shortly, the messenger boy dashes into the barroom, grabbing the doorjamb to stop himself. He pants for breath a moment before blurting out, "They's holed up in the high school. Ol' Wallace, he's barricaded hisself in the schoolhouse door. The Hun's got 'im treed."

The bartender shakes his head. "He's facing a platoon of the Regiment Groszherzogthum Baden. That's the gang that hit the beaches on Honshu. I doubt the high school is as impregnable as Tojo's fortress. What do you say, Stevenson? About fifteen minutes and it's over?"

Stevenson raises a shaky finger. "You. You're Tricky Dick."

The man smiles a devil's smile, but does not deny it.

"What are you doing here?"

"Everyone has to be somewhere." The guerilla leader is relaxed and confident, yet his gaze shifts constantly and he never looks Stevenson directly in the eye. Stevenson sets his glass softly on the bar top. What better place to sift for information than in a bar. A man will tell his bartender things he conceals from his wife.

"You've been behind all of this."

"Me?" The affect of great surprise. "Behind all of what?"

"Everything! The bombing . . . Rommel coming to town . . ."

Tricky Dick laughs. "You think I order provost-generals around?"

"You didn't order him. You lured him."

Dick's grin broadens into a smile. "I thought Wallace's attack on the guard shack brought Rommel here."

"And why did Wallace attack the guard shack? He's hot-tempered, but he's not stupid."

"Jury's still out on that. But if I have to guess, I would say the rumors about the guard threatening the baby and assaulting the wife must have outraged him beyond reason."

If he has to guess. . . . Tricky Dick is as convoluted as a snake. A master manipulator. "And who spread the rumors?"

Tricky Dick pulls out a bar rag and begins wiping the counter top. "It's funny," he says. "When a man believes the worst of someone, he'll credit anything bad he hears. He won't even stop to ask if it makes sense or not. That's a man's weak spot. We all have one: King, Rommel, you . . . Wallace thought the Germans were the devil's spawn, profaning . . ." And here Tricky Dick places a solemn hand over his heart. " . . . the sacred heartland of the Southern people. You could have told him that the expletive-deleted Huns ate Belgian babies or burned people in ovens and he would believe it. He didn't need me to feed him rumors."

Stevenson has actually begun to admire Tricky Dick's lies. There is an artistry to them that excites respect. He is a master of prevarication. Never so uncouth as a straightforward, bald-faced fabrication, his lies are fashioned by intaglio, the lie lying in what is not said, questions answered by the manner in which they are dodged.

"I know it was you who told King to steal the contraband weapons."

A shrug of dismissal. "That's always been his strategy. All I passed on was when and where an opportunity lay. Like I said, if you tell people what they want to hear, they're more likely to act on it."

"They say you have the greatest tactical mind since General Miles or General Crook."

Tricky Dick dips his head modestly. "Well, I am not a Miles."

Maybe not, Stevenson muses. More like Machiavelli than a military man. Tricky Dick's genius lay in scheme, not rifles in the field. His band of operatives—known as "The Plumbers," because they worked to "plunge the crap out"—was probably a small, tight-knit band. Had to be, for the man to be seen so little when sought so much. "How'd you get Wallace to barricade himself in the schoolhouse?"

Dick has been polishing the bar top. He looks up, sees Stevenson's knowing, just-us-chickens smile. He folds the rag and tucks it in his apron cord. "Ol' George, he's a Romantic. What he sees in his mind are the heroic poses, the grand speeches; not the bayonet sliding into the gut, not the slugs ripping and tearing the flesh and splintering the bones. So, a bunch of them were in here yesterday, griping like they always do; and Wallace compares the way he's standing up to the Hun to the way Washington and them stood up to the Brits. So, I told him about the heroic stand the Irish made in Dublin back about the end of the Great War. It really inspired him."

"The Brits stomped the Irish good," Stevenson points out. "Those that weren't killed were executed."

The Dick wags a finger. "Ah, but it led to the revolution and the Republic. The inspirational value of martyrs," he adds with a wink. "Ol' George really thinks his heroic stand will inspire others to follow him."

"Like Custer."

Tricky Dick shrugs. "It really is inspiring, you know. If Wallace and his cause weren't a bucket of expletives deleted, it might be even viewed as a noble sacrifice. A man capable of such an act is capable of redemption—if the world allows his heart the time to change."

Stevenson has been memorizing Tricky Dick's face so he can describe it to Daley's police artists. The Dick's greatest asset until now has been his invisibility. A man can be hard to find when no one knows what he looks like. Even Dick's last name or his native state are unknown. It is part of his mystique. Revealing himself to Stevenson is a major misstep; but if every man has a weakness, Dick's lies in his own cleverness. It is not always what a man believes of others that makes him vulnerable, but often what he believes of himself. Pleased with his own cleverness, the guerilla leader has succumbed to the desire to preen before a mind capable of appreciating that cleverness.

"What I don't understand . . ." Stevenson leans over the bar and taps it with a stiff forefinger. " . . . is what you hope to accomplish. As far as I can tell, you're just making things worse by stirring the pot." By pushing the pride button, Stevenson hopes to elicit some careless revelations.

Tricky Dick takes Stevenson's now-empty glass and dunks it in a sink full of dishwater. "I have a plan," he confides. "A secret plan to end the Situation." He wipes his hands on a bar towel, then turns on a small radio on a shelf on the back wall. In a few minutes, the tubes have warmed up and he twists the tuner to put the receiver back on frequency. Stevenson catches a brief moment of "hepcat jive" in four-part harmony before the radio settles on a fainter, more distant signal playing nondescript dance tunes.

The sound of the radio makes Stevenson aware that the distant gunfire has fallen silent. When his head cocks, Tricky Dick makes a show of checking his watch. "Seventeen minutes," he says with some satisfaction. "A little longer than I expected, but Elvis will be back soon with a battle report."

Stevenson forms a plan. The Germans are just as anxious to lay hold of Tricky Dick as the Democrats. His raids and sabotage have come down hard on Wallace's supporters, and occasionally have frustrated King's dreams of vengeance; but his mere existence is an affront to the German sense of Law and Order. *Alles in Ordnung* is the most satisfied remark a German can make. German lovers tell each other that after sex.

The masterstroke slowly comes clear through the bourbon haze. A way to discomfit the League, please the Sparkman-Bankhead faction, neutralize Tricky Dick, mollify the factions he means to unite by showing them another common enemy.

Stevenson excuses himself and weaves his way to the jakes, where he takes care of business before stopping at the writing stand in the lobby on his way back and scribbling a hasty note: Tricky Dick is the bartender at the Stonewall Hotel. He places it in an envelope and seals the envelope with his tongue.

Then he pauses under the weight of a great sadness. In many ways, he and Tricky Dick are brothers, sharing a single vision. Outrage over the racial clearings; and distrust of Wallace's ability to control them. Sympathy for King's people; but not for vengeance and retribution.

Satisfaction that the Germans have brought justice; but fierce anger at the violation of sovereignty. Had the dice rolled another way, he thinks, it might be "Agile Adlai," the "fighting perfesser," out there exacerbating the Situation while "Senator Richard" desperately seeks to bring the factions together.

Young Elvis comes dashing back in, breathless with news of the battle. Stevenson stops him and hands him the message. "Take this to Rommel. Quick. I forgot to tell him something earlier."

But the lad is not to be deflected. "I gotta tell the Man," he says. "You shoulda seen it! Ol' Wallace, he took a slug right in the spine. You shoulda seen him twist and shout before the Dutchies tied him into a stretcher and carried him out. That poor sumbitch'll be in a wheelchair for sure—if the Dutchies don't hang him first." And with that, he ran into the barroom to tell Tricky Dick.

And Stevenson runs into the lavatory, where he pukes his guts into a stained and smelly toilet. One rolling heave follows another until he is dry and his stomach is a shriveled cramp within him. Afterward he leans on the sink to steady himself, taking long, slow breaths. He stares at the reflection in the mirror, wondering who the bastard staring back is to have so calmly written other men's death warrants.

It's the times, he tells himself. Had the Situation not happened, he would have been a different man; just as King or Wallace or Tricky Dick. A better man, he hopes; something more than a hireling of Boss Daley. The Party needs a strong leader, who can tame both the machines and the Southern families. Franklin had had that dream—of welding the Party into a single, coordinated, national force. But the Great Panic had put paid to those dreams; and shortly after, the polio made running for office unthinkable.

Nuts. You play the hand you're dealt. Stevenson turns on the faucet and cups the water in his hands to rinse his mouth. He spits into the sink several times, but the sour taste does not leave his tongue.

Returning to the barroom, he sees that the boy has gone to run his errand. Shortly, the Germans will be coming to seize Tricky Dick. Best not to be here when that happens. "I'm calling it a night," he says, but the barman waves him over.

"Not without signing your tab, you're not." He shoves a paper at Stevenson and Stevenson scrawls his signature at the bottom. As he turns to go, the music on the radio cuts off abruptly and a faint, scratchy voice begins to speak.

"This just off our wire services: A major gun battle has developed in the town of Selma, Alabama, between a right-wing militia group apparently led by the state's attorney general, George Wallace, and the German peacekeepers. Details are not yet clear, but casualties are said to be heavy. More news as it develops. On a personal note, let me say that never have two combatants so deserved each other. Self-appointed partisans impatient with the considered wisdom of our leaders in Washington versus merciless militarists who came to bring justice to the oppressed, but did so with such callous brutality that people are apt to forget the true victims. All I can say is, 'There they go again.' This is Dutch Reagan for CBS News Radio."

The music returns and Tricky Dick laughs as he turns the knob off. "I get a hoot out of that guy. You ever catch his A.M. TV show, *Morning in America*? Someone has to uphold liberalism in this country against the corrupt machines, the racists, the goose-steppers. . . . Hey . . . !" He looks down at his feet, puzzlement on his face. "I'll be . . . Come back here a second and look at this. What do you make of it?"

Stevenson grimaces and staggers around the end of the bar. "What?" Tricky Dick points to the sink, but when Stevenson leans his hands against the edge he suddenly finds them bound by handcuffs. "What the hell?" He yanks and pulls, but the cuffs are fastened to solid brackets. They clack and rattle. "What is this?" Puzzlement has not yet given way to irritation. His mind, awash in bourbon, has not yet grasped the situation.

"There he goes." Tricky Dick points to the outside window and Stevenson looks up to see Rommel's car speed by. "Going off to round up King, I suppose."

Stevenson jerks his head around to look at the man, who is now untying his apron. "How do you know that?"

Dick's smile is pure venom. "Because you sold him out just to have a martyr, you expletive deleted. You don't think my boys will carry messages without showing them to me first, do you? Or that you can say anything in your room that I don't tape record? I keep tapes of everything. I know what you discussed with Sparkman, and with Wallace, and even out back in the alley with King. And it's all for nothing. When people see how you sold everyone out to everyone else, any hope of Democrat unity will vanish for a generation."

"How would they know I—"

"Your note to Rommel, you fool."

"I didn't sign it."

Tricky Dick holds up a sheet of paper. "You just did, right here, a few minutes ago. We copied your note and kept the original. Just the sort of thing to send Dutch, so he can show the whole country on TV. They may join forces, like you thought. It's a long shot, but if they do, they'll join with us. They'll join with the progressive party of Lincoln and TR and LaFollette and Warren, not the Party of their betrayer." He steps behind Stevenson and decks the apron over him, tying it up in back. Then he tucks the bar rag in the cord. "There," he says in satisfied tones. "Now you look like a genuine bartender." He opens a cabinet underneath the liquor rack and mirror. Stevenson feels a cool draft and, twisting to look over his shoulder, sees that the cabinet is really a stairwell to the storage basement.

The Dick looks at his watch. "You thought you could come down here," he says with some heat, "and meet with me and manipulate me like you did the others. You thought you could kick me around. Well, when the going gets tough, the tough get going. You won't have ol' Dick to kick around much longer."

An explosion rattles the entire barroom. Stevenson feels the floor beneath him shrug. The window on the street cracks. There is a moment of total silence, then the screams begin. A man runs past the window. His shirt is torn and his glasses are shattered. Blood runs from cuts on his scalp. Stevenson turns horrified eyes on his captor.

"That was the bomb we planted under a manhole cover," The Dick says. "My boy Elvis set it off by radio when Rommel's car passed over it."

"Rommel . . ." Stevenson's soul turns to ice. The man is a hero of the Second Reich, idolized by his troops. He tries to imagine what retribution the Germans will take over this latest atrocity. His eyes lock again on Tricky Dick, who has climbed halfway down the ladder to the basement.

"You!" Stevenson gropes for truth, finds a shard of it. "You're no better than me. You talk about betrayal . . . But you passed my note on to Rommel. You're as responsible as I am. And your manhole bomb must have killed bystanders. And Rommel . . . How many hostages will they round up and shoot over this?"

The guerilla leader laughs. "Enough," he predicts, "that the British and French will turn against them." He grasps the door handle, ready to pull it down over him. "You think too small, Stevenson. You want martyrs to unite the country? The Germans will oblige." Then the door closes and the latch turns from the other side.

Tricky Dick is the bartender at the Stonewall Hotel.

Frantic, Stevenson rehearses what he will say when they come for him. "Freunde! Freunde! Nicht shieße! Ich heiße Stevenson; nicht der 'Tricky Dick'!" And yet, it was a note from Stevenson that lured Rommel into his fatal ride. It is diabolical, the way the Dick has boxed him in.

There are two fascinating details he notices when the storm troopers burst into the barroom screaming, "Hände hoch! Hände hoch!"

The first is that these tough, pitiless men, whose bootheels have pressed the streets of Moscow and Tokyo, have tears streaming down their cheeks.

The second is that, when he tries to raise his hands, the rattle of his chains sounds remarkably like the cocking of a pistol.

Uncle Alf

Harry Turtledove

7 May 1929

My very dear Angela,

You will have seen, I am sure, from the stamp and the postmark that I am now in Lille. I have not seen this place for almost fifteen years, but I well remember the pounding we gave it when we drove out the damned Englishmen. They fought hard, but they could not hold back the All-Highest's victorious soldiers. And even to this day, I find, the lazy Frenchmen have not bothered to repair all the damage the town suffered at that time.

But the Frenchmen, of course, are never too lazy to make trouble for the Kaiser and for the German Empire. That is why the *Feldgendarmerie* sent me here. When they want results, what do they do? They call on your uncle, that is what. They know I get the job done, come what may. And I aim to do it here, too, though I do not think it will be easy. Of course, if it were easy, they would send an ordinary fool.

Here in Lille, they call *Feldgendarmerie* men *diables verts*—green devils—on account of the tall green collars on our uniform tunics. I tell you for a fact, darling, I intend to send some of them straight to hell. They deserve nothing less. They lost the war, which proves how naturally inferior they are to good German men, but now they think they can reverse the inescapable verdict of history with tricks and plots and foolery. I am here to show them how wrong they are.

You can write to me at the address on this envelope. I hope all goes well for you, and that you never have to trouble your lovely little head about the schemes of these degenerate Frenchmen. I send you many kisses, and wish I could give them to you in person. With much love, I remain your—

Uncle Alf

9 May 1929

My dearest sweet Angela,

It is worse here than I imagined. No wonder they sent for me. Lille is one of the most backward cities in France. Dazzling riches and loathsome poverty alternate sharply. Side by side with commercial wealth dwell the homeless in gloom and mud. And, though it shames me to do so, I must tell you that at least half the *Feldgendarmerie* men here are as corrupt as any Frenchman.

I suppose it is inevitable that this should be so. Many of these men have been in their places in Lille since the days of the war. I am not lying or exaggerating a bit when I say they have become more French than German themselves. They live off the fat of the land. They have taken French mistresses and forgotten the good German wives they left back home.

Such degeneracy should be punished. Such degeneracy *must* be punished! I have made my views on this subject very clear. If only I held rank higher than *Feldwebel*, something might be done. But a small, ruthless clique of officers has shamelessly held back my advancement. When I think I turned forty last month with no more to show for my life than this, I know how unjust the world is. If only I had been allowed to show what I might do, everyone would hold his breath and make no comment. Of that you may be certain!

Still, I serve the German Empire with a loyal and honest heart. It is the last and best hope of mankind. French revanchism must be, shall be, mercilessly stamped out. Heads will roll here in Lille, and I shall rejoice to see it.

Meanwhile, I hope your own pretty head back there in Munich is happy and content. I send you kisses and hugs, and I will try to send you and your mother some smoked duck as well. You would be healthier without it, though. This I truly believe. It is one of my cardinal principles, and I shall go on trying to persuade you till the day I die. Meanwhile, in this as in all things, my honor remains true. I am, fondly, your—

Uncle Alf

11 May 1929

Sweet darling Angela,

I hope to hear from you. In this miserable place, a letter would mean a very great deal indeed. Your love and kisses and the thought of you in my embrace could help me forget what a hole Lille is and what a pathetic lot of bunglers the local *Feldgendarmerie* men have proved to be.

They look ever so impressive as they strut through the town with big, fierce Alsatians on a leash at their side. But here is the truth: the dogs are braver than all of them and smarter than most of them. They see nothing. They want to see nothing, to know nothing. So long as they can get through the day without noticing anything, they are content. Then in the evening they settle down to cigars and to wine or foul apple brandy from one of the local *estaminets*, of which, believe me when I tell you, there are a great many. Men with more disgusting habits would be difficult to imagine.

Yet these are the ones who are supposed to root out treason! It would be laughable if it were not so dreadful. No wonder they had to call in someone whose belly does not hang out half a kilometer over his belt! *Gott mit uns*, our belt buckles say. With these men, their bulging bellies hide God from the world, and surely the Lord on high does not much care to look at them, either.

With them all so fat and sluggish and useless, it is up to me to go into the workers' districts and sniff out the treason growing here. And I *will* sniff it out, and we *will* cut it out, and the Second Reich *will* go on ruling Europe, as it was destined to do.

And when I have done my duty, how I look forward to seeing you again, to hugging you against me, to running my hands through your golden hair. Truly the reward of the soldier for doing what he must is sweet. The thought of coming home to you makes me struggle all the harder here, so I may speed the day.

Also tell your mother I remain her affectionate half brother, and that I will write to her as soon as I find time. As always, I am your loving—

Uncle Alf

14 May 1929

My darling and beloved Angela,

By now I had hoped to receive at least one letter from you, yet the field post brings me nothing. Without word that you still feel kindly towards me, life seems very empty indeed. I do my duty—I always do my duty, for the enemies of the German Empire must be rooted out wherever they are found—but it is, I must tell you, with a heavy heart.

The French, though . . . *Gott im Himmel*, they are and shall always be our most implacable foes. The hatred on their faces when they see us go by! They may act polite when we are in earshot, but how they wish they had another chance to fight us! You can tell by the looks they give us that they believe the result would be different in a second match. The essence of German policy here is to make sure that second match never comes.

How I thank God that General von Schlieffen was so resolute during the war, and kept the right wing of our advance through Belgium and France strong, stronger, strongest despite the unexpectedly quick Russian invasion of our eastern provinces. Once we wheeled behind Paris, knocked the English out of the war, and made the mongrel Third Republic sue for peace, we easily regained the bits of territory the Czar's hordes stole from us. Soon enough we bundled the Slavic subhumans out of the Fatherland and back to the steppes where they belong! We still have not exploited Russia so fully as we should, but that day too will come. I have no doubt of it; those Cossack hordes must not be allowed to threaten civilized Europe ever again.

But to return to the French. Here in Lille, as elsewhere in this country, endless schemes of revenge bubble and trickle and fume. I must get to the bottom of them before they grow too poisonous. I shall not find much help here—that seems plain. But I am confident regardless. The superior man carries on to victory, alone if necessary, and lets nothing obstruct him in the slightest. This shall be my plan here in Lille.

I wish I would hear from you. Knowing that you feel towards me as I do towards you would steel my resolve in the death struggle against the enemies of the *Volk* and of the Kaiser. May we soon see each other again. I would like to take you out to a quiet supper and walk with you in the moonlight and kiss you until we both are dizzy. I shall look forward to my hero's homecoming while holding off Reds and Jews and others who so vilely plot against the Fatherland here on foreign soil. With all my love and patriotic duty, I remain your—

Uncle Alf

17 May 1929

Dear lovely Geli,

So good to hear from you at last! When I got your letter, I first and foremost kissed the postage stamp, knowing it had touched your sweet lips but two days before. I am glad all is well in Munich, although I do not know that I ought to be glad you sang in a café. This does not strike me as being completely respectable, even if it might have been, as you say, "fun." Duty and discipline and order first, always. The people lacking them is surely doomed. These Frenchmen were frivolous before the war. Now they pay the price for their folly, and they deserve to pay it.

Which is not to say they are much less frivolous now. Walk into any of dozens of clubs and cafés here in Lille and you will see things that would never be allowed—would never be imagined!—in Germany. I shall say no more, drawing instead a merciful veil of silence over brazen French degeneracy.

But I do begin to make progress. In one of these smoky dens, while saxophones brayed out American music straight from the jungle and while dancers cavorted in ways I shall not—I dare not—discuss further, I heard two Frenchmen speaking of a certain Jacques Doriot, who has come to visit this town.

He is the man I principally seek, for he has been schooled by the vile Russian Reds who tried to overthrow Czar Nicholas in 1916. Had the Kaiser not swiftly sent soldiers to his cousin's aid, those devils might have succeeded in their criminal scheming, and then who knows what a mess this sorry world would find itself in now. But a whiff of grapeshot is always the best answer to such vermin. If the Czar had hanged a few hundred more of them after the troubles of 1905, he would have been spared his later difficulties, but he was and is only a wooly-headed fool of a Russian.

Meanwhile I listened as never before. I cannot speak French without showing myself a foreigner, but I understand it quite well. I had better, after so long tracking down enemies of the Kaiser! At any rate, I heard his name, so now I know he is indeed here in Lille spreading his filth. If I have anything to do with it—and I do—he will not spread it long. Good riddance to bad rubbish, I say.

After I return to Munich, perhaps you will sing for me—just for me. And who knows, my darling, what I might do for you? I am a young man yet. Anyone who says forty is old, forty is not vigorous, is nothing but a liar. I will show you what a man of forty can do, you may rest assured of *that*. My hair is still dark, my heart is still full of love and resolve, and I am still, and shall always be, your loving—

Uncle Alf

20 May 1929

Dear sweet kindly lovely Geli,

Still only one letter from you, and now I have been in Lille almost two weeks. It makes me sad. It makes me terribly sad. I would have hoped for so much more. A lonely soldier needs all the help from those behind the front he can possibly get. And I am, I must tell you, a lonely soldier indeed.

There are those who call me a white crow, a monkey in a jacket, because I do not fit in well with the other men of the *Feldgendarmerie*. They let so many things get in the way of their duty: their hunger for gross food and tobacco and strong drink, their coarse lust for the Frenchwomen with whom they defile their pure and vital German manhood, and sometimes—too often, I fear!—their venal appetite for money in exchange for silence.

None of these distractions holds the least appeal for me. You may be sure of that, darling! I live and work only to do harm to the foes of the German Empire. The others in this service, the worthless and shiftless ones, know it and envy me my dedication. They resent me because I do not care to pollute myself as they have polluted themselves. They resent me, yes, and they envy me, too. I am sure of that.

I went to the commandant. Brigadier Engelhardt and I go back some years now. When he was making observations at the front in 1914, a fellow named Bachmann and I stood in front of him to shield him from British machine-gun bullets (he was but a lieutenant-colonel then). None struck us, but that is the sort of thing a man of honor will remember. And so he saw me in his office, though I am but an underofficer.

I spoke my mind. I left nothing out, not a single thing. I told him exactly what I think of the sad state of affairs now obtaining in Lille. We might have been two brothers resting side by side in a trench during the Great War. And he listened to me. He heard every word I said, as though our respective ranks meant nothing. And they did not, not for that little while.

When I was through, he looked at me for a long time without saying anything. At last, he muttered, "Ade, Ade, Ade, what shall I do with you?"

"Hear me!" I said. "Do what needs doing! Drive the money changers from the Temple! Be a thorn in the eyes of those who would stand against the Kaiser. Not just Frenchmen, sir—the *Feldgendarmerie*, too!"

"They are men, Ade. They have the failings of men. They do good work, taken all in all," he said.

"They consort with Frenchmen. They consort with

French*women.* They take money to look the other way when the French want to smuggle. They ignored almost every regulation ever drafted." I grew more furious by the moment.

Brigadier Engelhardt saw as much. He tried to calm me down. "Don't chew the carpet at me, Ade," he said. "I tell you again, they mostly do good work. They don't have to follow every jot and tittle of the rules to manage that."

"But they should! They must!" I said. "We must have order in the ranks, obedience and order! Obedience and order are the pillars of the Second Reich! Without them, we perish!"

"We do have them here—enough of them," Engelhardt replied. Can he be corrupt, too? It makes me sad, terribly sad, even to imagine it. Shaking his head as if he were the font of righteousness, he went on, "Ade, you can't expect to bring the conditions of the front, where everything was an emergency, to an occupation that has gone on for fifteen years and may go on for another fifty."

Corrupt! So corrupt! A whited sepulcher of a man! Rage and indignation rose up in me. Only fools, liars, and criminals can hope for mercy from the enemy. Endless plans chased one another through my head. Furiously, I demanded, "If your precious men are as wonderful as you say, why was I sent for? Couldn't you track down this Red devil of a Doriot with your own green devils?"

He flushed. I knew I had struck home with a deadly shot. Then, with what might have been a sigh, he answered, "For special purposes, we need a special man." A special man! Even though, at that moment, he was far from my friend—was, in fact, much closer to being not only my enemy but an enemy of the *Kaiserreich*—he named me a special man! Recognizing my qualities, he continued, "This Doriot has a strong streak of fanaticism in him. It could be you are the right one to hunt him."

"We all need to be fanatics in service to the Kaiser,"

I declared: an obvious truth. "Moderation in the pursuit of Germany's enemy is no virtue, while iron determination to see the Fatherland thrive is no vice."

"All right, Ade," Brigadier Engelhardt said with a sigh. He did not like having an enlisted man outargue him. But, no doubt for old times' sake, he did not shout at me for insubordination, as he might have done. "Bring me Jacques Doriot. You may say whatever you like then, for you will have earned the right. Meanwhile, you are dismissed."

"Yes, sir!" I said, and saluted, and left. That is the superior's privilege: to end a discussion when he is not having the better of it.

Give me the chance, my dear, when I come home to Munich, and I will show you just what a special man is your loving—

Uncle Alf

23 May 1929

My sweet beloved Angela,

It pours rain here in Lille. And there is rain in my spirit as well, for I have still had no new letter from you. I hope that all is well, and that you will bring me up to date on what you have been doing back in the civilized and racially pure and unpolluted Fatherland.

Here, everyone is gloomy: *Feldgendarmerie*, Frenchmen, Flemings. There are more Flemings—of excellent Germanic stock—here in the northeast of France than one might think. Regardless of whether they speak the Flemish tongue, all those whose names begin with *van* or *de* show by this infallible sign their ancient Germanic lineage. A priest hereabout, *l'abbé* Gantois, has some excellent views on this subject. Few, though, seem to wish to lose their French and reacquire the Flemish of their long-ago forebears. It is a great pity.

Few people out and about today—certainly few of the so-called *diables verts*, who might catch cold, poor darlings, if they went out in the rain! So you would think, at any rate, to hear them talk. But I tell you, and you may take it as a fact, that rain in a city, even a sullen French industrial city, is as nothing beside rain in a muddy trench, such as I endured without complaint during the Great War.

And so I sally forth as usual, with an umbrella and with the collar of my greatcoat turned up. It is a civilian coat. I am not such a fool as to go out into Lille dressed as a German *Feldgendarmerie* man. One does not hunt ducks by dressing as a zebra! This is another truth some of my comrades have trouble grasping. They are fools, men unworthy of the trust the Kaiser has placed in them.

I sallied forth, I say, into a working-class district of Lille. It is in such places that Doriot spews his poison, his lies, his hateful slanders against the Kaiser, the Crown Prince, and the Second Reich. There are, no doubt, also French agents pursuing this individual, but how can the German Empire rely on Frenchmen? Will they truly go after the likes of Doriot with all their hearts? Or will they, as is more likely, go through the motions of the chase with no real hope or intention of capturing him?

I have nothing to do with them. I reckon them more likely to betray me than to do me any good. I feel the same way about the *Feldgendarmerie* in Lille, I must say, but I have no choice except working with them to some degree. Thus ordinary folk try to tie the hands of the superior man!

What a smoky, grimy, filthy city Lille is! Soot everywhere. A good steam cleaning might work wonders. Or, on the other hand, the place might simply fall to pieces in the absence of the dirt holding everything together. In any case, steaming these Augean stables will not happen soon.

I can look like a man of the working class. It is not even difficult for me. I wander the streets with my nose to the ground, listening like a bloodhound. I order coffee in an *estaminet*. My accent for the one word does not betray me. I stop. I sip. I listen.

I find . . . nothing. Have I been betrayed? Does Doriot know I am here? Has my presence been revealed to him? Is that why he is lying low? Has someone on my own side stabbed me in the back? I would give such a vile subhuman a noose of piano wire, if ever he fell into my hands, and smile and applaud as I watched him slowly die.

Hoping to hear again from you soon, I kiss your hands, your neck, your cheek, your mouth, and the very tip of your . . . nose. With much love from—

Uncle Alf

25 May 1929

Dearest adorable Geli,

What a special man, what a superior man, your uncle is! Despite having to carry on in the face of your disappointing silence, I relentlessly pursue the Red criminal, Doriot. And I have found a lead that will infallibly betray him into my hands.

One thing you must know is that the folk of Lille are most fond of pigeons. During the early days of the war, we rightly confiscated these birds, for fear of their aiding enemy espionage. (Some of these pigeons, I am told, ended up on soldiers' tables. While I hold no brief for meat-eating, better our men should enjoy them than the French.)

Now, though, we have in France what is called peace. The Frenchmen are once more permitted to have their birds. *La Societé colombophile lilloise*—the Lille Society of Pigeon-fanciers—is large and active, with hundreds, it could even be thousands, of members, and with several meeting halls in the proletarian districts of the city. And could not these pigeons still be used for spying and the conveying of intelligence? Of course they could!

I know something of these birds. I had better—as a runner in the war, did I not often enough see my messages written down and sent off by pigeon? I should say I did! And so I have been paying visits to the pigeon-fanciers' clubhouses. There I am Meinheer Koppensteiner—a good family name for us!—from Antwerp, a pigeon-lover in Lille on business. My accent will never let me pass for a Frenchman, but a Fleming? Yes, that is easy enough for them to believe.

"Things are still hard in Antwerp," I tell them. "The green devils will take away a man's birds on any excuse or none."

This wins me sympathy. "It is not so bad here," one of them answers. "The *Boches*"—this is what they call us, the pigdogs—"are very stupid."

Nods all around. Chuckles, too. They think they are so clever! Another Frenchman says, "The things you can get away with, right under their noses!"

But then there are coughs. A couple of fellows shake their heads. This goes too far. I am a stranger, after all, and what sounds like a Flemish accent could be German, too. I am too clever to push hard. I just say, "Well, you are lucky, then—luckier than we. With us, if a bird is caught carrying a message, for instance, no matter how innocent it may be, this is a matter for the firing squad."

They make sympathetic noises. Things must be hard there, they murmur. By the way a couple of them wink, I am sure they deserve a blindfold and a cigarette, the traitors! And maybe they will get one, too! But not yet. I sit and bide my time. They talk about their birds. Meinheer Koppensteiner says a couple of things, enough to show he knows a pigeon from a goose. Not too much. He is a stranger, a foreigner. He does not need to show off. He needs only to be accepted. And he is. Oh, yes—he is.

Before long, Meinheer Koppensteiner will appear at other clubhouses, too. He will not ask many questions. He will not say much. But he will listen. Oh, my, yes, he will listen. If I were back in Munich, I would rather listen to you. But then, after all, I am not Meinheer Koppensteiner. Thinking of the kisses I shall give you when I see you again, I am, in fact, your loving—

Uncle Alf

28 May 1929

Dear sweet adorable lovely Angela,

Three weeks now in Lille and only two letters from you! This is not the way I wish it would be, not the way it should be, not the way it must be! You must immediately write again and let me know all your doings, how you pass your days—and your nights. You must, I say. I wait eagerly and impatiently for your response.

Meanwhile, waiting, I visit the other pigeon-fanciers' clubhouses. And I make sure to return to the first one, too, so people can see Meinheer Koppensteiner is truly interested in these birds. And so he is, though not for the reasons he advertises.

The workers babble on about the pigeons. They drink wine and beer and sometimes apple brandy. As a Fleming, Meinheer Koppensteiner is expected to drink beer, too. And so I do, sacrificing even my health in the service of the Kaiser. At one of the clubs, I hear—overhear, actually—quiet talk of a certain Jacques. Is it Doriot? I am not sure. Why is this pestilential Frenchman not named Jean-Hérold or Pascal? Every third man in Lille is called Jacques! It is so frustrating, it truly does make me want to chew the carpet!

And then someone complained about *les Boches*—the

charming name the Frenchmen have for us, as I told you in my last letter. A sort of silence ensued, in which more than a few eyes went my way. I pretended to pay no particular attention. If I had shouted from the rafters, *I am Belgian, not German, so say whatever you please!*—well, such noise only makes the wary man more so. A pose of indifference is better.

It worked here. Indeed, it could not have worked better. Quietly, sympathetically, someone said, "Don't worry about him. He's from Antwerp, poor fellow." In fact, he said something stronger than *fellow*, something not suited to the ears of a delicate, well-brought-up German maiden.

"Antwerp?" someone else replied. "They've been getting it in the neck from the *Boches* even longer than we have, and there aren't many who can say that."

This sally produced soft laughter and much agreement. I memorized faces, but for many of them I still have no names. Still, with the help of the immortal and kindly *Herr Gott*, they too will be caught, and suffer the torments such wretches so richly deserve.

Seeing me make little response—seeing me hardly seem to understand—made them grow bolder. Says one of them, "If you want to hear something about the *Boches*, my friends . . . Do you know the house of Madame Léa, in the Rue des Sarrasins, by the church of Sts. Peter and Paul?"

I suspected this was a house of ill repute, but I proved mistaken. This happens even to me, though not often. "You mean the clairvoyant?" says another, and the first fellow nods. Madame Léa the clairvoyant? *There* is a picture for you, eh, my dear? Imagine a fat, mustachioed, greasy Jewess, telling her lies to earn her francs! Better such people should be exterminated, I say.

But to return. After the first pigeon-fancier agrees this is indeed the Madame Léa he has in mind—heaven only knows how many shady kikes operate under the same surely false name in Lille!—he says, "Well, come tomorrow at half past nine, then. She gives readings Friday, Saturday, Sunday, Monday. Other days, other things." He chuckles knowingly.

Tomorrow, of course, is Wednesday. Who knows what sort of treachery boils and bubbles in Madame Léa's house on the days when she does not give readings? No one—no one German—knows now. But after tomorrow, she will be exposed to the world for what she is, for a purveyor and panderer to filth of the vilest and most anti-German sort. Such is ever the way of the Jew. But it shall be stopped! Whatever it is, it shall be stopped! I take my holy oath that this be so.

Maybe it will not be Doriot. I hope it will be. I think it will be. No, it must be! It cannot be anyone, anything, else. On this I will stake my reputation. On this I will stake my honor. On this I will stake my very *life*!

When the mothers of ancient Greece sent their sons into battle, they told them, "With your shield or on it!" So it shall be for me as I storm into the struggle against the enemies of the German Empire! I shall neither flag nor fail, but shall emerge triumphant or abandon all hope of future greatness. Hail victory!

Give me your prayers, give me your heart, give me the reward of the conquering hero when I come home covered in glory, as I cannot help but do. I pause here only to kiss your letters once more and wish they were you. Tomorrow—into the fray! Hail victory! for your iron-willed—

Uncle Alf

29 May 1929

My dear and most beloved Geli,

Himmelherrgottkreuzmillionendonnerwetter! The idiocy of these men! The asininity! The fatuity! How did we win the war? Were the Frenchmen and the English even more cretinous than we? It beggars the imagination, but it must be so.

When I returned to *Feldgendarmerie* headquarters after shaking off whatever tails the suspicious pigeon-fanciers might have put on me, I first wrote to you, then at once demanded force enough to deal with the mad and vicious Frenchmen who will surely be congregating at Madame Léa's tonight.

I made this entirely reasonable and logical demand—made it and *had it refused*! "Oh, no, we can't do that," says the fat, stupid sergeant in charge of such things. "Not important enough for the fuss you're making about it."

Not important enough! "Do you care nothing about serving the Reich?" I say, in a very storm of passion. "Do you care nothing about helping your country?" I shake a finger in his face and watch his jowls wobble. "You are worse than a Frenchman, you are!" I cry. "A Frenchman, however racially degenerate he may be, has a reason for being Germany's enemy. But what of you? *Why do you hate your own Fatherland?*"

He turned red as a holly berry, red as a ripe tomato. "You are insubordinate!" he booms. And so I am, when to be otherwise is to betray the *Kaiserreich*. "I shall report you to the commandant. *He'll* put a flea in your ear—you wait and see."

"Go ahead!" I jeer. "Brigadier Engelhardt is a brave man, a true warrior . . . unlike some I could name." The fat sergeant went redder than ever.

The hour by then being after eleven, the brigadier was snug in his bed, so my being haled before him had to wait until the following morning. You may be certain I reported to *Feldgendarmerie* headquarters as soon as might be. You may also be certain I wore uniform, with everything in accordance with regulations: no more shabby cap and tweed greatcoat, such as I had had on the previous night for purposes of disguise.

Of course, the other sergeant was still snoring away

somewhere. Did you expect anything different? I should hope not! Such men are always indolent, even when they should be most zealous—especially when they should be most zealous, I had better say.

So there I sat, all my buttons gleaming—for I had paid them special attention—when the commandant came in. I sprang to my feet, took my stiffest brace—my back creaked like a tree in the wind—and tore off a salute every training sergeant in the Imperial Army would have admired and used as an example for his foolish, feckless recruits. "Reporting as ordered, sir!" I rapped out.

"Hello, Sergeant," Brigadier Engelhardt replied in the forthright, manly way that made him so much admired—so much loved, it would not go too far to say—by his soldiers during the Great War. I still tried to think well of him, you see, even though he had thwarted my will before. He returned my salute with grave military courtesy, and then inquired, "But what is all this in aid of?"

Having only just arrived, he would not yet have seen whatever denunciation that swine-fat fool of a sergeant had written out against me. I had to strike while the sun was hot. "I believe I have run this polecat of a Doriot to earth, sir," I said, "and now I need the *Feldgendarmerie* to help me make the pinch."

"Well, well," he said. "This is news indeed, Ade. Why don't you come into my office and tell me *all* about it?"

"Yes, *sir*!" I said. Everything was right with the world again. Far from being corrupt, the brigadier, as I have known since my days at the fighting front, is a man of honor and integrity. Once I explained the undoubted facts to him, how could he possibly fail to draw the same conclusions from them as I had myself? He could not. I was certain of it.

And, again without a doubt, he would at once have drawn those proper conclusions had he not chosen to look at the papers he found on his desk. I stood to attention while he flipped through them—and found, at the very top, the false, lying, and moronic accusations that that jackass of a local *Feldgendarmerie* sergeant had lodged against me. As he read this fantastic farrago of falsehoods, his eyebrows rose higher and higher. He clicked his tongue between his teeth—*tch, tch, tch*—the way a mother will when confronting a wayward child.

"Well, well, Ade," he said when at last he had gone through the whole sordid pack of lies—for such it had to be, when it was aimed against me and against the manifest truth. Brigadier Engelhardt sadly shook his head. "Well, well," he repeated. "You *have* been a busy boy, haven't you?"

"Sir, I have been doing my duty, as is expected and required of a soldier of the *Kaiserreich*," I said stiffly.

"Do you think abusing your fellow soldiers for no good cause is part of this duty?" he asked, doing his best to sound severe.

"Sir, I do, when they refuse to do *their* duty," I said, and the entire story of the previous evening poured from my lips. I utterly confuted and exploded and made into nothingness the absurd slanders that villain of a *Feldwebel*, that wolf in sheep's clothing, that hidden enemy of the German Empire, spewed forth against me.

Brigadier Engelhardt seemed more than a little surprised at my vehemence. "You are very sure," he remarks.

"As sure as of my hope of heaven, sir," I reply.

"And yet," says he, "your evidence for what you believe strikes me as being on the flimsy side. Why should we lay on so many men for what looks likely to prove a false alarm? Answer me that, if you please."

"Sir," I say, "why did the *Feldgendarmerie* bring me here to Lille, if not to solve a problem the local men had proved themselves incapable of dealing with? Here now I have the answer, I have the problem as good as solved, and what do I find? That no one—no one, not even you, sir!—will take me seriously. I might as well have stayed in Munich, where I could have visited my lovely and charming niece." You see, my darling, even in my service to the kingdom you are always uppermost in my mind.

Brigadier Engelhardt frowns like a schoolmaster when you give him an answer he does not expect. It may be a right answer—if you are clever enough to think of an answer the schoolmaster does not expect, it probably *will* be a right answer, as mine was obviously right here—but he has to pause to take it in. Sometimes he will beat you merely for having the nerve to think better and more quickly than he can. Brigadier Engelhardt, I will say, has not been one of that sort.

At last, he says, "But Ade, do you not see? No one has spoken Doriot's name. You do not *know* that he will be at Madame Léa's."

"I know there will be some sort of subversion there," I say. "And with Doriot in the city to spread his Red filth, what else could it be?"

"Practically anything," he replies. "Lille is not a town that loves the German Empire. It never has been. It never will be."

"It is Doriot!" I say—loudly. "It must be Doriot!" I lean forward. I pound my fist on the desk. His papers jump. So does a vase holding a single red rose.

Brigadier Engelhardt catches it before it tips over. He looks at me for a long time. Then he says, "You go too far, Sergeant. You go much too far, as a matter of fact."

I say nothing. He wants me to say I am sorry. I am not sorry. I am *right*. I *know* I am right. My spirit is full of certainty.

He drums his fingers on the desktop. Another pause follows. He sighs. "All right, Ade," he says. "I will give you exactly what you say you want."

I spring to my feet! I salute! "Thank you, Brigadier! Hail victory!"

"Wait." He is dark, brooding. He might almost be a Frenchman, all so-called intellect, and not a proper German, a man of will, of action, of deed, at all. He points a finger at me. "I will give you exactly what you say you want," he repeats. "You can take these men to this fortuneteller's place. If you bring back Jacques Doriot, well and good. If you do not bring back Jacques Doriot . . . If you do not bring him back, I will make you very, very sorry for the trouble you have caused here. Do you understand me?"

"Yes, sir!" This is it! Victory or death! With my shield or on it!

"Do you wish to change your mind?"

"No, sir! Not in the slightest!" I fear nothing. My heart is firm. It pounds only with eagerness to vanquish the foes of the Reich, the foes of the Kaiser. Not a trace of fear. Nowhere at all a trace of fear, I swear it. Into battle I shall go.

He sighs again. "Very well. Dismissed, *Feldwebel.*"

Now I have merely to wait until the evening, to prepare the *Feldgendarmerie* men who shall surround Madame Léa's establishment, and then to—to net my fish! You shall see. By this time tomorrow, Doriot will be in my pocket and I will be a famous man, or as famous as a man whose work must necessarily for the most part be done in secret can become.

And once I am famous, what shall I do? Why, come home to my family—most especially to my loving and beloved niece!—and celebrate just as I hope. You are the perfect one to give a proper Hail victory! for your proud, your stern, your resolute—

Uncle Alf

30 May 1929

My very dearest and most beloved sweet Geli,

Hail victory! I kiss you and caress you here in my mind, as I bask in the triumph of my will! Strength and success, as I have always said, lie not in defense but in attack. Just as a hundred fools cannot replace a wise man, a heroic decision like mine will never come from a hundred cowards. If a plan is right in itself, and if thus armed it sets out on struggle in this world, it is invincible. Every persecution will only make it stronger. So it is with me today.

After fifteen years of the work I have accomplished, as a common German soldier and merely with my fanatical willpower, I achieved last night a victory that confounded not only my superiors who summoned me to Lille but also the arrogant little manikins who, because they did not know what I could do or with whom they were dealing, anticipated my failure. All of them are today laughing out of the other side of their mouths, and you had best believe it!

Let me tell you exactly how it happened.

That fat and revolting sergeant had finally reached his post when I came out of Brigadier Engelhardt's office. Laughing in my face, the swine, he says, "I bet the commandant told you where to head in—and just what you deserve, too."

"Not me," I say. "The raid is on for tonight. I am in charge of it. After that, we'll see who gloats."

He gaped at me, gross and disgustingly foolish. Such *Untermenschen*, even though allegedly German, are worse foes to the *Kaiserreich* than the French, perhaps even worse than the Jews themselves. They show the *Volk* can also poison itself and drown in a sewer tide of mediocrity. But I will not let that happen. I will not! It must not!

Would you believe it, that *lumpen*-sergeant had the infernal and damnable gall to ask Brigadier Engelhardt—Brigadier Engelhardt, whom I protected with my own body during the war!—if I was telling the truth. That shameless badger!

He came back looking crestfallen and exultant at the same time. "All right—we'll play your stupid game," says he. "We'll play it—and then you'll get it in the neck. Don't come crying to me afterwards, either. It'll do you no good."

"Just do your job," I say. "That's all I want from you. Just do your job."

"Don't worry about it," he says gruffly. As though he hadn't given me cause enough for worry, God knows. But I only nodded. I would give him and his men the necessary orders. They had but to obey me. If they did as I commanded, all would be well. I could not be everywhere at once, however much I wanted to. I had discovered the foul Red plot; others would have to help snuff it out.

When the time came that evening, I set out for Madame Léa's. The Lille *Feldgendarmerie* would follow, I hoped not too noisily and not too obviously. That stinking sergeant could ruin the game simply by letting the vile Marxist conspirators spot him. I hoped he would not, but he could—and, because he was so disgustingly round, there was a great deal of him to spot.

The church of Sts. Peter and Paul is lackluster architecturally; the house Madame Léa infests even more so. A sign in her window announced her as a LISEUSE DE PENSÉES, a thought-reader—and, for the benefit of German troops benighted enough to seek out her services, also as a WAHRSAGERIN, a lady soothsayer. Lies! Foolishness! To say nothing of espionage and treason!

I knocked on the door. A challenge from within: "Who are you? What do you want?"

"I'm here for the lecture," I answered.

"You sound funny," said the man behind the door—my accent proved a problem, as it does too often in France.

"I'm from Antwerp," I said, as I had at the pigeon-fanciers' clubs.

And then Lady Luck, who watched out for me on the battlefields of the war, reached out to protect me once again. If one's destiny is to save the beloved Fatherland, one will not be allowed to fail. I was starting to explain how I had heard of the lecture at *La Societé colombophile lilloise* when one of the men with whom I had spoken there came up and said, "This Koppensteiner fellow's all right. Knows his pigeons, he does. And if you think the *Boches* don't screw over the Flemings, too, you're daft."

That got them to open the door for me. I doffed my cap to the man who had vouched for me. "*Merci beaucoup*," I said, resolving to thank him as he truly deserved once he was under arrest. But that could—would have to—wait.

To my disappointment, I did not see Madame Léa there. Well, no matter. We can round her up in due course. But let me go on with the story. Her living room, where I suppose she normally spins her web of falsehood and deceit, is quite large. The wages of sin may be death, but the wages of deceit, by all appearances, are very good. Twenty, perhaps even thirty, folding chairs of cheap manufacture—without a doubt produced in factories run by pestilential Jews, who care only for profit, not for quality—had been crammed into it for the evening's festivities. About half were taken when I came in.

And there, by the far wall, under a dingy print of a painting I suppose intended to be occult, stood Jacques Doriot. I recognized him immediately, from the photographs on file with the *Feldgendarmerie*. He is a Frenchman of the worst racial type, squat and swarthy, with thick spectacles perched on a pointed nose. His hair is crisp and curly and black, and shines with some strong-smelling grease I noticed from halfway across the room. I was right all along, you see. I had known it, and now I had proof. I wanted to shout for joy, but knew I had to keep silent.

Several men, some of whom I had seen at one pigeon-fanciers' club or another, went up to chat with him. I marked them in particular: they were likely to be the most dangerous customers in the room. Doriot took no special notice, though, of those who hung back, of whom I was one. Why should he have? Not everyone is a leader.

Most men would sooner go behind, like so many sheep. It is true even among us Germans—how much more so amongst the mongrelized, degenerate French!

More would-be rebels and traitors continued to come in, until the place was full. We all squeezed together, tight as sardines in a tin. One of the local men did not sit down right away. He said, "Here is Comrade Jacques, who will speak of some ways to get our own back against the *Boches*."

"Thank you, my friend," Doriot said, and his voice startled me. By his looks, he seemed a typical French ball of suet, and I had expected nothing much from him as a speaker. But as soon as he went on, "We can lick these German bastards," I understood exactly why he has caused the *Kaiserreich* so much trouble over the years. Not only are his tones deep and resonant, demanding and deserving of attention, but he has the common touch that distinguishes the politician from the theoretician.

No ivory-tower egghead he! He wasted no time on ideology. Every man has one, but how many care about it? It is like the spleen, necessary but undramatic. Theoreticians always fail to grasp this. Not Doriot! "We can make the *Boche*'s life hell," he said with a wicked grin, "and I'll show you just how to do it. Listen! Whenever you do something for those damned stiff-necked sons of bitches, *do it wrong*! If you drive a cab, let them off at the wrong address and drive away before they notice. If you wait tables, bring them something they didn't order, then be very sorry—and bring them something else they didn't ask for. If you work in a factory, let your machine get out of order and stand around like an idiot till it's fixed. If it's not working, what can you do? Not a thing, of course. If you're in a foundry . . . But you're all clever fellows. You get the picture, eh?"

He grinned again. So did the Frenchmen listening to him. They got the picture, all right. The picture was treason and rebellion, pure and simple. I had plenty to arrest him right there for spouting such tripe, and them for listening to it. But I waited. I wanted more.

And Doriot gave it to me. He went on, "The workers' revolution almost came off in Russia after the war, but the forces of reaction, the forces of oppression, were too strong. *It can come here.* With councils of workers and peasants in the saddle, I tell you France can be a great nation once more. France *will* be a great nation once more!

"And when she is"—theatrically, he lowered his voice—"when she is, I say, then we truly pay back the *Boches*. Then we don't have to play stupid games with them any more. Then we rebuild our army, we rebuild our navy, we send swarms of airplanes into the sky, and we put revolution on the march all through Europe! *Vive la France!*"

"*Vive la France!*" the audience cried.

"*Vive la révolution!*" Doriot shouted.

"*Vive la révolution!*" they echoed.

"*Vive la drapeau rouge!*" he yelled.

They called out for the red flag, too. They sprang to their feet. They beat their palms together. They were in a perfect frenzy of excitement. I also sprang to my feet. I also beat my palms together. I too was in a perfect frenzy of excitement. I drew forth my pistol and fired a shot into the ceiling.

Men to either side of me sprang aside. There was no one behind me. I had made sure of that. To make sure no one could *get* behind me, I put my back against the wall, meanwhile pointing the pistol at Doriot. He has courage, I say so much for him. "Here, my friend, my comrade, what does this mean?" he asked me.

I clicked my heels. "This means you are under arrest. This means I *am* the forces of reaction, the forces of oppression. *À votre service, monsieur.*" I gave him a bow a Parisian headwaiter would have envied, but the pistol never wavered from his chest.

Indeed, Doriot has very considerable courage. I watched

him thinking about whether to rush me, whether to order his fellow traitors to rush me. As I watched, I waited for the men of the Lille *Feldgendarmerie* post to break down the doors and storm in to seize those Frenchmen. My pistol shot should have brought them on the run. It should have, but where were they, the lazy swine?

So I wondered. And I could see Doriot nerving himself to order that charge. I gestured with the pistol, saying, "You think, *monsieur*, this is an ordinary Luger, and that, if you tell your men to rush me, I can shoot at the most eight—seven, now—and the rest will drag me down and slay me. I regret to inform you, that is a mistake. I have here a Luger Parabellum, *Artilleriemodel* 08. It has a thirty-two-round drum. I may not get all of you, but it will be more than seven, I promise. And I will enjoy every bit of it—I promise you that, too." I shifted the pistol's barrel, just by a hair. "So—who will be first?"

And, my sweet, do you want to hear the most delicious thing of all? *I was lying!* I held only an ordinary Luger. There is such a thing as the *Artilleriemodel*; it was developed after the war to give artillerymen a little extra firepower if by some mischance they should find they had to defend themselves at close quarters against infantry. I have seen the weapon. The drum below the butt is quite prominent—as it must be, to accommodate thirty-two rounds of pistol ammunition.

A close look—even a cursory look—would have shown the Frenchmen I was lying. But they stood frozen like mammoths in the ice of Russia, believing every word I said. Why? I will tell you why. The great masses of the people will more easily fall victim to a big lie than to a small one, that is why. And I told the biggest lie I could possibly tell just then.

Nevertheless, I was beginning to wonder if more lies—or more gunshots—would be necessary when at last I heard the so-welcome sound of doors crashing down at the front and rear of Madame Léa's establishment. In swarmed the *Feldgendarmerie* men! Now, now that I had done all the work, faced all the danger, they were as fierce as tigers. Their Alsatians bayed like the hounds of hell. They took the French criminals and plotters out into the night.

That fat, arrogant *Feldwebel* stayed behind. His jowls jiggled like calves'-foot jelly as he asked me, "How did you know this? How did you hold them all, you alone, until we came?"

"A man of iron will can do anything," I declared, and he did not dare argue with me, for the result had proved me right. He walked away instead, shaking his stupid, empty head.

And, when I return to Munich, I will show you exactly what a man with iron in his will—and elsewhere! oh, yes, and elsewhere!—can do. In the meantime, I remain, most fondly, your loving—

Uncle Alf

31 May 1929

To my sweet and most delicious Geli,

Hello, my darling. I wonder whether this letter will get to Munich ahead of me, for I have earned leave following the end of duty today. Nevertheless I must write, so full of triumph am I.

Today I saw Brigadier Engelhardt once more. I wondered if I would. In fact, he made a point of summoning me to his office. He proved himself a true gentleman, I must admit.

When I came in, he made a production of lighting up his pipe. Only after he has it going to his satisfaction does he say, "Well, Ade, you were right all along." A true gentleman, as I told you!

"Yes, sir," I reply. "I knew it from the start."

He blows out a cloud of smoke, then sighs. "Well, I

will certainly write you a letter of commendation, for you've earned it. But I want to say one thing to you, man to man, under four eyes and no more."

"Yes, sir," I say again. When dealing with officers, least said is always safest.

He sighs again. "One of these days, Ade, that damned arrogance of yours will trip you up and let you down as badly as it's helped you up till now. I don't know where and I don't know how, but it will. You'd do best to be more careful. Do you understand what I'm telling you? Do you understand even one word?"

"No, sir," I say, with all the truth in my heart.

Yet another sigh from him. "Well, I didn't think you would, but I knew I ought to make the effort. Today you're a hero, no doubt about it. Enjoy the moment. But, as the slave used to whisper at a Roman triumph, 'Remember, thou art mortal.' Dismissed, Ade."

I saluted. I went out. I sat down to write this letter. I will be home soon. Wear a skirt that flips up easily, for I intend to show you just what a hero, just what a conqueror, is your iron-hard—

Uncle Alf

Horizon

Noreen Doyle

. . . he granted the request of the Lady and
concerned himself with the matter of a son.

—Deeds of Suppiliiuma, King of Hatte,
recorded by his son, Mursili

Nomads bring word of the Hittite prince's progress, nomads who not long ago laid themselves seven times on the belly and seven times on the back before the Great King of Egypt, whose widow has bade the Hittites come. "Through Kizzuwadna we tracked them," they tell Horemheb, General of the Army. "Make ready, because the prince, he comes."

Hearing this, soldiers put away their games of twenty-squares and lay aside letters written home. They have been at war with the Hittites for a very long time. "How soon?" they ask. "Tomorrow? The next day?"

"Soon enough," Horemheb says, wondering if it can be soon enough, for he is afraid. Will the Queen betray Egypt, betray him who was her husband? He does not know. When he is certain of the Queen's will, then he will act.

The Egyptian army, camped along the Syrian frontier, waits in eager anticipation.

I shall make it as the horizon for the Aten, my father.

—Speech by Akhenaten, King of Egypt,
on a boundary stela at Akhet-Aten

Nebmaatre Son-of-Re Amenhotep was, no denying, an old man. It seemed impossible that once he had sailed to Shat-meru and there, in the span of dawn to dusk, slain fifty-five wild bulls, or that he could have dispatched any of the lions credited to his arrows. When he sat upon the throne, rolls of fat obscured his belt. Now, illuminated by a broken pattern of sunset passing through a stone grille, they merely spread like half-melted wax across the wooden bed.

It was a waste, Akhenaten thought. Indolence. O, but here was his father, his god, the Dazzling Sun, spoilt by such common pleasures as even peasants might have: bread and beer and the pleasures of the bed. But even the peasant tempered himself with labor.

Not weakness, Akhenaten thought. It could not be weakness. It was the fading colors of dusk. What appeared to be softness and indolence was the inevitable bloating of the disk at sunset.

The Great Queen Tiye sat beside him, grim and patient, indulgently suckling her newborn Tutankhaten. But even so, she was no longer an image of youth. "Amenhotep will never see your new city again. He is dying."

"Does it truly please him, mother, what he has seen?"

"The god told you to build the Horizon of the Aten. How could anything so created fail to please him?"

Neferkheprure-Sole-One-of-Re Son-of-Re Akhenaten longed to return to his new city, to Akhet-Aten. For seven years now he had overseen its construction on a virgin plain to which the self-created Aten had directed him, following the dictates of the one god and none other. Here in Thebes Akhenaten felt smothered beneath the long shadow of Amon, the Hidden One, whose priesthood had long ago eclipsed Righteousness. At Akhet-Aten Egypt was being born anew, purged of the darkness and the weakness of falsehood.

Akhenaten replied, "The Aten rises from the eastern horizon and fills every land with his beauty. His Righteousness demands to be recognized."

"The Aten is strong in Akhet-Aten."

Akhenaten knew what Tiye was thinking: if Tushratta, Great King of Mitanni, sent Ishtar of Nineveh to Egypt again, perhaps Nebmaatre might rally. But that statue had not cured the King's illness, nor had the hundreds of statues of the lion goddess Sekhmet that his father had erected throughout Egypt. That had proven that there was no power in such things. Power emanated only from the disk of the sun, the Aten, creator of life.

What had been radiant would become black. There would be a night. Then there would be a tomorrow. There would always be a tomorrow, for so long as it was the will of the Aten to rise.

Nebmaatre died as Akhenaten knew he would: in the hours of darkness, when lions came forth from their dens and all serpents bit.

In the roofless temple ambassadors waited while Akhenaten, Nefertiti, and their daughters sang hymns before scores of altars laden with fruit and flowers. Beyond the walls could be heard the sounds of block slid upon block, of bronze struck against stone, of men laboring to expand Akhet-Aten. Some years ago Nefertiti had asked Akhenaten when the Horizon of the Aten would be wide enough. "It will never be," was his reply. "Too long has Righteousness been neglected on the earth."

When at last they gathered beneath the Window of Appearance, where a wall might provide a little shade, the ambassadors complained amongst themselves that for too long had *they* been neglected. From the Window, with Nefertiti at his side and the little princesses at his feet, Akhenaten could see their robes were soaked in sweat, their faces reddened, their tongues grown thick in their mouths.

Had they no endurance? No, they too were soft, like those graven images of wax once used in the false temples. Arrayed alongside the ambassadors, the courtiers, soldiers, Egyptian princes and foreign hostages of the Royal Academy displayed no such weakness, not anymore. The rays of the sun annealed the Egyptians.

Tutu the chamberlain read a letter from Ribaddi of Byblos, who complained, as he had for years, about Aziru, the new ruler of Amurru. The city of Sumura had fallen to Aziru's siege, and Byblos might be next. Send archers and ships, Ribaddi begged. Why had Egypt let Sumura fall?

"This is only as it should be," Tutu said at the end. "Aziru is merely reclaiming his patrimony. He has your anointing. Aziru also writes to you and promises to rebuild Sumura."

Akhenaten remembered Aziru. Years ago they had stood shoulder to shoulder in Thebes among the youths of the Royal Academy while Nebmaatre held court. Akhenaten remembered a quiet, crafty boy, good at games of chance. Like Aziru, many of the rulers in Nubia, Canaan and Syria had grown up like brothers to Akhenaten, hostage princes in Egypt. Fight amongst themselves though they did, they all swore loyalty to Egypt. It was best this way, Nebmaatre had said: a fragmented Syria and Canaan could not effectively rebel.

But how each fragment warred with the other, overwatched by the Aten! How could this be pleasing to the god who had given life to each in the womb?

"Everyone wants troops from me today," Akhenaten said, "just as they wanted them from my father yesterday. Is there even one among you who does not want soldiers?"

Of all the men assembled below, only one came forward. Akhenaten knew him well: Keliya, Tushratta's trusted ambassador. "The Great King of Mitanni asks for no troops, your majesty."

Tutu snorted. "No, not troops!"

"Years ago, your majesty," said Keliya, "your father promised Tushratta—who loves you as he loved Nebmaatre—two statues of solid gold. I saw them before your father died. They are very fine."

Tutu said, "My lord, it is always the same from Tushratta, with you or with your father: 'Gold is like dirt in your country, as plentiful as dust,' he says, and it is! But a house may be swept clean."

Keliya implored, "Your father himself promised this gold! How has Tushratta, my lord, failed you, O King of Egypt, to cause you to deny him this gift? Tell us, for we know of nothing!"

"How has he failed?" Akhenaten pointed the royal flail at Keliya and shook it so it rattled. "Keliya, you are no fool. You know that Nebmaatre became unhappy with Tushratta and withheld those statues for good cause. Tushratta cannot even hold together his own country. Your vassals rebel and make peace with the vile Hittites. It was because of Tushratta that the Hittites captured my father's vassal Shutarna of Kadesh and his son Aitakama and brought them as hostages to Hatte. For ten years Tushratta has slept like a lion in his den while dogs scavenge Syria!"

Keliya pressed his forehead to the floor. "Have there never been troubles in Egypt? Has your majesty never sent soldiers out into your own countryside to make things right?"

"Don't listen to the man of Mitanni!" A Canaanite man flanked by two Nubian spearmen broke from the ranks of Asiatics. "I am Ilumilku and I speak for Abimilki of Tyre who is your loyal servant! I kept my tongue, your majesty, because like everyone else here I have come to beg for soldiers. I'll not deny it, but listen to me, your majesty. You wrote to Abimilki asking what he has heard. He himself would have come here to tell you, but Zimreda of Sidon covets our mainland and plots against us with Aziru. Your good servant Horemheb saved us from Zimreda and dispatched Nubians from his garrison to guard my caravan, so important is what Abimilki sent me to tell you." Ilumilku dropped to his knees but raised his voice: "Half of the palace in Ugarit was burned by Hittite troops! And Aitakama has become prince of Kadesh."

A shadow passed over the Window, as if darkness hovered before its appointed hour. Aitakama, long a hostage of the Hittites, had returned to Syria? Akhenaten remembered Aitakama in the Royal Academy, too.

Tutu stood over the prostrate Keliya. "Aitakama in Kadesh! The Hittites at Ugarit! And to think that Tushratta would claim to guard our interests in Syria against the Hittites! He has brought them to our threshold!"

Against this Keliya said nothing.

The King asked, "And who would do better, Chamberlain?"

"Aziru of Amurru, your majesty. His capture of Sumura and the other cities speaks well for his competence. He pledges loyalty to you and will rebuild the city."

Keliya sat back on his heels. "The goodwill of Mitanni goes forth to every loyal vassal of Egypt, may they prosper from your generosity. Even as Tushratta sent the statue of Ishtar of Nineveh with blessings for Nebmaatre, would it not be in the spirit of goodwill and kindness for Nebmaatre's son to send these two gold statues to bless Tushratta?"

Akhenaten said, "Your king made a gesture without substance. There are no blessings but from the Aten."

"And do gifts from the King's hands account for nothing?" Keliya pressed his belly hard to the floor. He rolled over onto his back, arms outstretched. "May the Son of the Sun grant blessings upon Mitanni!"

Blessings, indeed. The statues would pay for Tushratta's

chariotry and infantry. They would inspire fear in the hearts of Mitanni's restless vassals. Such a gift from Egypt would renew Mitanni's standing in the world, but what good would it do Egypt? Gold had gone to Tushratta before, and what did Egypt get in return? Hittites in Syria.

"I will take the matter under advisement."

The King stood, Nefertiti and their daughters following. The crowd prostrated itself.

"Let us give thanks to the cause of all being, and let us pray for Righteousness."

And he brought them all out into the sun.

> But my brother has not sent the statues of solid gold. . . . You have sent ones of gilded wood.
>
> —Letter from Tushratta to Tiye

Akhenaten presented two statues to Keliya for his lord Tushratta. Finely gilded cedar they were, well appointed with colored stone, rock crystal, and glass, but they were wood nonetheless. Keliya, under Egyptian guard, accepted them. He had no choice.

"The statues that your father had made," Nefertiti asked, "what have you done with the gold?"

"In the beginning of time, Re said that gold was his flesh. Gold is as dust in Egypt, my beloved," Akhenaten replied. "The world will see."

> May the King come forth as his ancestors did!
>
> —Letter from Ribaddi,
> ruler of Byblos to Akhenaten

Akhenaten did not deny the truth of what Keliya had said: the army was everywhere in Egypt. Since the death of Nebmaatre, temples had been stripped of gold and silver and every precious thing, their estates had been seized, their ships had been confiscated. Everything now belonged to the Aten and to the King. Everywhere the name of the Hidden One occurred, wherever gods were written of, such was hacked out. Even in the birth-name of Nebmaatre it was not spared.

As if pursuing some lingering shadow of the Hidden One, Akhenaten drove every weakness from the backs and limbs of his soldiers, hardened them with labor, sparing neither prince born to the chariot nor conscripted peasant boy.

Daily they quarried stone and trimmed it and expanded Akhet-Aten. Under the watchful gaze of Ay, Master of the Horse, Akhenaten's young brother Smenkhkare and the other youths of the Royal Academy—noble Egyptian boys and hostage sons from Asia and Nubia alike—drilled to perfection in their chariots. Soldiers paraded and wrestled and fenced before their commanders. Under the scorching sun they stood to worship the Aten, the King, and the Queen.

In time, commanders, standard-bearers, the chariotry, the infantry and all the army scribes converged at harbors and riverbanks, in Upper and Lower Egypt alike.

Since the days of Akhenaten's grandfather, some fifty years ago, a king had not stirred from Egypt into Asia. But that was yesterday.

This was today.

And soon tomorrow would dawn at Byblos.

Horemheb remembers his astonishment when he learned that the King was in Byblos at the head of an army. At last, the King of Egypt was doing what his father never properly did! The army would be effective. How Horemheb had prayed for that.

Today he knows that his prayer was granted. Today the army is strong and ready for the Hittites approaching at the Queen's request.

At dusk Hapiru scouts come into camp with new word of the Hittite prince's progress: Hani, the Queen's messenger, travels with him as guarantee of safety through the kingdom of Kizzuwadna.

The Hapiru also say: "And we met the Ignorant along the way." That is the word the nomads use for those who have not pledged loyalty to Egypt. They hold out a bag, which Horemheb instructs a scribe to weigh. Shortly there is the sharp ting of small bits of metal being dumped onto the ground.

Horemheb also remembers the first time he heard exactly this sound.

Ianhamu, the highest commissioner in Syria, was leading him through Byblos to meet with the King. They passed a native smith working under the direction of an Egyptian soldier. People passed by, dropping before him little statuettes and amulets of bronze. Horemheb used to see vast quantities of such things offered for sale in the markets. The smith was melting them again, casting images of gods, of Reshef, Baal, and Baalat, into tips for arrows, blades for daggers and axes, and scales for armored shirts.

What pleasure that sound gave him, assurance that the troops would be well armed. Ianhamu assigned him reinforcements, a bureaucracy of scribes and workmen under the direction of Hotep, whose father had been commissioner of Sumura. Despite his promises, Ianhamu said, Aziru had not rebuilt Sumura. Hotep would correct that oversight.

The efficiency of it all, the promise of arms, a competent bureaucracy, blinded Horemheb.

He sees well enough now, even though darkness hovers over the land and the Hittite prince comes closer yet. Sumura opened Horemheb's eyes very wide, and he must pray that it likewise opened the Queen's.

❖ ❖ ❖

> You know that the King does not fail when he rages against all of Canaan.
>
> —Letter from Akhenaten
> to Aziru, ruler of Amurru

Sumura indeed remained in ruins.

The siege had been hard. The surrounding plain, once fertile cropland and pasture, had been churned up by horses and charred by flames, and was only now coming to life again under the half-hearted efforts of farmers and herdsmen. Much of the city had burned. Plague had claimed many. Those who remained shuffled along, their faces slack, their hearts as broken as their city. The sky itself wept for Sumura.

Amurrite chariots and foot soldiers swarmed through the ruined ramparts to meet Horemheb. Among the chariots Horemheb recognized none of Hittite make, which gave him small comfort. Ribaddi and Abimilki had claimed that Aziru honored a treaty with the Hittites.

Horemheb demanded: "Where is Aziru?"

"In Tunip," said an Amurrite. This was one of Aziru's brothers, Pubahla. "The Hittites are near Ugarit, which is not far from there."

"Would Aziru prefer to be near the King of Hatte or the King of Egypt?"

Pubahla blanched. "Near . . . ? We had heard such a thing but did not believe."

"Did not believe or did not want to believe?"

Horemheb struck Pubahla with his staff and had him tied behind his chariot. Pubahla trotted along wretchedly, ordering the Amurrites to lay down arms and to dismount. "Aziru your lord is an anointed vassal of Egypt and these are royal troops! Obey!"

The Amurrites obeyed, warily. Horemheb led his troops in, dragging Pubahla along when he fell.

The people of Sumura stared. They who formerly cooked in ovens now made open fires like nomads. Those who had lived under timber roofs now slept beneath tents of uncured hides of animals butchered prematurely for food during the siege. Women cried and wept, tears of joy for the presence of the Egyptian army commingled with tears of anger that they had not come sooner. Why, they asked, O why had Sumura been handed to the Amurrites? Why had Egypt abandoned them?

Horemheb had his officers round up the Amurrite troops, who had little choice but to cooperate as Pubahla lay bleeding and shackled beneath Horemheb's foot. By nightfall the Amurrites had been evicted and encamped outside the ramparts, corralled by Egyptian soldiers, while Nubians roamed the city so that the destitute did not loot each other. Soldiers and masons cleared rubble from the streets and brought baskets of earth to begin repairs on the ruined ramparts.

The troops of Hotep, the ones with writing-boxes tucked under their arms and rolls of papyrus in their hands, walked through the city like tax assessors. Everything that they could find for bread and beer, all the butchered flesh and fowl, they brought to an altar Hotep had constructed from stones dragged from the temple.

There Hotep summoned the city elders, who received amulets of gold, bright disks hung on braided gold chains.

One of the army officers, Troop Commander Sety, spoke with Horemheb that evening while they ate sitting in the shadow of the half-ruined temple. "Hotep's men carry gold as one Great King might give to another. I've seen the likes of this only when I brought royal caravans from Egypt to Babylon, and the Babylonian King was pleased indeed."

"Much gold for one Great King, or many little ones. Sumura will not be the end of our labors," Horemheb said, and Sety could only agree.

As they watched, Hotep redistributed the offerings from the altar to all the households of Sumura. "Ah, grain." Horemheb bit off a mouthful of bread. "Now that is the poor man's gold. And Amon goes hungry, even if the commonest lad of Sumura never does." He made a silent prayer to Amon now. What good, Horemheb wondered, was a common man's prayer without the rituals of the temples? What strength had an army without the blessings of the gods? He was afraid to learn.

"Hey, now," said Sety, "what's this?"

To each household in which a man or his wife could read, Hotep's men passed a clay tablet. This was something neither Horemheb nor Sety had ever seen before. Horemheb would ask Hotep about this, come morning.

Sety roused Horemheb before dawn. "There has been bloodshed."

Horemheb rolled from his camp bed, cursing. "How dare you engage in action without consulting me!"

When he emerged from his tent, it at once became apparent that neither Sety nor any of his men had shed this blood.

Bodies hung from the wall of the temple. Bodies not of Pubahla's men, nor even Egyptians or Nubians. Farmers and potters these were, housewives and priests, fourteen citizens of Sumura.

Horemheb raged: "The Amurrites will pay for this with their lives, and every Egyptian or Nubian lax at his guard shall lose his hand!"

Sety stayed Horemheb's hand and pointed to another wall.

The sun had emerged from the eastern horizon from which it drove away the clouds. Long rays of dawn reached over the hills to embrace the men who stood atop and below the wall with ropes, stringing up a fifteenth corpse by its feet.

At the ropes were men dressed in white linen. They were scribes and masons. Hotep's men.

To the elders of Sumura Hotep explained that Sumura had been abandoned to Aziru because the gods to whom they prayed were false. To Horemheb Hotep said, "They were vessels of treachery. This is the will of the King."

Citizens came forward, begging the Egyptians, but not for the bodies of their loved ones; they were afraid, Horemheb suspected, to admit kinship to the dead. Nor did they beg for gold, nor for their share of the morning's offerings of bread. The literate begged for tablets, the rest for spoken words.

By the time the King of Egypt arrived from Byblos with Prince Smenkhkare and a large retinue, none in Sumura wanted for shelter or for food. These had been provided in the name of the god the Egyptians worshipped and their King.

God, they had learned, was good. God provided all.

God, they had learned, was the Aten, and Neferkheprure-Sole-One-of-Re Akhenaten was his only son.

❖ ❖ ❖

All eyes observe you in relationship
to themselves.

—Hymn to the Aten

At last, at the direct command of the King, Aziru came south from Tunip. He bowed low and lower before the King, and never did Horemheb's archers lose their sight on him. Horemheb himself never ventured farther from Aziru than arm's reach, and his dagger was always near to hand. From the cities he had seized, the Amurrite chief brought gifts and, by the King's demand, his own young son as another hostage for the Royal Academy.

Akhenaten received him in the palace of Sumura. In exchange for Aziru's gifts, Akhenaten presented a large offering table bearing a single loaf of bread.

"I have heard," Akhenaten said, "that you have shared food and strong drink with Aitakama of Kadesh."

Aziru raised his hands in supplication. "O, but I am

like a son to his majesty of Egypt. We were youths together in the Royal Academy."

"As was Aitakama. Then the Hittites took him in."

"O, but I am a vassal anointed by his majesty of Egypt," Aziru protested, touching his forehead to the ground at the King's feet. "I am loyal."

"Aitakama says the same, and Aitakama is an enemy. He and his father were captured years ago by Suppililiuma, King of Hatte, and now Aitakama is as a son of Hatte's royal academy. While protesting his loyalty to me he honors a treaty with the Hittites. Ribaddi and Abimilki and others say that Aziru does the same. They beg me to deal with him, just as they begged me to deal with his father. Remind Aziru of his father, Horemheb."

Horemheb, who remembered how Abdi-Ashirta had died, grabbed up Aziru by the shoulder. His dagger touched Aziru in exactly the same place it had pierced his father, near the liver.

Aziru shook with fear, but fear was not loyalty.

At the King's nod, Horemheb released the Amurrite, but not before pressing his blade a little into Aziru's flesh. Aziru cast himself at the King's feet, seven times on the belly and seven times on the back. "It has been so long since your majesty's forefathers came forth into Asia! Aitakama has firsthand seen the strength of Hatte and forgets the might of Egypt!"

"The sun is everywhere," Akhenaten said. "He created the earth according to his own desire. Without the Aten we would not exist. How can Aitakama doubt the Sole-One-of-Re?"

"He is an ignorant dog, my lord."

"And Hatte holds his lead. You will break bread with him again."

"My lord! I would not break your trust, not even give the appearance."

The King held out the loaf of bread. "You have perceived the Aten, Aziru."

"It is the sun, my lord, your god, the creator of life."

"You observe the Aten in relationship to yourself. Every man does." The King dropped the loaf to the ground and crushed it beneath his heel. "When the Aten is gone, nothing can exist. There is no perception, for there is no thing."

The King dismissed everyone from the hall but Aziru. Horemheb began to protest—this was the bandit chief of Amurru!—but what could he say against the King's command? Obedient, Horemheb made his way back to his tent that night, keenly aware of his own hunger, and keenly aware of the dark.

Aziru's troops departed Sumura with Horemheb's, heading for Kadesh. They displayed no knowledge of military discipline in the Egyptian fashion, but Horemheb did not underestimate their effectiveness. They had, after all, seized a great deal of territory under Aziru's command, and some had served Aziru's father equally well. Their proficiency, in fact, caused him some concern, which he made known to his officers. The Amurrites were not prisoners in tow. They were fighting men, properly armed, to be treated as such.

Six days they marched, six days in which the sky was as dull as tarnished silver. "Is this the strength of your Aten, that he cannot even shine in summer?" Aziru said. "For a long time Syria has been like this, cool and damp. There is illness afoot, too many rats."

Horemheb said, "Too many Amurrites."

Each night they camped with the Amurrites in the midst of the Egyptians. Aziru dined with Horemheb and his officers, hostage as much as guest, and slept under Nubian guard. Without Aziru the Amurrite army was like a brick without straw, and the Amurrites themselves knew this.

Three hours' travel from Kadesh, the army made camp for the night. Again Horemheb dined with Aziru, for perhaps the last time. Dislike the King's command though he did, Horemheb was about to cut Aziru's leash.

"We will be an hour's ride behind you; scouts will be even closer."

"I rely on that," Aziru replied. "Aitakama may have Hittite troops with him."

"And do you rely upon that too?"

Aziru smiled around the meat in his mouth. "General, do you doubt my intentions to do the King's will?"

"Yes."

Aziru's smile faded. "The King of Egypt resides in Sumura and I am to defy him? He speaks of the oneness of god, rebuilds a city nearly overnight, and I am to disobey? He is the Son of the Sun. I do not doubt him."

"He has paid you."

Aziru shrugged and laid aside his meal unfinished. "What is gold compared to Righteousness?"

That evening Horemheb prayed that the King was right, that the Aten alone was god, because if the other gods were not false, then the Hittites, the Amurrites, none of them were hindered by heresy.

The King had instructed Aziru to lay a trap, and indeed he was doing just so. But, Horemheb wondered, for whom?

The Egyptians lay beneath cover in the pass that led through the hills to Kadesh. Like so many before it, this day too dawned cool and damp, the sky veiled by clouds as it almost never was in Egypt. On the plain before them, west of the River Orontes, Aziru and Aitakama had joined their troops and exercised together like brother princes. As brothers they once might have been in Egypt, but they were no longer sons of the Royal Academy. Aitakama had among his troops Hittite chariotry.

Horemheb ordered Sety forward with a light force, the sort that would pursue a fleeing enemy on the road. Aitakama's men saw Sety at once. Troops fell into a defensive formation about Aitakama with startling precision.

"In the name of the King of Egypt, Neferkheprure, I come for Aziru son of Abdi-Ashirta!" Sety called. "Aitakama, you swore loyalty to the King of Egypt. Aziru is a dog who has slipped his lead. Return him to prove your loyalty to the King in deeds rather than words."

The audacity of this challenge—in the face of Hittite troops at Aitakama's flank—amused the prince of Kadesh. Not, however, Aziru, who fervently begged Aitakama's protection.

Horemheb admired how well Aziru was playing his role, if indeed it was a role at all. Suspecting nothing, Aitakama moved his troops between Sety and the Amurrites. "It would violate the laws of hospitality to surrender one who is as my brother. Would you take him by force?"

Sety's troops—six chariots, twelve men in all—fanned out in a line. As Sety raised his hand, his archers raised their bows. When his hand dropped—

Horses of Aitakama's guard fell or bolted as arrows struck them. Confusion seized the enemy, who had not expected so small a force to attack. Aitakama quickly restored order and commanded the Hittite chariots to swing about.

The heavy Hittite chariots charged the light Egyptian ones, raining arrows before them. They came around wide and drove eastward, forcing the Egyptians toward the Orontes, where Aziru's troops blocked the ford. If Aziru's men did not give them quarter at the riverbank, Sety would have to make a stand, and with such numbers a stand would be brief and fatal.

But now Aitakama's forces had turned their backs on Horemheb.

At Horemheb's command, the Egyptian troops abandoned their cover. Asiatic foot soldiers staggered with Egyptian arrows pinning their backs. At first these losses went unnoticed by the charioteers, the cries of the wounded lost in the thunder of wheels and hoofs. But soon shieldmen began to shift their positions to guard the backs of their archers and drivers, who did not understand what was happening until a slingstone picked off someone nearby or an arrow stung their shoulders. Enraged by this blatant trickery, Aitakama's officers bellowed orders to reverse! reverse! but the heavy Hittite chariots needed room to turn. More perished as the Egyptian chariots, built for the hunt as much as for battle, darted through the enemy ranks and cut commanders from soldiers, severed chariotry from infantry.

New infantry poured from Kadesh, men with slings and bows and daggers, and fresh arrows for the charioteers. The balance was swiftly tipping back to Aitakama, who had what Horemheb realized he himself lacked: reserves and reinforcements at hand, for Aziru remained passive at the river.

So the fighting fell into two battles: an outer of chariots and arrows, of which Horemheb struggled to retain the upper hand; and an inner, near the river, in which Sety's dwindling force fought to stay alive against the crush of Aitakama's troops. Sety himself had lost his chariot.

Aitakama bore down upon him.

As the sun was now high and strong, its rays at last pierced the thick cloud cover. A flash of light—the glint of the sun from Sety's gilded shield, perhaps, or the bronze scale of his armor—startled Aitakama's horses, which reared and bolted. Aitakama fell and, as if tied to his shoulders, the clouds cleared away to the horizon, burned off by the sun. Horemheb lost sight of Sety and Aitakama as the battle surged in again.

Now through the din came another sound, faint but unmistakable in its cadence. As Horemheb drove nearer to the river, smiting chariot runners and slaying horses and drivers in his path, he could hear it:

You are beautiful, great, dazzling,
and high above every land,
And your rays embrace the lands to
the limits of all you have created,

For you are Re, having reached the limits and
subdued them for your beloved son,
For although you are distant, your rays are
upon the earth and you are perceived. . . .

The King's words. Aziru's voice.
And the Amurrites fought.

Hotep has come, bringing the gracious and sweet words of the King.

—Letter from Aziru
to Tutu, Chamberlain

Kadesh surrendered, its people begging for the installment of Aitakama's brother, Biriawaza, who was ever loyal to Egypt. Aitakama they declared to be a criminal and a traitor who had destroyed much of the city when he returned from Hatte. He now sat with his wrists thrust through a wooden shackle strung from his neck. Aziru asked to cut off Aitakama's hand for the King, but Horemheb refused him the honor. He wished it for himself: his trusted Sety was dead. The sun had inspired Aziru's determination too late.

"The King will decide what to do with the traitor of Kadesh. Even," Horemheb said, "as he decided what to do with you."

"Aitakama you spare, yet me you would have slain when I entered Sumura."

"I would have slain you when I slew your father."

"And now?"

"The King declared you to be a loyal vassal. I did not believe him then. But as the King speaks, so the world becomes."

Before nightfall, more Egyptians approached Kadesh in chariots and on foot.

Hotep and his men.

Horemheb let them in, and by dawn blood ran down the walls of Kadesh.

> The Aten causes him to plunder every foreign land
> on which he shines.
>
> —Hymn to the Aten

Throughout Canaan and Syria cities fell before Akhenaten's army and the Amurrites who had joined him. Cities whose ramparts were damaged, whose homes and workshops were burned, whose fields were ruined, these Akhenaten renewed. He sent physicians to treat those ravaged by war and hunger and disease. At his command scribes took stock of livestock, food, copper, slaves, everything, and restored order. His troops were tireless, enduring, generous, for this was the will of the Aten who rose from the horizon every morning for the sake of all humanity.

True, old men, youths, and suckling mothers, tanners, smiths, and glassmakers sometimes died in the night with knives in their backs, arrows through their throats, amulets ripped from their fingers and necks. Akhenaten deeply regretted that this had to be. But those who abandoned these little bits of bronze and clay and wood and falsehood received greater things. By the grace of the Sole-One-of-Re, they received the flesh and the prayers of the sun, Righteousness, and they also received their lives.

The King of Egypt and his army met the King of Hatte and his army outside the city of Ugarit, invited there by King Niqmandu and his Egyptian wife. Niqmandu spread offerings between them, fish, flesh, fruit and wine for the troops, gold and ivory and other precious things for the Great Kings. Their war had much disrupted commerce, the lifeblood of Ugarit. Niqmandu begged Egypt and Hatte for peace.

This meeting did not please Horemheb, but Niqmandu King of Ugarit was a faithful ally of Egypt, no friend of the Hittites who had burned half of his palace. Moreover, Akhenaten had long wished to see his enemy Suppililiuma of Hatte.

Horemheb and his men kept close watch on the Hittites; he permitted the soldiers to drink none of the wine offered by Niqmandu's servants and to eat none of the fish or fruit, lest they become sated and slow.

To honor their host's hospitality, like brothers the Kings spoke about their wives at home, the sons and brothers who sat beside them here today.

"There is a god you favor above all others, I hear," Suppililiuma said through his interpreter.

"He is the only god, my brother," Akhenaten said. "He is the creator, mine as well as yours. He appointed your skin and your tongue."

"And my kingdom?"

"The Aten has appointed every man his place."

"Then I like this god of yours, my brother!" And Suppililiuma laughed. "All is from the Aten, then?"

"Everything."

"Including this?"

Suppililiuma gave a signal with his hand, and as he did so, Horemheb's men, who had been waiting for such a thing, rose up with spears and daggers and axes and rushed to shield their King. Niqmandu's servants dropped their jugs of wine and platters of food and withdrew behind the Egyptian line. The Hittites stood behind their shields, motionless.

"What is this?" Akhenaten demanded. "You would defy the hospitality of Niqmandu, my loyal ally?"

"We destroyed half of Niqmandu's palace," Suppililiuma said. "The other half we did not destroy. We made it ours. This, then, is the will of your god, my brother."

A great pain seized Horemheb's side. The cupbearer beside him held a bloody knife. Horemheb shouted,

"Kadesh!" and his men understood. As Aitakama had fallen, so were the Egyptians to fall, impaled on the blades of their allies. The Hittites withdrew from the banquet.

Horemheb was struck again, and he fell upon the body of another. On his back he lay, blinded by blood, while above him the Egyptians and Amurrites rallied around the King and butchered Ugarit's army of servants. Then an arrow struck Horemheb's thigh. Horemheb shouted for all to fall back. Hittite archers had come up to finish the battle.

Someone pulled him to his feet and thrust a shoulder beneath his arm. Horemheb wiped an arm across his face to clear away the blood, and found Aziru at his side. And at his feet, in a pool of crimson that spread from his neck like the Nile in flood, lay Prince Smenkhkare.

The Hittites retreated from Ugarit, scarcely beaten but it was late in the season, time to head home. They would return.

Whereas the Hittites had burned half the palace, Akhenaten burned the entire city. Everything in the treasury, all the copper and tin and glass, was put aboard ships seized at the harbor and sent straightaway to Egypt. The bodies of Niqmandu and his Egyptian wife, of all the royal family and all the servants and all the servants' families, hung from the city walls.

And then the King beat Aitakama with his own hands, Aitakama's blood spreading like sacred oil upon his skin. When would this war end? His brother! His beloved brother!

"It will not end," Aitakama said. "The Hittites will always return. In Hatte they are strengthened and refreshed. There is no relief."

"No night is eternal. Dawn always comes to the horizon."

"Likewise dusk."

The King broke Aitakama in the end. To do it he removed both hands and one ear, and pinned Aitakama's severed nose to a wall. "In the city of Hattusa, their capital," Aitakama said with the tongue Akhenaten had left him, "there is a tunnel leading to the south, to safety, for Suppililiuma greatly fears what lies to the north."

And he told Akhenaten of Kaska, of the tribes there who harried shepherds and merchants and burned Hittite crops, and how they had ever been the bane of Hatte. In the days of Suppililiuma's father, the Kaska-tribes had destroyed the kingdom of Hatte. "Don't you remember that once your father called for them? But the Kaska-tribes never came, my brother. Not for Nebmaatre Amenhotep."

At that instant Akhenaten killed him.

He hung Aitakama's body in a cage suspended from the rudder of his royal ship and sailed north and then south again, so that all from Kizzuwadna to Libya might see the wrath of the King of Egypt, and that word of it might travel to Nubia and the Isles in the Midst of the Sea. Then he returned to Akhet-Aten to bury his brother Smenkhkare in the hills from which the Aten rose every day.

Send me the Kaska-tribes!

—Letter from Nebmaatre Amenhotep

The Hittites delayed the next campaign in Syria. Akhenaten remained in Egypt, learning from Horemheb's letters that the Hittite Upper Lands had been overrun from Kaska, and that Tushratta of Mitanni had at last reclaimed his rebel vassals. Akhenaten dispatched messengers through the lands of Mitanni. They rode tirelessly to Kaska and back again, bringing with them the flesh of Re stripped from the false temples of Canaan and Syria.

Hittite troops came into Syria that summer and several summers thereafter. Harried from Kaska, they could do little more than burn fields before Horemheb's chariots and infantry fell upon them and cut them up. In the wake of destruction, as always, came renewal: Hotep, tirelessly at work, establishing Righteousness in the name of the Sole-One-of-Re. Seated beside Nefertiti, with the princesses at their feet, Akhenaten heard of all of this from Tutu. It pleased him, as it pleased the Aten.

Then one campaign season was not delayed. It did not come at all. Tutu announced that the Kaska-tribes had destroyed a holy city and wrecked a number of outposts. Lands to the west had rebelled. Kizzuwadna joined its border with Mitanni, so now if the Hittites wished to enter Syria, they would have to fight through every pass, do battle on every plain, and risk leaving their homes open to attack. And there was, too, the plague.

It struck Egypt no less than Hatte, carried in the breath or the sweat of supplicants, messengers, and prisoners. The youngest princesses died, and soon thereafter Tiye as well. Akhenaten himself took ill throughout his entire body, and today, seated at the Window of Appearance, shivered with cold as though the warmth of the Aten could no longer reach him.

"I feel enveloped by night, but it is not yet noon," he whispered to Nefertiti, who held him and fondled him as she had always done.

Below, the hostage sons and royal princes of the Royal Academy paraded before the ambassadors to present the newly orphaned prince, Tutankhaten. The three remaining princesses leaned over the ledge of the Window, curious to see the youths whom they might someday marry. Already they looked to tomorrow.

The King said, "It is too soon for this. O my father who gives breath to all you create, it is not yet noon!"

The next day he died, collapsed upon an altar, thin and wasted before the ambassadors of Asia, as the sun descended to the horizon on the shortest day of the year, never to know whether there would be another tomorrow.

Encamped outside Aleppo, where Hotep had strung more bodies from the wall, Horemheb received news of the

King's death. His widow had shed her old name and, as Ankhetkheprure-Beloved-of-the-Sole-One-of-Re Neferneferuaten, sat alone upon the throne of Egypt.

"The war that you have waged is to end," Ankhetkheprure wrote to Horemheb. "I have written to Suppiliiuma, King of Hatte, to send a son."

At the hour of dawn, one of Horemheb's aides, Paramessu son of Sety, comes to him. "General, they are here. Shall I go out to meet them?"

Horemheb studies Paramessu. He is much like his father, hawk-nosed and tall. "No. This time let the Hittites come to us." He orders his troops into formation, a show of strength and precision.

Into the camp Hani, the Queen's messenger, leads a caravan of laden carts and asses, chariots and horses finely arrayed. Riding in a heavy chariot of the sort defeated at Kadesh, the prince, scarcely in the flush of adolescence, wears weapons tucked in his belt, but it is the gold amulet around his neck, a pendant in the form of some Hittite god, that most worries Horemheb. The length of Canaan and the breadth of Syria are the horizon of the Aten. What will become of it without the Sole-One-of-Re on the throne? What is the Queen's will?

Horemheb greets the prince in the names of Ankhetkheprure and of the Aten. "Which son of Suppililiuma are you?"

"Mursili, his second," replies the boy in a voice still high and fine.

Hani reaches out and snaps the amulet from around Mursili's neck. In two hands he holds it high, to the east, and, uttering the name of Ankhetkheprure-Beloved-of-the-Sole-One-of-Re, rolls his knuckles together. The soft gold bends in his hands before he drops it to the ground, where it glitters in the dawn. Mursili stares at it, brokenhearted.

But Horemheb's heart rises with the sun into the expanse

of clear sky. The Horizon established by the Sole-One-of-Re shall indeed be preserved by his Beloved. The Aten is god.

"Your coming is a great occasion for me," Horemheb says to Mursili as the soldiers break camp. "I have not been home to Egypt in a very long time."

"Bring me home to Hattusa."

"My prince, now your home is Akhet-Aten."

As the sun rises toward its height, Horemheb directs the soldiers and the caravan and the prince southward.

He will obey Mursili, but not yet. Not until the tutors of the Royal Academy have taught the prince to pray to the Aten and his only bodily son. Not until he is returned to Hatte as a loyal vassal duly anointed by the Queen of Egypt.

I looked this way and that way and there
was no light. Then I looked towards the King,
my lord, and there was light.

—Letter to Akhenaten, King of Egypt

Devil's Bargain

Judith Tarr

Richard Coeur de Lion, King of the English, Duke of Normandy, Count of Anjou, and numerous other titles that his clerks exercised themselves to remember, was enjoying a great rarity in this country: a day without one of his endless fevers. His new physician was taking the credit, but he rather thought that the thing had simply run its course. This man, however, was remarkable in prescribing, not noxious potions, but cups of sherbet cooled with snow.

The snow came from Mount Hermon, and the Saracens imported great quantities of it, sealed in straw; one of his raiding companies had brought in enough to keep him in sherbet for a good month. He was not at all averse to the regimen. Cold sweetened nectar of lemon or orange or citron was more than pleasant in the hills near Jerusalem in June.

He sat in the shade of a canopy, sipping his medicine and watching a knight from Burgundy and a knight from Poitou settle a dispute by combat. The Burgundian was getting the worst of it: he was not as young or by any means as thin as his adversary, and the heat, even this early in the morning, was taking its toll. Richard watched with professional interest, because the Poitevin was a jouster of some renown; but when he laid a wager, he laid it on the Burgundian. The lesser fighter had the better horse, lighter and quicker and, though it sweated copiously, less visibly wilted by the heat. The Poitevin's charger was enormous even by the standard of the great horses of Flanders, and although it lumbered and strained through the turns and charges of the joust, no sweat darkened its heavy neck.

Having handed his gold bezant to Blondel the singer, who was keeping track of the wagers, Richard let his mind wander even as his eye took in the strokes of the fight. He liked to do that: it helped him think. And there was much to think about.

He would not camp in sight of Jerusalem. If it happened he must ride where he could see it, he had a squire hold up a shield in front of his eyes. He had sworn an oath: he would not look on those walls and towers or the golden flame of the Dome of the Rock, until he had come to take it for God and the armies of Christendom. But scouts who kept the city in sight said that it had been boiling like an anthill since shortly after sunset the evening before.

None of his spies had come in with reliable news. They did know that all the Saracen raiding parties had begun to swarm back toward the city, and messengers—all of whom, damn them, had escaped pursuit—had ridden out at a flat gallop on the roads to the north and east. Rumors were flying. The Sultan Saladin was preparing a killing stroke against the Franks; Islam was under siege from some hitherto unforeseen enemy; Jerusalem had been invaded in the night by an army of jinn and spirits of the air. There was even a rumor that no one credited: Saladin himself was ill or wounded or dead.

Richard had prayed for that. He was not fool enough

to expect that it was true. The Old Man of the Mountain had sent his Assassins against Conrad of Monferrat the month before last and thrown the succession of the Frankish Kingdom of Jerusalem into great disorder, but if anyone was to be thought of as the Assassins' next target, that was Richard himself. He refused to live in fear because of it; that was not his way. But he did not turn his back on the possibility, either.

The Poitevin's horse collapsed abruptly, just as the Burgundian flailed desperately at the rider's head. The heavy broadsword struck the great casque of the helm with a sound like a hammer on an anvil. The Poitevin dropped like a stone.

The horse was dead—boiled in its own skin, without the relief of sweat to cool it. The knight was alive but unconscious. The unexpected victor sat motionless on the back of his heaving and sweat-streaming destrier, until his squire came running to get him out of the stifling confinement of the helm and lead him dazedly off the field. His face in its frame of mail was a royal shade of crimson.

As men from the cooks' tents hauled the dead horse off to the stewpots, a different disturbance caught Richard's attention. "See what that is," he said at random, waving off Blondel and the winnings of his wager. Several of the knights and squires nearby sprang up to obey, but Blondel was quickest on his feet.

Richard's eyes followed him as he went. He had the grace of a gazelle.

He came back so swiftly that he seemed to fly, and with such an expression on his face that Richard rose in alarm, half-drawing his sword. "Sire," he said. "Lord king, come. Please come."

Richard only paused to order his attendants to stay where they were. They did not like the order, but they obeyed it. With Blondel for guide and escort, Richard strode swiftly toward the camp's edge.

One of his scouting parties had come in with a captive: a slender man in desert robes, with the veil drawn over his face. He seemed not to care where he was or who had caught him. He sat on the rocky ground, cross-legged in the infidel fashion; his head was bent, his shoulders bowed. He had the look of a man on the raw edge of endurance.

"He was headed here, sire," the sergeant said. "He didn't resist us at all, except to stick a knife in Bernard when he tried to pull off the face-veil."

Bernard nursed a bandaged hand, but Richard could see that he would live. Of the infidel, Richard was not so sure. He reached out; his men tensed, on the alert, but the infidel made no move to attack.

He drew the veil aside from a face he knew very well. It belonged to a man he trusted more than most Franks, a loyal and diligent servant whom he had thought safe in this very camp, serving as interpreter for the clerks and the quartermasters. Although, come to think of it, Richard had not seen him for a day or two. Days? A week? The damned fever had taken Richard out of time.

"Moustafa!" Richard said sharply.

At the sound of his name, Moustafa came a little to himself. His skin had the waxy look of a man who had lost too much blood; there was wetness on the dark robes, and the stiffness of drying blood. His eyes were blank, blind. He was not truly conscious; all that held him up was the warrior's training that let him sleep in the saddle.

Richard called for his men to fetch a litter. While they did that, he sent Blondel to fetch the physician. "Tell him to attend me in my tent. And be quiet about it."

Blondel barely remembered to bow before he turned and ran. This time Richard did not pause to watch him. The litter was taking too long. Richard lifted Moustafa in his arms, finding him no great weight: he was a slender man as so many infidels were, compact and wiry-strong, without the muscular bulk of a Frank.

Richard sought his tent quickly, almost at a run. Even so, Judah bar-Samuel the physician was waiting for him, with a bed made and a bath waiting and all made ready for the care of a wounded man. Moustafa was all but bled out; Judah scowled at the wound in his side that had bled through the rough bandages beneath his robe, and the others here and there that might have been little in themselves, but all together had weakened him severely.

Moustafa began to struggle, as if swimming up through deep water. This time when his eyes opened, they saw Richard. They saw precious little else, but they fixed on his face with feverish clarity. "*Malik Ric,*" he said. "Lord king. The Sultan of Damascus is dead."

How peculiar, Richard thought with the cool remoteness of shock. The one rumor everyone had discounted, and it was true. "Assassins?"

Moustafa nodded.

Richard drew a breath, then let it out. He sat beside the bed, leaning toward Moustafa. The infidel groped for his hand and clutched with strength enough to bruise. With that for a lifeline, he said, "Lord king, I pray you will pardon me. I left my place. I abandoned my duty. I went spying in Jerusalem."

"So I gather," Richard said dryly. "What possessed you to do that?"

Moustafa sighed, catching his breath on an edge of pain. Judah scowled, but Richard was proof against the disapproval of physicians and nursemaids. "Lord king, it was foolish. You were sick, and I was bored. Nobody knew what was going on inside the city. I decided to see for myself."

"What did you see?"

"I visited al-Malik al-Adil—the lord Saphadin. He was glad to see me. He sends you his greetings, and says that he hopes you won't mind that he doesn't also wish you good fortune in your war against his brother."

Richard's lips twitched in spite of themselves. "You

know," he said, "that I should have you executed as a deserter and a spy."

Moustafa did not even blink. "You probably should, my lord," he said. "I stayed with the lord Saphadin, and I watched Saladin's caravans fill the city. It's provisioned for a great siege. Yesterday—yesterday I stood with the Sultan while the last of the supply-trains came in, and afterwards I followed him as he went with his brother to pray in the Dome of the Rock. And in the hour of the evening prayer, while we all performed the prostrations toward Mecca, two of the Sultan's mamluks, the most trusted of his servants, whom he had loved like sons, rose up and killed him.

"I was there beside him, my lord. I killed one of the Assassins. The other almost killed me, but the lord Saphadin cut him down."

"You weren't paid well for the service, from the look of you," Richard observed.

Moustafa shook his head, perhaps more to clear it than to shake off the chill of Richard's words. "I didn't give anyone time to be grateful. I left as soon as I could. The city was in terrible disorder. The lord Saphadin was doing what he could, but it was like a madness. People were running wild, shrieking and striking at one another—crying out that every man was an Assassin. They set fire to a street of houses near the Wailing Wall, and tried to loot the storehouses, but the garrisons were able to stop that. I escaped when the messengers went out to summon the Sultan's emirs and his son and the rest of his brothers from Damascus. I came to you as fast as I could. I would have been faster, but my horse was shot from under me, and it took a while to steal another."

Moustafa fell silent. He had run out of strength; he was unconscious again—and none too soon, said Judah's glare. Richard rubbed an old scar that ran along his jaw under his beard, letting that narrow dark face fill his vision while the tale filled his mind.

Blondel was still there, crouched in a corner, watching and listening. The round blue eyes were narrowed a little, the full mouth tight, but then they always were when he saw Richard with Moustafa. It was a pity, Richard thought, that two of the people he trusted most in the world were so intractably jealous of one another.

"Blondel," Richard said in a tone that he knew would catch and hold the singer's attention. "Go to Hubert Walter. Tell him what you heard here. Have him call the war-council, and quickly. There's no time to waste."

For an instant he thought Blondel would refuse to move, but the boy was a good enough soldier, for a lute-player. He nodded, bowed just a little too low, and ran.

Richard set guards over the wounded man, sturdy English yeomen whom he trusted implicitly. Then he went to order the attack on Jerusalem. He was too old a soldier to skip like a child, but his heart was as light as air.

They would move toward evening and march by night, taking advantage of the cooler air and the cover of darkness. In the meantime the watchers in the hills reported that the city's gates were shut, but there were ample signs of disarray: sentries missing from their usual walk on the walls, sounds of fighting, and smoke and flames from more than the single fire that Moustafa had spoken of.

Richard found that encouraging, but he was not about to rely on it. Saphadin was a wise and canny man. Whoever, whatever had roused and sustained the uproar in the city, he would devote his every resource to restoring order. Jerusalem was too vital, too sacred, and much too well prepared for a siege. No general worth the name would let it go.

Time was short and Richard's resources thin, but if he moved quickly enough, he would win a city filled to the brim with provisions. It was a gamble, but one well worth taking.

It did not take overly long to inform the war-council

of his plan, and give them their orders. Not all or even most of them were overly eager for a fight, but Richard had not asked them for their opinions in the matter. Judging from the alacrity with which the army itself moved into position, the troops were of Richard's mind: now or never. Strike fast or give up the war.

Richard took an hour in the worst heat of the day to rest: soldier's wisdom, and he had seen a good number of his men taking the same opportunity. Judah was still occupied with Moustafa, but the canopied porch in front of Richard's tent was both cooler and airier. Blondel, apparently recovered from his fit of the sulks, had lowered the veils of gauze that kept out the flies and some of the heat, and brought in a fan and a fan-bearer to cool Richard while he dozed.

Richard slept for a while with his head in Blondel's lap. He did not know exactly what woke him: whether it was the sound of a footstep or Blondel's sudden, perfect and rigid stillness.

He took stock before he opened his eyes. One person—no, two, but the second was of no account. Under cover of his body, he let his hand slip toward the dagger at his belt. His fingers closed round its hilt as he opened his eyes.

There were two strangers sitting under his canopy, as calm as if they had every right to be there, and never a sign that his guards or sentries had marked their coming. They were both dressed all in white. One was very young and surprisingly fair-skinned, almost as fair as Blondel, with grey eyes full of dreams. The other was white-bearded and old, and might have seemed frail, except that he was sitting here in the heart of Richard's camp, watching Richard with a dark and steady stare. His lips smiled, but his eyes had the cold glitter of a snake's.

By that Richard knew him. Richard judged it wise not to move, but to remain where he was, hand on the dagger's hilt, ready to attack or to defend if the moment presented itself.

The Old Man of the Mountain spoke, and his companion rendered the words into fluent French. The young Assassin's accent, Richard noticed, had a strong flavor of Provence. "A good day to you, king of the Franks," he said.

"I am the king of the English," Richard said.

"You are all Franks," the Old Man said mildly. He seemed a harmless creature, no more strength in him than a bundle of sticks. And yet, like a spider crouched in the center of its web, he kept watch over all the strands of power in this part of the world.

He did not frighten Richard. If death had been on the Old Man's mind, he would have sent a party of his Faithful, armed with daggers. He had come himself—which was half a gesture of contempt for the strength and vigilance of Richard's army, and half a signal honor. For the Old Man to leave his mountain was a rare and significant thing.

Richard settled more comfortably, yawned and stretched and said, "I see you're keeping me in reserve."

"That is a way of putting it," the Old Man said dryly. "I see you're taking advantage of the opening I gave you."

"Did you expect that I wouldn't?"

"Franks are sometimes hard to predict," the Old Man said. "I've come to offer you a bargain."

Richard raised a brow. "Oh, have you? And what would that be? Pack up and go away and you won't kill me?"

"If I had wanted that, I would have left the Sultan alive."

Richard sat up. He was not a master of nuance—that was his mother's gift—but this was obvious enough. "You think he would have defeated me."

"I know he would have kept Jerusalem. And you would have left with your Crusade unfinished."

Richard felt the swift rush of heat, the temper that, if he let it, could rip this monstrous old man apart. But he was not ready to do that, not yet. "So now he's gone—and I'm going to mourn him. He was my enemy and it serves me well that he's dead, but he was a worthy adversary."

"Surely," the Old Man said. "Here is your bargain. I can give you Jerusalem: weaken its commanders, lure off its troops, and open its gates at your coming. As an earnest of my good faith, I've already begun to act on my promise. The riots are my doing, and the disturbances that refuse to be quieted for anything the emirs and the princes can do. In return, I ask a simple favor."

"Is any favor simple?" Richard demanded.

"They're all simple: I profit you, you profit me. I give you the city you prayed to win. You give me a simple thing: freedom. Take all of this country that pleases you, except those territories and castles that are mine. Leave me free to do my duty to Allah and my Faith."

"And if that duty is to destroy everything I build?"

The Old Man shrugged, a fluid roll of the shoulders. For an instant Richard saw not a feeble old man but a veteran warrior, all cunning and whipcord strength. "I can give you what you want most. Whether I later take it away . . . that is in the hands of God, and your own conduct toward me and mine. It's a gamble. But what in this life is not?"

"You bargain like the Devil," Richard said, but he laughed. "And this is a devil's bargain—but I'll take it. For Jerusalem I'll take it."

"So be it," said the Old Man of the Mountain. "Wait as you planned, march as you planned. When you come to the city, dispose your troops as you intended, but wait for a signal."

"And what will that signal be?" asked Richard.

"It will be unmistakable," the Old Man said. "Go with God, king of Franks. And may God give you all you pray for."

Richard could swear that he only blinked; that no one moved. But one moment the Old Man and his interpreter were there, and the next they had vanished into the heatstruck air.

★ ★ ★

Richard's army came to Jerusalem by starlight. They had met only one troop of defenders on the way, a party of Turkish archers who must have been late in receiving word of the sultan's death. Richard loosed the Templars on them; the warrior monks cut them apart with holy glee.

He had told no one of the bargain he had made. That there was treachery in the city, yes; but not whose doing it was. None of them would understand. None of them was a king.

Philip of France, that supple snake—he would have understood. But he had called this Crusade a fool's errand and taken himself back to France. Barbarossa of the Germans was dead. There was no clearly acknowledged King of Jerusalem, now that the Assassins had taken Conrad. There was only Richard here, on this march, disposing his troops along the barren hills and through valleys so holy that they could barely support the weight of living green.

He rode last, leading the rearguard, as if to thrust himself to the front would turn all this to mist and dream: he would wake and find himself prostrate with another fever, and Saladin still alive, and no honest hope of winning the prize he had dreamed of for so long. But even as slowly as he rode, in the end he topped the stony summit of the hill and looked on the Holy City.

It was a darkness on darkness, shot with streaks of fire. When he looked down, he found his army more by feel than sight. There was no moon; the stars were hazed with dust and heat. His skin prickled with it under the weight of padding and mail.

His horse snorted softly, pawing with impatience. Its steel-shod hoof sent up a shower of sparks.

In almost the same moment, a comet of fire arched up over Jerusalem. Then at last he saw the outline of walls and towers, and the golden flame of the Dome. And more to the point, he saw David's Gate open below the loom of the tower. There were no lights visible in the tower, no sign of guards on the wall or in the gate. Torchlight gleamed within, casting a golden glow across the meeting of roads that led up to the gate.

It could be a trap. Richard was ready for that. He had focused his attack on the gate, though the rams would not be needed after all; in their place he sent a company of crossbowmen. They took their positions out of ordinary bowshot, and sent a barrage of bolts into the open gate.

Nothing moved inside it. No hidden troops fell screaming from the towers. The gate was empty, open and inviting.

Richard gambled as he had with the Old Man: he ordered the first wave into the city. With a cry of trumpets and a thunder of drums, they swarmed out of the hills and fell upon Jerusalem.

Richard had intended to go in with the rearguard, but as the vanguard swarmed toward the gate, he could not bear it. He clapped spurs to his destrier's sides. He barely cared if anyone went with him; all his heart and soul were fixed on that flicker of torchlight.

He was not the first to pass beneath that echoing gate, but he was far from the last. Although he had never been in the city, he knew its ways as if he had been born to them. He had committed them to heart against just such a day, praying every night and every morning that it would come to pass.

This was David's Gate, the gate of the north and west, guarded by the Tower of David in which the kings of Jerusalem had lived and ruled and fought. The Tower seemed deserted, empty of troops and even of noncombatants. The street of David that ran inward from it, nearly straight through the middle of the city till it reached the Beautiful Gate of the Temple on the other side, was as empty as the Tower, but for crumpled shapes that proved to be bits of abandoned baggage: an empty sack, a heap of broken pots, a chest with its lid wrenched off and nothing within but a scent of sandalwood.

He was deeply, almost painfully aware of the holiness of this place, the sanctity of every stone. But in this hour he was a fighting man, and there was a fight ahead—that, he was sure of. But where? Not, he hoped, in every street and alley of this ancient and convoluted place.

The Old Man had woven this web and, Richard had no doubt, cleared this sector of the city for the invasion. Both he and Moustafa had spoken more than once of the Dome of the Rock. That was the Muslims' great holy place, the rock from which their Prophet had been taken up to heaven. Like the Holy Sepulcher for the Christians, it was the heart and soul of their faith.

It was also a great fortress and storehouse, built as a mosque and then transformed into the stronghold of the Knights Templar: the Templum Domini, the Temple of the Lord. Saladin had died under its splendid dome. It would be like the Old Man's humor to drive Saphadin's troops there and pen them like sheep for Richard to slaughter. Saphadin might even hope to withstand a siege, until hordes of reinforcements could come from his kinsmen in Damascus.

Richard gathered his vanguard and the second wave of forces behind it, ordered the lanterns lit to guide them, and led them into the city. The third rank would go in after a pause, and sweep the city behind them, taking it street by street if need be.

Beyond the gate, at last, they met opposition: a barricade across the broad street, and turbaned Saracens manning it. The Norman destriers ran right over them. It cost a horse, gut-slit by an infidel who died under the hooves of the beast he slew, but none of Richard's men fell, even when the archers began to shoot from the rooftops. They were ready for that: shields up, interlocked as they pressed forward.

There were two more barricades between David's Tower and the Latin Exchange, where half a dozen skeins of streets met and mingled. One barricade they broke as they had the first, but at higher cost: there were more men here, and more archers. They lost a man-at-arms there, arrow-shot in the eye. The other barricade was broken when they came to it, all its defenders dead—Assassins' work, quite likely. Past that, as they marched warily round the looming bulk of the Khan al-Sultan, they found the way clear, and only dead men to bar it. Walls on either side rose high and blank, windows shuttered, gates shut and barred.

Richard was preternaturally aware of the force he led, as if it had been a part of his own body. He felt as much as heard the troop of Germans who ventured to creep off and begin the sack before the city was won. An English voice called a halt to them, and English troops barred their way. They snarled like a pack of dogs, but they were quelled, for the moment.

Morning was coming. The sky was growing lighter. He could see the Dome of the Rock floating above the walls, seeming no part of earth at all.

No time for awe. Not yet. It was as he had expected: the Beautiful Gate was heavily manned. There were turbaned helmets all along the wall, archers with bows bent and aimed downward at Richard's army.

He had siege engines. He had the city. He could take the bait the infidels offered, and be snapped up in turn by the massed armies of Damascus.

"No," he said to no one in particular. He had been promised Jerusalem. This, to an infidel, was the heart of it.

He rolled the dice one last time. He sent for the rams—but when that messenger had gone at a gallop, he brought up the heaviest of his heavy cavalry, the German and Flemish knights on their massive chargers. The beasts were as fresh as they could be on this side of the sea, with the cool of the dawn and the slowness of their progress through the city.

Richard addressed them in a voice that was low but

pitched to carry. "I've heard that a charge of armored knights could break down the walls of Babylon, and those are three lance-lengths thick. This gate's not near as thick as that. There's not much room to get going, but we'll give you all we can, and we'll cover you with crossbow fire. Just break that gate for me."

"*Deus lo volt*," they replied: the war cry of the Crusade. "God wills it."

The rest of the army drew back as much as it could. It must have looked like a retreat: Richard heard whooping and jeering on the wall. So much the better. The charge prepared itself behind a shield of English and Norman knights.

When it was ready, the crossbowmen in place, Richard raised his sword. As it swept down, the knights lumbered into motion. Their shield melted away, then came together behind them.

Crossbow bolts picked off the Saracen archers with neat precision. The knights beneath them were moving faster now, building speed from walk to an earth-shaking trot. Lances that had been in rest now lowered. The few arrows that fell among them did no damage, sliding off the knights' armor or the horses' caparisons, or falling harmless, to be trampled under the heavy hooves.

The Saracens above the gate were brave or desperate: they hung on, though more and more of their number fell dead or wounded. The charge struck the gate with force like a mountain falling. Lances splintered. The destriers in the lead, close pressed behind, reared and smote the gate with their hooves. The knights' maces and morningstars whirled and struck, whirled and struck.

They broke down that gate of gold and forged steel as if it had been made of straw, trampled over it and plunged through. The second, less massive but still powerful charge thundered behind them, Richard's English and his Normans chanting in unison: "*Deus lo volt! Deus lo volt!*"

There was a battle waiting for them in the court of

the Temple; mounted and afoot, the dead Sultan's gathered forces under command of a prince in a golden helmet. That helmet had been Saladin's, and the armor had been his, too; but he had never ridden that tall bay stallion, Richard's gift to the great knight and prince of the infidels, al-Malik al-Adil, the lord Saphadin. The first light of the sun caught the peak of his helmet and crowned him with flame.

Richard's knights plunged deep into the waiting army of infidels. His lighter cavalry, his archers, his foot soldiers were close behind them. The court could not hold them all. Over half waited in reserve outside, or had gone up on the walls and dealt with the archers whom the crossbowmen had not disposed of.

It was a hot fight. The enemy had been herded and trapped here, but they had not been robbed of either their courage or their fighting skill. They contested every inch of that ancient paving, right up to the gate of the golden mosque.

Richard faced Saphadin there, the Saracen prince with his back to the barred door, and Richard too on foot, man to man and sword to sword. Richard was taller, broader, stronger; his reach was longer, his sword heavier. But Saphadin was quicker, and he had far more to lose. He drove Richard back with a flashing attack. He was smiling, a soft, almost drowsy smile, deep with contentment.

It was the smile of a man who had decided to die, and had chosen the manner of his death. He was wearing himself into swift exhaustion. It was a grand and foolish gesture, showing off all his swordsmanship; he would know, none better, that Richard would simply wait him out.

Richard waited, keeping sword and shield raised to defend against the whirling steel. He was aware, while he waited, of the battle raging around him. His men were gaining the upper hand, but they were paying for it. There were too many of them in too small a space, and their heavier horses, their heavier armor and weapons, were beginning to tell on them as the sun climbed the sky.

It had to end quickly. Richard did two things almost at once: he firmed his grip on his sword as Saphadin's swirl of steel began to flag, found the opening he had been waiting for, and clipped the Saracen prince neatly above the ear; then, not even waiting for the man to fall, he spun and bellowed, *"Now!"*

They had all been playing the waiting game. Now they struck in earnest, as his reserves charged in through the Beautiful Gate, swarming over the enemy, surrounding him and bringing him down.

By noon it was done. The Temple of the Lord was taken. The defenders paid the price that the knights of the Kingdom of Jerusalem had paid at the slaughter of Hattin, where the kingdom fell and the Crusade was born: the high ones died or were held for ransom; the ordinary troops were chained and led away to be sold into slavery.

Saphadin was alive; Judah the physician had taken him in hand. Richard did not intend to let him go, not while he had value as a hostage. For the moment he was safe, and heavily guarded; Richard did not fear for the prince's safety among his own men, but the Old Man of the Mountain was another matter.

When Richard was certain that his army was under control, the packs of looters caught and hanged where they stood, and the cleansing of the city and particularly the Temple well begun, he went at last to the place he had dreamed of. He entered the Church of the Holy Sepulcher, that he had won back for Christendom, and laid his sword on the tomb in which the Lord Christ had risen from the dead.

It was near dark when he emerged. A flock of people waited for him, but he only took notice of the squire who knew where he could find a bath, dinner, and a bed for an hour or two before he went back to securing the city.

Those were in the Tower of David, in what might have been the king's lodgings: rooms both wide and airy for a castle, fastidiously clean, and about them still a hint of eastern perfumes. Richard cared only that the basin for the bath was full and the water hot, and dinner was waiting, and the bed was ready, clean and fresh with herbs.

The bath was bliss on his aching bones, his bruises and the few small wounds. The servants were deft and quiet; one of them was adept at soothing away aches and the raw strain of exhaustion. He sighed and closed his eyes.

"So, king of Franks," said a soft voice in his ear, speaking Latin with an eastern accent, "are you satisfied with your bargain?"

Richard was abruptly and completely awake. He kept his eyes shut, his body slack. He was completely vulnerable here, naked in the bronze basin, and no weapon in the room, not even a knife for cutting meat.

The Old Man of the Mountain went on bathing him with a servant's skill. He shuddered in his skin, but he would never, for his life's sake, let this man see him flinch. "Did I not do well? Have you complaints of the gift I gave you?"

"I have no complaints," Richard said, deep and slow, as if half in a dream. So, he thought: the Old Man had never needed an interpreter at all. It was all part of the game he played, deceit upon delusion upon deception.

"Now you will do your part," the Old Man said.

"Yes," said Richard; a long sigh.

"Truly," said the Old Man. Richard felt a cold soft kiss at his throat, and the faintest, barely perceptible sting of the dagger's edge. "Remember. I can follow you wherever you go, find you wherever you hide. Keep your bargain, and your life is sacred to me. Break it, and you die."

"I understand," Richard said. He gathered himself inside, still in the dark of closed eyes, vividly aware of the steel pressed to his throat.

In the instant that it yielded, he struck: up, round, in a whirl of water. The dagger flew wide. The Old Man fell headlong into the basin. He was fully as strong as Richard had expected, but Richard was stronger. Barely; he was near to drowning himself when the thrashing slowed and mercifully stopped. He held the old monster underwater for a long while, not trusting even the letting go of the bowels that was a clear, and redolent, mark of death.

When his hands began to shake with weariness and the water began to grow chill, he let go, and called his guards and squires. They stumbled at the door: the servants' bodies were there, one stabbed to the heart, one strangled. "Bury them with honor," Richard said, "but hang this carrion from the wall."

They did his bidding, nor did he care what they thought, or what they said once they were out of his presence. Let them think what they pleased, as long as they rid him of the Old Man's body.

The Old Man's presence lingered long after his earthly remains were taken away, the basin emptied and scoured, and the room blessed by the nearest convenient prelate, who happened to be the Patriarch of Jerusalem. When all that was done, at last Richard could lie in the bed that had been prepared for him. Guards stood at the four corners of it; Moustafa, recovered, armed to the teeth, and grimly determined, lay across the foot.

Richard had not tried to dissuade them. It soothed their guilt, and let them feel that they were doing their duty after he had done it for them. He let sleep take him, even knowing who stood on the other side of it.

The Old Man of the Mountain was sitting as Richard had first seen him, under a screened canopy. In dream or in death he spoke all the tongues of living men;

Richard heard him in good Norman French, with a fine grasp of ironic nuance. He sounded, in fact, a great deal like Richard's mother. "So, king of Franks. What of our bargain?"

"I kept to the letter of it," Richard said. "You asked me to set you free. I did exactly that."

The Old Man's mouth twisted. "And you said that I bargained like the Devil."

"So you did," said Richard, "and I bargained like a good Christian. We Franks are simple men. We do as we say we will do."

"Except when it suits you to do the opposite."

Richard shrugged. "The Devil is the Father of Lies," he said. "You didn't honestly think I'd let you run wild in this kingdom, did you? You gave me Jerusalem, and for that you have my perpetual gratitude. In return I gave you what all your Faithful yearn for: a swift death, and a speedy ascent into Paradise."

"*Malik Ric*," said the Old Man, shaking his head. "O king of Christian devils. Savor your victory; it's well earned. But watch your back. I may be dead, but my Faithful survive—and there is the whole of Islam waiting to descend upon you. Did you hope to see your England again before this year is out?"

"I will see it when God wishes me to see it," Richard said calmly. "It's a good war, old man, and a grand victory. I'll remember you in my prayers."

The Old Man's brow arched. "You'd pray for me?"

"I'd pray for the Devil himself if he'd given me Jerusalem," Richard said.

The Old Man's smile held for a moment the hint of a fang; and the foot beneath the white robe, for a moment, had the shape of a cloven hoof. But he was, after all, only a dream. Richard was waking already, roused by the sound of bells in the tower of Holy Sepulcher, and clear voices greeting the dawn. For the first time since Jerusalem fell to Saladin, Christians chanted the Psalms in the holy places, and in place of the muezzin's cry, Richard heard the morning hymn in the sonorous cadences of Rome.

He rose only to kneel, and crossed himself and began to pray. He thanked his God for this gift of Jerusalem, for this splendor of victory. And he prayed for the soul of Sinan ibn Salman, lord of Assassins, Old Man of the Mountain, who had given him his heart's desire. "For even the Devil may do good," he said to the numinous Presence in his heart, "and even the Devil's familiar may serve Your will."

He drew a deep breath, drinking in this air that was most holy in the world, and let it out again in a long and blessed sigh. "God wills it," he said.

Editorial Note: George Patton was dyslexic, and did not learn to read until he was twelve. His bad spelling was notorious, and is preserved in this chronicle.

George Patton Slept Here

Roland J. Green

Sicily, 1943

Patton's Diary, July 27:

All roads don't lead to Messina, or at least they shouldn't. Ought to be just enough for Seventh Army to get there first. Two roads for us and two for Monty means it's still anybody's fox.

If the British get to Messina first, it will still be as hard as ever to convince them that Americans are worth a damn as fighters. That will mean we go on fighting the war with the British tail trying to wag the American dog.

Divine Destiny [Eisenhower] may like this. It surely gets him a lot of bootlick from the British. I don't.

Just heard that Mussolini has "resigned." Be happier to hear that he's been arrested and shot, or even better turned over to the Krauts. (They don't like losers.) We still have to push the Italians so hard that, running away, they'll block all the roads and keep the Germans from bringing up reinforcements.

The ballroom in the Royal Palace is large enough to maneuver jeeps. My bedroom could hangar a couple of fighters and the bed has four mattresses, all mildooed. What a waste to have a bed that size all to myself.

Patton's Diary, July 28:

Slept badly. Even if we have the roads to reach Messina first, do we have the guts? Our veterans are about as good as the Germans. Our reinforcements are about as green as ever. I hear stories about more cases of "combat exhaustion." Somebody needs to knock some guts into men like that, if they can be called men.

Al Stiller [junior aide] says no wonder I couldn't sleep in this palace. He claims he's seen muskitos as big as the ones in Texas, and cockroaches the size of jeeps. He wants to find me a nice clean modern boarding house down by the harbor. I told him that he has no sense of history.

Will try no booze and only one cigar before bedtime, also some Swedish exercises. The best kind of exercise for an old married man can't be had when you're in Sicily and your wife is in Massachusetts.

Patton's Diary, July 29:

Slept alone again in the same bed, but a lot better. After breakfast, inspected the salvage and repair work going on down by the harbor. I would feel sorry for the Sicilians living with all that noise if I hadn't seen everything else they live with. They are down at the level of the Arabs, which is pretty damned low.

Seeing the port gave me some ideas. I had a mix of Army and Navy engineers in for a good dinner and decent liquor. Asked them a few questions about how fast the port will be back in shape. Right now we are tied to the roads up from the south for most of what we need, and the ammo expenditures are already going up. 1st and 45th Divisions are both coming up against Germans in rugged territory. Will talk to the Air Force tomorrow, but that's probably still going to be like teaching a pig to sing.

Patton's Diary, July 30:

Slept fine until the air-raid sirens went off. Turned out to be a German snooper, who was shot down by the antiaircraft. Crashed down by the harbor, and wrecked three apartment buildings. No loss, except to the people living there. Will ask the Cardinal about a joint effort, us and the Church, to find roofs for the people and arrange a funeral for the dead.

The engineers tell me we should be able to stage a fairly big shore-to-shore operation out of Palermo within a few days, if the Navy can provide the ships. The Navy engineers wouldn't promise anything. I told them *they* didn't need to promise anything; it was their bosses I wanted. Did promise the engineers Distinguished Unit Citations if we brought it off.

Turns out that a colored supply battalion helped rescue the people from the wrecked buildings, including the one that was on fire. Some of the colored boys were hurt because they wouldn't leave some people to be burned. That took guts.

I visited them and some of the Sicilians in the hospital. One colored boy had gone on moving rubble with a broken arm. He said that after picking sugar beets in Louisiana since he was eight, there wasn't anything the Army or the Krauts could do to make him sweat. I gave him a Bronze Star.

That colored boy should talk to some of the "combat exhaustion" cases.

Tomorrow I talk to the admirals.

Patton's Diary, July 31:

Another good night's sleep. Just as well. I talked to the admirals until I nearly lost my voice. Then I kissed their asses until I have a sore lip and will probably get some sort of mouth fungus as well. I think it paid off, though. They're promising enough for a reinforced battalion. I want to make it two battalions, one infantry and one tank, but they think the best they can do is a company of tanks and some towed AT guns.

The Navy isn't what it was in the days of Stephen Decatur. They talked about the sykological effect of having even a small force in the German rear. I told them without using too many rough words that you can't do anything to the Germans with sykology (?). None of the ones I've fought scare easily. You need a physical effect, like shooting the sons-of-bitches in the guts or running over them with tanks.

To top it all off, somebody must have read my mind. They're going to call the landing OPERATION DECATUR!

Maybe his ghost will haunt them.

Patton's Diary, August 1:

No chance today to beg and plead with the admirals. Flew to 1st Armored Division for a quick inspection. They are not much dirtier than I had expected, and they are doing a fine job on vehicle maintenance under very bad conditions.

Back by way of 3rd Infantry Division. Lucian [Truscott] looks tired, even though I would still call him the best division commander in Seventh Army. I asked him if he was getting enough sleep, and if he lacked confidence in his staff and regimental commanders. He said he had complete confidence in his division—and also in the Germans' ability to require a total effort by everybody in it!

Even if the British say it, "He who has not fought the Germans, does not know war," may be true. What's completely true is that the British screwed up their early campaigns as badly as we did ours, and they got their "greater experience" by killing a lot of their own men. But try to tell Ike that.

We will just have to kick the Germans in the pants so hard that even the British will notice when they see a lot of bare-assed Germans running for their lives, crying for their mothers and their goddamned Fuehrer!

Warned Lucian to get more sleep, since he'll be the senior ground commander for Operation Decatur. No problems likely with Clarence [Huebner, commanding 1st Infantry Division] tomorrow. He's as tough as Black Jack [Pershing].

Patton's Diary, August 2:

I haven't felt so good in months. The planning for Operation Decatur is going forward at a gallop. Lucian may not be getting the extra sleep he needs, though. I hope he won't wear himself down to the point of being cautious. *L'audace, l'audace, toujours l'audace!* [boldness, boldness, always boldness!] has to be our motto. Give the Germans five extra minutes and they'll counterattack. Give the Navy ten minutes, and they'll find excuses for not doing something.

Visited 1st Infantry Division. Clarence is what they need, even though I suspect it will be a while before they know it and a long time before they like it. You could sum up his General Orders in two sentences: you will look like soldiers and you will stop feeling sorry for yourself. I still want to go over my indorsement to Terry's and Ted's [Terry Allen and Theodore Roosevelt Jr., former commander and assistant commander of the 1st Infantry Division] relief, to make sure there's nothing in it that might prejudice their getting new commands. The Big Red One hit the Torch beaches ready to fight, and it is about the only goddamned division we had that you can say this about.

Went to a field hospital after lunch with Clarence. They

had several new admissions, one with a leg just ampotated, another blinded. I pinned Purple Hearts on both of them. I added for the blind boy that he had one consolation—he didn't have to look at my ugly old mug while I was decorating him.

One of those "combat exhaustion" cases was sitting on the last cot. At least that's what he looked like. No wounds and when I asked him what he was here for, he said, "I guess I just can't take it."

I glared at him, and he started crying. I looked at him a second time, and it looked to me like he might be really sick. Malaria or cat fever or the runs can turn almost anybody into somebody who thinks he can't take it which is exactly what I told him. I also asked him if he'd been examined, loud enough so that all the medical people should have heard me.

Then I told Al to bring in the emergency supplies, because if an American soldier crying because he thinks he's a coward isn't an emergency then what the hell is? I apolegized to the nurses for the language and also for prescribing without a license but I told the combat exhausted boy (I never did get his name) that he shouldn't drink any of what I was giving him until he'd seen the doctors and had a good meal and maybe some sleep.

Then I told him that everything looks different after a night's sleep or a few. Even if it was something like seeing your buddy blown to pieces, after you sleep you remember that you have other buddies who might live if you go back and be there. It's not being a coward to be scared sometimes, when you're sick or hurt or you've really been in the shit (another apology) and in fact there aren't any cowards in the American Army. I ordered him to never think of himself as a coward and he stood up at attention and saluted.

Then he looked more like he was going to laugh than cry, and I thought I was going to get carried away and start crying, and that would have been a hell of a thing to happen to a general. I remembered all the boys I'd led in the Argonne, where just me and Joe Di Angelo came out alive. I handed over the whiskey and got out of there.

I felt almost all right by the time we got back to Palermo. I felt completely all right after I heard that the Navy was borrowing back some landing craft from the British for Operation Decatur. If the Germans do bomb Palermo or any of the other assembly ports, we still go on time and with everything we need.

Letter, Lt. Col. Perrin H. Long, Medical Corps, to the Surgeon, NATOUSA, August 4, 1943 subject: Visit to Patients in Receiving Tent of the 15th Evacuation Hospital by Lt. Gen. George S. Patton:

Exhibit #1—Pvt. Joseph L. Shrieber, K Company, 26th Infantry, 1st Division— . . . concluded visit by saying that there are no cowards in the American Army and that he ordered Pvt. Shrieber never to think of himself as one.

Subj. pvt. stood to attention and saluted Gen. Patton, and so did all other ambulatory patients and medical personnel. Gen. Patton appeared extremely moved by this and became inarticulate. 1st Lt. Gayle Hadley asked if he needed any help, but he smiled and shook his head, then left the tent.

Lt. Hadley immediately asked me if Gen. Patton might require medical attention.

Then she said that she had been trying to find something to say to combat fatigue cases, because very few of them seemed to be happy about getting out of the lines. Subj. pvt. had been ordered back three times with a diagnosis of combat fatigue and each time asked to return to unit. He had been in the Army eight months and with the 1st Division since June 1943.

Private Shrieber's diagnosis was acute dysentery, possibly

amoebic, with a temperature of 102.5 degrees, frequent headaches and stools, and severe dehydration. His stool test was negative for malarial parasites. Bed rest and fluids were recommended.

I have advised all personnel present during Gen. Patton's visit to treat his words as entirely confidential. I also sincerely hope that it will be possible for Gen. Patton to grant permission for his words to be circulated, if not generally then at least among medical personnel. He may have found a much more effective way of telling combat fatigue cases that they are still soldiers than any the Medical Corps has yet developed.

Interview with Captain Gayle Hadley Jorgensen, U. S. Army Nurse Corps (Ret.), November 25, 1963:

I suppose you'd have to say I was the guilty party in letting what General Patton said get out. Many of us who heard him were almost in tears when he left, and some of us did break down afterwards. I think his aide, Major Stiller, knew that, because he left two bottles of whiskey, not one, even if the second was something from Texas and pretty awful.

But anyway, I wasn't quite myself when I got off duty, or when I got to my boyfriend for our date. He was married, so I won't tell you his name. It was just one of those things that happen in wartime, when you're both alone a long way from home. I was also thinking of how after one Luftwaffe raid it might have been me sitting on a cot shaking and crying, and nobody to tell me that being scared wasn't the same as being a coward.

So I told my friend, and he said he was glad to hear that some high brass understood what it could be like, when you had to fly straight and level on the last ten miles of a bombing run with fighters coming in from all sides except the one that the flak was using, and sometimes even that. He also promised not to tell.

That's why we broke up, incidentally. He really didn't keep the promise. Like a lot of Air Force officers, he knew a reporter. He talked to the reporter, the reporter decided that this was too good a story to sit on, and it wound up embarrassing General Patton, or so I've heard.

It's too late to apologize to Old Georgie. But I hope he'll understand that ever since that day, all of us who heard him are just a little prouder of having worn the same uniform as he did.

From The New York Times, *August 6, 1943:*

PATTON STRIKES BLOW FOR MORALE
SAYS "NO COWARDS" IN AMERICAN ARMY
CHEERED AT PRESS CONFERENCE IN PALERMO

Letter to Beatrice Patton, August 7, 1943:

Don't worry about the old "death wish" coming back, but right now I would rather lead the first wave of Operation Decatur ashore than give another speech or answer another question from a reporter. Anyone would think I was running for office (when I retire after the war I am more likely to run from office) and the reporters say they are on our side but I don't think all of them are telling the truth.

Of course, neither am I, in public. You are the only one I'm going to tell about the whole thing. I was all ready to chew Private Shriver's ass up one side and down the other, and maybe kick him right out of the tent. But I had a tickle in my throat, and I knew that if I started shouting I would cough myself silly.

So I put on my fighting face, which looked as if it was going to scare the poor little SOB right off his cot. I started to raise my riding crop, and I could see people flinching.

Then something grabbed my wrist. It was as solid a

grab as I ever felt from you. It pulled my wrist back to my side and then I heard a voice whisper, "Wait." It was the same voice I heard when I was wounded in the Argonne.

I looked over Pvt. Shreever's head, and saw Papa standing there. He was about the age you remember him when we met, but he was wearing his VMI [Virginia Military Institute] cadet's uniform.

"Look at me, son," he said. I hoped nobody else could hear him, and that I could reply without anybody else hearing me. Right then, I didn't want anybody thinking I was crazy.

"I wore this uniform a lot longer than that young man has worn his," Papa went on. "But I never set foot on a battle field. I never smelled powder smoke. I never had a single man die beside me. You honor my name, but let me tell you that Private Shrieber is braver than I ever was."

"But Papa—your own father died because his brigade—" I didn't really care if the living heard me.

"Was running away?" That was another voice, not as familiar. I looked beyond Papa, and saw my grandfather standing there. He was the one who'd wondered out loud if it was time for another Patton to die, at the Meuse-Argonne. The same as the other time, he was wearing his Confederate uniform like in the pictures my grandmother left us.

I didn't know what to say. My grandfather grinned. "Oh, some of them were running. Most of them were trying to find somewhere behind a fence or wall, instead of standing out there to be targits for the Yankee artillery. Even the ones who were running away, they've apologized and asked me to forgive them.

"I did just that. This boy hasn't even run away. Nobody's died because he was sick, and nobody will. *If* you send him back to his regiment with his pride intact. And if you go back to your post so as to make us prouder still. You've already done honor to the Patton name, grandson. Go and do more."

He saluted. So did Papa. Then they were both gone.

That is exactly what I remember, no more and no less. It must have happened in some way outside of time, because it was only a few seconds according to my watch.

Thank God nobody else heard or saw anything. Or maybe they did, and they are too afraid of everybody thinking their crazy to say anything.

Anyway, that's Grandpa, Papa, and you who all think I'm a pretty good soldier. We shall see what happens with Operation Decatur.

Your George

PS—The British seem to be reading the papers.

All of a sudden, Monty wants a meeting tomorrow, to coordinate Operation Decatur with a landing on the east coast of Sicily. I hope there's enough air cover for two, and that the Limeys move out of the beachhead fast. They will be closer to Messina than we will be, and they might get there first, but that does not bother me as much as a lot of British soldiers getting killed because they squatted long enough for the Germans to bring up artillery or even counterattack. Oh well, if nothing else moves them, the Royal Navy will give them a kick in the ass. They've been trying to get Monty to try an end-run for weeks.

PPS—Don't show this to anybody else.

From The New York Times, *August 11, 1943:*

A Pincer for the Panzers
Double Allied Landings Cut Off
Germans in Northern Sicily
Ferocious Luftwaffe Counterattacks

Patton's Diary, August 12, 1943:

So far, so good. Lucian has gone ashore at Brolo to personally supervise the three-ring circus they have there.

If the Germans weren't so convinced that we still have a second wave or a whole second landing force in Palermo and weren't trying to bomb the city flat, we might be in trouble.

It did help that the first companies ashore moved right out and up on to the high ground around the beaches. Right away they had good observation for the Navy and the mortars, and good fields of fire for everything else.

Between the AA [antiaircraft] we've landed and the fighter cover the Air Force is actually providing, not just promesing, the boys ashore don't have to look up too often. They have one road blocked and the other under fire, and German prisoners say the 29th Panzer Grenadiers is redeploying to clear their rear. They think we've landed an armored division.

The Navy hasn't been so lucky. They've lost two transports, the light cruiser *Savannah*, and a destroyer, plus some landing craft and PT boats. *Savannah* blew up and went down with most of her crew. I'm endorsing a recommendation for the Medal of Honor for her captain.

The British only went ashore with one battalion, near Taormina north of Mount Etna. They've already lost a monitor, *Erebus*, and a destroyer escort. Hope they don't have to evacuate. That sort of thing draws the Luftwaffe like shit draws flies, and if Monty is blamed for another Dieppe he may be out on his skinny ass before you can say "Dunkirk."

Patton's Diary, August 14:

Department of Utter Goddamned Confusion. Fortunately, both sides have one. Also, I don't think the Italian alliance with the Germans is going to last much longer.

The air raids of the last three days have really hurt Palermo. They've also wrecked the Luftwaffe—nearly a hundred planes lost—and kept it off the backs of our landing forces. The Krauts even tried a parachute drop of commandos against harbor facilities and ammunition dumps.

Didn't work. Our base troops hid behind the rubble and shot back with everything they had. This included some of the first tanks to be unloaded directly at Palermo. They may also be the last for a while. The port is pretty well wrecked all over again. But the Germans lost five hundred crack troops and nearly all the transports they sent in.

Rumors running around that some of the colored supply boys did really good fighting. Did they accidentally ship the 10th Cavalry over here by mistake? If they did, I am damned well going to have them orginize a mounted column for when we cross the Straits into the Italian mainland. The French are already supposed to be sending over some of their mountain guns with a mule train.

And I've recommended the Presidential Unit Citation for the two DECATUR battalions and oak leaves to his DSC and a third star for Lucian Truscott. Damn, but we're getting good!

Patton's Diary, August 15, 1943:

Remind me not to play poker with Monty. He keeps an ace up his sleeve.

When we met to plan the DECATUR/BROKE landings, I noticed a lot of airfield construction going on near Monty's HQ. They'd even put a couple of new infantry battalions to work lengthening runways.

It turns out that BROKE force (named after a *British* navy captain of the War of 1812, not because it's going to end up that way) faced nothing but Italians around Taormina, and they surrendered faster than the Brits could haul up the rations to feed them. So pretty soon there was lots of elbow room, with the Germans not doing anything except long-range artillery shoots and a few patrols.

Inside their perimeter was a partly finished airfield. They filled in craters, hauled wrecked enemy planes away, and got a bumpy runway long enough to land gliders and fighters. Then last night fifty Wellington bombers flew over, towing gliders with troops and antitank guns. As soon as the runways were clear, the RAF started landing P-40 Kittyhawks.

Meanwhile, the Wellingtons flew back to the just-extended runways, landed, bombed and fueled up, and took off for a maximum-effort raid on Messina. They hit the port facilities so damned hard I doubt if we'll be able to use them to jump the Straits. Just maybe, though, the Germans won't be able to use them to evacuate Sicily!

So now we have stuck our fingers all the way down the Krauts' throat. So they'll have to either choke to death or bite back hard!

Patton's Diary, August 16, 1943:

Germans definitely trying to evacuate. They've broken contact along at least half of the Allied line, stopped raiding the BROKE and DECATUR beachheads, and aren't trying to give air cover to anything much south of Messina.

Reports coming in, from Italian prisoners, that the Germans have been keeping Italians off German vehicles at gunpoint and even confiscating Italian vehicles. They've also started blowing up heavy equipment.

Rumors going around that some Palermo Communists stole guns from Italian Army depots and helped round up the German paratroops. I am giving orders to squash those rumors. Right now the Germans have to treat Italy as some kind of ally. If they learn that even some Italians have changed sides, they'll retaliate all up and down the penensula, occupy everything they can, and wreck everything they can't.

Not as worried about squashing the Palermo Communists.

Right now, anybody who wants to fight Germans is doing more good than harm. We can sort them out after the Germans are down for the count.

Don't know what the politicians are doing. At least the Palermo Communists have the guts to come out shooting. But if the politicians won't give us orders, Ike and Alex [Field Marshal Sir Harold Alexander] and Monty and I are all going to have to sit down and make up our own.

Decorated several Air Force pilots today. One of them had been with Eagle Squadron during the Battle of Britain. Said that he felt he'd earned this Distinguished Flying Cross even more than the first one. The air fighting was just as heavy and you couldn't be sure of landing in friendly territory!

Patton's Diary, August 17, 1943:

Mass surrenders of the Italians. Surviving Germans are going to be lucky if they escape with their clothes and personal weapons. The British aren't ready to send heavy ships into range of the big shore batteries at the Straits of Messina. But they are bombing the ports on both sides every night, and have sunk quite a bunch of the lighters and coastal freighters the Germans will need to evacuate artillery and vehicles.

Already beginning to capture German supply dumps before the rearguards can destroy them. Not so many Italian supplies, but the Italians may not have much left to capture!

Note from Monty—we should meet to suggest modifications in the existing plan for knocking Italy out of the war on August 20. I have asked the engineers if we can mount *anything* out of Palermo before the middle of September. It would be a good deal easier if the Italians would surrender now. Then we could enlist all the POWs into the Royal Italian Army Engineers and watch the dust fly.

From The New York Times, *August 19, 1943:*

SICILY FALLS TO ALLIES
25,000 GERMAN, 150,000 ITALIAN POWS
RUMORS OF CRISIS IN ROME

From Field Marshal the Viscount Montgomery's Mediterranean Campaigns:

—triumphal entrance into Messina was simply not on, because there was hardly any Messina left to enter, triumphantly or in any other manner. It is more than a little difficult to maintain a conqueror's pose when one stumbles over rubble at every step and coughs on the smoke of burning buildings at every third breath, if one wishes to do so at all.

None of the Allied commanders wished it. It seemed a vulgar display worthy of the former *Duce*, and not of liberators. Had we known at the time the debates among Italian and German leaders (each keeping their debates secret from the other), we might have taken even further measures to adopt a conciliatory position toward the Italians.

If I had known at the time how little diplomatic intelligence Eisenhower was receiving, I would have been less hostile to his apparent obliviousness to political considerations. I now think better of him, and rather less well of those parties responsible for his ignorance. One would almost think they were prepared to sabotage any American support for a joint Mediterranean strategy, lest it threaten the primary emphasis on the cross-channel attack.

Fortunately Eisenhower also seemed willing to find excuses to continue the pressure on Italy, at least until the country surrendered and remaining Germans were expelled or neutralized. Possibly this was the beginning of an awakening sense of field strategy, or perhaps he was as lacking in initiative as ever, but even more willing to listen to Generals Patton, Bradley, and Clark.

I was least surprised at Patton's commitment to forcing Italy out of the war. Since Operation Torch, he had exhibited a singular instinct for seeking and severing the opponent's jugular vein, even if he also wished to adopt methods for doing so that enlarged his own role. We had fewer objections to a larger role for Patton now than a year ago, when Alan Brooke [Chief of the British Imperial General Staff] said that the American could only be useful in a situation requiring boldness, even rashness. From appearing to be fit for no larger command than a regiment of cavalry, he had developed higher military qualities in abundance. He was also noticeably more agreeable in person than he had been previously. The burdens of command over the previous month seemed to sit lightly, even gracefully, on his shoulders, and he was firm and fair in his praises of the British share in the greatest Anglo-American victory of the war to date. I began to see him as one who would return in full measure all the respect shown to him—and to his officers and men, toward whom his loyalty was, then and ever afterward, utterly unswerving.

To be brief about General Clark, on the principle of *nihil nisi bonum:* since his recently activated Fifth Army would include all the American and some of the British ground forces assigned to the invasion of the Italian mainland, it was clearly in his interests to execute that invasion. The bitter fighting in Sicily had also put us somewhat behind schedule for the next operation, and used a number of transports, landing craft, and warships intended for that operation, so both suitable weather and suitable sea transport might be lacking. Finally, one can only conjecture at this date, but Clark might well have possessed more information than the rest of us about the political circumstances in Italy.

Last, Omar Bradley, a man who might fail in genius but never in diligence and seldom in diplomacy. Loyalty to his superiors was written on his heart, and he also had no reason to wish to be translated to the remote northern mists of the British Isles to plan a cross-Channel invasion when he could continue fighting in a sunnier Mediterranean clime. Furthermore, sooner or later Patton or Clark would be elevated to the command of an Army Group, and at that point Bradley would surely succeed to the vacant Army command.

What we planned will become obvious to the reader shortly. But this is the appropriate time to quote a remark by General Eisenhower that has not, as far as I know, found its way into any other memoirs.

Looking at General Bradley, Eisenhower frowned and said, "Brad, I thought you grew up in the infantry. But less than a year with George, and you've grown hooves and a tail."

Then, turning to Patton, he said, "George, as far as I understand your proposals, we are to land in twice as many places over three times the distance with two-thirds of the resources we had planned for the original operations."

Patton bowed his head. "Sir, although an old cavalryman, to that charge I cannot say *neigh.*"

Letter from Beatrice Patton, September 2, 1943:

I hope you are too busy planning the invasion of Italy to read the papers. It might not be good for you, to learn just how highly everybody else thinks of you. But of course you *are* the outstanding American field commander of the war so far, and I think that the same will be said when the war is over.

I also hope that you will continue to let enemy fire seek but fail to find you, rather than "chasing the bubble reputation at the cannon's mouth." These days, I think your reputation is made of cast iron, and as firmly fixed in place as Grant's Tomb. I have also received a letter from General Eisenhower, warning that he will have to pull rank if you do become a casualty, and does not guarantee that he will leave enough of you for me to do anything with or to.

Please do not try to walk across any of the bodies of water that you have to pass over to reach your objectives. There are sharks and minefields in the Mediterranean, and meeting either one would at the very least ruin your boots. Sergeant Meeks has been faithful at repairing your boots all these years, and now that you are no longer putting your foot in your mouth quite so often he deserves a rest.

I hope you feel wonderful, being at last (or again) the happy warrior. I know it feels slightly wonderful to be married to him.

Letter to Beatrice Patton, September 7, 1943:

If you read this letter, it will be the last one you read from me, for the usual reasons that cause the writing of "last letters." However, I don't think this time being "a conqueror or a corpse" are mutaually exclusive. We are conducting parts of this operation on a shoestring, but even if I fall, before I do we should have the shoestring pulled tight around the throats of the Germans in Italy, as well as any Italians stupid enough to get in the way.

I could never embrace the better angels of my nature, because they weren't very damned good. So I embraced you instead. That has worked. Without you, I think I would be known only through the footnotes in biographies of other men.

If I do fall, I want to be buried beside the men I led. There my mortal remains can crumble away without bothering anybody. My immortal part will wait somewhere else, for you to join me so that we can take morning rides together once again.

From The New York Times, *September 11, 1943:*

AMERICANS LAND IN SARDINIA

NAVAL GUNS, PARATROOPERS SUPPORT AMPHIBIANS AT CAGLIARI

HEAVY AIR RAIDS STRIKE NORTHERN ITALY

Patton's Diary, September 11, 1943:

Aboard *U.S.S. Augusta*: It looks like the gamble on using paratroops again so soon has paid off. This time we were careful to have the transports approach and leave well clear of the landing beaches, and we borrowed lead navigators from the bomber boys, one for each flight of transports. The only gamble was on the paratroops' morale and the possibility of the Germans having moved in some extra AA.

But Jim Gavin is the kind of general most men really will follow to Hell. I think the jump boys might have followed Ambrose P. Burnside if the alternative was sitting out the war or going back to what they call "straight-leg" infantry. Rather like cavalry being dismounted, I suppose.

Anyway, the 82nd boys are keeping the engineers secure while they work on the airfields. We should have two ready for fighters tomorrow, or at least ready to stage through on the way north. After that we need at least one strip good for C-47s and B-25s. Then we start on the roads and bridges out to the edge of our planned peremeter.

We could never have risked Operation MINETAUR if we'd needed to take the whole island from the Germans. But we only have to take enough of Sardinia for the air bases, and that mostly from the Italians who are ready to hand over just about anything and gift-wrap it too!

So far, anyway. The Italians are certainly surrendering rather than retreating, which smells to me as if they want to stay away from the Germans. So far the Germans and the Italians haven't come to open shooting yet. I wouldn't mind if they wait a few days. By then, any German south of Rome will have his goddamned head in a meat grinder, and the Allies will have hold of the handle!

From The New York Times, *September 13, 1943:*

ITALY SURRENDERS

ITALIAN FLEET SAILS TO MALTA; U-BOATS SINK ONE CRUISER

ALLIED FIGHTERS FROM SARDINIA STRIKE ROME

Patton's Diary, September 14, 1943:

Moved ashore into the old Bishop's Palace in Cagliari. Parts of it go back to the seventeenth century and look as if they haven't been cleaned or painted since then. At least the Italian staff is willing and trying to look eager. I got them all together and talked to them through a translator who I told to not soften anything I said, or he would be the first one shot!

I told them that no doubt some of them were Fascists. I didn't care. Fascism was dead, whatever they thought. The Germans had always treated Italians like dirt, and were now too busy to reward anyone who tried something stupid, like shooting me.

Besides, I added, anybody who tries to shoot me probably won't even live to be hanged. These pistols aren't for show. I think the translator got everything through the way I wanted it.

The first A-20 landed today. Emergency landing—pilot got off course after the flak shot him up and holed a fuel tank, didn't have enough gas to make it back south, so flew out our way and landed safely with no brakes and damned little fuel. I think that proves our runways work. I won't really be happy until we can land a B-17—or even better, launch a raid of B-24s all the way to southern Germany.

I still keep hearing people fuss about the Foggia Plain around Naples. Fogg the Foggia plain! We can run a nice little air force out of Sardinia, another one out of Corsica (if we can keep the Corsicans from stealing everything that isn't nailed down), and then wait for the rest of Italy to get ripe and be ours.

I hope, for their sakes, that all the Germans in southern Italy who want to see the Fatherland again are on their best behavior. For our sakes, they can run wild with the *vino* and the *signorinas* so that they end up with their balls decorating the gates of all the local houses.

I think the Italians really wouldn't mind fighting the

Germans, if they could do so without much danger. But there's no way you can fight the Germans without danger. The next best thing for them would be some modern equipment, which I understand, seeing what they were fighting with (or without). But all their factories are still in German hands, and we're still going for the Mediterranean knockout on a tight budget.

Note from Ike says that Marshall is beginning to worry about the expindeture of landing craft that we'll need in the Channel. Have to do up a very careful reply, not telling Marshall or Ike their business, but God knows somebody has to! We're going for a knockout in the Med not to put off the Channel crossing, but because we've got a good grip on a whole lot of Germans and can kill them more conveniently now rather than later.

Every German we kill here in Italy is one less we have to worry about facing somewhere else in Europe. Territory doesn't matter. Burying Germans in it does.

Evening—Beedle [Lt. Gen. Walter Bedell Smith, Eisenhower's Chief of Staff] flew in aboard a B-25. Runway turned out to be just about long enough for a safe landing, if you don't mind having a heart attack. Beedle looked rather shaken when he climbed down. Maybe his ulcer as well as the flight? I wish he would either get better and not snarl at everybody, or get worse and have to go home.

Showed me a MOST SECRET (it was British) map about where everybody is.

The Germans are definitely moving south. But they don't have more than six divisions south of Rome. The air forces are keeping those fairly busy, so they haven't occupied too many key points. Italian units being disarmed where it's safe, but some are supposed to be just hiding their weapons and going home. Germans don't have enough strength to hunt runaways through every village.

Situation north of Rome turning nasty. The Germans are definitely holding on to industrial northern Italy, and being pretty rough about disarming Italians and arresting resistance. The SS has been in action. Total up there is about ten divisions, three of them panzers.

Beedle said he favors a landing at Salerno, in fighter range of Sicily. I said we'd have fighter cover over Civitavecchia all the way south to Naples by the time we needed it. He said we'd damned well better, or we'd lose three divisions and half the Navy.

The Salerno/Civitavecchia landing force is at sea out of Bizerte. The British are ready to cross the Straits of Messina and also land near Taranto tomorrow. I hope they move out fast again, because they'll need Italian *support*. The Italians obviously won't support anything or anybody who doesn't stand between them and the Germans, and I told Beedle as much.

He accused me of "defeatism." I did not say what he was doing, when he moaned about needing to land at Salerno. Going ashore north of Rome might put us up against strong German forces, but the Navy can hold the ring until we get air cover from Sardinia over them. *The Luftwaffe has had it* and anybody who thinks otherwise hasn't looked up lately.

North of Rome, we are squarely in the rear of more than twice as many more Germans as we bagged in Sicily. We are also north of several mountain ranges where the Germans could hold until winter just by rolling rocks downhill. Then nobody would go anywhere.

Salerno is *south* of all these places you don't want to visit and enough Germans to hold on to them until hell froze over.

If Beedle was as good a staff officer as he thinks he is, he'd know this. But he's mostly just Ike's hatchetman rather than a real staff officer. One of many reasons I hope we continue to wipe up the floor in Italy is that if we do that, I will swing as big a hatchet as Beedle.

So to bed—alone, in case anybody who shouldn't reads this diary after a while.

From The New York Times, *September 15, 1943:*

BRITISH LAND ON ITALIAN MAINLAND
ONE CORPS IN CALABRIA; SECOND NEAR TARANTO
A NEW ALLIED PINCERS MOVEMENT?
WILL ROME BE AN OPEN CITY? POPE, GERMANS SILENT.

Patton's Diary, September 16, 1943:

Al Stiller wants to shoot a few reporters. I told him that any German who can read a map has probably figured out where the nutcracker is going to squeeze. If he can't get his nuts out in time, that's his problem.

Cod [Colonel Charles Codman, Patton's senior aide] arrived this afternoon with the first PT boats to be based at Cagliari. He's looking well. I told him that he doesn't need to worry about us running out of war.

Dinner of C-rations and coffee, while we watched the first Sardinia-based air strikes take off. Heaviest is A-20s, but we're supposed to have a B-25 group as soon as they finish paving Runway Q.

Word is: landing at Civitavecchia. Next word: convoy with French divisional task force for Corsica coming in tonight. Told Navy to be sure swept channels stay swept. Final word: Bradley going ashore with earliest possible wave. Good for him. Fifth Army (or any other) does not need two headquarters operators. Hope he isn't sticking his head into a buzz saw!

From The New York Times, *September 17, 1943:*

ALLIES LAND NORTH OF ROME
HEAVY LUFTWAFFE RAIDS ON BEACHES
WILL ROME BE DEFENDED?

Patton's Diary, September 17, 1943:

The Luftwaffe has not shot itself dry. I should have remembered that Kesselring used to be in it, and was damned good. They seem to have pulled back to airfields safe from anything shorter-ranged than a B-17, risking us going ashore unopposed at Salerno. But we went ashore right up by Rome at Civitavecchia, and they are now all over us like what you might expect.

Germans probing hard at Sardinian perimeters and raided two airfields in broad daylight. Only seven planes destroyed, five of them A-36s; we can't afford losing even that many very often. Need to clear the rest of Sardinia sooner rather than later.

Placed French *Deuxieme Division Coloniale* under Lucian, with their first mission to secure Sardinia. Lucian asked permission to arm released Italian POWs to help. Okay, as long as he keeps them and the French well separated.

French thoroughly pissed at not being allowed to land in Corsica immediately. Understand their frustration, but no hope. We need to keep every spare ton of amphibious lift available, to reinforce Civitavecchia.

Sent Cod over to sweet-talk the Frogs. He knows all the fancy French, plus all the plain French needed to get mules, French generals, and other stubborn types moving. Drafted a message for the French, pointing out that they will have the honor of being the first French North African troops into action *and* the honor of liberating the first French soil. (Foreign Legion has a battalion with the British at Taranto, I've heard, but I've also heard that the Germans are hauling ass out of the Italian heel as fast as they can.)

Message from Forward HQ, Fifth Army, Lt. Gen. Omar N. Bradley, Acting CG, to HQ, Seventh Army, Lt. Gen. George S. Patton, CG, September 18, 1943:

HEAVY LUFTWAFFE ATTACKS HAVE SUNK COMMAND SHIP *ANCON* WITH HEAVY CASUALTIES INCLUDING GEN. CLARK, TWO TRANSPORTS, ONE DESTROYER, NUMEROUS LANDING CRAFT. CASUALTIES ON SHORE PRINCIPALLY

FROM SNIPERS, BOOBYTRAPS, AND ARTILLERY. WILL ATTACK AS SOON AS POSSIBLE TO EXPAND PERIMETER TO PERMIT LANDING OF FIRST ARMORED DIVISION AS SOON AS AIR SITUATION ALLOWS. ITALIAN CIVILIAN SENTIMENT STRONGLY ANTI-GERMAN.

COPIES TO: CG EIGHTH ARMY
CG FIFTEENTH ARMY GROUP
HQ MTO

From Charles Codman, Audacity (Boston, 1961):

"Not standard form, is it?" General Patton asked.

I had now been with Patton long enough to know a rhetorical question when I heard it. "It conveys all the necessary information to everybody who needs it," seemed a neutral and accurate reply.

"So it does. But I remember a Brad who would rather be court-martialed than send an irregular message." He frowned. "But then, he's in irregular circumstances. At least for him."

I thought that was also neutral and accurate. Bradley's message certainly didn't sound like a cry for help. Of course, he would know that we could reinforce him faster than the Germans could reinforce their Rome garrison, once we regained complete command of the air, and that was a job for somebody else.

"Cod," the general said, "I'm going to hitch a ride over to Civitavecchia and get Brad's shopping list. As far as I'm concerned, supporting him is now Seventh Army's top priority. I'm taking Al Stiller and a couple of enlisted bodyguards."

I must have looked disappointed. "Cod," he said, "if the Luftwaffe starts hitting here, you'll have your hands full. Even if they don't, once the French move out Lucian will need a French-speaking liaison officer. You have just been volunteered for that post. While you're at it, see if you can trade a couple of jeeps for some good brandy.

I've never known any French outfit larger than a platoon to go to war without a few bottles in reserve."

I gave him a particularly crisp salute. Neither of us wanted to admit the possibility that he might not come back from this particular excursion.

Patton's Diary, September 19, 1943:

Getting over to the mainland was a *long* hundred miles.

No way to fly, because nothing fast enough to avoid the German flyboys could land on the one emergency strip they had in the Civitavecchia perimeter. The maps showed a couple of fighter fields, but I guessed they'd be too cratered and too close to German artillery to be safe.

So I rode a PT boat, one of four with a destroyer escort carrying medical personnel. They were going to have to go ashore in DUKWs or even rafts, but that didn't seem to be bothering them.

Don't know if we were escorting the DE or it was escorting us. The skipper said that the Germans were trying to either reinforce or evacuate Corsica by night, while our air is all tied up supporting the landings. They escorted the convoys with E-boats, and sometimes the E-boats swung south to take a crack at our routes to Civitavecchia.

I told him that I was too old to enjoy midnight swims and that I'd already been in one naval battle, off Casablanca, so if the E-boats stayed home I wasn't going to complain to Admiral Doenitz. The skipper said he wasn't going to complain to Doenitz either, but he would have a beef with Marshal Kesselring if the Germans hauled out before his squadron could get in at least one good fight.

He also said that he was a Catholic, but he still wished the Pope would piss or get off the pot as far as Rome being declared an open city. I said that we'd probably confused both Pius and Kesselring, practically landing in their bedrooms, and neither of them had been dropped on their heads as babies, from what I'd heard. Neither of them would want to go down in history as the man who got Rome burned down for the first time since somewhere around 1500, so they'd probably do the right thing.

The skipper agreed, as long as they damned well did it soon!

I asked him if he couldn't move along faster. He said he didn't want to outrun the DE, and anyway, over twenty-five knots the boats gizzled fuel and made a big white wake that the Luftwaffe could pick out even at night. And our own flyboys weren't much better at target recognition. . . .

From Richard Tregaskis, "Campaigning in the Campagna," Baltimore Sun, *September 20, 1943:*

The tourist guides say that Civitavecchia, the main port of Rome, is on the Tyrrhenian Sea, and is the major ferry port for Sardinia. By the time they allowed reporters into the beachhead, most of the city was *in* the Tyrrhenian Sea—or the harbor, or the rivers and canals that fed the port. What our air force and the bombardment supporting the landings hadn't wrecked, the German artillery was finishing off. No ferries were running to Sardinia either, partly because it was in Allied hands and partly because most of them were sitting on the bottom of the harbor.

General Bradley had made his headquarters in the basement of a half-wrecked warehouse. The rubble was just as good a hiding place for our machine guns as it was for the Germans, and we had smoke pots, booby traps, and a few strings of barbed wire laid out. The basement also had several entrances, so that if the Germans decided to come in one, we could leave through one of the others—and, as the general said:

"If there aren't too many of them, we can slip around behind them and—ah, dispose of them, then get back to work. This isn't the Old West. Nobody will complain about us shooting them in the back."

Bradley looked ready to help that project along. He carried an issue .45 and a couple of spare magazines for it, and he had a carbine and another pile of spare magazines on one corner of the Italian worktable he was using for a desk. He also looked more like a company commander than an army commander, and even a little like a militarized and clean-shaven Abraham Lincoln. He didn't have Old Abe's wit, but he certainly had a knack for making everyone around him feel that it would be insubordinate to get excited when the general was so calm.

The only time I saw him upset during those three days was when General Patton visited. I don't know if it was wondering if Patton had come to relieve or at least criticize him, or worrying about keeping Patton alive. The German snipers kept trying to infiltrate, we had lost battalion commanders and hospital personnel, and Patton wore all his ribbons, three stars everyplace they would fit, a polished helmet and boots, and a riding crop and two ivory-handled pistols. It was all a little messy from his PT boat ride, but it still made him a target visible three hundred yards away in the light of the fires and flare bursts.

Patton grinned. "Brad, you owe the Relief Fund about a hundred dollars in fines. Boots dirty, no tie, no helmet, and when did you last shave?"

"When I went down to the evacuation hospital yesterday. My own razor didn't make it ashore. Most of the rest went in a shell burst. If the shell had been five yards closer, you'd be talking to Troy Middleton."

Bradley was smiling, but there was also an edge in his voice. He probably was not in a mood for Patton's jokes. After sleeping maybe five hours in the last three days, my sense of humor wouldn't have been in particularly good shape either.

Patton blinked, then actually apologized. "Sorry, Brad. I didn't come to tell you how to do your job. I came to find out how we could help you do it better."

"Well, we did have a little list," Bradley said. "Let's pull it out and see what we still need."

The bodyguards chased all the reporters and juniors out, to let the two generals talk. I learned afterward that Bradley only asked that a bomb line be drawn far enough forward so that the heavy bombers could strike the German artillery, if necessary. Patton was concerned about civilian casualties, particularly since the Italians were beginning organized assistance to the Allies. Civilian opinion in Rome was sure to influence whether it was declared an open city or not.

It was while we were trying to stay hidden from snipers and in jumping distance of a ditch or foxhole that we heard ragged cheering from down toward the waterfront. Then we heard the squeal and grumble of tanks, growing steadily louder, and the first of a line of Shermans nosed around the corner, knocking loose a shower of bricks from a stub of wall.

A sergeant scrambled down from the turret of the lead tank. "Company C, 3rd Battalion, 66th Armored Regiment reporting for—Oh, you're a civilian." He looked around. "Anyone I can report to?"

"You can report to me," came a high-pitched gravelly voice from the shadows. "It's good news to see you gentlemen. We hadn't expected you for another twenty-four hours."

A tank lieutenant stepped forward and saluted. "We decided that we might be safer—" Patton glared "—and more useful ashore, than bobbing around, getting salt in the transmissions and wondering when the Luftwaffe was going to get lucky."

"Get some hot food and a couple of hours' sleep,"

Patton said. "You'll have a busy day tomorrow, because we want to push out the perimeter far enough to get rid of the German artillery and bring in some air support."

"What about Italian civilians?"

Patton's grin got wider, which I wouldn't have thought was possible. "We just heard. The Italians have risen against the Germans in Naples, Salerno, Ravenna, Cassino, and several towns in Apulia that the operator couldn't spell and I can't pronounce. I don't think we have much to worry about with Italian civilians—except hitting them by accident. They may not be Allies yet, but they damned sure aren't enemies any more!"

There must have been a lot of Italians within earshot, and some of them knowing English. The cheering from all around us sounded like a football crowd just after the home team scored the winning touchdown. Then we heard:

"*Vive America! Vive Generale Patton!*"

Patton cupped both hands over his mouth, "*Vive Generale Bradley!*"

We went on cheering the Allies and their generals until the whole tank company had rolled off to their bivouac. We might still have been out there cheering, if a plane hadn't buzzed the warehouse, too fast to let us identify it.

"Could be one of ours, or it could be a German out of bombs," Patton said. "But I'll take a small bet from anyone who cares. In another forty-eight hours, if you hear a plane overhead, it will be ours."

From The New York Times, *September 21, 1943:*

ROME DECLARED OPEN CITY

ALLIES BREAK OUT OF CIVITAVECCHIA BEACHHEAD

WILD GREETINGS FOR ITALIANS' LIBERATORS

★ ★ ★

Excerpts from Patton's Press Conference, Rome, September 28, 1943:

Q: How did the Germans end up leaving a corridor between Rome and the sea that let us attack them in the rear?

A: I think they had it in mind to do the same to us. Remember, if a territory is "open," neither side can conduct military operations in it or against it. The Germans are good soldiers; as long as they have one man and one bullet left they'll be thinking of attacking. But we were doing the same, and we had more tanks, the Allied navies offshore, and air superiority.

So we struck south before they could strike north, and that's how we ended up encircling them at Anzio.

Q: Didn't we take heavy naval losses?

A: We did lose *Augusta,* two more destroyers, an ammunition ship, and quite a few landing craft. But the British were ready with reinforcements by the time we started south, and let me tell you, battleships make damned good tank destroyers. *Warspite*'s already drydocked in Malta, and she'll fight again.

Q: Have you found Marshal Kesselring yet?

A: No, and I suspect that when we do the only thing we can offer him is a military funeral. In his situation, I wouldn't be alive by now. We'll mark his grave and hope to be able to return his body to his family after the war.

Q: I don't suppose—

A: That I'd be willing to predict when that would be? That gets into politics, and so many people tell me that I don't know anything about politics that I'm ready to believe them.

All I can say is that we'll have to win several more campaigns bigger and bloodier than this one before the Germans are beaten, and we'll need all the men and weapons we have and all the strength of our allies to win those victories. The war is a long way from over, and anybody who says otherwise is even crazier than I am!

Q: What about the Medal of Honor for General Gavin?

A: I can't comment on awards that haven't been officially recommended. I can say that he certainly did a heroic job completing the Anzio encirclement with his link up to the British. I can also say that if he doesn't receive it for the Anzio jump, he will have other chances. His wounds were serious, but they won't keep him off jump duty. Just as well, for the sake of the doctor who would be stuck with the job of telling him otherwise!

Q: What's next for you, General Patton?

A: That has the ultimate secret classification—nobody knows. There are going to be enough Germans to go around, though, so I'm not worried. (Looks at watch) Our time is just about up, so rather than take any more questions, I'd like to call for a minute of silence, in memory of the dead of the Italian campaign, starting with Lieutenant General Mark Clark.

(Silence)

Letter to Beatrice Patton, October 10, 1943:

. . . actually assigned me a plane and crew to start my trip home, so it's just possible I may be calling on you only a little while after this letter does. If they send me home by way of England, it may be quite a while, but they won't dare risk my using up all the parades and other goodies that Montgomery will want them to save for him. (Get right down to it—I think the little weasel deserves most of them. I think we puny piffling colonials taught him a few things about war.)

They have told Bradley that he can keep Fifth Army, which smells to me of his having an Army Group for routing the Germans out of the industrial North or doing some other things I can't talk about. That in turn implies something fairly imposing for your old cavalryman. You know what I want, but if the decision is to give me Army Ground Forces, it won't kill me.

One request—consider it an order, if you wish. Reserve a nice comfortable hotel suite, someplace hard for reporters to get to but with good room service. Don't pack a lot of clothes. Do pack some extra money, so we can bribe the staff to silence instead of my having to get out of bed and shoot them.

Your affectionate Georgie

P.S. I expect to be well-armed enough, even without a pistol.

Tarnished Glory: Custer and the Waffen SS

Chris Bunch

More than fifty years have passed since the death of Lieutenant General George Armstrong Custer at the height of the Battle of the Bulge, yet the endless array of books and essays continue, analyzing his life, his flaws, and his downfall.

I think I've read them all, and find none exactly delineate the man the press sometimes called "Gloryhound George."

I think I can say that for I was Custer's chief aide from my discharge from an English hospital in early 1944 until his death, and spent many hours with him, both on and off duty.

Those who actually knew Custer seem to fall into one of two camps—those who think he was one of the great tactical geniuses of the Second World War, whose death was an almost-crippling blow to the postwar United States Army; and those who think he was as dangerous an egomaniac and cold-blooded politician as ever held an officer's commission, and his death was a great blessing that should have come years earlier.

So there is no misunderstanding, I will admit I fall into the latter group, even though I also remember Custer as one of the most charming and charismatic officers I've ever known, let alone served under.

His fatal flaws reach far back into the past, which is where, I'm afraid, most of our virtues and vices are rooted.

Beginnings

I can skip over Custer's early years as a small-town farmer's son, born in 1885, for these are all well known, and how he fought hard for an appointment to West Point, personally appealing to one of his state senators, even though the Custer family was staunchly Republican to the point of leafleting during campaigns, and the senator was a Democrat; and how his father sold their farm to give Custer money to attend the Academy.

Custer's grades in high school weren't particularly prepossessing, and his athletic performance was not that remarkable, although his football team was fairly successful. It's been noted that Custer's quarterbacking was frequently at direct odds from his coach's orders, so George's willingness to follow orders he found convenient and to disobey others came early.

Regardless of political affiliations, Custer was given the choice appointment to the class of 1909. Custer said later that he did very well in certain classes, chose to sleep through others, which gave him his standing near the bottom of his class. This is untrue—*all* of Custer's grades were uniformly low. He preferred his friends and pranks to his studies, and was generally popular.

At this point, he met what I consider the biggest influence in his life, the now utterly forgotten George Smith Patton, Jr.

Patton, four years older than Custer, was everything George was not. He was from an enormously rich California family, and seemed half centaur, with his string of polo ponies and race horses. He was also most reserved, again the opposite of Custer.

It was said that Patton already had the chill eye of a general, a man who could dispatch men to death without a qualm. Such might have been the case but, like many other officers who die young, that quality was never to be shown.

Custer and Patton made an ideal partnership, each having virtues the other did not, although book studies couldn't be considered a prime virtue for either of them. When they chose to work hard at something, they did very well. But mostly they did not, at least not in what the Academy considered productive. One such time-waster was their swearing competition, each trying to come up with the most colorful and obscene set of oaths. Custer told me that before that began, "I was one of the cleanest-mouthed boys in America. Afterwards . . . " He shook his head, then brightened. "But it surely stood me in good stead when I was dealing with those mule skinners when we were after Pancho Villa."

Patton had already been dropped a class for failing mathematics in his plebe year. But somehow the pair struggled through the Academy, and were given their lieutenants' bars in 1909. They were both commissioned into the glamorous cavalry, in spite of their low standings. Neither, in spite of accusations and sometimes boasts, was the lowest graduate, the so-called "goat."

They were posted to different regiments, but kept their correspondence fresh. Both men wrote long letters, to each other and, later, to their fiancées and then wives.

Custer took leave twice in Washington, seeking a better assignment than the dusty Western posts he was sent to.

Patton also took leaves, to play polo and, in 1912, to

compete in the Stockholm Olympics, in the modern pentathlon, placing a very respectable fourth.

World War I

The beginning of the Great War found both of them, like most career soldiers, champing to see combat, worried that somehow the Allies would defeat Germany before they would have a chance at action.

But then revolutionary Mexico surprised everyone. General John J. Pershing, after assorted border outrages by the sometimes-bandit, sometimes-soldier Pancho Villa, took 10,000 men, mostly cavalry, across the border.

Patton's unit managed to trap one of Villa's main generals, General Julio Cárdenas, and Patton supposedly killed Cárdenas. Or so the story has it.

Custer, on the other hand, claimed that a column he led came "close, very damned close" to Villa himself, even though none of the reports from Pershing's expedition mention it. In any event, Pershing retired back into the United States in a bit under a year, the Mexicans probably chastened a bit if hardly defeated in detail.

Then came the real war, and both men went to France. Patton was an aide to Pershing, commander of the American Expeditionary Force, while Custer was assigned to a troop of the Second US Cavalry. Patton asked Pershing for a combat assignment, and was put in charge of the first American tank brigade, as a lieutenant colonel.

He looked up his friend, and told him that horses were doomed. Unless Custer wanted to spend his war like the British cavalry, eternally waiting for a breakthrough in the trenches, he'd go with Patton.

Custer refused.

He told me three times, late, in his quarters, after he'd been drinking, that this was "the biggest damned fool mistake I ever made, and thank God he gave me a chance to change things."

This, by the way, brings up another of Custer's meaningless prevarications. He claimed that he'd gotten drunk once, when a young lieutenant, made an ass of himself, and never touched alcohol again. He was, indeed, piously temperate among civilians and politicians, but would have three or four whiskey-and-waters in the officer's club, although I never saw him more than mildly intoxicated. Why he bothered to tell this lie, other than to further set himself apart in a hard-drinking Army, is beyond me.

At any rate, Patton went on to have "a hell of a war," as Custer described it, gaining respect, medals and recognition. He was badly wounded in the battle of Meuse-Argonne. Custer claimed he visited him in the hospital, just as the great influenza epidemic was beginning.

Patton realized he was dying and, again according to Custer, made him swear to pick up the torch of the newly invented tanks and bring the Army into the Twentieth Century.

Custer, like most liars, couldn't leave well enough alone, and told me he was one of the casket bearers at Patton's funeral. Some years after the Second World War, I happened to see an old photograph of the pallbearers as they carried Patton's casket onto the transport that would take his corpse back to the United States. George Armstrong Custer was not one of them.

His oath to Patton is also suspect because, with the war's end, the tanks were given to the infantry, and Custer, rather than go with them, chose to return to the horse cavalry.

After the War

Custer's service between the wars was somewhat undistinguished, although he gained a reputation for not suffering fools gladly. Unfortunately, all too often the fools he wouldn't suffer were his commanding officers or post commanders, and he was constantly in trouble.

However, he saved his career by becoming an intensely political officer, making close friends with high-ranking Republican politicians, or at least as much as a soldier and a politician can be friends.

Needless to say, this did not endear him greatly to his fellow officers. But in the tiny peacetime Army, one learned to keep one's mouth shut, particularly as the Depression roared around the gates of the camps, and the advantages of a civilian career looked very bleak.

Then Custer was chosen for his first staff post, and his behavior changed. Now there was no one smoother, more ready with a colorful story of what it was like "out in the field," or to agree with a superior's opinions. Custer was now considered a man who was headed for the top.

There were also murmurs from his conservative political friends that anyone this handsome and well-spoken might, in time, make an interesting senator or representative.

He married well, to the beautiful and flamboyant Reynolds-tobacco widow Libby Holman. But she was hardly the perfect Army wife, especially in those days, with her loud espousal of such causes, radical to the military, as civil rights, black music and the arts. Their relationship has been written about extensively, particularly considering Holman's suicide in the late 1940s, and I feel no need to invade their privacy, in my speculations, since I never met Libby. I do wonder, if Custer had lived through the war, if the marriage would have survived, given the different directions their lives would almost certainly have taken.

In late 1939, with war again ravaging Europe, Colonel Custer was given a battalion of tanks, although half of them were no more than trucks with signs proclaiming their tracked status.

Then came the huge 1940 war games, in Louisiana, that

ended some officers' careers and made others. Custer had been commanded to hold a flanking position for an infantry division's attack. Instead, he led his "tanks" in a long, looping maneuver around the "enemy," and romped through the rear lines, bringing havoc.

The blitzkrieg and the destruction of the Polish army by the Wehrmacht was much in the headlines, and George Armstrong Custer became a bit of a hero, enough so those who muttered about his disobedience or behaving as if he were leading a saber charge did so quietly, especially after Custer was summoned to the White House, congratulated by President Roosevelt, and given his first star.

Africa and Sicily

Two days after Pearl Harbor, Custer was ordered to form the Second "Hell on Wheels" Armored Division, and given his second star.

He took the Second into combat in North Africa. Where other generals hemmed and stumbled, Custer and firebrands like Terry Allen, Lucian Truscott, Ernie Harmon and others smashed into combat as if it was what they'd been born for.

Custer loudly thought just that. He was beginning to become a reporter's darling, always ready with a controversial quote or interesting perspective.

He said he believed in reincarnation (as, interestingly enough, had George Patton). Custer thought he'd been first a caveman, defending his tribe; an infantry commander in ancient Atlantis; a centurion at Cannae; a Crusader in the Holy Land with the Knights Templar; and most recently a subaltern in the Indian Wars, dying when the Seventh Cavalry, under Major Marcus Reno, was wiped out by the Sioux at the Battle of the Little Big Horn.

Custer fought the Second Armored like it was a cavalry squadron, hitting the Germans when and where they least expected it. The vastly more experienced German

Panzer soldiers were impressed by Custer, dubbed him the "Cavalryman From Hell."

Custer became the best-known general of the African campaign, although there were whispers that he was too ready to fight, taking his tanks and men into head-on assaults when he could have saved many lives by waiting until a flank opened, or until the enemy's intentions were more clear before he attacked.

But he won every battle he fought, and people spoke of "Custer's Luck."

He and General Eisenhower had a few disagreements during that campaign, but nothing serious. Eisenhower made him Commander of the Western Landing Force for the Sicily invasion.

Custer took his Seventh Army north and west, and the Germans and Italians retreated steadily east, toward the Straits of Messina and the short passage across to Italy.

Then Custer almost ruined his career again. He had always been a little loose with his mouth, particularly as his fame grew, and now was more than willing to comment on what he thought of the British Allies—"Our Brit brothers seem to have two speeds, slow and stop."

He and British General Montgomery became bitter enemies when the British forces became stalled at Catania. Custer said, "The only thing good about General Montgomery is that he had the balls to stand up against Churchill at El Alamein until Winnie gave him enough troops to have ten-to-one odds when he finally attacked Rommel. Frankly, he doesn't appear to me to be the bravest of men when he doesn't have those kind of odds on his side."

Eisenhower told him to hold his tongue and attack west, giving him various units for small amphibious landings along the north coast.

In a little over a month, the Seventh Army took Messina. However, almost all the Axis forces managed to escape to the Italian mainland.

Now Custer made his first large-scale rewrite of history. He claimed that he hadn't been able to stop the Germans because Montgomery was moving so slowly, and he knew better than to leave a flank exposed to the Germans.

Also to blame were the new divisions arriving from America—"There's nothing wrong with our fighting boys," he said in an interview. "I just wish their damned generals would get some of their spirit."

In fact, Custer split his forces, trying to not only hold to the coastal route as ordered, but to clear the mountains to the south, the same mountains holding up the British.

The Germans, always masterful in the defense, would fall back, counterattack again and again, ridgecrest by ridgecrest, and Custer's units were badly battered, even as the advance slowed.

But finally the campaign was over, and plans were made for the Italian invasion. Eisenhower, newly named Supreme Commander of Allied Expeditionary Forces, decided he would have enough prima donnas in the Mediterranean, between Mark Clark, Montgomery, other British Generals like Alexander and Leese, New Zealanders like Freyberg, and took Custer with him to England, to prepare for the Normandy Invasion.

In Britain Custer busied himself, building what he called "An Army that's the way it's supposed to be,"—Third Army.

As for me, Captain James Casady . . .

I'd graduated from the Point in 1942 and ended up as a tank platoon commander in the muddy nightmare as we slogged up the Italian Peninsula toward Rome, in a campaign noted for not just the bravery of the soldiers, but the stupidity of the Allied Commanders.

I had three tanks left when I was ordered to support the Fifth Army's crossing of the Volturno River in October of 1943. Clark and his staff, luxuriating in their villas, never considered that it was raining in the mountains, and all the Italian rivers were flooding.

The Germans held the far bank of the Volturno, and were committed to keeping it. We attacked and attacked again, each time being driven back.

I went forward with my tracks to support a retreating company pinned down in the muddy swamps by a German machine-gun nest. My Shermans' 75mms took care of the Spandaus, and then the Germans unmasked two of their deadly 88mm cannon.

Before I could order a pullback, two of my tanks were hit. I stayed in the open, bringing fire on the 88s, long enough for the infantry and my surviving tankers to get out. I thought I'd gotten away with it, and then the world exploded. The aviation-fuel burning M4 was well, and correctly, known as a "Ronson lighter," lighting up every time.

I was burned badly enough to be evacuated by hospital ship to Britain, where the best burn specialists in the world were. They laboriously rebuilt the skin of my chest, arm and the right side of my face, made me a major and said I could go back to combat duty if I wished.

I did wish. There were still Germans fighting, and I figured I owed them. But instead of being given a company of tracks, I was offered the chance to become one of Lieutenant General George Armstrong Custer's aides. It was, frankly, less of an offer than a command.

A soldier follows orders and so, somewhat dreading things, I reported to Custer's headquarters in April of 1944.

The Invasion of France

When I met Custer, he was just short of fifty-five years. He was a bit taller than the average, of good build, which he didn't seem to have to work at. Years before, he'd been known for his curly hair, which he wore a little longer than customary in the Army, more like officers of an earlier age. Now, his hair had darkened from blond, and was receding, and he was a bit sensitive about it. He wore a unique hair oil that smelt highly of cinnamon.

He was most friendly and outgoing, and I relaxed a bit, feeling that this assignment might not be as onerous as I'd feared.

I found it odd that Custer kept two pictures of generals on his office wall—one was of Douglas MacArthur, who he'd made friends with through his political friends, the other of himself. But then, most generals are a bit egotistical. Custer was just more so than the others. There was also a third, very small, very battered, sepia-tone print, dimly showing two lieutenants in campaign hats, one grinning at the camera, the other looking most solemn. It was, of course, Custer and George Patton.

Custer drove himself and his men hard, preparing for the invasion. They loved him, with some justification, for he was very solicitous of their welfare, always inspecting mess halls and the tent cities we lived in. He was a holy terror with higher-echelon supply officers, wanting the latest and the best in arms and equipment, and accepting no excuses.

Another reason Custer was popular with the enlisted men was he was hardly a spit-and-polish soldier, unlike some others in the European Theater of Operations. He required only that his men be clean and in good fighting order. Beyond that he cared little what they wore or the arms they carried. The only exception was no one was permitted German uniforms or helmets, for obvious reasons.

He himself, in the field, always wore an old slouch hat, such as the cavalry wore on the border, and a leather belt with the cavalry emblem and an old-fashioned .45 Colt Peacemaker.

His enemies . . . beyond other, possibly jealous, generals, the British and some Democratic politicians . . . were all commissioned. I noted, with interest, that some of his bitterest foes were those who'd served under him since the landings in Africa, and took good note of that fact.

One of his divisions, the Fourth Armored, was scheduled for the second wave at Omaha Beach, backing the 28th Infantry.

Some of Custer's tanks had been modified to be amphibious, given extended exhausts and canvas skirts extending from the hull to the turret, a British invention. Custer thought these tanks would be unlikely to make it to the beach, and cozened and bullied several Landing Craft Tanks with conventional M4 Shermans and M10 tank destroyers as far forward in the landing order as possible. Behind them were larger Landing Ship Tanks with more of the Fourth.

No one could ever slight Custer's courage. He should have stayed on a command ship, as most other generals did, to keep the clarity of distance, at least until D-Day Plus One. Instead, he, and certain elements of his staff, including myself, were aboard one of the LSTs.

As he'd predicted, the amphibious DD (Dual Drive) tanks were almost useless, only a handful making it ashore. The issue on Omaha Beach was very much in doubt, and Custer ordered his tanks in, ahead of the landing schedule.

The Germans had emplaced artillery behind the beaches, and the guns struck at our tanks hard. The sand was littered with smoking, burning Shermans, their crews sprawled in death behind them, or pinned down by the German machine guns.

The day was a blur of incoming artillery, screaming soldiers, chattering MGs, the flat blast of mines. The Navy came in close, bringing direct fire on artillery positions, and the tanks kept pushing on. By dusk, we held the plateau behind the beach, and were reforming to move inland. The casualties, both in tanks and men, were terrible and, later, there were mutterings about Custer's ambition. No one at Normandy on that Sixth of June talked much, then or later, about "Custer's Luck."

Custer rode a tank to the top of the ridge, with me standing on the back deck behind the .50 caliber turret machine gun, watching for snipers. He looked back at the beachhead and the troops swarming ashore, and said in a low voice, "How's that, George?" I pretended I didn't hear.

The lead elements of the Fourth were decimated, almost destroyed, and it took several weeks before they were rebuilt and could join the rest of the Division as it pushed on, into France. Their exploits on D-Day and later gained them the nickname, from the Germans, of "Roosevelt's Butchers."

Then the slow battering began, as we pushed the Germans out of Normandy. Custer seemed almost delighted when Montgomery was handed a bloody nose at Caen, was angry when we went on the defense to give Joe Collins and his Seventh Corps the supplies and reinforcements to take Cherbourg.

The Allies regrouped and, while Omar Bradley's First Army took St. Lô, Third Army was finally unleashed on the right of the Allied Line. We smashed through the Avranches Gap, cleaned Brittany out, then headed south, to the Loire River. Somewhere in the blood and the mud, I got my silver leaves, and Custer was made Lieutenant General.

General von Kluge, under Hitler's direct orders, struck back hard, hoping to isolate the Third Army and wipe it out. We fought them to a standstill, then, with the Canadian and Polish forces, sent them stumbling back, trapping them near Argentan, the famous "Falaise Gap." Our tanks and fighters savaged the cornered Germans in a nightmare of steel and fire.

It was impossible to walk down any road in the area without stepping on German corpses. Allied pilots flying hundreds of feet overhead could smell the stink of the corpses. The statistics were numbing: 50,000 Germans captured, 10,000 dead, and those who survived left their tanks and vehicles behind and walked out. But there were those who sniffed, and said it wasn't enough: "only" one German division had been completely wiped out. Of the twenty others, eleven divisions had to be withdrawn to be rebuilt, and the other nine, including the deadly SS Panzer Divisions, were held on the front and rebuilt as they fought.

There was also our butcher's bill—we took 20,000 casualties, and a cynical journalist said, "as far as I can tell, General Custer is even better than Hitler at killing young Americans."

When Custer heard this, he went into a rage. "Goddamit, Jimmy (a nickname I'd always loathed), what do these shitheels want? First they're pissed that I wasn't able to lock the Krauts up at Messina, now I'm supposed to win this frigging war by myself!

"Next time, the hell with what they want me to do. I'll do it . . . and go another ten or fifty miles, and there won't be any of these rear echelon second-guessers to piss in my ear.

"I've learned my lesson, Jimmy, learned it well, although I'll bet they're still going to make me pay!

"The way things are going, they probably won't even let me take Paris!"

They didn't. For sensibly political reasons, Custer's Third was kept in pursuit of the retreating Germans, while Free French General LeClerc's Second Armored Division, with the US Fifth Corps in support, was the first to rumble down the Champs Elysees.

Custer was even angrier when Eisenhower gave Montgomery permission to take Antwerp—we were running beyond the range of the French ports we'd captured. That meant the gas that Custer felt should've gone to his tanks, that would've taken him to the Rhine River, went to the British.

Montgomery took Brussels, then Antwerp, but evidently

didn't look at his maps and realize the Belgian port was sixty miles from the ocean. That land was firmly held by the Germans, not to be taken until that winter.

Third Army crossed the Meuse River and sat there, out of gas, watching the Germans retreat and then build up defensive positions.

Custer cloaked his bitterness with humor, or what he called humor, and was always on the move, from Command Post to Command Post, cheering his men, telling them they were the best, and the rest of the Allies couldn't, as he said, " . . . pour piss out of a boot with a 1:50,000 projection map printed on the heel." I wondered how wise this sort of talk was, either for the men's morale or for his own good, but kept silent.

Custer got into the habit of having a nightcap—a cup of strong coffee with cream—with me, and telling me his real thoughts.

He spoke a lot about Patton: "Before I go into any battle, after I make my tentative plan, I always try to figure out what George would've done.

"Poor sorry bastard, to have to die so damned young, only having fought with those boiler-plate tanks in pissyass quantities. I tell you, Jimmy, he would've been in hog heaven if he'd lived.

"Hell, he probably would be where I'm sitting right now if he had."

"And," I once chanced, "where would you have been?"

Custer grinned. "If I was unlucky, I'd be his Chief of Staff. If I was lucky . . . who the hell knows. Maybe running Fifth Corps.

"Now, that would've made a combination, wouldn't it? Two generals with their eyes on the ball . . . we'd be in Berlin by now!"

All the Army knew Custer was ambitious, that he would have loved to see Eisenhower and Bradley die in a plane crash and he picked to take over Supreme Headquarters, Allied Expeditionary Force.

But his ambition ran beyond that.

Several times he sat staring at his picture of MacArthur, and musing what would come after the war: "We beat the Krauts by the end of this year, then we'll go to the Pacific, invade Japan, and the war'll be over, except for mopping up, by late '46 or '47, I figure.

"MacArthur comes home covered with glory, and the Party (that always meant the Republicans) will need somebody strong.

"Roosevelt will be dead by then . . . my friends in Washington say he's hanging on by his fingernails, hoping to see the end of the war . . . and one of his weak-ass Vice Presidents will take over, and get run for the Presidency in '48.

"Mac goes against him . . . and he'll need a running mate."

I once said I thought America might be a little sick of following military men around.

"Not a chance, Jimmy," he said. "People get used to doing what they're told, and start liking it. You think they're going to vote for some damned war profiteer if they've got a couple of war heroes on the ticket?" He snorted laughter. "Plus we'll have people like Taft on our side.

"Life'll be interesting then, Jimmy. MacArthur's not exactly a spring chicken, and maybe 1952 will be my year."

He had pronounced ideas on what the postwar world should look like.

"Another reason we'll need another strong man like Roosevelt . . . except Republican . . . in the White House is we're going to have to deal with the damned Bolsheviks sooner or later.

"Stalin's our buddy now, because he's killing more Krauts than we are. But the minute peace breaks out, there'll be some hard looks at things.

"We'll have to rebuild Germany and Poland to be able

to stand against the Russians first thing. Then we'll have to step in and make sure Italy and France have strong governments.

"Britain? The goddamned Limeys are a thing of the past, and we're going to have to learn that, first thing.

"Naturally, we're going to have to keep a strong Army, once the war's over. Anybody who thinks we'll just go home and bury our heads in the sand like we did after the last war is a fool.

"Just like we'll have to deal with those damned Commies we've got at home. There'll be enough enemies in the world without worrying about being stabbed in the back. We soldiers will know how to give them a short sharp shock. Send those who won't recant back to Russia, like Palmer tried to do, and the muffleheads wouldn't let him."

Listening to Custer and his grandiose plans, I remembered what my father had said: "We should thank the Good God that American soldiers mostly aren't politicians. Politics is nothing but shades of gray, and no soldier worth a hang sees anything in colors other than black and white."

Perhaps being Irish and Catholic gave me a better perspective on Custer's ambitions. I'd grown up hearing enough tales of having British soldiers in Ireland always riding up your lane with their bayonets and torches to shiver at the notion of America putting any political authority in the hands of its military.

Ideas like this, I think, are one reason that Custer has become an icon to the radical conservatives in the Constitutionalist Party. "If only he'd lived . . ." is something I've heard again and again, and am most tired of.

One thing Custer was not, which many of the racist Constitutionalists would prefer not to hear, was a bigot. He'd never liked serving in the South, seeing the way African Americans were treated and, now, despised the Germans for their treatment of the Jews.

"From what I've heard, the Krauts are trying to kill off all the Jews wherever they go. As soon as the Nazis run up the white flags, we'll have to deal with them.

"I think the Commies have the right idea on what to do with the Nazi Party. We don't need any kind of trials like some people are talking about. Walk 'em all, from Adolf down to the last goddamned SS man, down a corridor, like the MVD does, and put a bullet in the back of their necks and throw 'em in unmarked graves."

I asked if that might not leave Germany a little short of politicians.

"Screw 'em," Custer said. "That's another reason we need a strong army. These AMG units that are hanging about back of the lines . . . we'll use them to run Krautland for twenty, thirty years, and let the Army train the kids how to think right."

Eventually Eisenhower realized Montgomery'd run his course, and unleashed the American armies. But by then, summer was creaking past, and it was fall before we were closing on the German border.

And Hitler had one great surprise waiting.

The Battle of the Bulge

In October, we began operations against the Siegfried Line, on Germany's border, and in November Eisenhower ordered the November Offensive, intended to smash all German units west of the Rhine and then cross the great river into the heart of the Nazi homeland.

It was bitter going as the weather grew colder. Ninth and First Armies smashed themselves against the Hurtgen Forest, and even battle-loving Custer told me he was very damned glad none of his divisions had been sent into that frozen hell.

We pushed on, south of the Hurtgen, and by mid-December we'd taken Metz, not thirty miles from the German border.

"Now," Custer rejoiced. "Now, let Ike turn us loose,

and we'll bust across the border and have the Rhineland before Montgomery has time to pin his beanie emblems on and have a cup of tea."

The next offensive would take us across the Saar River, into Germany.

And then Hitler moved first.

Twenty-four German divisions, ten of them armored, attacked to the west, through the supposedly tank-impassable Ardennes, on 16 December. At their head was Sixth SS Panzer Army, under Hitler's pet thug, Sepp Dietrich. Hitler's insane orders were to cross the Meuse, then continue on to take Antwerp. Hitler thought this unexpected attack would shatter Allied cohesion, and in the confusion he could find a way to end the war victoriously.

It was nonsense, certainly, but the Germans, as they almost always did, obeyed their orders.

They had utter surprise on their side—Hitler somehow felt German codes were penetrated (they were, of course, by ULTRA, but almost no one knew that). The first wave, eight Panzer divisions, broke the Seventh Corps. The 106th Division was destroyed, and the 28th, one of Custer's former units, broken.

The weather was terrible, and our invincible fighter bombers couldn't get into the air.

The Panzers pushed on, past St. Vith, taking back most of Luxembourg.

Eisenhower threw in his reserve divisions, including the 101st Airborne, which took and held the road hub of Bastogne.

In the meantime, Sixth SS Panzer moved steadily on to the west, killing civilians and US prisoners as it went.

Eisenhower, after a few befuddled days, put Montgomery in charge of all troops to the north of the "Bulge" the Germans had created.

Eisenhower called a conference at Verdun on 19 December, giving Custer new orders: Take charge of Seventh Corps, and relieve Bastogne.

Custer smiled grimly, and said he'd do it.

Ike appeared unshaken by the German surprise. "I think this is an opportunity for us, actually."

"Exactly, sir," Custer said eagerly. "Let's let them run us all the way back to the Atlantic, then slam the door on the bastards and destroy them in detail. Assuming we've got the nerve."

Eisenhower smiled, a bit frostily. "I have the nerve, and I know you do, as well. But I doubt if anyone in Paris, London or Washington would appreciate it if we did that."

"The other option we could do," Custer went on, unfazed, "is have me keep pushing past Bastogne, right on up until I run into the limeys. Cut off this damned Bulge, and all the Krautheads in it, like it was a boil."

"General," Eisenhower said, "remember your Shakespeare, and the lion hunter who kept thinking about what he'd do with the lion's skin, when the animal was still alive. You just relieve McAuliffe at Bastogne, and then we'll worry about the next step. Understood?"

"Yes, sir," Custer said, but I noted his voice was grudging.

Custer, his assistant Chief of Staff, Colonel Paul Harkins, and I, in the battered old staff car he preferred to a jeep, went back to our headquarters and, the next day, visited seven of his divisions, and told them we were changing the axis of their attack through 90 degrees, moving north against the Germans instead of west.

Custer may have been a braggart, but there have been very few generals who could turn 350,000 men in a single day without panic and utter confusion, which he'd done.

"I wonder what Patton would think of that," he said, as we pulled into his headquarters at Nancy. I was bone-exhausted, but he seemed untouched by the day's freezing weather and the bouncing miles over icy, rutted dirt roads.

"Now," he said gleefully as he bounded up the steps toward his quarters, "now we'll see what we shall see about that famous next step."

I managed a salute, told the driver we were through for the night, reported our return to one of his staff officers, and fell into my sleeping bag across a camp cot, knowing I'd have to be awake and alert before dawn the next morning.

One of my unspoken duties was to keep Custer and the press separated, especially when Custer was either bouncy or angry, for that was when he wasn't as careful with his words as he should be.

The next morning, I was getting Custer a cup of coffee and a croissant from a basket an old Frenchwoman had brought to us. It was black outside, with flurries of snow tapping on the windows. I thought of the poor bastards who were out there on the line, crouched in icy foxholes, looking for movement, waiting for a bush to turn into an SS man in a white camouflage cape, aiming a burp gun at them.

I was starting out of the general's mess with my tray when Colonel Harkins hurried in. He was angry and upset.

"Good morning, sir."

"I'm not sure if it is or not. I just got a call from Beetle Smith, and he's pissed."

I waited. Major General Walter Bedell Smith was Eisenhower's Chief of Staff.

"Last night our noble boss, after we thought he was headed for bed, ran into Ed Kennedy of Associated Press."

"Uh-oh," I said.

"Uh-oh is right. He told Kennedy what he said to us last night, about turning almost half a million men around. And then he kept talking. He hopes that Ike can hold the course, and not let his mind get changed by the next general he talks to . . . good thing Omar the tentmaker Bradley didn't get this assignment, or it'd be spring before he started moving . . . Montgomery's in the right spot, being the anvil and sitting on his ass, rather than having to figure out how to maneuver.

"Naturally, Kennedy called SHAEF to get comments on

what General Custer said, and naturally the shit has hit the fan.

"Beetle said that Ike's about as angry as he'd ever seen him, and told me that Custer had better pull this one off in roses, or his ass is liable to be running a replacement depot in Scotland somewhere."

"Oh brother," I managed.

"Now, the question I've got," Harkins went on, "is, do we tell Custer?"

I thought about it.

"I don't think so, sir," I said. "I know Kennedy pretty well. He's a good man and won't hold back his story, and there's no way we can change what he said."

"That's what I thought," Harkins said. "And we've got a battle to fight, and our George needs to have a clear head and not worry about other things. Go take the General his coffee."

Custer was awake, and in his comfortable, if rather civilian, fur-lined pants and knee-top boots. There were maps pinned on the walls, with arrows and markings. I glanced at one, which had Bastogne in its center, and saw, with a sinking feeling, that the arrows went on beyond the besieged city.

Custer saw my expression.

"Now's our chance, Jimmy. I'm tired of taking pissant chances, when there's a war to be won here! Hitler's got his ass out there in the wind, wiggling at us, and we're going to run a division or two right up it, and see what he thinks of a little blitzkrieg himself!"

"Yes, sir," I said neutrally, thinking that, with what he'd told the reporter, this could either be the icing on the cake, or else Custer's salvation. Oh well, I thought. I'd always been curious to see the lochs and if I'd look good in a kilt.

"Look," Custer said, and took me to another map, very large-scale, that was a little less scrawled than the others. I decided this showed his final battle plan.

"Bastogne here," he said, pointing. I nodded. "And look at all these little roads to the west. I'll bet a good man, like Bill Roberts, could push CCB through them. All that he'd be facing are those punks of Fifth Parachute Division, who haven't fought worth sour owl crud so far."

"Little roads are right, sir."

"If the goddamned Heinies could do it to start this mess, so can we."

We'd fallen into the practice of setting up Combat Commands within a division, composed of armored infantry, tanks, tank destroyers, engineers, and so forth, each able to fight independently.

"Yessir," I said skeptically.

"We put Tenth Armored over here, to the west of Bastogne, heading up the road from Neufchateau.

"Then you and I ride with CCR and CCA straight on up the Martelans road to Bastogne. We relieve the Battlin' Bastards of Bastogne, link up with CCA and the Tenth north of the city, keep going north and give the Sixth SS a big fat bite in the ass.

"They should be running low on gas, and if we hit 'em hard, immobilize 'em, then we can tell Ike to get Monty off his butt and come on down to finish them off.

"Or maybe," Custer said, and he licked his lips, "we'll be able to hit them hard enough so there won't be anything for Monty to police up.

"I'd like that. I'd like that a lot.

"Plus I've got a little plan to keep anybody from screwing the deal up for us, like the Brits did last time around by hanging on to all the gas."

I looked at the map carefully. I could see Custer's temptation. If all went perfectly, there was a chance we'd not only relieve Bastogne, but break the back of the German offensive. Without the SS Panzers, the rest of the Germans, name-only paratroopers and volksgrenadier units made up of recruits and middle-aged men for the most part, could well fall apart.

If everything went perfectly.

In war, nothing goes perfectly.

But lieutenant colonels, if they wish to stay at their present rank, aren't recommended to tell lieutenant generals that they are, in the words of the popular song of the time, "Wishing on a Star."

"Call the staff, Jimmy. I want the troops in the saddle by noon."

We were, in a driving snowstorm, wheeled vehicles skidding in the slush and ice. At least no one was afoot. The infantry was either in 6x6 trucks, halftracks or on the backs of tanks. That sounds grim, but the rear deck of an M4 Sherman, with its gridded ventilation ducts, is a lot warmer than a lot of other places.

Custer's secret was that he'd gotten every gasoline tanker that Third Army had filled to the brim, and following us in a guarded convoy. If I felt sorry for the men in the foxholes, I felt doubly so for those incredibly brave drivers in the thin-skinned tankers with no armor, thousands of gallons of explosive fuel behind them, and no protection except an occasional ring-mounted antiaircraft machine gun above the cab.

Custer's driver ditched the staff car after five miles, and we stopped an M20 armored car, and squeezed into the open troop compartment. The rest of the staff was, sensibly, already riding halftracks to our rear.

We were moving fast, almost five miles an hour when we could, and the roadblocks the Germans threw up were smashed aside.

The weather got worse, but we kept moving. It became a pattern: make contact, the infantry drop off and move forward under covering tank or tank destroyer fire, smash the strong point, remount and move on.

But each time, there were a few less infantrymen and tanks. The stink of burning men and tanks pulled at my nostrils as we'd pass some motionless figures in olive drab, blood staining the snow beside them.

We went on until dusk, made crude laagers, ate half-frozen K rations, stayed on 50% alert, started off again before dawn.

CCA and CCR were moving steadily, but Tenth Armor was running into trouble from the Panzer Lehr division and, to our east, CCB was not only having trouble with the icy, narrow tracks, but Fifth Parachute Division had suddenly changed their style, and were fighting like German paratroops had on other fronts.

But, slowly but surely, we ground west, toward Bastogne.

To our north, the Sixth SS Panzer Army's offensive was bogging down against tough stands by Custer's old commands, the Second Armored and the Fourth Infantry. Its general, Sepp Dietrich, was plaintively asking Hitler for permission to turn south, and find another way toward the Meuse and Antwerp.

And the Panzers were running low on fuel. . . .

I've made my dislike for Custer clear, but I'll never forget, on Christmas Eve, his giving me a tiny bottle of schnapps someone had liberated in one of the villages we passed through. I tucked it in my parka, determined to drink it when we relieved Bastogne.

On the day after Christmas, we broke through, and the 101st and the other, less famous but equally hard-fighting units, were safe.

Custer ordered us to stay the night and refuel and rearm. He hoped that CCB and the Tenth would join us the next day, but they were still being held back by stiff German resistance, the roads and the weather.

Colonel Harkins asked if we shouldn't hold in Bastogne until the other two columns reached us.

Custer thought for a moment, then shook his head.

"We stooge around here, and sure as hell Ike'll hear about my plan and pull the plug.

"No, Paul. We move out at dawn."

"The roads look pretty terrible, General."

"I've got confidence in my boys," Custer said. "They've

done okay so far on the cowpaths. The Tenth and CCB should link up with us . . ." and he checked his map " . . . at this place called Houffalize, if not sooner."

Custer had gotten away with splitting his forces in Sicily and, so far, here. But luck only holds for so long.

And so we were on the road at dawn, Colonel Creighton Abrams' 37th Tank Battalion on point. I drank my little bottle of schnapps before we moved. I wonder if I sensed something, and figured I'd better drink it then, rather than not be able to drink it at all.

That day, heading toward Foy and on north, was a horror as we moved past burned-out US vehicles abandoned in the retreat toward Bastogne when the battle began, and saw the unburied bodies of our soldiers scattered everywhere, and the destruction of the farms and villages on either side.

I'll never forget seeing a jeep, parked beside the road. Its driver was turned to his passenger, a colonel, who held a map in his lap, possibly asking for instructions. But both of them were headless, the Panzerfaust that had blown the jeep's engine out neatly guillotining the two.

German resistance was light, but determined, and we drove them back from the roads into the snowy wasteland.

"Another two days, maybe three," Custer promised, "and we'll be hanging some SS scalps on the lodge pole."

For the first time since Sepp Dietrich had joined the Nazi Party and the SS, in 1928, he disobeyed an order of Hitler's. He ordered his Sixth Panzer Army to turn south, toward Bastogne.

Custer's feared presence on the battlefield, and his reaching Bastogne and continuing his attack had been reported by German scouts. Dietrich decided he couldn't chance having the mad cavalryman in his rear. No one knows if he heard of the pot-sweetening convoy of tankers trundling along behind CCA.

His decision, and disobedience, was reported to Hitler

in Berlin. The Fuhrer went into one of his typical screaming rages, then quieted, and examined the map.

"No," he is reported to have said. "Perhaps my Sepp is right in this. Perhaps, when he smashes the American Third Army, takes whatever fuel they might have, and then renews the attack . . . perhaps this might be the real surprise that turns the tide."

Of course, he didn't communicate his semi-approval to Dietrich. Hitler never admitted he might be wrong.

The SS was on the move—four armored divisions, about 30,000 men, First SS Panzer "Liebstandarte Adolf Hitler," Second SS Panzer "Das Reich," Ninth SS Panzer "Hohenstauffen," and Twelfth SS Panzer "Hitler Jugend," plus one division of paratroopers, Third Parachute Division.

They were heading south, toward us . . . and we didn't know it.

The first sign of trouble was in a nameless little village. We took fire from well-positioned heavy machine guns and some light cannon. The infantry came off the tanks, and started forward, using the shattered building walls for cover.

Then three Panthers ground into sight. They'd been hiding, hull down, in a covert just below the village, a scattering of panzergrenadiers covering them. Two Shermans exploded as they opened fire, then an M10 blasted one and a second with its 90mm. The third German tank had time to reverse back for cover, and somebody hit its turret in the rear with a bazooka round. The round exploded, doing little damage, and the Panther was gone. The German soldiers were quickly gunned down by our machine gunners, and scouts darted forward to check the bodies.

In a minute, Custer's radio cracked.

"Curly Six, this is Arrowhead Six."

Curly Six was Custer's call sign, Arrowhead Six Abrams.

"This is Curly Six," Custer said.

"Those troops who just hit us were SS," Abrams said. "They've got the sleeve tabs of the Twelfth Division."

The troops of Hitler Jugend Division were known for

their ruthlessness, as well as suicidal fanaticism in combat. And, as far as we knew, they were supposed to be miles away, to the northeast.

Custer looked worried, told Abrams to push on, then ordered his commo officer to make contact with Tenth Armored and CCB. "Tell them hubba-hubba one time," Custer said. "The game's afoot."

We went on, the road winding past small farms and fields. To show how memory is tricky, I remember it being deathly quiet, with the only sound the low rumble of engines and the ominous grinding of treads on the frozen ground, but of course this is absurd. There would have been shouts, the occasional blast of gunfire as a machine gunner reconned some building he wasn't sure was empty by fire, the crackle of radios and other sounds of an army on the move.

We approached another village, little more than a dirt crossroads with a scattering of walled farmhouses around it, trees not yet torn apart by shellfire around the farmhouses.

The land opened on the other side, climbing through virgin snow to trees and a second group of buildings that appeared abandoned.

Then German 88 shells exploded around us, too fast for us to hear their approach, greasy black against the snow.

"Son of a bitch," Custer said. "They're up there, in those buildings."

Foot soldiers were coming off the tanks, finding any cover available. More 88s came in, airbursts in the trees, and I saw men pirouette, go down, be scattered like bowling pins. Inexperienced soldiers went flat, experienced ones stood close to the trees, giving a narrow target to the overhead bursts.

Abrams didn't need any orders. He put the 37th on line, and the M4s went up the hill, men stumbling through the deep snow behind the tanks.

There was another explosion . . . a 75mm, I think . . . against the brick wall our armored car sat beside. The driver stood up, turned back to us without a face, fell dead, and the engine died.

"Unass this pig," Custer shouted, and the surviving crew obeyed.

A staff halftrack rumbled toward us, Paul Harkins standing next to the driver. An 88 drilled through its engine compartment, and Harkins vanished in the blast. Flames rose out of nowhere, and a Panther rumbled from behind a barn, smashed over the halftrack toward us.

A self-propelled gun had a clear field of fire, and put a 105mm shell into the Panther's belly, and it exploded.

"They're in a damn' minefield," Custer shouted, and I looked upslope, and saw explosions, men falling, a Sherman's track rolling, like a huge rubber band, back downhill as the tank flamed up.

There were men pushing, shoving, some trying to get forward to fight, others to get the hell out of the way. A man screamed, the scream abruptly cut off, as a tank backed over his legs.

Custer ran for an M4, pulled himself up on the deck, grabbed the track commander's mike, got through to the command net.

He gave swift orders—bring the road units up on line, and support Abrams.

"Get those damn' SP guns up here," he ordered.

Custer had a tight smile on his face, was clearly enjoying himself.

I would have thought there was nothing left to burn in this ruined village, but flames crackled, and greasy smoke boiled down the lanes.

Another scream came, this one in terror, and a King Tiger, the Germans' biggest tank, rumbled slowly toward us, tearing the barn it'd hidden in apart.

Its huge 88mm cannon slammed, and a Sherman blew up, turret spinning high into the air, then crashing down on a group of machinegunners.

I was on the Sherman's deck, beside Custer, as he

ordered the tank commander to take the Sherman behind a house, and come back in on the Tiger's rear.

The TC obeyed, and the front horns of our tank crashed into the ancient stone of the building, pulling it toward us. I ducked behind the turret, saw, falling from an upstairs window, an old woman in white. She was screaming, waving her arms, but the air wouldn't hold her, and she fell in front of our tank.

The Sherman ground over her, leaving a patch of blood and entrails in the slush, and we were around the corner and could see the Tiger's stern.

"Don't miss," Custer advised. Our tank fired its 75mm cannon, the shell going just over the Tiger's turret. The gunner corrected, and his second shell hit the turret at its base. The Tiger lurched, then smoke poured out. Machine-gun fire chattered from the street as our infantry took care of the crew.

"Good boy," Custer shouted. "Now, let's go get those cannon that're giving Abrams a hard time."

We moved forward, into the open again, and I looked up the slope. The 88s up there weren't cannon, or even SP guns, but more Tiger tanks.

A handful of Abrams' tanks scuttled back toward us, through the smoldering ruin of ten, no, fifteen, M4s on the slope, and the attacking infantry was tumbling back down the hill.

But we had bigger, closer problems. SS soldiers were streaming into the street, and the battle was suddenly swarming hand-to-hand. There was no order, no organization, just a swirling mass of fighting, killing, dying soldiers, Germans and Americans intermingled.

Two Americans sprawled, hit by submachine-gun fire, and an SS man running past them paused, and put a deliberate burst of Schmeisser fire into them.

I was at the .50 on the tank, and cut the bastard in half, swung the big machine gun and slashed through a formation of his fellows.

There was another Tiger coming through the smoke behind the bodies, its commander in the open hatch. Our gunner fired, and his cannon shell hit the solid forward plate of the Tiger, ricocheting off as the Tiger fired.

It took us in the bow, and I was flipped backward off the Sherman as it slewed to a halt, smoke wisping from its hatches.

I looked around for Custer, saw him as he jumped off the side of the destroyed tank, the tank commander's Thompson gun in hand.

"Come on, George," I heard him shout . . . I think.

The Tiger's turret swung toward him as Custer fired, and the German tank commander slumped. Custer staggered, and an SS officer came from behind the tank, submachine gun firing.

Custer's tommy gun was empty, and he clawed out his antique .45 six-gun, and shot the German down.

Another bullet hit him, and he turned, lifting his pistol, as the monstrous Tiger turret swiveled on him.

Insane, goddamned insane, and he fired at the tank, completely unafraid, and the Tiger's coaxial machine gun chattered, and Custer sprawled in the mud.

The turret swung, looking for another target. I saw a dead panzergrenadier in a doorway, his Panzerfaust beside him.

I ran to it, not letting myself look, not letting myself see that huge turret aim at me.

I had the Panzerfaust, spun, didn't need to aim, pulled down on the firing lever, and nothing happened. I was very calm, able to look down the 88mm barrel as I realized the rocket launcher still had the safety clip in, yanked it out, and pressed the lever down again.

The rocket hit the driver's slit, exploded into the Tiger's interior, and the blast knocked me back into the ruined house. There was no smoke, no flame, only a blackened hole on the front of the Tiger, but it was dead.

I ran to Custer's body. He was very dead, most of his

upper body missing from the machine-gun bullets. Rounds whistled past my head, and I grabbed his pistol, rolled twice, saw an M1 rifle in the street, had it and dropped the German who was busy reloading his Mauser for another shot at me.

Then I was up, limping, not knowing when or how I'd been hit, moving back. I shoved Custer's pistol in my belt, found a bandoleer of ammo, shoved clips into the M1, fired when I saw a field gray target.

We pulled back, out of that village, as more and more German tanks, SP guns, and halftracks rumbled toward us along the country lanes.

Custer's luck had finally run dry.

Aftermath

More than Custer's CCA and CCR took a beating that day and the next few. The Tenth Armored Division was bloodied by Second SS Panzer, and CCB was hit hard by First SS Panzer. We couldn't hold, but fell back on Bastogne, Dietrich's Sixth Army on our heels.

They captured our fuel tankers for desperately needed gas, came on.

The 101st Airborne and its allied units, the bravest of the brave, could only take so much after the siege. The SS hit them hard, and the Division shattered.

They were forced to break up, and escape and evade. There were about 15,000 men still in and around Bastogne. Of those, 8,000 were captured, 3,000 were casualties, and the rest escaped in ones and twos.

Most of the officers, including the acting commander, General McAuliffe, were killed or captured.

In addition to General Custer, Third Army lost General Gaffey, Colonel Abrams, Colonel Harkins, and other fine officers.

Other units in the Bulge were hit very hard, particularly Ninth Division. Its command post was overrun, and the Division Commander, General Craig, and the promising Chief of Staff, Colonel Westmoreland, were killed.

However, Custer's arrogance and disobedience may have actually shortened the war.

Sixth SS Panzer, and other units around Bastogne, including Panzer Lehr and the Fifth Parachute Division, turned northwest again, toward the Meuse, and there was almost no one to stop them.

But then the weather broke, and the Royal Air Force Tempests and American Army Air Force Mustangs went after the German supply lines around St. Vith.

Custer was not the only one who remembered the "mistake" at Falaise. Montgomery noted the extended German lines, and brought the 21st Army Corps down, and other American units stopped the SS in their tracks.

Now there would be no suggestion of escape. Tactical air swept the roads and forests, and almost all of the German Panzers and their transportation, support and artillery were destroyed.

Sepp Dietrich was killed in one air raid, and his replacement, Herman Priess, ordered the remnants of the army to fall back toward Germany, in spite of Hitler's raving. But the soldiers trudging through the snow still fared badly.

There were fragments of the 101st in the forests, and they tore at the Nazis like wolves, getting the last drop of bloody revenge. More than ten Germans moving in a group were asking to be strafed.

Of the twenty-four German divisions ordered into the Watch On Rhine offensive of the Bulge, all were obliterated, and their names stricken from the German rolls. Only a few thousand of the Germans who marched west ever came back to Germany. While not as disastrous as the collapse of Army Group Center in Russia, this debacle definitely shortened the war.

German losses were over 120,000; American just under 100,000.

Other effects of Custer's disaster are fairly well known. Montgomery, who was almost as incautious in his words as Custer, commented loudly and repeatedly on how, once again, it took the few British divisions in the ETO to save the Allies.

That was the final straw for Eisenhower. He declared it was either Monty or him. Roosevelt went to Churchill, who reluctantly relieved Montgomery. However, Eisenhower was forced to resign as well, and Omar Bradley became Supreme Commander.

There are those historians, particularly recently, who see the effect of Custer's death ranging even further.

They blame Custer for the 1948 Republican presidential debacle, when Vice President Harry S. Truman and his running mate, Omar Bradley, demolished Senator Dewey and Eisenhower.

Still further, they say this positioned Bradley to run in 1952, when he publicly shamed the Republican candidate, Eisenhower, for not squelching the ultraconservative right for, among other things, calling Eisenhower's mentor, General Marshall, a Communist.

This sparked Taft, McCarthy and others of their ilk to flee the party to form the Constitutionalists, and shatter the Republicans so badly that, from Roosevelt's era to the turn of the century, only one Republican has gone to the White House, and that for a single term.

Perhaps.

But I think not.

I don't think any single man can affect history that deeply. Even if Custer had not been in the position he was, and, say, George Patton had lived to see the Second World War, and there had been no disaster in the snow, I don't think matters would have been changed that much.

History, in spite of the popular phrase, is, in fact, a rather constant jade.

Compadres

S.M. Stirling & Richard Foss

The man who would be President in half an hour hopped into the open carriage with boyish energy and eyed the still figure who sat waiting for him. The big, somberly dressed man was as quiet as a cat, a relaxation that was complicit of motion, ready without tension.

"Are you ready, Senator?"

"Can anybody ever be ready for something like this?" The soft accent of the southern desert was still strong in his voice. "Twenty thousand people staring at the son of a mule driver while he takes the oath that means he is one heartbeat away from the Presidency?"

The Vice President flashed his famous grin, and the Senator noticed a few more gray hairs in his bushy reddish mustache. "We faced nearly that many at San Juan Hill, or at least it seemed so at the time. The Spanish were better armed, and considering the acumen of Senator Bryan, I should say they were also better led. Buck up, Francisco."

The Senator smiled. "You know, Theodore, you are the only one who calls me that."

"And you are about the only one courteous enough to remember my Christian name as well, no matter how I may correct the others when they shorten it. Back when I was Police Commissioner a pressman told me that as I was always making news, printing my name in the briefest manner possible saved paper and ink."

I have been called many things, Francisco thought. *All the way back to the day at the mine . . .*

"Git yo' back into it, y'fuckin greaser!"

The miner rose, slowly. He was a dark young man of medium height, turned browner still by the desert sun. The great open-pit mine around them rang with the sounds of pick and sledgehammer and shovel, with the clang of ore thrown into steel cocopans, with the voices of men and the hooves of mules. Distantly, a *crump!* came as dynamite shattered stone; the air smelled of rock dust, hot stone, sweat. Harsh southwestern sunlight streaked sweat through the white dust on the miner's face, bearing the bitter taste of alkali to his lips; heat reflected back from the white stone in an eye-squinting glare. Those lips quirked in the beginnings of a smile as he thought how it must sting the skin of the foreman, which had turned boil-red and hung in strips despite the wide hat he wore. He was from Alabama, with a cracker's long, lanky build and pale, washed-out blue eyes.

"I cannot haul the cocopan myself, senor," he pointed out reasonably. "And the mules need water and rest."

Then his hand moved with blurring swiftness, up under the rear of the baggy, dirty peon blouse he wore. His face broke into a smile, showing teeth nearly as bright as the stubby-bladed knife now resting in the soft skin beneath the foreman's throat. The tip was right next to the artery, just dimpling the surface, and a bead of sweat curved as it ran past. The dark man's voice sounded as calm and patient as before.

" . . . And if you call me a fucking greaser again, hijo da puta, I will cut your throat. Do you understand this?"

Hatred glared back at him, through the eyes of a man driven to the edge of madness by prickly heat rash and fatigue. "You're finished here—finished," the man croaked.

"I quit," the miner said succinctly. "And because you are a brave man to speak so, with a knife at your throat, I will let you live this once."

He stepped back and lowered the weapon, looking around at the circle of silence that had fallen among those who could see the little drama.

"Adios!" he called, grinning at the cheers that rang out; cheers from hispano and Anglo and the few Chinese as well. Then he cut the mule's traces with a few swift jerks of the steel, vaulted to its back (how unfortunate that it was not a fine stallion with a long sweeping mane) and flourished his sombrero.

"Go with God! I'm going to Cuba!" he called to the miners, and there were cheers as he clapped his heels into the mule's flanks.

The Senator blinked at his friend, shaking off the memory. A long time. Much time, much change since then. The proverb he had heard so often as a child ran through his mind: *Sin Novedad*. May no new thing arise.

But perhaps this should be discarded, this saying. For have not many new things arisen in my life, and most of them fortunate?

One of the horses at the front of the carriage shied as a photographer's flash gun misfired, tossing sparks in all directions. The two men inside looked on approvingly as the driver expertly calmed his team.

"That one would have been an asset at Santiago, when we lost our supplies thanks to bad horsemanship," observed the Senator. "We shall have to see that the army can pay men as good as this one to handle their wagons."

"They just up and died," the young teamster whined, tears in his eyes. "They just up and died."

The officer controlled his own mount with effortless skill, stroking a hand down its arched neck. Sweat lay heavy on its skin, and on his.

This was not like the mesquite country where he had been born. The land south of El Paso was hot, yes; the very anvil of the sun, drying men to jerky and making women old before their time. But at least it was dry. The air sucked the sweat off your skin, and if you drank much you would not die of the sun-fever.

Here . . . He looked around. Here you felt that something was growing on you, like a mold on a rawhide. The rank green growth around him gave shade that did not refresh; all the trees whose names he did not know were overgrown with shaggy vines, sugarcane rippled in the fields at the height of a mounted man's head, flowers in the ditches beside the rutted mud track flourished in great bursts of purple and crimson.

The air was heavy in his lungs, thick and wet and hot, full of the buzz of insects and the rank smells of lush growth, full of birds with gaudy feathers. Only the houses of the village in the distance had anything familiar about them, tile roofs and whitewashed walls.

Unconsciously, his hand touched the long machete strapped to the left side of his silver-studded charro saddle. The guerilleros were pro-American and anti-Spanish, but they were also half-bandit, and the supply train was a temptation to such starvelings.

And my men are hungry! he thought angrily, and swung out of the saddle. A quick examination of the foundered animals brought his temper to a boil. There were deep weeping harness-galls on their gaunt hides, and the hooves were splintered where the shoes had come off.

"Son of a whore!" he shouted as the wagoneer shrank trembling against the slatted boards of the vehicle. "Don't you know enough to check for footrot? When was the last time you fed these poor beasts?"

He reined in his fury; tongue-lashing the incompetent

would not bring the animals back to usefulness. Instead he turned to the patrol that had ridden in with him.

"Sergeant!"

A tall Montanan straightened in the saddle. "L'tenet?" he asked, shifting his quid of tobacco to the other cheek.

"Take five men and go back to the hacienda we passed. There will be animals: horses, mules, oxen. Round them up and bring them here. If there aren't enough, bring the workers in the ingenio; yes, and the haciendado himself. My men will get these supplies, on the Cubans' backs if no other way!"

"Yessir!" the sergeant said, and pulled his Winchester from its saddle-scabbard. "You heard the man, boys! Yo!"

The officer drew his pistol and turned to the horse that lay in the mud before him, its eyes glassy and blank. Some of the others might be saved, but this one he could give only the mercy of a bullet.

The Vice President was speaking, in that high-pitched voice that went so strangely with his burly chest and big-toothed grin:

"We shall see to the army and much more, Francisco, in the next few months. But we shall do none of it if we do not get on our way to the Capitol."

He adjusted his glasses—two small lenses on the bridge of his nose, without earpieces—and directed his attention forward to the driver. "We are ready, sir. Onward to the inauguration!"

Crowds lined the broad avenues of Washington. They cheered as they saw the carriage approach, with its mounted escort before and behind in a glitter of polished brass and steel. The Vice President acknowledged them solemnly, as befitted the occasion. He had gotten his first term because McKinley had fallen to an assassin's bullet, but he had won his second fair and square, after proving that he could indeed uphold the dignity of the office. On this day in 1905, he was more restrained than his usual ebullient self, more formal and proper than anyone had ever seen him.

Yet his companion could sense the coiled eagerness there, the will to command and the certainty of what to command.

Theodore always seems to be urging men forward, thought the Senator. *And because he is who he is, they will follow him, even though the path he leads is through Hell. Now he is urging a whole country forward, and I pity the ones who do not want to go in the same direction. Luckily, I agree with him, at least so far. We have ridden together a long way since the Rough Riders. And now we ride to the White House. If he had not needed an officer who spoke Spanish, where would I be riding now? Among the mesquite and saguaro of home, perhaps fighting the bandit gangs, perhaps joining them?*

Theodore's voice broke in on his thoughts. "Thinking back, Francisco? You have a look on your face that reminds me of the night before the charge."

"Yes, I was there for a moment," the Senator replied. "Seven years ago, and sometimes it seems like yesterday, sometimes another life entirely. We have come far indeed."

"And we shall go farther still once we get to the dais, which I hope we shall by Christmas," Theodore observed flatly. "Driver, your pardon, but what is the reason for this delay?"

The coachman's deferential answer was in such a low tone that Theodore had to lean forward. Francisco leaned back, studying the blustery gray sky. Whoever had suggested the District of Columbia for a capital city had been mad or malevolent, he decided. Too wet in spring, too humid in summer, barely tolerable in fall and hell in winter. It would be better to be fighting in Cuba again than sitting under a blustery March sky in Washington. It would almost be better to be working back at the mine again . . . no, nothing was worse than that, or he wouldn't have left to join the Rough Riders in the first place.

Such a madly assorted bunch of men those warriors were, roughnecks from the West, adventurers from the East, Englishmen, Germans, Indians, Negroes from both America and Africa, even a few Chinese who held their heads up and fought and cussed just like everybody else. He had come to Theodore's attention thanks to his horsemanship, stayed in his awareness because he, Francisco, had that something that made men follow. He had stayed because Theodore had that something that made even leaders follow, made them glad and grateful to do so.

He had said as much the night before San Juan Hill, the Senator remembered. Francisco had been bent over the hoof of a horse that a picket had found wandering loose when he heard someone coming up behind him.

"Inspecting the animals again, Lieutenant? Bully! Where do you think that one came from, an American unit or Spanish?"

"Local, Colonel Roosevelt, and unfit for anything but pack work as he stands. There isn't a well-shod horse or a well-maintained rifle on this whole island, except the ones we brought with us. Or a well-cooked meal, including the ones we brought with us."

"Blame the outfitters who sold the army that vile tinned beef, not the poor souls who have tried to make something of it. Corporal Hang Ah has thrown away the stuff that came out of the tins green, and he has done all that can be done with the rest."

"I have no doubt he works miracles with what he has, and I will remember to compliment him on his skill the next time I see him."

"You will, Lieutenant, and he will take heart from it. Do you know, you are the only one of my officers who would think to do so. Though you first served me as an interpreter, I will have you know that I consider you an able leader of men, one whose instincts I trust. You have the gift of command, and I shall rely on you to give the men courage tomorrow."

"I will give all that I have, Colonel. I swear it on my honor," Francisco said earnestly.

"That men such as you will take such an oath assures us of victory. It is the job of a commander to inspire competent men, so that the whole army may be led with both valor and skill. God has given me the gift of command, and God or Divine Providence has sent me a man such as you who will be my strong right arm. It could not be otherwise."

"It could have been different, Colonel Roosevelt. Remember, there were two drafts of the treaty after the war with Mexico in my grandfather's time. If the commissioners had signed the other one, with the borderline drawn to the north instead of to the south of Chihuahua, I would have been born on the other side. There are Mexicans fighting us here, you know, volunteers and irregulars. I found one of them dying on the beach yesterday—he begged me for water in a Veracruz accent. Only a hundred miles from where I was born, a hundred miles and a border."

"You have no second thoughts? No feeling of kinship for those with whom your people shared a language and culture?"

"You and I share a language as well, one I have spoken since I was a child. The officers we capture have the accent of Castille, of the grandees who have their position because of their birth, not the plain Spanish my parents spoke in their stables and kitchens. As for culture, Chihuahua was never truly part of Mexico. My father told me tales of the old days; the taxmen everywhere, the police so corrupt that we feared them more than the bandits in the hills. No, I am with you. I will live or die with you, and I will be able to tell my children that I had the honor of riding with Theodore Roosevelt, whom they will call Teddy like everyone else."

A grin stretched the Colonel's red mustache, and he put out his hand. "And I will be honored to tell mine that I have ridden with Lieutenant Pancho Villa, though tomorrow we shall ride apart. You shall have the left flank, I the right, and I shall meet you atop San Juan Hill."

The carriage was moving slowly, to allow the maximum number of residents and visitors to view the newly elected President. The majesty of the moment affected even the naturally buoyant Roosevelt, who sat erect and waved to the crowd with more restraint than usual. He perked up at the sight of a pair of boys still in the short pants of childhood who shrieked in excitement, evidently as much at seeing the fancy coach and mounted guards as the occupants of the carriage. They ran between the militia who were trying to keep the crowd back, and Theodore laughed at the awkwardness of the police trying to catch them.

"Those boys are as excitable as a pair of freshly minted privates," he chuckled.

"And as much use in a charge," agreed Francisco.

He had expected fear, on the day of battle. He had not expected such confusion. The tall grass on the hill ahead waved in the breeze that blew the smoke of the Americans' black-powder weapons into a haze around the troops. All around him he heard the slow barking of single-shot carbines, the ripping-canvas growl of the Gatlings, the occasional bark of a fieldpiece. The Spanish forces on the ridge above were returning fire with their smokeless-powder Mausers, invisible to eyes or field glasses, the high-velocity bullets passing with a vicious flat whipcrack sound. Over it he could hear men shouting, the horses neighing in terror as they were led over the mushy ground toward territory suitable for a gallop. A few American pickets who had been scouting the area withdrew from the field at something which approached but wasn't quite a dead run.

The flight of the well-dressed soldiers was a marked

contrast to the motley but disciplined Rough Riders, who surged forward toward the hidden enemy.

"Forward! *Arriba!*" Francisco shouted.

He raised his voice in a high yipping war-cry and waved his hat towards the Spanish positions. There was fear in his own heart, but pride drove it out as he saw men take heart from his example and surge up the hill behind him. Their eyes upon him did not banish fear, but they made it so much easier to overcome.

The Colonel will not fail me, he thought. *And I will not fail my men.*

The dome of the Capitol came into view, and an instant later they saw the wooden platform which had been erected for the occasion. The black robes of Chief Justice Fuller stood out among the morning coats and striped trousers of the dignitaries and diplomats, the contrast magnified by his shock of white hair waving in the light breeze. Fuller wore his customary air of cool reserve, a marked contrast to the celebratory air of most of the men around him.

One other expression was different—Mark Hanna, the Republican Senator who fancied himself the party's kingmaker, stared at the men in the carriage with unconcealed disgust. When Roosevelt met his eyes, he turned abruptly and started talking to one of his aides.

"Our friend Senator Hanna seems to have eaten something which disagrees with him," mused Theodore happily.

"His hopes, perhaps," suggested Francisco. "He will be an old man in four years, too old to run for President himself, and you will have that time to change this country. You will fight the big corporations and trusts that are dear to him, the railroad barons who are his friends. You will take the country in a direction he does not understand."

"We will do that," exclaimed Theodore, clapping a comradely hand on his shoulder. "Both of us," he affirmed as the carriage came to a stop.

A crush of people surged forward, local dignitaries mixed with Pinkertons, military officers, and a few garishly dressed men with notebooks. In a moment they were surrounded by the crowd. Most converged on Theodore, but one singled out Francisco.

"Mr. Vice President . . ." he began.

"Not yet, but in a while," replied Francisco.

The man stopped a moment, twisted his long blond mustache thoughtfully, and continued. "Ah, yes, that's right. I ask your pardon. Well then, Senator Villa, I'm Ambrose Bierce of the *Sacramento Bee*, and I'd like to ask you a few questions . . ."

Both men were distracted as a scuffle broke out nearby. The military police were taking no chances after President McKinley's assassination, and a squad was shoving the crowd back toward the sidewalk.

The reporter hesitated a moment, and Francisco took his hand. "Now is not the time, my friend. Come to my office this afternoon, and I will talk to you then." The reporter nodded gratefully,then hopped toward the sidewalk as a sergeant brandished his baton.

"Making friends with the press?" asked Theodore as the two men walked toward the dais.

"He had good manners, and was the first person to call me Mr. Vice President," answered Francisco. "I have just gotten used to being called Senator, and now I must get used to this new title. Besides, he was a Westerner, and I like them better than the Eastern newspapermen, who are always too cynical."

"Now Francisco, we are one people," chided Theodore gently. "Even if I do agree with you in favoring Westerners, and would take a Colorado farmer or Montana ranch hand over twenty Mark Hannas. Still, I would not have you judge even all Democrats by him."

"There were good men from everywhere at San Juan Hill . . ." agreed Francisco as they ascended to the platform.

★ ★ ★

"Now!" cried Theodore and the bugles blared. The Rough Riders started moving forward slowly, gaining momentum with every step like a tightly wound spring uncoiling. A tall dark Metis trapper who wore a red sash over his uniform whooped as his horse picked up speed, and fired his revolver at the distant Spanish, then jerked back in the saddle as a bullet hit him in the chest. The wet slap of lead on flesh was unpleasantly audible as blood gouted.

A wiry redhead who wore a green bandolier grabbed the reins of the trapper's horse, keeping the animal under control and steadying the wounded man.

"Sure and I have him now, Pancho," the smaller man called in a thick brogue. "You'll have to shoot two for me, then!"

Francisco grinned and waved his hat while deftly maneuvering his horse past a shell crater, then spurred forward, his horse first in the line by a nose, racing toward the barbed wire at the base of San Juan Hill. A bullet went over his head with a flat, ugly crack, and he pulled his pistol and fired in the general direction of the Spanish redoubt without aiming, as a gesture of defiance as much as anything. More shots rang out around him, along with a ragged cheer mixed with shouted slogans, wordless yelps, and Apache war cries.

He joined in with his own yells of "Viva Teddy Roosevelt! Viva los Rough Riders!" and was surprised when the men around him took it up as a cheer.

The House Chaplain had been unusually brief at his oration, a prayer sprinkled with classical references that left a few people on the dais scratching their heads. Chief Justice Melville Fuller was speaking now, his nasal Maine accent making his formal invocation sound like a foreign language. His delivery was so flat that it took a moment after he had finished to realize that his most recent words had been:

" . . . preserve, protect, and defend the constitution of the United States?"

Roosevelt's ringing "I shall!" was such a contrast that several people jumped, startled despite the inevitability of the response. . . .

"And furthermore," Roosevelt continued, facing the crowd and projecting his voice in the eager strains which had carried over battlefields, "I shall endeavor to bring about a continuance of the march to greatness that was the mission of my predecessors in the glorious office."

For the first time the applause was more than polite, and the crowd standing below moved forward to hear as he continued his speech. "No people on earth have more cause to be thankful than ours, and I say that reverently, in no spirit of boastfulness of our own strength, but with gratitude to the Giver of Good who has blessed us with so large a measure of well-being and happiness . . ."

He has them now, thought Villa, *just as he did when we stood at the top of San Juan Hill amid the stink of blood and powder, and I cheered him with the rest of the men. This Easterner with the vigor of the West is going to take this country and stitch it together, from Alaska in the North to Sonora and my Chihuahua in the South, and he will make it one, and make it proud. He is going to take on the best of the Democrats and the worst of his own party, and he will vanquish them both and they will never know why or how, and the most able of them will follow him, will give up everything else as I did, will make themselves better men in the process as I did. When I retire to my hacienda in Chihuahua, as I will someday, flattering men will say I was destined for greatness. The men who remember the miner with the knife, the bandito I once was, they are all dead now, and maybe nobody but me will know that the smooth-talking men are lying. I could have joined the ones in the hills, been their Teddy Roosevelt perhaps, worked against all I now hold dear. Whatever I could have been, I am the man you trusted your flank to at San Juan Hill, and I will defend you through shot and shell and congressional committees and whatever else the world sends . . .*

The President finished his speech and paused for effect, his famous grin wide on his face.

And I will hail you in the way of my tradition, so when the news gets back to Chihuahua they will know I have not become entirely a creature of this filthy Northern city of pale people.

Francisco seized Theodore's hand in his own and raised it high, shouting with all his might the same phrase that had rung out over the battlefield by the Santiago road. "Viva Theodore Roosevelt!"

And the Glory of Them

Susan Shwartz

Again, the devil taketh him up into an exceedingly high mountain, and showeth all the kingdoms of the world, and the glory of them.

Matthew, Chapter 4:8

June 27, this year of Our Lord 1098

Bohemond stood with his knights near God's table. In sad truth, the table was a ramshackle bit of carpentry rendered temporarily splendid by a bolt of brocaded silk liberated after Antioch's fall from a man-at-arms who wouldn't have appreciated it anyhow; and Bohemond didn't so much stand as try not to lean on his nephew Tancred, but if that old death's head Count Raymond de Saint Gilles could get through one of Adhemar's services without sitting down, Bohemond was damned if he'd show weakness—even if he *had* taken a cut in the final battle for the city that damn near had made a Greek official of him.

The wound hurt like Greek fire, which was, frankly,

a subject he didn't like thinking of. It was one thing to roast a spy or two and make his men yell "*Voici Mardi Gras.*" But that damnable clinging stuff you didn't dare get close enough to cut away—it would take a Greek to come up with such a thing, dishonor at long range, and a Greek like that fox Emperor Alexius to use it.

Bohemond was hardly the only one to wobble through the mass. None of the peers who'd taken Antioch were particularly steady on their feet.

The Papal Legate elevated the Host. It looked like a giant eye and smelled like bread. The men tracked it with hollow eyes, more a case of hunger than piety.

His Grace Adhemar of Puy had imposed yet another of his favorite three-day fasts. So communion would be the first food anyone had had for three days unless some sly bastard had sneaked off to gorge on some of the spoil from the city. If Bohemond had had a moment alone since they raised his banner—as purple as the Emperor's—near the citadel that had yet to fall, he'd probably have tried to sneak a little food himself. He'd have bet his second sword his nephew Tancred's belly didn't growl with emptiness. But, he told himself, hole-in-corner gluttony was hardly the feast worthy of a Prince who had won his city by the sword. The time for wine and fat roasts would come.

Are you surprised, Father? You told me, if I wanted an Empire, I would have to fight for it.

Marcus Bohemondus, named after the giant in the folk tale, son of Robert, called the fox, crossed himself, then swiped his hand over his face. Sweet Jesu, he was tired. Fasts too damn often and scant rations the rest of the time were a hell of a thing to heal on, let alone if a man had to fight four wars at once.

He counted them out. One against Kerbogha, camped beneath the city walls right where Bohemond had camped less than a month ago. A second against those stubborn bastards who'd holed up in the citadel after the rest of Antioch fell. A third, and a disgraceful one, against those pigeon-hearts among the Franks who tried to escape the siege by sliding down the walls on ropes—by God, he'd make the next coward *dance* at the rope's end! And finally, a secret war against Alexius of Constantinople and anyone—like Raymond—who thought that the wily Emperor of the Greeks who'd deserted them had a right to the city Bohemond had bled to take for himself.

I wonder if the wine in that chalice—not that it's worth drinking—will set Adhemar reeling. Now that would be a sight.

Just that day, Peter the Hermit and Herluin had ridden back through the gates with the not-completely-unexpected news that the emir Kerbogha had rejected peace terms. So, it all boiled down, like last week's stew (assuming the plague of locusts Bohemond called his men had *had* meat to stew last week) to a fight. God wills it, God save the right, but Bohemond was glad he had sharp swords, good armor, and some damn useful spies to rely on.

He only hoped Kerbogha had bigger stones than Yaghi Siyan, whose head stank on a post above the stinking city engulfed by stinking camps. When they'd arrived here over a damn nasty hill passage, the plain before the city had looked like it was full of milk and honey. They'd eaten all the food, and now it was full of carrion instead. Not even the stinking Tafurs could haul the bodies out fast enough, and when Bohemond had tried to talk with *le roi Tafur*, who'd become in some strange fashion a vassal of his, that crazed death's head on legs had damn near raised his scythe to him.

Yaghi Siyan's son had tried to use the citadel to retake the city and failed. So he'd been deposed by Achmed ibn Merwine, another of those damned unpronounceable names. Son of a pagan whore could fight, though.

Adhemar was still praying, which was no surprise. Bohemond let his eyes unfocus. Torchlight glowed on the lance that Raymond de Saint Gilles always kept near him, making it shimmer. Finding that piece of scrap and calling it the Holy Lance that pierced Christ's side had been one of Raymond's better ideas, much as Bohemond hated to admit it. To think it was *Bohemond* who called himself the son of the Fox! Crafty Raymond had set a dozen men with more piety than sense to dig for the Holy Lance.

What if Raymond could outmatch him? Bohemond broke into a sweat. Thoughts like that could make a man defeat himself just when he stood on the threshold of the principality he'd fought for all his life.

Bless me, father. Bohemond crossed himself. At least, his hand didn't tremble. You've got to keep the men in heart. Hell, a good meal would do better than all these pious mutterings. Did anybody really think they could take Jerusalem and keep it anyways?

It wasn't as if he could challenge Raymond on a fake relic; there was always the chance there really had been a miracle, and there Bohemond would be—out of luck. Again.

He'd fought too hard for that. He didn't particularly like leaving Raymond, who had this superstitious reverence for the oaths he'd sworn His Imperial Majesty Alexius Autokrator of the Romans, and whatever other titles the man could hang around his overdecorated neck, behind in the city while he rode out yet again to fight, but my lord the Count of Toulouse was a sick man and someone had to stay behind to keep an eye on the citadel.

No man could fight like Adhemar and still claim to be a milky innocent, but Bohemond would have bet half the bribes Alexius had lavished on him that the Papal Legate thought they wanted to receive the Body of Christ, rather than a round of bread. Even if it did look like a very eye of God.

It was Bohemond's turn to limp forward and receive the Host. Christ, he could have swallowed the whole loaf without chewing!

Bohemond only saw bread, tasted bread, and not enough of it. What did Adhemar see?

Whatever, it was none of Bohemond's business, and if

that's how he was thinking, he was taking fever from his wound and they'd have to burn it again tonight. If he had half the brains that had gotten him from a younger son's fealty in Taranto to the point where he could claim to be Prince of this city and be half believed, he'd take to his bed tonight alone, drinking little, and eating less.

But he knew he'd be out, prowling his city as he'd done every night since the gates opened to him and his banner went up.

Steady there . . . the peers were watching him. He might have wound-fever, but those others—they'd taken the infection of plotting from the Greeks, even though Alexius' pet Turkish general Taticius had long since abandoned the armies. Plots, nothing but plots. Give Bohemond an honest battle any day.

Antioch at night, Bohemond thought. *I lift up mine eyes unto the hills, whence cometh my help*—from the strength of my right arm and the valor of my knights. He'd pushed away a host of knights turned nursemaid and insisted that, yes, by Jesu, he was going to walk about his city, maybe up as far as the approach to the citadel, and who among them was man enough to stop him?

When they'd fallen back, murmuring among themselves, he'd flung a cloak about himself, picked up his sword, and set out. And damned glad to have done so, he thought as he paused, breathing hard, to look down at his city.

Surely not even Jerusalem could be more magnificent than his city with its walls, higher than Jericho's, with their hundreds of towers; his city, lying in the lap of the mountains. The night winds had blown the stink away. If you ignored the sections laid waste, the quarters burned by Bohemond himself to force Frankish slackers out of their houses and into the streets where they could be put to the serious work of fighting, his city was beautiful.

Do you see, *Father?*

Robert Guiscard had acknowledged Bohemond's quality. But he had chosen to make Roger Borsa, Roger the Purse, his heir. Well, my lord Roger shouldn't have one of those ungainly copper coins the Greeks called a *follis* to put in his purse—much as Bohemond would like to watch him try.

He could see men going to and fro on the plain, Tafurs dragging bodies out of the city, his nephew Tancred riding in a cloud of knights and dust to whatever errand he had tonight. He didn't trust him, not as far as he could throw him, fully armed, and his horse, assuming Tancred hadn't eaten it on the sly. His nephew's pride was too hot and his Arabic too good. Not that Bohemond was above profiting from it. If Tancred hadn't been able to speak to that turncoat Firouz, who'd turned a blind eye to the knights who climbed into the tower he commanded, they'd still be outside the city walls, and Kerbogha, coming down from the hills, would have cracked them against the walls like eggs.

And he'd have had no new godson. Firouz, who'd opened the city to him, had agreed to receive baptism and had taken Bohemond's name.

Bohemond looked up from the Orontes in its silvery flow to the greater silver of the moon. Milk and honey? The others could have Jerusalem and the hereafter, and he'd take this and the power and the glory of this world.

The moon was making him dizzy, like one of those fools who faints at Mass, mazed with sanctity. Or maybe it *was* the fever.

But the river Orontes running through the plain wasn't the only water for leagues; Antioch was a city rich in water. That had helped it hold out under Yaghi Siyan and was helping them now.

A stream . . . two steps forward and he'd damn near have measured his length in it. He knelt, a movement painful enough to force a grunt out of him now there was no one to see and to whisper he was losing his strength.

He scooped up a palmful of water and slopped it down, dripping onto his cloak and armor: another, and another; and it wasn't enough. Taking off his helm, he filled it and lifted it. A moment longer and he'd have sluiced its contents over his head and maybe have quenched the fire in him that seemed to be turning his face and hair ruddier hues . . . But the image of the city, reflected in the water, beautiful as one of those mosaics in the Greeks' churches, captured him, and he stared at the city, his city, while the wind whipped up about him and he was alone, truly alone, as he hadn't been since his vigil before his father knighted him. Knighted him and sent him off to make his own fortune while making Roger Borsa, Master Purse with his little puckered mouth, his heir.

Bohemond shivered in the moment. He supposed it ought to be shared with the men who'd fought for him, with him: not to mention the ones who'd never see dawn and those who'd already died.

Bohemond didn't want to share this. Or his city. Damn, for once, he would have something, something magnificent, something that was only his. All his life long, he'd all but turned himself into coin. He'd helped Tancred deck himself out like a warrior prince. He'd armed and horsed as big a troop as he could borrow money to support, not that he'd been doing so well until Alexius had tossed him that roomful of treasure with no more thought than he'd have thrown alms at a beggar. Damn the man, to have so much and to rub Bohemond's nose in it, and dole out never a crumb of *real* power.

Before setting out for the Holy Land, he'd had little more than his sword, his horse, and his armor. But he'd torn his best cloak into crosses the day he vowed to go on what his-holy-lordship Raymond, who'd never had to worry where his gold would come from, called a pilgrimage and he knew, perfectly well, it would be the struggle that would win him land and lordship or lose him his renown and his life.

The man who should see you take seisin of this land is dead. Take it for yourself. Ignoring the now-familiar pain of his wounded leg, Bohemond lowered himself to one knee and scooped up a handful of earth, which crumbled in his hand: rich, well-watered, his. He set it down gently, with more respect than he'd been using for the spoils he'd won, rubbed his hand on his cloak, then dipped it in the stream. This damnable fever made him thirsty, made him dizzy . . .

. . . *made him think he was seeing ghosts . . . and what was* that, *creeping up stealthy as a cat behind him?*

Dark-skinned, white-clad, the smell of fresh-baked bread about him, the man was fast but, even faster, Bohemond ripped sword from sheath and hurled himself to the ground (and halfway into the stream, if the truth be told). And when the pagan pounced with one of those blood-curdling yells with Allah in it that always meant all hell had broken loose again, Bohemond spitted him on his outthrust sword.

Blood from the death wound spurted out, fresh stains against the others that stained his cloak. *Le roi Tafur* would call this a baptism, but *le roi Tafur* was probably the craziest thing to come out of France, notwithstanding the competition.

"What an emir you'd be if only you weren't . . ."

Another voice.

Whirling, Bohemond tugged his sword free of the man he'd slain. Another pagan to be slaughtered. Next!

"Show yourself!" Bohemond ordered. Perhaps he should order them to get in line.

"If that will content you, Lord Bohemond," said this new enemy. "*Dominus meus excellentissimus ac gloriosus Boamundus inspiratus a Deo*. You will pardon, I hope, any errors in direct address. Your own fellows stumble in your holy language, separate as it is from the common speech. Your hair betrays you. And your courage, to come out alone at night so close to your enemies."

Sarcastic, sneering bastard, making free with honest knights' errors. They were warriors, not scholars.

"I told you, show yourself!" he snarled, hand on hilt.

The stranger moved out from the shadows into the light. Clearly, he was no mean fighter; Bohemond could see that from how the newcomer carried himself. One hand rested almost casually near the hilt of a sword that could probably chop good Frankish steel into slivers without taking a nick itself. Clearly, the man was either sure enough of his skill, or he had men in hiding (in which case Bohemond was in deep trouble, if not neck deep in a midden). Or both.

There was always the possibility that he was even crazier than the king of the Tafurs. But Bohemond didn't think so.

Madmen didn't wear heavy robes of bronze-and-green silk, embroidered with those symbols the pagans claimed were honest letters, that hung with the weight of the armor they concealed. Madmen didn't watch mortal enemies with steady eyes above a mouth and chin and throat concealed by the same glittering silks.

And madmen didn't laugh like nobles in a quiet room, didn't move their hands away from their weapons, and above all, didn't detach and unstopper richly chased flasks, silver and gold over leather, hanging from their belts.

A sapphire glinted black on the stopper in the starlight as the man pulled down the scarf that masked his face, drank, then passed the flask to Bohemond.

Bohemond tasted, then downed a lusty swallow. Wine, and good wine at that, not the combination of horsepiss and vinegar that even Adhemar called wine these days. "I thought you pagans didn't . . ."

"Virtue is what Allah pours into your heart and mind, not down your throat," said the stranger. He was well-armed, well-dressed, if not with the elaboration of Yaghi-Siyan or his son. One was dead, the other fled.

Incongruously, the man laughed, then went on in the blend of Frankish, Latin, and Arabic that had become the common tongue of the pilgrimage, "Just because your lord turned water into wine doesn't mean you're drunk all the time. You couldn't fight like that if you were."

"Maybe we'd fight better," Bohemond said with a chuckle that startled him. He nudged the assassin's body with one muddy boot. "Would *he* have drunk?"

"I think not," said the stranger. "But then, I also thought he would not fail me."

Bohemond laughed and planted his fists on his hips. "Let's work that one out. You had such faith in this . . . this assassin of yours that you followed him to make sure he carried out your wishes. That doesn't sound like faith to me."

He looked down, found the flask in his hand, and had another gulp of the wine before, a little belatedly, handing it back to its owner.

"For that matter, what *was* his errand?" Bohemond asked. "Or would it be safer to ask *who*?"

"He was to seek the life of a man named Firouz, that filthy traitor with horns on his head."

Bohemond barked laughter. "The man you seek's died to that name. Washed in the blood of the Lamb or whatever. He's my godson Bohemond now. You'll just have to give up your grudge," he added and held out his hand for the flask.

The man shook his head. "You are too trusting!" he chided. "How do you know I haven't poisoned the wine?"

"You drank," Bohemond pointed out.

"And that is incontrovertible proof that I did not poison the wine? I think not. I might be willing to assure your death with my own. Or, like the ancient King Mithridates, I might have accustomed myself to poisons, a little at a time, until what would kill you and your knights would affect me no more than a surfeit of sherbet."

Bohemond shrugged, trying to shift his position so he could get a glimpse of the face beneath the silks *and* ease the ache in his leg. "Poison's for Greeks. If you'd wanted me dead, your assassin there would have taken me out. Or tried. You pagans fight like men. Look at you now, come down from up there—" he gestured at the citadel, "—rather than hide like a woman . . ."

"Or like one of your—you call them ropewalkers, who run away?"

Bohemond bit his lip. Even in the East, they knew that red hair meant a temper of fire, and it would help him not at all if this shadowy emir provoked him into losing his judgment.

He heard a ghost of a chuckle, which improved his temper not at all.

"And what makes you so sure," said the stranger, "that I am from . . . up there, as you say?"

The night wind erupted, whistling through the charred remnants of the trees on the ground here between city and citadel. Bohemond felt his cloak billow around him, but the other man's garments scarcely stirred. Good metal hidden within them: best not fight him. And a fine mail scarf probably lay beneath the silk that now concealed all of the man's face except his eyes, exceptionally piercing, and so pale for a pagan that Bohemond thought he could practically peer within the fellow's skull.

The wind roared again. Bohemond shifted position, but his enemy moved not at all.

His mouth suddenly dry, Bohemond lifted the flask he still held to drain it.

That was when he saw the interlocked triangles, above and below, forming the six-pointed stars he'd seen in Jewish quarters before his men ran wild with fire and sword. Solomon's Seal, it was called hereabouts, and attributed to mages and to the demons called djinn.

Bohemond let the flask drop from his hand, then crossed himself. It was a costly toy; a human man would bend to retrieve it, and then Bohemond would have the advantage. A djinni . . . possibly a djinni could beckon, and the flask would fly through the air to his hand and be miraculously filled.

"Such a conclusion you jump to," said the stranger. "I offer you peace and wine. You take the wine, then let my flask fall on the ground, and make holy signs as if I were some creature sent by Shaitan to confound you, not an honest warrior."

The moonlight struck him, turning his burnished splendor all pale. His long eyes gleamed, and he lowered the scarf over his mouth, revealing a jaw fully as stubborn as Bohemond's. He drew his sword, a beautiful movement accompanied by the sweet sound of steel, water patterns glistening down its deadly length. Slowly extending it, he caught up the flask's strap, and held it, dangling from the point, out to Bohemond again.

"Look within, I tell you. There are no djinn in my flask. And no wine."

Bohemond barked laughter. "Of course not. You already left your bottle." His heart sank about the level of the repairs to his boots. If this emir or whatever he was were sorcerer as well as warrior . . .

Then Adhemar would have been Bohemond's best defense this night, assuming the Legate were in shape for so long a walk. Or Tancred, whose Arabic might have been good enough for a feeble curse or two.

Bohemond leapt forward, though his leg felt as though it had been wounded all over again, and grabbed the stranger. What felt like honest steel and flesh lay beneath his gripping fingers. The man held firm. Either he had a dagger—a deadly little final weapon, poisoned or not—tucked in among those folds of costly robes, too clean for a proper man, or he really was one of the unclean creatures known as djinn.

"Have you come to offer me all the kingdoms of the earth?" Bohemond demanded.

The djinni, if such he was, twisted free.

"Well asked, my lord Bohemond," he said. "So you read

the Book of which you are a child, in which the saint we call Issa fasts in the wilderness and is visited by Shaitan. Walk with me now, and let me show you all these kingdoms of the earth."

I am a fool and the son of a fool, Bohemond told himself, knowing both to be a lie. *Nevertheless, as if he had been bespelled by the moon or—the wine! This son of Satan may not have poisoned it, but put some drug in it to render me witless!*

Christ, it would be hard to be Prince of Antioch and then cut down with no more of a fight than Yaghi Siyan put up, fleeing after he'd lost the city.

Or maybe it was just the fever, playing tricks with the light and his judgment. He heard himself murmuring, "Again, the devil taketh him up into an exceeding high mountain, and showeth him all the kingdoms of the world, and the glory of them, and saith unto him, all these things will I give thee, if you will fall down and worship me. Then saith Jesus unto him, Get thee hence, Satan, for it is written, Thou shall worship the Lord thy God and him only shalt thou serve. Then the devil leaveth him and behold, angels came and ministered unto him."

But he found that he'd taken a few steps to an outcropping of rock, built up with a wall on which it was possible to lean out and overlook the entire valley. Unsteady as he was, the djinni probably could pick his moment to push him over. Well, he could try.

The djinni nodded.

"But you haven't left."

He gestured at the city lying at their feet. "What will you ask?" he demanded. "A princedom? The Emperor's crown?" He took a deep breath. "The Holy City of Jerusalem itself? Will you beg for it?"

"Antioch is mine by right of conquest," said Bohemond. "And I beg for nothing."

He was Antioch already, if he could hold fast, despite

Godfrey and Adhemar's holiness and Raymond's mewlings that Antioch belonged to the Emperor. And Jerusalem? A dream men had died for. Bohemond preferred gold and honest stone to dreams.

"You wouldn't care to step off this height and let me help you fly?" There was laughter in the stranger's voice.

"You offer me cities, honor, gold," said Bohemond. "Emperors have done that, and I've taken what I chose and only what I thought I could hold. You offer me more than any man could guard, and for what price? My soul? Poor scarred thing that it is, assuming I have one at all. I would not bargain with you for so little."

"Then if your soul means nothing to you," said the djinni, if such he was, "why not clasp hands and say 'done' on our bargain?"

He held out his hand, scarred with battle, but long and fine. Would those fingers be ice-cold or warm as honest human flesh?

Knocking his hand away might make the djinni bring down the lightnings, or whatever weapons besides steel that djinn used. Instead, Bohemond put his own hands behind his back. A boy's gesture, and it would leave him vulnerable for a perilous second or two, but it went with what he was about to say.

"If Jesus Christ appeared on that rock over there right now and offered me Antioch, all unearned, I'd say 'thank you very much, my Lord, but I cannot accept honor I have not earned for myself.' Do you understand that?" Bohemond demanded. "I won this city with fire and sword and sweat and blood, and no one, human, djinni, or God Himself, is going to take it from me!"

He heard his voice echo off the rock walls of the citadel. In the valley below, men raised a cheer. He had heard them cheering like that, "Bo-he-mond! *Bo-he-mond*!" at dawn when they looked down from the city's walls and realized that they'd won it, at least until Kerbogha could arrive. Screamed like fugitives from the Pit, their faces black with smoke and sweat and rust, their eyes red, and blood pouring from unfelt wounds. He'd beggared himself to bring them here, cursed them for gaping mouths, greedy guts, and weaklings when their courage faltered; yet here they were, in Antioch, and he loved every one of them.

Would anyone lower himself to win Antioch by magic or even the gift of God when he could have this ferocious glory? Not Bohemond.

"You poor, miserable bastard," he all but purred at his adversary. "Let me explain it to you. See this city? It's mine. Won by *my* hand, *my* sword, *my* men, *my* blood and my bone and the courage God gave *me* as a knight. And you offer me trickery instead. As well offer me water and call it wine, or a leather glove and oil when I want a woman. You know about the wine, at least. Do you damn djinn have any balls, or are you like Greeks that way, all cut off?"

Those were fighting words. If the man drew, as he expected, he'd have God's own battle on his hands. Roused as he was, he thought he could take him. And if not, it was better than wondering if his leg wound would rot.

Sweat was breaking out all over him. His matted hair was drenched with it. Waves of hot and cold rushed over him, but he managed not to reel until they subsided and he realized: *I've got the turn. My fever's broken, and I'm going to live. Live and rule Antioch.*

He drew his sword and waited.

And waited longer.

His adversary laughed. "My lord, if you could see the expression on your face! I believe you're actually disappointed we won't be able to hack each other to pieces."

Bohemond found himself laughing, with relief among other things. "It would be a shame to spoil that pretty coat. Maybe, when we take the citadel, I can get me one as spoil."

"I will remember that," said the other man and saluted him in the pagan fashion—touching heart, lips, and brow with a grace that any perfumed courtier from the south of France might envy.

He drew in a deep breath, looked up at the sky, flying the same banners it had flown the night Bohemond won his city, and veiled the lower part of his face once more.

"I have found out what I wished to learn," he said. "Are you well enough to walk down alone to where you're quartered?"

"Walk?" Bohemond replied, as he gazed down the way he had come a long night before. "I could fly!" Then, as the other man laughed, he added hastily, "But I won't!"

"I never expected it," he answered. "But I am pleased to hear you are well. If you feel the need, send a messenger to the citadel. Some physicians still survive. May God be with you."

To Bohemond's surprise, he used the proper word, not "Allah."

Tancred came riding toward Bohemond and the assembled lords with the sort of eagerness you beat out of pages and worked out of squires. His horse's hooves struck sparks from the city's stones, but though it stumbled, it didn't fall.

"Hell of a way to use a good horse," Bohemond muttered. Didn't Tancred realize this idiocy reflected badly on his uncle?

"Uncle! My lord!" he was shouting.

Splendid. Now, he was interrupting a council to which he hadn't been invited, and Raymond was already shooting Bohemond little "control-your-nephew" glares that Adhemar was bound to have to back up.

Tancred reined in so suddenly that the horse reared, sending him into a fall that only a knight's skill turned into a form of dismount.

"They're surrendering up there!" he shouted. "The citadel! The flag's up, not Raymond's but my lord uncle's! The gates are open, and the commander swears he'll yield to Bohemond or no one."

Adhemar rose, his face transfigured.

Jesu, *not another three-day fast*, Bohemond thought and cast round for a distraction.

"Assemble our men, nephew."

"They're coming," Tancred said, his eyes ablaze. He, like Bohemond, knew what it was to be poor, to want, and to hack and fight to win one's heart's desire.

Bohemond could hear heavy footsteps. He could see crowds approaching, faces he knew, voices he recognized, and some he saw only in his heart.

"My lords, with your permission," he began. Christ, he was a boy again, on his first campaign, with all his dreams untarnished. Joy erupted in him. Generous enough to give the others grace, even the sour, disappointed Raymond, Bohemond shouted, "Not by my hands, not by our hands . . . *non nobis, Domine* . . . sing it, you bastards! Sing with all your hearts!"

As the knights, any one of whom would have regarded the name of bastard as sufficient reason to fight to the death, burst into song, Bohemond marched them up the battered streets of Antioch and didn't halt before he reached the citadel. The hell with the leg. He'd have time to collapse later, and skilled pagan physicians to attend him.

Behind them rose the cheering of the host. For some, the cheer would be their last word—no bad way to go. *Do you see that, Father? First, a princedom, and now this public glory.*

Adhemar would counsel him to avoid the sin of pride. He would try not to show just how proud he was.

And please God he could manage not to burst out laughing.

The pagans formed up in a double line from the

citadel's gates. Even in surrender, they were splendidly tricked out in fine silks and gleaming mail and swords the knights would make them surrender unless Bohemond stepped in. The wailing of those weird pipes they carried and the rapid beating of their round drums erupted all about the citadel as their commander walked through the gates.

So this was Achmed ibn Merwine: a bronzed man, silk-robed, long-eyed, his face half-veiled. As Bohemond waited, he unhelmed and removed the scarf that hid his face.

"You!" Bohemond gave in to the great shout of laughter he'd felt building since Tancred almost fell off his horse and bounded forward.

"Some soldiers told me you were the true commander, the only leader, of the Franks. And then I met you and saw for myself that, truly, you would not be defeated."

"And they were right," Bohemond said. It wasn't his fault if this emir wanted to rub salt in Raymond de Saint Gilles' wounds, now, was it?

"I cannot endure the destruction of more of my men. Or of this city. It is written that you shall rule Antioch, and thus . . ." The man removed his sword from his belt, knelt, and offered it to Bohemond.

He took it, drew it and heard the sweet rush of fine steel cutting air, then held it over the enemy commander, who was certainly no djinni.

"So," he asked, "what shall it be? We can give you safe conduct out of here—no doubt Kerbogha will receive you. Or will you stay with us and be baptized in the True Faith?"

Achmed ibn Merwine saluted Bohemond, heart, lips, and brow, the way he had the night before. "My lord, I offer you another godson named Bohemond. If you are willing to stand with me before the altar."

Heedless of Tancred's sudden watchfulness or Raymond's glare, Bohemond strode forward.

"I would be honored," he said.

He raised the emir, drew him into an embrace.

"My son," he intoned formally, and damned near broke his hand thumping him on the back, thanks to the fine steel sewn into ibn Merwine's fancy coat. Despite the ache in his hand, he could feel laughter under the silk and the steel.

Another one from whom I'll have to guard my back, thought Bohemond, Prince of Antioch. The sounds of rejoicing rose all around him. The killing would probably resume tomorrow.

Twelve Legions of Angels

R. M. Meluch

"What the hell am I reading here?" The Reichsmarschall turned back to the cover page of the offensive manuscript. *Twelve Legions of Angels* the damned thing was titled. Small eyes glinted blue tracer rounds at the Oberstleutnant who had brought it. "What is this slop?"

The Oberstleutnant blanched. May have made a mistake coming here. Still, he had drawn the short straw. Nowhere to go but forward. "It is a work of—oh, what to call it?—*speculative fiction,* I suppose."

"It's sedition! Why did you bring this to me? Turn the swine over to the Gestapo!"

"The swine is one of ours."

The small eyes grew as wide as they could. "German?"

"No, Herr Reichsmarschall. Air man."

The flare of anger subsided to a troubled scowl. The Gestapo thugs were out of the question now. The Luftwaffe took care of its own problems. "English?"

The Oberstleutnant gave a brisk nod. "Former C in C of the RAF Fighter Command. Air Chief Marshal Hugh

Dowding—retired. The RAF sacked him directly after Dunkirk."

The scowl deepened. Dunkirk. Not Hermann Goering's finest hour. He had let the British Expeditionary Force escape across the Channel—even with the lack of British air cover.

That lack got the RAF flyboys rightly spat upon in their own streets, while all of England exalted the miracle of the boats.

Always astonishing what the British will call a miracle. They had abandoned thousands of French allies on the beach, and though they had managed to ferry a quarter million British soldiers across the Channel, it was still a bloody retreat! Those quarter million soldiers had not been enough to turn away Goering's Eagle Attack! Nor that of the Sealion. Queer sort of miracle, that.

"Why was this Dowding relieved from command?" Goering demanded.

"The RAF forced him into retirement for refusing to send Spitfires to France."

"Do you mean he had Spitfires to send and he didn't? His best aircraft? Was he trying to help the Reich?"

"No, Herr Reichsmarschall. The opposite according to this." The Oberstleutnant gave the manuscript a gingerly tap. "It was part of his strategy."

"Oh, *strategy* was it."

"From what I could read. This seems to be a treatise on how Herr Dowding would have run the British air campaign."

"Another armchair expert." Goering sniffed.

"He flew in France," the Oberstleutnant advised quietly.

"Old enough to retire and he was still flying?"

"In the Great War, Herr Reichsmarschall."

"Ah." Had all of Hermann's attention now. A shared history there. The Blue Max gleamed under the Reichsmarschall's chins. He could sense an instant warmth toward this brother under the cowling. An addled, idiot brother on the wrong side, but a brother all the same, from a time when real men flew in open cockpits, the wind and prop wash bitter in their faces, grit clattering against goggles, when your kite could turn on a thought, and there were no parachutes.

The Fat One became magnanimous. Victors could afford to be. He looked forward to marshaling a combined force of Spitfires and Messerschmitts against the Bolshevik menace.

A clack of heels in the doorway demanded attention. An adjutant: "It's time, Herr Reichsmarschall." Further questions regarding angels, however many of them, must wait.

Out to the balcony festooned with red, white, and black buntings, to take up a place flanking the Fuhrer and the British king.

Crowds surged like the stormy ocean with thunderous *sieg heils.*

Down below, within the palace gates, a semicircle of VIPs stood up from their chairs.

Beyond that, the Mall stretched like a runway between fields of raised salutes. And here came the airplanes.

The procession extended twenty-five miles for the flyover at Buckingham Palace on this, the first anniversary of the end of the *Kanalkampf*, the conflict which the losing side had called the Battle of Britain.

You saw them first, a blot upon the sky. Then their roar shook the ground, the kind that throttled your throat, shook the heart in your chest.

Pride of place went to Hitler's bombers. The HE 111s' cut-out wing roots gave them a distinctive silhouette, unlike the JU 88s, looking from the ground unnervingly like British Blenheims. Their radial engines' clatter gave them their German accent.

Only then came the ME 109s, radiators whistling. Hard- lined, vicious shapes, in *geschwader* strength, they peppered the low cast sky for miles.

A lull, then, on the horizon with a signature purring you need only hear once to know immediately, advanced British Rolls Royce engines—a *schwarm* of Hurricanes in Nazi colors. Stable gun platforms, those. The Hurricanes had delivered a convincing punch to their erstwhile adversaries, and they could take a beating. Shooting them was like shooting a wicker basket. But the Hurri was not a nimble crate. With Spitfires cleared from the sky, the ME 109s had chewed them up.

Next came the Spitfires, emblazoned with swastikas. A single surviving vic of them liberated from the crushed RAF. The lead craft wore a Geshwadercommodore's stripes and a Micky Mouse emblem on his cowling. That one broke formation and rolled.

Unexpected. Hermann growled disapproval, but his eyes gleamed. Boys will be boys.

Elegant, agile crates. The Spitfire was the ME 109's graceful, Britannic twin.

"Pretty kites," someone said.

Apparently too pretty for Air Chief Marshal Dowding to use. The stingy man had only sent a handful of them to France to aid his allies. True, he had only a few Spitfires at any one time, but he hoarded all he had. For what? A rainy day? The storm had come!

And this the man who wrote a book on how the battle for Britain should have been run?

Nothing, thought Hermann Goering, nothing could have stopped his Luftwaffe.

Unnoticed in the crowds, near a bench in St. James's Park, a drab, forlorn gent watched Stukas advance in plague swarms. They were not diving today, so the crowds would not hear their screamer whistles. Not for terror this pass. Yet they terrified. The sky blackened with masses of crook-winged monsters.

Slow. They were slow. But once England spent her Spitfires and Hurricanes, there had been nothing to stop these slow monsters from lining up their attack runs from up high. And once they bunted over, nothing could hit a Stuka in a dive. The dive-bombers had picked off the ships of the proud British Navy at will, clearing the way for invasion.

All the fibres in his body quivered with pain as though he was burning alive at the utter horror of the sight. The Stukas blotted out the meagre sun.

Someone who had seen an American cinema said, "Run Toto, run!" The Stukas became flying monkeys in a little girl's nightmare. Yes, that was it. This was all unnatural. Not right. *Not right.*

Still trembling in the lull that followed the horrific Stukas, he had to acknowledge the logistical feat involved in this procession. There were airfields and assembly areas to organize, times aloft and varying speeds and ranges of aircraft to be calculated. Times required to reach altitude. All the difficulties of Big Wings.

Of course, these pilots knew exactly where they were going, and no one was even shooting at them.

Next, perhaps most hideous of all, came a lopsided vic—one Lancaster, one Hurricane, and one Spitfire—in red, white, and black.

The program called them the Fuhrer's Flight.

Vision blurred as he tried to watch them pass over the palace—blurred the swastikas from the heroic shapes, blurred the colours back to those they had worn in defense of Britain.

Bleary gaze dropped to the balcony.

He saw Union Jack buntings in place of Nazi flags. And instead of that evil man, a queen in a green dress. And in place of Reichsmarschall Goering, a very pretty princess.

And down below, within the palace gates in those chairs where Hitler's favored sat, a bunch of old men called the Few.

He did not know what the Few were. The word just popped into his grief-addled head along with the thought that it was fifty years later and he was dead.

He had become quietly unhinged.

He fled, pushing through the crowds with barely audible requests for pardon.

His picture and his name had long since disappeared from the press, so he was not a widely known figure anymore. He passed unrecognized and scarcely noticed. He was not the first grown man to leave the aerial display in tears.

Hermann Goering blew back into the palace with an energized swagger. Dashed the offending manuscript off the table with his baton. *Twelve Legions of Angels* strew the Persian carpet. "How did you come by this work?" he demanded of the Oberstleutnant.

"The publisher turned it over to us, Herr Reichsmarschall."

Stopped the big man mid-strut. "He is *publishing* it!"

"Trying to. Yes, Herr Reichsmarschall."

"Would anyone take this Dowding seriously?"

"Difficult to say. Herr Dowding is not a particularly lovable figure. His most influential supporter—one Keith Park, very popular fellow—went down with his boys in the battle."

"So the man is not lovable," Goering dismissed that. "His words—are they dangerous or lunatic?"

"I . . . haven't the English to say."

"Then get English!" Goering bellowed. "Tell me what all this says!" Gestured about with his baton. "Briefly!"

The Oberstleutnant glanced sorrowfully at the scattered pages of angels. Noted with some small relief that Herr Dowding was a detailed, exacting man and had the pages numbered and clearly typed.

"Tell me if what he says in this book could make sense to anyone, or does Hugh Dowding come off the complete fool he seems to me. No use shooting an old man unless we have to. Someone could decide he was lovable!"

★ ★ ★

Hugh Dowding moved without direction, oblivious to his surroundings until his soles crunched on a pavement aglitter with glass shards.

He lifted his gaze to a storefront. Had been this way before, yet was slow to recognize the jeweler's shop where Sarah's young man had bought the ring with which he had asked for her hand. The shop was dark within, all chaos and ruin.

He stepped carefully through the gaping opening that should have been a window. "Mr. Rose? Mr. Rose?" Searched the shambles.

A curt bark from the street: "Here now! You there! *You there!*" The silhouette of a bobby at the window. "I see you! Out with you now!"

Hugh Dowding picked his way back through the glass and splinters to the window. Inquired, "Mr. Rose. Where is Mr. Rose?"

The bobby sized him up. Decided the older gent was not the looter he had first taken him for. "Here now." Reached over the sill for Dowding's elbow. "Mind the step."

"Did Mr. Rose get out before this happened? Is he well?"

"I wouldn't worry about that much, sir, if I were you. Move along now." He motioned with his nightstick. The armband, de rigueur these days for men in uniform, waved a spidery cross.

Hugh Dowding hurried home.

Lights in all the windows welcomed him. The door opened to an oasis in the horror of the day, the house warm and alive with gay feminine chatter. Sarah and her bridesmaids practiced hooking that eternal train of satin onto Sarah's bustle.

Sarah turned at her father's entrance. Beamed, showing off her assemblage. "What do you think?"

Tears again. Found his wife at his side. His arm fit naturally around her waist. "Clarice, can this vision possibly be mine?"

She gave his chest a tender slap. "No one else's."

Their daughter was radiant.

Clarice carried a lot of sewing stuff under one arm. A work in progress. "What's all this?" Rather late to be constructing another dress.

"We've had a bit of a disaster," said Clarice. "My dress got burned at the cleaner."

Hugh Dowding bristled. What had the clot been thinking to use that kind of heat on antique silk? "I shall have words with the bounder."

But no. There were no words to be had with the proprietor.

The dress had burned along with the rest of the cleaner's establishment.

Dowding drew the curtains closed. The world outside had gone to hell.

Dick Trafford, the British air attaché upon whom the task had been foisted, turned another tedious page. Groaned. Ground his teeth at every self-righteous paragraph.

What made Stuffy Dowding think that anything *he* did could have made a difference? He would have forced us into a defensive battle. His strategy involved avoiding casualties rather than inflicting them on the enemy. His plan was to hold out until the Channel became too rough for the Germans to launch a crossing. Not the sort of military objective that wins wars.

He found fault with everything the RAF did. Especially with the RAF's finding fault with that Heath Robinson defensive organization Dowding left behind him.

Trafford did not appreciate the accusatory tones with which Stuffy dressed down those who sabotaged *his* RDF system.

Sabotaged. He had the nerve to use that word!

The Radio Direction Finding system successfully detected enemy aircraft approaching England, but that information had not arrived where it needed to go. The links of Dowding's complex communication system broke down. *Our fault.*

He blames us for lack of intercepts. Likens us to inept runners in a relay race, bobbling the baton pass.

Does this man not realize how difficult it is to route information in times like that? There was no time! The information could change in a moment.

The system would have needed to work like a clock, and Dowding certainly had a clocklike mind. No fighting man here.

Had Dowding still been in charge, he would have eliminated standing patrols, and instead waited until his RDF detected enemy craft on their way. This (he says) would lessen the chance of the Luftwaffe catching us on the ground between patrols.

Kept harping on the harsh reality that a Spitfire needed twenty minutes to climb to effective altitude. True. But might the humble air attaché point out to the esteemed ACM Dowding that the RDF apparatus point *outward*? Once the Luftwaffe crossed the coast, they were out of electronic sight. What point having the altitude advantage over the enemy if you did not know whether he had turned?

To this problem, Dowding answered with his Observer Corps. A true scientific marvel there. Involved men and women with binoculars going outside and looking up.

This Stone Age organization would have telephoned vectors to Ops who would track the plots on a map. Ground Controllers would radio the course changes to fighter aircraft already aloft.

Did the man not read his own words? Could he not see how *stuffy* he was? The whole concept ran so counter to the RAF fighting spirit that one could not read more than a page of it without needing to get up and walk off the insult.

Dowding wrote in highly critical terms of the aggressive leadership that followed his tepid reign. He found fault with RAF attacks on the Luftwaffe bases in Normandy.

Well, Stuffy, if we had not hit their airfields, there would have been still more of them camping on the French coast in still closer striking distance of our shores. We would have lost *sooner*.

Dowding's contention was that we should have preyed on the weakness of the ME 109, which the Spitfire shared; its lack of range. A fighter going either direction had only minutes over enemy territory in which to do battle before it must turn around, else risk ditching in the Channel. A fighter over its own homeland could battle until it dropped out of the sky into friendly soil, the pilot free to fight again.

Dowding wrote that we need never have crossed the Channel to have won the conflict, but that the Luftwaffe must. Said we should have let *them* ditch in the Channel after tangling with our Spitfires. After the Spitfires had sent the MEs packing, the Germans' underpowered bombers would have been easy fodder for the Hurricanes and the Ack Ack guns. Said we threw away our advantage.

Dowding would not even have dispatched interceptors for those German fighters who came over two by two on free hunts. Just let the pairs of MEs come buzzing over for a jolly, stitch up the tarmac, and return to France. Those Dowding would have left to the sector guns. Said he would not have been provoked into an aerial battle. Did not want to expend the aircraft.

"Stuffy, you wouldn't have spent them at all!" Dick Trafford shouted at the manuscript. Provoked. "Aircraft are not a defensive weapon! The RDF faced *out*! You use it to guide bombers and fighters to their target and home again, you pompous twit! The Hun knows how to use aircraft!"

Had come out of his chair. Sat back down. Glanced self-consciously about. Hoped his shouts had not carried through the walls.

Returned to his labour, reading how we should have sat and let the Germans shoot us. Wait for the bombers before we did anything.

Dowding criticized the RAF's lack of adherence to a single coherent plan—his.

Hit nearly home with that one. Plans. The RAF had no want of plans. Everyone was an expert. Too many plans and no commitment to *one*. That killed us.

But to say that *this* one, Hugh Dowding's, was the one that would have saved England was as absurd as it was arrogant.

Stuffy had particularly strong words for the Big Wing approach, wherein vast numbers of enemy aircraft were met with vast numbers of interceptors. A natural plan of action. But Stuffy faulted the time it took to muster a Big Wing, then to find the enemy without the help of an Observer Corps.

A Big Wing put all one's resources in one place. When that place had been on the ground, refueling, a second huge wave of the Luftwaffe's limitless attackers had destroyed much of our Big Wing on the ground.

Did not hindsight make any man appear brilliant?

In what was surely the most bald stroke of impudence, he called Douglas Bader a truly heroic young man of unquestioned courage and ardent patriotism with a faulty grasp of tactics and none of strategy. A junior officer given too much credence.

Trafford snarled at the page: *Douglas Bader died in defense of his country. How generous of you not to question his courage.*

In parting, this mother hen complained bitterly of the RAF's sending up untrained pilots. Did he think he could have told the Hun to wait while we got enough air under our pilots' bums to qualify? The battle would have been lost by the time Dowding let them fight!

Turned the last page. The end, none too soon. The anger stayed. Felt like telling the Reichsmarschall to shoot him.

They should have put Stuffy out to pasture long ago. The unmitigated conceit of this old man that he could be one of those rare souls upon whom events of the world pivot.

★ ★ ★

Dowding returned to the jeweler's shop. Like the tongue that probes a chipped tooth again and again, making sure that nothing changed in the instant between visits, he could not stay away. He stood, helpless, before the gutted, blackened wound.

Sensed someone pass behind him on the pavement. Glanced after passerby.

A young man kitted up like a Pilot Officer at dispersal, complete with yellow Mae West over his wool jersey. No swastika on his arm. He wore his second-best blue trousers and fleece-lined boots.

Wondered if the young man knew he was dead.

Dowding had never before seen a ghost, but knew one when he saw him. A little startled that he was not more alarmed.

Followed the young man into a church. Took off his cap. Slid into the pew beside him. "Are you lost, son?"

The Pilot Officer nodded, gaze far away. "I was looking for heaven, actually. It should be here."

"*Here?*" Dowding asked.

The Pilot Officer nodded again. "Here. This. This *England.*" Depth of feeling in the name. "But it's not here."

"No," Dowding said sadly. "It is not." Eyes to the cross, "How could He let this happen?"

"How could you?"

Dowding floundered. "How could *I*?"

The Pilot Officer looked at him at last. "It is your fault."

Deeper and deeper under water Dowding floundered. "How is this my fault?"

"You weren't here for us."

"I—I was retired." How very puny and unacceptable that sounded to his own ears.

And deeper. "Are you sure you did not ask for it?"

Dowding coughed, surprised. "I never! Would never!"

"Did you not?" said the youth, then, in a voice not his, " 'Almighty Father, anything but this. I cannot bear it. Let this cup pass away from me.' Did you not? As the bombs fell and we flew to our deaths, with only you piloting this ship through the worst storm of its existence. Did you not let go the tiller, leave your heavy burden to someone else, and go merrily to attend your pretty daughter's wedding and sleep in your warm wife's bed?"

"How dare—" Stopped himself. This boy had died for England. And he, he was preparing his pretty daughter's wedding.

"Are you sure you did not ask to get out of what needed to be done? Did not say 'It is too much for me?' "

A searching moment. A croaking groan, "No. I didn't. I wouldn't. I would give anything for my country. Anything."

"Would you, Abraham?"

"My name is not—oh. Oh my." Gave him pause. Felt the quiver in his chin. The sacrifice of Abraham. "My family are dearer to me than life."

"Your life is not what hung in the balance."

"But . . . my son!"

"Your son. Your wife. Your daughter. Your happiness. Your sanity."

"Why them? Why my wife? Why my—" Could not talk. Was dangerously near to weeping again.

The Pilot Officer produced a sheaf of papers from his boot. Dowding recognized his manuscript. Part of it. "You say you should have devoted more effort to organizing communications and to developing the capabilities of the RDF. You should have. But it was not the task for a happy man to be wholly focused on the RDF, the links between the spotter corps and Ops and dispersal and the pilots in the air." He bounced the pages. "This calls for a strict taskmaster. Detailed. Blunt. Undistracted."

A man with a loving family was not so disagreeable and difficult as the time demanded.

"You weren't there, Hugh Dowding. And you were

needed. And now you *dare* say you could have made a difference." He presented *Twelve Legions of Angels.*

"I never had the chance! I feel there is no one else who could fight as I do!"

"To make the hardest decisions ever demanded of a man, when God Himself is silent? To stay the course without knowing for sure that all would be well in the end? With only the conviction of your own rightness and trust in what you cannot see?"

"I would have. By God, I would have. I *never* asked to be relieved! I never *would* ask, had I the chance."

"Your children will never have been born."

Too many thoughts ramming together. Dizzy between hope and crashing despair. Drew breath with difficulty. "You're saying it can be done again!"

"It can be done the way you decided. What *did* you decide?"

Would have jumped at the answer, but for the cost. "What of the souls of my children? If they are never born, do I condemn them to the outer darkness?"

"None of us has the power to damn any soul but our own."

Sat silent, gazing at the stained glass windows.

The Pilot Officer stood up. "Be here Saturday at eleven o'clock if you did not ask to be spared."

"Then what will happen?"

"Then you did not ask to be spared."

"My daughter's wedding is at eleven o'clock."

Met the Pilot Officer's silent stare. Not a surprised stare. Rather disparaging.

"I can't!" Dowding blurted.

"Then don't." The Pilot Officer stalked out of the church.

Dowding ran out to the street after him, but of course he was not there.

When Dick Trafford had his report ready for delivery, the Reichsmarschall was to be found at a hunt club.

The German airman who admitted the British air attaché to the hall found his name amusing—Dick. *Dick* was German for *fat*. Dick Trafford, a slight man, was not *dick*.

"Our Hermann is *dick*!" The German laughed, ushered Dick to the Presence.

The girth and breadth of Hermann Goering were encased in a foxhunter's bright red habit, complete with black helmet and riding crop. A pack of cheerfully subservient English foxhounds fawned about his black boots.

Surely he did not mean to inflict that bulk upon some unhappy steed!

But no. The Reichsmarschall stood regally still, posing for an artist with two full tubes of red oils in his arsenal. In the adjoining chamber, exuberant young Luftwaffe pilots drank liberated brandy and talked with their hands under a cloud of aromatic cigar smoke.

Without breaking pose, Hermann's little eyes slid Dick's way. "So, Fat Trafford. Tell me about Herr Air Chief Marshal Hugh Dowding. Would anyone take his stupid book seriously? You are hesitating. That means yes."

"Not precisely," Trafford found his tongue. "No one with any knowledge of the facts would. But to a layman— Who knows? He bandies about technical terms and numbers with such authority, someone might take him at his word. What with his rank."

"He does not admit that you lost to German superiority?"

"No one ever questioned the superiority of German strength and numbers."

"So his plot to defeat my Luftwaffe was to . . . do what?"

"Rather a lot of nothing, from what I gather. He would avoid fighting. Reserves everything he can."

"And *that* was going to stop the Stukas!"

"The Spitfires and Hurricanes he reserved could have neutralized the Stukas. He says. Truthfully, Mr. Goering, Stukas *are* slow."

"Not in a dive." Goering's wide chest expanded in pride.

"Mr. Goering, *you* would be quick in a dive."

Silence gripped the club. The pilots' boasting from the next room, the clinking of glasses, even breathing stopped. The thump of tails wagging became very loud.

Until Goering's lusty laughter sounded the all clear, scattered the dogs, and upset the painter.

Goering dropped his pose, shooed the painter away, and called for a drink.

Told Dick Trafford that the RAF must silence Hugh Dowding. "He is yours. You take care of him."

And he was off to join his lads with a snap of his riding crop. "Tally ho!"

Clarice turned over in the bed, shook her husband's shoulder. "*Mis*ter Dowding! You are thrashing and you've got all the covers!"

To his mumbled apologies she offered to heat some milk. He told her that would be very nice, and the two shuffled down the stairs to the kitchen.

In the mundanity of this place—of the motions of this beloved woman, no longer young, heating milk, of his own slippers on his blue-veined feet—the demons with which he wrestled lost their reality.

He had been agonizing: Did I do this? Did I sell England for my happiness?

And if I sell my happiness back for England, what of my Clarice? My Sarah? My John? Their children?

Did I really ask for the burden of command during England's darkest hour to lift from my shoulders? And it *did*?

Here, now, the idea that he should yet hold the balance upon which the fate of the world hung seemed weird, impossible.

Well, there it is. I have gone completely starkers.

Caught between hideous alternatives, to live in guilt or to live in sorrow, he had discovered the obvious third—that there was no choice. He was a deluded old man who could only embarrass his daughter on her wedding day by chasing angels.

He was free to let it all go as God's will. He could live with his loving wife and dote on his coming grandchildren with a clear conscience.

There was nothing he could do.

A package arrived from Germany for the bride. The father of the bride saw fit to take a look before passing it on to his daughter.

A framed portrait of Adolph Hitler.

"It's odious!" Clarice cried. "Who could have done this!"

"The German Air Ministry." Dowding read the card congratulating Sarah on her wedding and wishing her many healthy Aryan children.

"What can we do!" Clarice shrieked in a whisper. "We can't give it to Sarah!"

"Certainly not," said Dowding.

"But someone is sure to call on her! What can she say when they ask what she did with it!"

"She shall tell them it hangs in her father's study. And so it shall." He whisked it away, out of sight of tender eyes.

Dowding was tapping a nail into the wall when the callers entered his study like storm troopers in RAF blue.

One wore an Air Marshal's insignia, apparently only here to lend authority, for one of the other men actually led this sortie. That one shook a fat pile of papers at Dowding, demanding, "Have you any other copies of this?" While the other men ransacked the room.

"This" was *Twelve Legions of Angels*.

Dowding advised his visitors that their lack of civility was uncalled for. They need not conduct affairs like hooligans.

The ringleader grew purple in the face. "Don't get the rest of us shot because you can't face reality! Exactly what did you expect to gain from this—this appalling treatise? The love of a nation?" High incredulity in that question. "It is over! It is *done*. It cannot be undone! You have nothing to gain except a bullet for rehashing it! And may I say, sir, you should be ashamed of this! What makes you think you could have done better than better men than you! *We gave all we had!*"

Dowding, politely, "What I proposed was that a more careful, less glamorous man might have spent all we had more efficiently."

By then the henchmen had found the carbon. Crammed all the pages of both manuscripts into the hearth and set a match to them.

"Open the flue if you don't mind awfully," said Dowding.

The callers stayed to see the manuscripts well and truly burned.

The Air Marshal, stone white in mortal embarrassment, offered a private aside, weakly, "You are taking this rather well, Dowding."

"I shall rewrite it," Dowding said without excitement.

The Air Marshal found the courage to look the man in the eyes. "Don't. Dowding, you embarrass yourself. You have a charmed life. You got through this war unscathed. You have a lovely family. Don't ruin it for yourself. Get out of London. Go back to Moffat. Stay out of public life. For heaven's sake, *write a different book.*"

"Write nothing!" the other shouted. "You lost France for us! The world does not need a tract from you on how wars are to be waged!" Looked to the guttering fire. "We can go now."

Dowding returned to hanging his picture. "When you see your masters, thank them for this gift."

They found their own way out.

The day arrived on which Dowding was to give his daughter away. He was rooting through the desk in his study after his best cuff links, when he glanced up to lock gazes with Adolph Hitler. The image caught the melting madness in the eyes.

That picture did not belong there. Not right. Not right. This should not *be.*

The indecision returned. Adolph and the clock ticking closer to eleven. The hour of decision.

What if he had actually talked to an angel? Could he afford to toss away the chance—the most remote, feeble and pitiful of chances—that it was true?

Perhaps remote, feeble and pitiful chances were all one ever got when it came to changing history.

It was insane. He could not possibly fail his daughter on her day of days.

Days that would never exist for her at all were he to follow the angel. Were the dire promise to prove true.

Had he certainty, he might have steeled himself to the task. But the possibility, the *probability,* remained that he was deluded. And grasping at a false chance held consequences as dire as those of which the angel spoke—no less dire for their lack of global importance.

His daughter's confusion, anger, tears, humiliation in front of everyone. The question *why*? She would never forgive him. The pain in Clarice's eyes. She would carry the betrayal like a wound for the rest of her days. Walk in shame on his arm. Shrink from the whispers behind hands—*Did you hear what he* did? Even his enemies could not speak of it without wincing. *Poor Sarah. Poor Clarice.*

Fumbling fingers rattled the cuff links in the drawer. He could not fasten them. Had to ask Clarice.

She fit them tidily into his cuffs. Straightened his collar, while their son John went outside to bring the car.

"You look grand Mr. Dowding. But pale. You feel cold. Are you well?"

He took her palm from his cheek, kissed it, pressed it back to his cheek. "I have all a man could ever ask heaven for. Ah, here's the car."

John bounded round the car to open the rear door for his parents. Snugged up the armband required of men in uniform in public.

Hugh Dowding's throat constricted. Sweat broke in pinpricks on his scalp. He drew his pocket watch to check yet again the advancing hour. Clarice's hand touched his. "Do stop."

Time dwindled as they rode toward the church.

Needles of fear stung under his tongue. Heartbeat shook his throat.

An overturned lorry brought them to a halt behind a line of cars. Progress continued by creeping starts and stops. Even Clarice became anxious.

"Not to worry," John said, turning hard down a side street. He negotiated a few more turns to come out on a parallel avenue.

One block north of the angel's church.

"What time is it?" Clarice asked. "Hugh? Hugh!"

Dowding was clawing at the back of his son's seat. *Aryan grandchildren.* "Let me out of the car. I cannot breathe."

Was already opening the door as John braked.

"Hugh! Where are you going! We are *late*!"

Shutting the door after himself: "John, take your mother ahead. I— You won't even know I'm gone."

Tyres screeched. Stopped just short of the man who had stepped off the curb.

Heedless, he proceeded at an old man's fragile running gait, straight across the path of the Air Marshal's motor car.

Dick Trafford sat up. "Good lord, is that Dowding?"

"Can't be." The Air Marshal watched the huddled figure go, kitted up in his best, running to a church. "I thought his daughter was marrying today."

"She is. He's gone to the wrong ruddy church!"

He looked terribly fragile. Seemed to have shrunk from the days when they had been adversaries. The Air Marshal regretted the visitation. The words. The burning manuscript. "That was . . . harsh."

"Did he not deserve it!" Trafford cried. "Pompous coward! Old twit!" Angry at Dowding's presumption. Angry that he should land the task of shutting him up.

"Do you think he will stay quiet? What if he rewrites his book?"

"I don't care." Trafford snarled the gears. "It is not as if anyone of any importance will listen to him."

The Air Marshal nodded, sat back. "Still. I cannot help thinking we treated him shabbily."

In the Prison of His Days

Joel Richards

On Easter Monday, April 24, 1916 (a bank holiday), a band of seven revolutionaries and perhaps seven hundred men ignited an uprising in Dublin against British rule. Doomed by nonsupport from the Irish Volunteers and the country at large, the rebellion failed after a week of bloody house-to-house combat that leveled much of Dublin's center and resulted in 130 British soldiers dead.

The rebels had solicited German aid, and a gunrunning ship, attempting a landing, was scuttled by its crew outside Queenstown harbor to avoid capture. The British used this pretext to quickly try the leaders by military courts-martial for treason and abetting the enemy. They were shot, rather than hanged, before Irish or British public opinion could be mustered in their behalf.

The iron chair leg scraped across the pitted floor.

The poet looked up from his notebook to his cellmate. MacBride's eyes were calm, the mustache fierce. Perhaps ill tended was a better word. Prison cells—these kind, without mirrors and with little enough light—did not lend themselves to careful barbering or even routine maintenance of facial hair.

Yeats was clean shaven, or had been two days ago. His hand rubbed over his chin, feeling the rasp of his own stubble. He was unused to this, sleeping in unwashed street clothes, the inability to shape his outward image. He was unused to the larger implications of confinement and imminent death.

"How do you do it, MacBride?" he asked in a low voice, and got back a cocked eyebrow of questioning, no words. Yeats waved an arm about him.

"Does soldiering prepare you for this?"

"It does," MacBride said.

"And death, too?"

"Ever at a soldier's back."

Yeats stood up, took a step or two to stretch out the kinks. A hangman's rope would do that as well. But this was a military barracks, and the others had been shot.

"Sheehy-Skeffington, that harmless, fey man! Can one credit it? The man's a pacifist and still they shot him. So why are we alive?"

MacBride smiled thinly. "Your literary reputation with these barracks types? I doubt it. Maud has been agitating and stirring up her contacts here and in London, I'm thinking."

Yeats nodded and tried to make sense of this. Maud Gonne had been and was the love of his life. She had offered Yeats spiritual love and friendship. She had married Major John (Sean) MacBride, choosing the organizer and leader of the Irish Brigade of the Boer army over Yeats. Yeats had asked Maud to marry him many times. MacBride had asked once—had it been with more decisiveness, less diffidence?—and she had accepted. Though long separated, in the Church's eyes the two were still wed.

What the Church would not put asunder the Crown

might, and probably would. Little good that would do Yeats. He and MacBride would continue their link in death.

What had it been? The crowds, duty, or a lonely impulse? All these and the madness of what was Ireland.

What had led him to this tumult?

Sunday was not a day for selling pipes and cigarettes in Dublin. Most fellows might think a fine March afternoon the occasion for a walk on Stephens Green with a favorite girl, or a rougher time at it with the lads on the soccer pitch. Tom Clarke was rather too old for either. Too frail, some might say—but not many. Certainly not the military and constabulary powers at Dublin Castle who knew him well.

Tom Clarke was a naturalized American citizen who played a harder game than soccer. In his youth he had been convicted and imprisoned in London for bomb making. Now he was back in Dublin again, doing business in a modestly sized but highly aromatic tobacco shop on Great Britain Street that announced itself in Gaelic as belonging to T. S. O'Clerigh.

Another type of business altogether was being conducted this day. Present were seven rebels comprising the Military Council of the Irish Republican Brotherhood who would later elect one of their number, Patrick Pearse, as President and Commandant-General of the Irish Republic. Pearse was a poet, playwright and headmaster of St. Enda's Irish-Speaking School, himself possessed of a mystical but highly compelling vision of restoring Ireland to its days of splendor and heroism. In stark contrast was the trade unionist, James Connolly—hard-nosed and almost equally a socialist and an Irish revolutionary. He had organized and commanded his own Citizen Army, apart from the Irish Volunteers who made up the far larger body of Irishmen covertly under arms. Also in the conclave was Thomas MacDonagh, university lecturer and critic, and a dynamo of talk and action. Others included Joseph Plunkett, the movement's battle tactician and a man about to undergo an operation for glandular tuberculosis, and Sean McDermott, an upbeat but tough motivator of men.

There had been some good talk. Questions of military planning and logistics had been worked over in good Irish fashion. No amount of words, however, had been able to talk away the inadequacies in manpower and armament of the insurgent forces. Unsaid till now but hanging over the meeting was the palpable fear that this rising would likely be another bloody Irish failure.

Pearse addressed the matter.

"The Volunteers as a body will not be with us. At most we'll get those who are already IRB men, perhaps a few more. We need to rouse a citizenry of irregulars and turn them into a force of nature."

He paused and looked about him. Some of his compatriots stared back, puzzled and uncomprehending. Joe Plunkett opened his mouth in a roundfaced grin and spoke.

"You and MacDonagh are our academics, Padraig. I sense something in your line."

"Indeed," Pearse said. "I think we can get Yeats."

"The poet?" Clarke asked. "Are not the days gone when poets fought beside kings, devising *ranns* whose powers could shatter battlements and break spears? Would that such days maintained! Ireland is acrawl with poets—more of them than serpents before St. Paddy's time."

"And none better than Yeats," MacDonagh said. "He is not a great orator, but his words and reputation are power in their own right. He was one of our Brotherhood and a revolutionary in the days of the Centenary riots—he exhorted the crowd—and could be one again."

"A bit old, wouldn't you say?" Clarke said with a mischievous grin.

"Fifty-one to your fifty-seven," Pearse laughed. "As well you know."

"But are his fires as hot as Tom's?" McDermott asked.

"Banked, rather, I'd heard. What makes you think we can get him?"

"I spoke to him in the street yesterday. He's restless and anxious, asking himself the kind of questions a man does in his middle years, without a cause—as yet—as ours to answer them. You know of his love for the actress Maud Gonne. It's shaped many of his poems these last twenty years."

"She married Sean MacBride," Plunkett said.

"MacBride's back in town," Pearse went on. "And Yeats knows it. Maud has left MacBride these several years, and Yeats still burns to win her. He fears that he must act rather than versify or play consort to her nationalistic schemes. He told me so. We can marry the appeal of his love for his country and his lady."

Clarke smiled. "You're a poet, too, Padraig. Very noble of you to bring aboard Ireland's best. He's bound to upstage you in that department." His eyes turned deep. "But by all means let us have with us a man whose words and presence will raise the nation. And chronicle our fight. But can we get him?"

"I've asked him to join us." Pearse looked at the shop's walnut-and-brass sea captain's clock. "He'll be here in ten minutes—2:30."

"Risky, Padraig," Clarke said. "How much does he know?"

"Nothing concrete. But he's far from a fool. I think he has drawn the true conclusions."

"Can he keep his mouth shut if he doesn't buy in?" Plunkett asked.

"Yes," Pearse said. "But it's our job to sell him. Let me tell you how we'll do it."

William Butler Yeats stood at the mirror in his rooms at the Hotel Nassau on this fine spring afternoon and considered his appearance.

Augustus John had sketched him in 1908, giving him a wild "gypsy" cast, or so Yeats had thought, but rendering him alive and vigorous. Charles Shannon had painted him quite charmingly, resembling Keats. Best of all had been the charcoal drawing of John Singer Sargent, sharp-featured yet with a sensitive mouth, looking passive but verging on a decisiveness Yeats seldom could rouse. His hair was parted to a high and uncombed forelock that fell over one eye, lending a Byronic note overall. His body then had been lean.

And now, eight years later? The hair was still there, but it framed a face of more fleshiness and care. The eyes were more puffy than dark and deep set. What had George Moore said of him on his return from his American lecture tour? " . . . with a paunch, a huge stick and an immense fur overcoat."

"You left out the intestinal troubles, George," Yeats muttered, and turned toward the door.

Bright sunlight dappled the Dublin streets through shade trees and overhead wires. Open trams trundled boater-topped men and their ladies to the parks. Single men on cycles whipped in and around them and the occasional plodding horsecart. Yeats stood at the curb looking for a chance to step off.

William Butler Yeats did indeed have a good apprehension of what awaited him in a closed-for-business tobacco shop on a Sunday afternoon. Particularly when it was the shop of Tom Clarke and his invitation had come from Patrick Pearse. Pearse had ostensibly talked of literary matters, referring pointedly to Yeats' own poem, "September 1913," bemoaning the trading of Irish romanticism and nationalism for moneygrubbing. Pearse had let Yeats know that not all Irishmen had made that bargain.

Yeats had no illusions of the men he'd meet or of himself, not this day. He had written a more recent poem, "To a Friend Whose Work Has Come to Nothing." In a dark moment he felt he'd written it of himself.

But the prospect of redemption was at hand.

With resolve and vigor Yeats stepped off the curb. Today

he had no need of a fur coat against the March breeze nor a huge stick to support him.

"Gentlemen," Yeats said mildly.

"Mr. Yeats," murmured some of the assembly. "Willie," said MacDonagh and Pearse.

Yeats settled into the vacant chair, the only one in the room with arms, and clearly for him.

"I more than suspect that the IRB is planning a rising," he said, and held up a forestalling hand. "What do you want of me?"

"We have the shock troops to mount a rising," MacDonagh said. "We need the country behind us to make it stick. Otherwise the British will wear us down."

"Ah," Yeats said. "You want me to write your pamphlets, your addresses and exhortations. Odes to the rising. Maud was always after me for that in the '90s, and I wouldn't. I was more idealistic about the uses of my art then. But I suspect you want more."

"We want your pen, Willie, and your voice and your name," Pearse said, and smiled. "All three have increased in value since then."

"You have several jobs, it seems. Tell me in what specific capacity you want me, and convince me that this rising has a chance for success."

"We don't have a cabinet yet, Willie," MacDonagh said. "We shall once we declare a republic, and we can make you a cabinet minister. Minister of Information, perhaps. But for the moment we are a military organization. This is the Military Council of the IRB, and Pearse is Commandant-General. I propose a staff rank of general for you, reflecting the eminence that poets of ancient *Eireann* had to their kings."

"A general," Yeats repeated softly. "I've taken on roles, worn masks, but never one such as that."

He sat back in reflection. The others sensed his inward casting and held silence.

What am I? Yeats considered. *What have I truly done in this life? What is my legacy? I am a minor poet of narrative lyric work and plays. Verses and essays of a parochial Irish nature, written in the style and tradition of Rossetti, Pater, Herrick and others of an earlier day. I have no wife, nor am I likely to have one. Maud won't have me in that role. I leave no children. And in the modern, real world emerging, I have no credentials. Perhaps if I live through—and shape—this rising I can find a more forward-looking and expansive arena for my poetry. For we will be dealing with life and death in our time, and not Cuchulain's.*

And—an inward chuckle bubbled up—*perhaps* this *would win me Maud.*

If this is self delusion, well . . . perhaps I'm allowed an indulgence now and again.

He looked up. Pearse met his eyes, and spoke:

> "You'd cry 'some woman's yellow hair
> Has maddened every mother's son.'
> They weighed so lightly what they gave.
> But let them be, they're dead and gone'
> They're with O'Leary in the grave."

Yeats sat upright in his chair. "I take the point, Padraig, even when you make it with my words. There's work to be done, and we're not dead and gone. Not yet. So let me hear your plans for making this grand thing work."

While much of Dublin was enjoying the quiet of a bank holiday following Easter, a body of irregular soldiers poured forth from Liberty Hall, a large structure devoted to trade unionism on the banks of the Liffey. This was not the Irish Volunteers, a broader based group which commanded the largest number of armed and organized men in the country. Its leader, Professor Eoin MacNeill, had ordered his 10,000 men to withdraw from Easter Day maneuvers once he knew that leaders of the IRB had planned to escalate them into what he considered to be a disastrous and quixotic insurrection. Some of his men joined the rebels nonetheless.

This was the Citizen Army, headed by a more radical, bolder (some might say more impetuous) leadership. Patrick Pearse, James Connolly and Joseph Plunkett formed at the front of the HQ company, all self-proclaimed Commandant-Generals. Though not all of the soldiers were uniformed, or even armed with rifles, these three wore green uniforms crossed by Sam Browne belts and sheathed ceremonial swords.

Four city battalions had mustered elsewhere and were occupying their positions around the center of Dublin and Dublin Castle itself—administrative headquarters of the British occupation and (a complicating factor) also a Red Cross hospital. These city battalions were charged with impeding troops from the British barracks in the outlying reaches of the city from pinching in on the rebel command post, which would be set up within the General Post Office—once it was taken.

The generals formed up their column of perhaps fifty men, backed up by a couple of trucks and motorcycles and a late addition, Michael O'Rahilly—known as The O'Rahilly, himself being the head of that storied clan. Cofounder of the Irish Volunteers, he had arrived at the last minute in his green Ford touring car, which he helped load with homemade bombs and spare ammunition. Though his organization had attempted to abort this revolution, his addition to the force gave it a huge lift. With a sure touch for the apt word, he had announced, "I helped wind this clock. I've come to hear it ring."

At their leaders' command the column set off for O'Connell Street, a broad boulevard flanked by a few stately Georgian homes and an array of hotels, shops and public buildings. Dominating this scene was Nelson's

Pillar, 135 feet tall and capped by a statue of the naval hero. Ambitious view seekers could climb its winding steps for a fine outlook over the city and, near to hand, the GPO.

Bemused and largely puzzled bystanders watched this bizarre and faintly ragtag procession on its progress along Abbey Street, then up O'Connell. A bunch of British officers watched from the Metropole Hotel where they took rooms. They had seen such maneuvers, even mock battles, before, and regarded them as comic opera turns that afforded them much amusement. It came as a surprise to many when Connolly, in a loud, stentorian voice, brandished his unsheathed sword and yelled, "The Post Office—charge!"

His troops, those with rifles waving them and firing them in the air, poured through the main entrance. They met no defending force; for all its neoclassical splendor, it was a post office, after all. Within minutes the building was taken. Only two persons within sight were of even vaguely military status. One was a Dublin policeman, the other a British lieutenant sending a telegram to his wife. Pressing onwards, the occupying force found seven British soldiers in the upstairs telegraph office, the post office guard detail. They had been issued guns but no ammunition. They became the first prisoners of the revolution.

Connolly looked out through a pall of smoke toward the Liffey and his longtime bailiwick, Liberty Hall. A burning glow suffused the air, a false sunset to a long Wednesday not ending well.

"The bastards have shelled Liberty Hall. Well, that I expected, but never that the capitalist swine would shell their own factories and public buildings. Hotels, even!"

"You're thinking too much like a socialist revolutionary, Jim, and not enough like an Irishman. They hate us and what we're doing more than they love their property." Pearse nodded toward the Metropole, late billet of British officers and now a sniper's outpost of the revolution, and also in flames. "They'll destroy their property rather than have us use it."

The building shuddered from the shockwave of a nearby hit.

"A lot of those fires are set by looters," Connolly said, and shook his head. "I had hoped more of my class would have joined us than pillaged and burned."

Pearse wasn't interested in continuing this ideological discussion.

"That's an eighteen-pounder. They've brought a gunboat up the Liffey, too. Well, we've lasted three days, more than Emmett's rising, but we can't last much longer digging in to positions that'll soon be pulverized." He turned to the IRB's strategist. "What do you say, Joe?"

Plunkett looked up from his maps, looking every bit a man who was dying except for his piercing eyes. His neck was bandaged from his recent surgery, and his face was wan as if the bandages had served instead to block the blood from his cheeks

"I'd hoped for better than this. We're in defensive positions and we don't have the guns or men to mount a sortie, much less take another building. We need the country to rise with us."

Pearse turned to Yeats. "You can write us a *rann*, Willie, but we need a means to promulgate it."

"A newspaper," Yeats said. "I have friends at the *Irish Times*."

"Reactionary rag," Connolly growled.

"The publishers, indeed," Yeats said. "Not my friends."

Pearse gave him an intense look. Yeats had traded his billowing shirt and silk tie—the city clothes that Pearse had known—for rough country tweeds and hobnailed boots. He looked very much a man ready for hard and dirty work. His eyes had the raging look of a burning king of yore, fiercer than Plunkett's. Pearse could hardly credit his eyes.

"Forget their offices," Yeats continued. "Get me to their print shop and the type setters. If the telephones still work I'll get the night editor there. We'll publish your proclamation and my statement and—yes—a poem. Get some copies out of the city to Cork, Limerick, Tralee. Let that be the spark to fire the land!"

"Yes!" Pearse seized Yeats' hand. "We'll round up a squad."

"Smaller is better, Pat," Plunkett said. "I'll see if Ned Daly can spare some men to reinforce them once they've made it."

Pearse looked out over the abandoned street, raked by sniper fire of tommies and rebels alike at any sign of movement.

"Dusk is best," he said. "The smoke is bringing it sooner."

Yeats looked out at the mass of rubble that was O'Connell Street. Some of it was the wreck of gaping storefronts—shattered glass, occasionally glinting orange in the reflection of flames, tattered awnings, overturned counters and mannequins thrown out into the street. Horsecarts and trams lay on their sides. Two dead horses, killed the first day in a silly and bloody charge of mounted British lancers, lay stiff-legged and putrifying in the lee of Nelson's Pillar. Some of the rubble had been organized by the insurgents into a barricade—huge rolls of newsprint, mattresses, all or parts of drays and trams, furniture, even bicycles, all baled together by pulled-down tram wires and the one roll of barbed wire the rebels had rounded up.

Michael Carroll beckoned his men forward with a swing of his arm, then motioned to Yeats to fall in behind.

"Our men will cover us from the Metropole. There's a bolthole in the barricade by that bakery wagon." He grinned. "I dummy-wired it myself."

The squad streamed out into the twilit haze. The streetlights had been shot out, but a couple of snipers banged away nonetheless, their bullets skipping and whining off the cobblestones in puffs of stone dust. The rebels dodged their way to the barricade, and three of them flopped down in the cover of a tram's steel wheels.

"None of that, Joyce," Carroll yelled, pulling the nearest man erect and pushing an upended shop counter aside. He led his men through the gap. Yeats could hear the ring of his own nailed boots on stone as he ran hard to keep up. They burst through the barricade and veered for the corner of Abbey Street. A machine gun stuttered. Yeats strained forward, toward the head of the zigzagging line of men, reaching Carroll's shoulder. Carroll looked back over his shoulder and took a bullet in the throat. His mouth puckered to an "O" as he fell to his knees. Yeats moved to hold him from toppling over. The rest of the men turned the corner without looking back.

"The *Times*!" Carroll's voice was a mouthed rasp protracted by the whistling of air through the hole in his trachea. He held out his rifle to Yeats. "Go!"

Yeats took it, set Carroll down, then tore for the corner. Four remaining men waited there, winded and indecisive. Yeats passed them on the run. "With me!" he yelled, and fired his gun in the air. He looked back. The men were with him.

Yeats swung around, facing forward again. Turning into Abbey Street, advancing in a line abreast and at a slow trot, was a squad of fusilliers led by a florid-faced sergeant. There was no time for either side to fire. Yeats hit the gap between two tommies, swinging his rifle barrel across the cheekbone of the man nearest him. He could hear it crack as the man went down. Yeats was through with three of his men behind him. They were near the burned-out Liberty Hall now, and friendly fire covered them in their dash to the *Times*' print shop.

Lights blazed within. No low-country hearth had ever looked so beckoning.

"Good work with that rifle." Harry Joyce grinned at Yeats as Yeats pounded on the door with his rifle stock. Joyce nodded approvingly. "That's all she's good for now, General, until you reload. She's a single shot."

The place didn't feel like a newspaper office, but it was going to do for one. Print shop or no, there were desks there. Yeats had commandeered one and was writing away at white heat.

"What is it to be?" Doheny, the night editor asked, waiting patiently until Yeats had put down his pen.

"Narrative poem," Yeats said. "Not Wandering Aengus, Cuchulain, Cathleen ni Houlihan. A poem of modern times and modern men. Here are the first pages."

Doheny scanned them, then looked up.

" 'A terrible beauty is born.' Aye, but that's a good line, and true." He nodded. "Many fine lines."

The sky was lightening, the ruddiness of the sun playing over the glass shards by their feet.

"More light for their gunners," Doheny said gloomily.

The door below shook with heavy pounding. Joyce edged to the window, unslinging his rifle and edging it out before him.

"It's Ned Daly's men!" bellowed a voice below. "Let us in."

"Reinforcements," Joyce said. Yeats bent back to his writing. The sound of heavy boots broke his concentration and a draft of cold dawn air caused him to look up for his coat. His eyes met the black stare of a hard-featured, lean figure, erect in bearing and not the vainglorious lout Yeats wanted him to be.

"MacBride," he said, and felt sick.

"Yeats."

This was too much. Yeats knew quite well that though it was Ireland that he was fighting for, it was also the shade of the professional soldier—personified in his life by Sean MacBride—that he was fighting against. Or at least trying to outdo in his own head and perhaps in the affections of Maud Gonne.

But MacBride was no shade. He was here, very much alive and very much—so it seemed—a comrade in arms.

Yeats turned away to face the night editor.

"When can you go to press, Mr. Doheny?"

Doheny's answer was drowned in the explosion of an artillery shell's immediate impact. Yeats' eardrums felt like bursting as the explosion rocked the room. The shock knocked him to the floor, plaster and lath caving down on him from the ceiling above. A wave of heat followed behind. Men screamed.

"The paper rolls! The bastards have hit the newsprint!"

"Everybody out!" MacBride ordered, his body outlined by the inferno behind him. The smoke was roiling before the flames, turning the air black. Yeats crawled, then stumbled to the front door, MacBride behind him.

Yeats looked up at a squad of soldiers, khaki clad not green, rifles ready and bayonets deployed not six feet from him.

"Put up your hands," MacBride said softly behind him. "Or we'll be dead before your next breath."

"A visitor, Major," Banks said. His voice held a softer and even awed tone, one that Yeats had not heard before from the jailer. He looked toward the door.

A figure in black, taller than Banks, stood in the shadows by the jamb. A priest, perhaps?

"Maud!" MacBride whispered hoarsely.

"Sean, Willie," Maud Gonne said, and strode into the room. A backwards glance from those glittering eyes sent the jailer scuttling back, closing the cell door and locking it before tramping away.

"They let you in," MacBride said. A silly remark, Yeats

thought, saved from fatuity only by the heaviness of the situation.

"They've let me little else," Maud said, throwing her cape aside in a careless but graceful gesture. Stage manners without thought. "For once the Church is good for something. I'm your wife."

She moved between the two men and took the hand of each.

"Still your friend, Sean. And yours always, Willie." She paused. "You bold, foolish men."

Yeats nodded. "That we are."

"They're going to shoot you." Yeats felt Maud's grip tighten. She let drop her hands and turned away.

"I expected no less, Maud," MacBride said. "This is my second go at them. They've not forgotten the first."

"That I know, Sean, and little could I do for you. And I tried for you, Willie. So did our friends in England—Wilde, Pound, Shaw. They've tried to get the Prime Minister's ear."

"I've lunched with Asquith," Yeats said. "Little good that will do me."

"They fear the power of your pen, Willie. They'll take the heat of public indignation to your ongoing threat to rally Eireann."

"Bad news but expected. I'd rather hear it from your lips than any other's."

Maud took a step back to better survey them. Dark hair a helmet to that fairest of faces. Beautiful still and always.

"I come to deliver more than news. Ireland's love and mine. It's yours and always will be." She looked at Yeats. "And some words to water it down the years? Have you that for us?"

Yeats reached to the table behind him.

"Two poems."

Maud took the papers, turned away to read.

"They're grand, Willie. 'Easter 1916.' That will hold the

day green. But this second one. And what do you know of Irish airmen?"

"Little enough. But I know something of foreseeing my death. I learn more each minute."

Maud looked at him. "Ah, Willie—the poems you might have written! What a bargain you have made!"

Yeats focused on the pin at Maud's breast, Ireland's green and gold. He moved his eyes up to see in hers a respect and regard he'd not seen before.

"A good bargain, Maud." He paused. "The best."

Labor Relations

Esther M. Friesner

It was in the Month Without Gods, in the third year of the great invasion of the three Korean kingdoms, that Old One's great-great-granddaughter Snow Moon went out to fetch water and came home with a Japanese soldier. She found him slumbering behind some thorn bushes that grew on the mountain where Old One's special seeing-spring leaped forth from the rocks. He wore a *tankô* over his clothes—the short-bodied iron cuirass favored by the invaders—with his helmet and spear laid out on the ground beside him. It would have been an easy thing for even a child to grab the spear and spit him through the throat, then and there, but he was young and handsome and, since the war had begun, Snow Moon had come to an age when such things mattered.

So it was that Old One looked up from her iron tripod through the open doorway of her hut to see the child of her grandson's daughter come walking along the village path, prodding a shamefaced Japanese soldier along before her with his own spear, his bronze shortsword thrust awkwardly into the sash of her jacket.

"Now what?" she muttered. She rose from her stool, shook the wrinkles from her seer's robes, and came out into the sunlight, blinking like a toad.

The girl's route home from the mountainside took her and her prisoner through most of the village, so that by the time they reached her great-great-grandmother's house their progress was attended by every woman, child, gaffer, dog, pig, and chicken with time to spare and curiosity to waste. The young man's face grew pale as he trod the narrow path between rows of hostile faces. The war had gone on for long enough to drain the village of all its able-bodied males, leaving behind wives and sweethearts whose patriotism had soured more and more with every winter's night when all they had to occupy their minds was needlework. There was only so much embroidery a woman could do before she realized there were some itches that a dainty little needle was insufficient to scratch.

It was one such badly deprived lady who threw the first clod of pig manure. Others soon followed her example.

To his credit, the young man did not flinch from that less-than-refreshing rain. Instead, he turned in his assailants' direction and allowed his face to melt into the most charmingly regretful smile anyone in the village had ever seen. On so handsome a face, such a tender expression was utterly devastating. The village filled with the echoing plops of manure balls dropping from nerveless hands and of many women crying out to the young man in pity, apology, and invitation.

Old One saw all this and shook her head. "Idiots. First they threaten his life one way, then another. Can't they see he's one of our enemies? He may know things that will prove priceless to our own armies." She hastened forward, bulling her way through the sea of clamoring females, all the while shouting, "Fools! Headless chickens! This man is valuable! Will you kill him and waste what good he can do us?"

Most of the crowd stepped aside for Old One, but the blacksmith's wife—a woman as sturdy as her husband's anvil and as fearless of his hammer—stood her ground. "You don't have to tell *me* how valuable he is," she replied. "Just look at that back, so strong and young! And those arms! And those legs! He's healthy as a horse and twice as beautiful."

"And you'd be just the one to break him to the saddle, eh?" Old One spat deftly, so that the gob landed just an inch from the other woman's toes. "Wait until your man comes home and I tell him that."

"*If* my man comes home." The blacksmith's wife glowered. "It's been almost three years since the war began and no sign that it will ever end. And if it does, will there be a single man left alive in all the three kingdoms?"

"Well, they're not dead yet," the young man spoke up.

Old One and the blacksmith's wife turned to stare. "What did you say?" Old One asked. The Japanese soldier's grasp of the local tongue was serviceable but a trifle shaky and she wanted to be certain she had not misunderstood.

"I said that no one's dead," he repeated. "It is the will of our Empress, the serene lady Jingo, who leads us into glorious battle. Uh . . . more or less glorious. And I suppose you couldn't technically call it *battle,* but—"

" 'Us', you say?" Old One interrupted, regarding the young man closely. "I see only one of you."

The young man lowered his eyes. "I am in truth only one. I am called Matsumoto Yoshi."

"You are called worse things. You're a deserter, aren't you?" The young man did not reply, and his shamed silence was an eloquent confirmation. "I thought so," Old One said with satisfaction. "Just what this village needs: A pretty coward."

"I am not a coward!" Matsumoto Yoshi's eyes flashed angrily. "Ask anyone who knows me!"

Old One cocked her head to one side. "Here?"

The young man was not disposed to chop the logic of his declarations. "I did not leave our army because I feared death," he continued. "I left because I could no longer bear the insult to my manhood that this war has become. Who ever heard of battles without bloodshed, campaigns without corpses? How is a warrior to make his reputation without killing *somebody*? But such is the will of our Empress." He scowled, a grimace which did nothing to diminish his beauty. The village women sighed and murmured that it was very naughty of the Japanese Empress to deprive such a fine young man of the opportunity to advance his chosen career through applied slaughter.

Old One turned to Snow Moon. "My stool and my pipe," she said. When these were brought, she settled down, lit the gummy nubbin in the silver bowl, and inhaled the smoke deeply before addressing the visitor once more.

"What a great gift you have brought me, Matsumoto Yoshi," she said. "If I live to be two hundred I shall never be able to thank you enough."

"Gift?" the young man repeated, confused. "What gift?"

"At my age, anything new is a gift, for I awaken each day with the dreadful conviction that I have already seen all that this world has to offer. Only by encountering something new do I manage to go on living. Take your case, for example: You have given me not one but three fine gifts. First, you bring me word of a woman commanding troops. This is wonderful."

"The Empress is only doing what her late husband, the Emperor Chuai, should have done while he yet lived." Matsumoto Yoshi's tone was downright sulky. "He took a vow before his divine ancestress, the great sun-goddess Amaterasu, that he would subjugate this land, for such was her desire. But he kept putting it off and putting it off—doubtless because he did not yet have an heir who might assume the imperial throne—until it pleased the gods to take him into their company."

"A man who would rather make love to his wife than go out and steal another man's land?" Old One raised one tufty white eyebrow. "In that case, make it *four* gifts you've brought. How munificent!"

"What are the remaining two?" A distinct chill had come into the young man's voice. He looked down his nose at the old woman on her stool as if he had already conquered the village and all who dwelled in it single-handed, solely by the force of his having been born able to pee neatly while standing up.

"Don't take that tone with me, sonny," Old One said, chuckling. "You only enrich me. The other two unheard-of things are these: That a war is fought without killing and that a man is fool enough to think this is a calamity. I would like to meet your Empress; she sounds clever. Tell me, little fighting cock, how *has* she managed to keep a war going for three years without a single death?"

"By the favor of the goddess Amaterasu, of course," Matsumoto Yoshi said haughtily. "The divine one gave the Empress a pair of miraculous gems, the Tide Ebbing and the Tide Flowing Jewels. By these, the serene lady Jingo was able to subdue the very waves of the sea and to bring our armies here in safety. By these she continues to rule the waters, making seas and mighty rivers do her bidding."

"Is that so? *That* would be a sight worth seeing."

"I've seen it," Matsumoto Yoshi said dully. "I have done nothing but see it since we left home. Every time we have had the chance for a good, settled, murderous battle, the Empress calls upon the power of the Tide Ebbing and the Tide Flowing Jewels and suddenly there is a great and unwelcome incursion of water, preventing any combat. Your people pursue ours or ours pursue yours, only to have the Empress call a halt to the chase time and time again by invoking Amaterasu's tokens."

"A strange strategy for a general intent on conquest," Old One mused. "What can she have in mind?" Rising from her seat, she motioned for Snow Moon to approach. "Pack food and clothing and the apparatus of my profession. We will visit this Empress Jingo."

So it was that Old One, Snow Moon, and Matsumoto Yoshi soon left the village behind, retracing the path by which he had first reached them. The young soldier was in a foul mood, one which became fouler by the footstep.

"I don't know why I'm doing this," he grumbled as he led them along.

"You are doing this because you don't want to die," said Old One.

Matsumoto Yoshi gave a short, bitter laugh. "A true warrior does not fear death."

"A mad warrior does not fear death," Old One corrected him. "A true warrior fears death but faces it anyway. As for you, I see you are an idiot warrior, so I couldn't say what your attitude toward death would be."

"Oh! Grandmother!" Snow Moon gasped at such rudeness to one so young and strong and handsome. "How can you speak to him so? Isn't he doing your bidding willingly? Isn't he guiding us where we want to go?"

"Willingly," Old One repeated. "As long as you and I hold his weapons." Her hand closed comfortably around the hilt of his captive sword and she nodded at the great spear now in Snow Moon's keeping.

The girl seemed eager to take the handsome young man's part against her ancestress. "You know as well as I that if he tried to escape, he would easily outdistance you and that sword. As for me, I am intimidated by this powerful shaft; it's much too big for me to handle skillfully."

"You'll learn," Old One said. She turned to their guide and added: "I ask your pardon, Matsumoto Yoshi. By taking us to meet your Empress, you are indeed performing a great service for us, but a greater one for your own people, for I mean to put an end to this endless war."

"I don't see how you'll do that," he said sullenly. "When we reach the Empress' encampment, you will be taken prisoner. As for me, I can't even enter the precincts, for if I'm seen, I'll be arrested for desertion and my fate will be a dishonorable death."

"Oh, I don't think so," Old One said. "But if you do make good your escape a second time, take a miserable old woman's advice: Become a recluse and live alone. On no account make your presence known in any village or town in all Korea for, if you do, the women will get you, and then you will surely die."

"Ha!" Scorn contorted Matsumoto Yoshi's face. "I don't think any of you women knows what to do with a spear any more than this sweet maiden does."

Snow Moon blushed at the compliment, but Old One herself said, "You would not die by spear or sword. We women have a secret weapon. Like your precious Empress, we know that victory does not always go to the side that can command sharp, sudden sorties and incursions, but to the side with the most staying power. In other words, in a land where so many men are gone from home, you would be sucked drier than an old persimmon rind in a fortnight. Do you follow me, boy?"

Matsumoto Yoshi did. At first he leered, but the leer soon dwindled to a weak smile which quickly faded to a look of badly controlled panic. "You—you think that if I rejoin my troops, the Empress won't call for my death?"

"I promise it," said Old One. "For behold, have you not brought her a precious gift?"

"I have? What?"

"Me."

The Empress Jingo sat in her hilltop pavillion, contemplating her *tankô,* its iron shell adorned with a riveted skirt, every rivet on skirt and cuirass capped with gold. It had been made to her exact measurements, which gave her both comfort and protection, but absolutely no leeway when it came to gaining weight. It hung from a lacquered rack, attended by her bow and quiver. Beneath these, in a green box with a gold pattern of sea waves, resided the Tide Ebbing and Tide Flowing Jewels, Amaterasu's gracious gifts.

Two of Amaterasu's gracious gifts. Despite the awesome power contained within the small green box, there was still a third gift which the goddess had bestowed upon the Empress that left the mastery of wave and water looking dreadfully pathetic by comparison.

She rose and crossed the pavilion to where a polished bronze mirror on a wooden stand awaited her pleasure. She was not a vain woman, though her beauty gave her every right to be, and while her royal husband lived she had spent scarcely any time at all studying her own image.

"Three years changes much," she murmured to her reflection. "And nothing." She stood sideways and ran her hands down the front of her tightly cinched robe, over the perfect flatness of her belly. Incredible. The marvel of it all never ceased to astonish her.

She was thus wrapped up in her own thoughts when they brought her the news: Matsumoto Yoshi had returned with prisoners of war. For love of his Empress he had taken it upon himself to scout the land in hopes of finding something that might help the war effort. The gods had blessed him and he had found such a thing. He begged the Empress to honor his miserable efforts on behalf of the imperial house of Yamato by deigning to view his offerings.

The Empress Jingo sighed and called for her servants. They dressed her in her warrior's garb—a serviceable tunic and wide-legged trousers tied below the knee, both with the gorgeous embellishments proper to her rank—helped her don her *tankô* for effect, and laced on her leather arm-guards. Only then did she step outside.

"Women?" she exclaimed when she saw Matsumoto

Yoshi's "offering." Old One and Snow Moon stood one to either side of their supposed captor, each with a small bundle of possessions at her feet. "You have captured *women*? For *this* I put on armor?"

"Most excellent lady, this is no ordinary woman," the young soldier said quickly, pushing Old One to the fore. "She is a great power among her people, a seer of inestimable talent. She is also terribly, awfully, extremely and acutely old."

"How old is she?" the Empress asked, raising one mothlike eyebrow.

"I am so old that there are rocks who call me grandmother," Old One spoke up. "I am so old that the name my parents gave me at my birth got tired of waiting for me to die and preceeded me to the grave so that now I am known simply as Old One. I am so old that I remember when dragons were plentiful enough for housewives to have to use brooms to chase the smaller ones out of their gardens. I am so old that I recall the days when Japan was not the only land which the men of China called the Queen Country." She stared meaningfully at the Empress.

"That's old," the Empress Jingo admitted.

"She is a treasure," Matsumoto Yoshi went on. "If word reaches the Korean troops that we have her, they will at last accede to a peace parley. Your excellency will be able to set your own terms and acheive your goal of hegemony over the Three Kingdoms. The war will be won, the gods will be satisfied, and we can all go home!"

The longer he spoke, the more Matsumoto Yoshi began to believe his own words and the greater his enthusiasm grew until he was joyfully prophesying a swift and immediate victory. The Japanese troops, all massed in their ranks before the Empress' pavilion, took fire from him and began to cheer in a most raucous manner.

The Empress Jingo made a small mouth and gave Old One a sideways look that as good as said: *Men*! Old One shrugged and both women smiled.

"Honored guest in my land," Old One said when she could at last be heard above the soldiers' clamor. "If my age commands any respect at all from you, I beg you to grant me a private audience."

It was a simple request, innocent, and readily granted. Old One picked up her bundle and carried it into the imperial pavilion while the Empress commended the care of Snow Moon to Matsumoto Yoshi. Only when Jingo had been relieved of her armor, refreshments had been brought, and the last servant had been dismissed did the women speak.

"You're not his prisoner, are you," the Empress stated.

Old One chuckled. "And you are not going to have him put to death for saying I was."

"I should. His whole story is riddled with lies like a block of rotten wood with wormholes. More likely he was your prisoner—though how that came to pass I can not say—and bringing you to me was your idea alone. He didn't undertake an expedition to help us win the war; he ran away."

"True. But he has come back, and with me, and I am in fact the treasure that he paints me. You will not call for his death, O Empress."

"You sound sure of that."

"A war that drags on for three years with not a single casualty, all thanks to those Jewels of yours, and you want me to believe you'd be capable of ordering an execution?"

Jingo's brow darkened. "Don't underestimate me. If it is necessary, I will command that a life be taken. If needful I will take that life myself."

"You are not a coward, O Empress," Old One said, calmly raising a teacup to her lips and slurping contentedly. "You don't fear death, but like all good housewives you despise wastefulness."

"You dare to call me a housewife?" Jingo sprang from her seat, bristling. "I am the Empress of all Japan!"

"Same job, bigger house." Old One drank more tea. "You see to it that everyone under your roof is properly fed and clothed, you look to the future and provide for it, and you do your best to keep your beloved children from harming themselves or others."

Jingo held onto her anger for a few heartbeats longer, then slowly sank back onto her stool. "I see your point."

"Now if only I could see yours." Old One helped herself to some of the little leaf-shaped cakes that the Empress' servants had left behind on a tray. "A war without deaths—very admirable, but to what end?"

"The same end as all wars: Victory."

"Yes, but victory to be acheived by what means? We chase you, you chase us, we all get ready for a fight, and before anyone can draw his sword—*whoosh!*—an uninvited river. Nothing is decided and the chase resumes. This is a war with neither gain nor loss for either side. Let it go. Pack up your quarrelsome children and go home."

"I can't," the Empress replied. "Such is not the will of the gods."

"We have other gods in these lands. I have brought my tripod so that I may invoke our divinities. When they appear I'll ask them to pay a social call upon your gods and settle the whole thing amongst themselves."

"That would be futile. This is the Month Without Gods, the yearly time when the great *kami* gather at Izumo. But even if our gods were here, your offer would be rejected. This war is the will of Amaterasu, benevolent ancestress of the imperial house. She first entrusted it to my beloved husband—"

"—the Emperor Chuai, yes. That nice young man told me. Is that the only reason why you pursue this war? Because you fear that if you disobey, the benevolent goddess will kill you, too?"

All that Jingo replied to this was: "Bah."

"You are so certain of her good will?"

"Naturally. She did not order this war for herself—what need does the great *kami* of the sun have for mere mortal kingdoms?—but for the enrichment and advancement of her beloved descendants, the imperial house of Japan."

Old One's wrinkled face twisted into an expression compounded of disbelief, surprise, and unconditional rejection of every word she had just heard. "O wise Empress, with all due respect and every honor due to your position, I ask you: Are you out of your mind? *What* descendants? Your husband is dead, and you may correct me if I err but as I understand it *he* was Amaterasu's descendant, not you."

"I will not correct where there is no error," Jingo said. "He was in fact then the last of her line."

"And he died three years ago." Old One felt uneasy in her bones. Surely the Empress did not need to have such things spelled out for her? She *looked* sane enough.

"I know it well. I mourn him to this day and will forever honor his memory. All the more reason to win these kingdoms for our son."

Old One's mouth opened. No sound came out. She closed it again, then made another stab at expressing herself, but this one likewise came a cropper. Closing both her mouth and her eyes she took a deep breath, mentally rattled through the names of her eleven husbands to center herself, and finally was able to say, "Your husband died *three years ago*. Do they handle these matters *that* differently in Japan?" She pointed definitely at the Empress' flat belly.

Jingo laughed and placed her hands over her abdomen. "In the natural course of things, we women of Japan handle these matters much as do you women of Korea. I know I don't look like a woman with child, but—"

"Three *years*," Old One insisted. "He's been dead for three *years* not three *months*. You, a woman with child? By this time, you should look like a woman with water buffalo!"

"All thanks to Amaterasu. I fulfill her wishes and she permits me thus to carry her descendant, the Emperor-to-be, until this war is over."

Old One looked skeptical. She had had many years' practice at it. "Now let me see if I have this right," she said. "You are enduring a pregnancy of three years' duration, so far, that will not come to its natural end until you win a war that you are waging without bloodshed?"

Jingo graciously acknowledged that this was so.

"In that case, O Empress, I don't need to set up my tripod to read your future: You're going to be pregnant a long, long, *long* time."

"I disagree. In fact—" the Empress flashed Old One a playful smile "—the war is almost won. You see, I have within my power a weapon of such devastating strength, such awesome might, such—"

"I know, I know: The Tide Ebbing and Tide Flowing Jewels."

Jingo lightly waved away Old One's mention of Amaterasu's miraculous gifts. "Beside *this,* they are nothing. For this is a weapon that slowly but surely devours from within, and against which there is neither protection nor remedy."

"Poison?"

"Boredom."

The Empress stood up and began to pace the rice-straw mats that floored the imperial pavilion. "You have lived long, Old One; you know the way of things. A man begins a war with his head befogged by dreams of winning everlasting glory in battle. Soon enough he learns the truth, that every battle is an island of rousing terror surrounded by a sea of spirit-drowning tedium. I have found the way to sink those islands and cover all the land with a war so dull, so inert, so uneventful, that it is only a matter of time before *everyone* deserts just to escape the monotony!"

"If everyone deserts, how can anyone win?" Old One demanded.

"By the old rule of the last man standing. Only in this case, he will be commanded by a woman."

"What! You think your forces will triumph? They'll be as bored as ours!"

"Yes, but when my men debate running away, they will remember that they have a much longer road home, over a sea whose tides *I* control. Your men, on the other hand, will think of their wives and sweethearts, the comforts of their homes which stand oh, so much closer at hand! And that's to say nothing of the lure of home-cooking over army food. One fine day your kings and generals will wake up to face a sea of empty encampments. They will surrender out of pure embarrassment. All we need to do is outwait that day. It is only a matter of time."

Old One stared in awe at the Empress. *Brilliant,* she thought. *She may be crazy—a* three-year *pregnancy?—but she's right. A war without battles can only endure for so long until even the most glory-blinded man gives it up as a bad bargain. And there are practical matters to consider as well: Our kings can not feed their soldiers forever, not when those soldiers are the same men who must be home to till the fields. But the Japanese will be fed with supplies from their own land, carried on ships sped across the waters by those accursed Jewels. An empty belly swallows dreams of glory quickly. It is only a matter of time indeed, and then . . . defeat.*

Old One got down on hands and knees and pressed her forehead to the mats. "O Empress, who can stand against the truth? I concede your eventual, inevitable victory and humbly offer you my services." Sitting back on her haunches, she added: "I have seen the banners of our armies raised on the hillside opposite this one. Let me go there to speak with the kings and the generals, let me explain to them the futility of prolonging this war. I am sure that we may reach an accord whose terms will satisfy both our peoples."

"Don't be silly," said the Empress. "What terms? I win, I get Korea. Well, my son the Emperor-to-be will get Korea, but I'll take care of it for him until he's old enough to appreciate it."

Old One did not care to hear her country spoken of as if it were a piece of Chinese porcelain to be kept out of reach of a rambunctious toddler. "Unconditional surrender? Is that all you will accept?"

"It's all I need to accept."

Old One scowled. The Empress met her angry look with an expression of utter composure. Both women knew that there was only truth behind Jingo's words, a truth that the Empress saw no need to honey-coat in order to make it more palatable.

The Empress could not know that Old One was as fond of honey as any bear, and just as liable to make reprisals if deprived of it.

You are as arrogant as a fortified town, O Empress, safe behind the walls of your goddess, and your Jewels, and your indisputable strategy, Old One thought, closing her eyes lest the sight of Jingo's complacent face should make her lose her temper at a diplomatically inadvisable juncture. *I have never cared for walls. I swear that I will be the one to bring them down around your ears. Have I lived this long, mastered so much lore, learned so many spells, gathered so many memories and not one among them all will save my homeland? May the gods close my eyes with earth if that is so! The answer lies within me. The question now is only . . . where?*

Old One retreated deep within herself, searching for the solution she knew she must find. With her eyes thus closed and her breathing slowed by deep contemplation, she lost all track of time. She was unaware that she had become the picture of an ancient woman who had grown weary of the world's commotion, had settled her dignity around her like a cloak, and simply had taken her leave. Her sudden silence and immobility alarmed the Empress, who grabbed her by the shoulder and called out her name in a most distracted manner.

"*What?*" Old One snapped like a turtle at this imperial interference with her meditations.

The Empress had not expected the presumed corpse to speak. She gasped and tottered back a few steps, her hands on her stomach. "Oh! Praise all the gods, you're still alive. For a moment, I thought— Don't ever do that again. Whenever I'm scared, it goes straight to my belly, makes my insides shake like *tofu*. Bad enough I've had morning sickness three years' running. You should apologize."

Old One's eyebrows twitched just the smallest degree. The three silver hairs that sprouted from the wart on her chin quivered. It was all the outward sign she gave to acknowledge that her prayers had been answered: She had her weapon.

Swiftly she clapped a look of the utmost concern over her face and shuffled forward on her knees to seize the Empress' hands. "A thousand pardons, august lady!" she wailed, swaying like a willow in a gale. "May the gods forgive me! What hideous harm have I perpetrated upon your royal beneficence? Oh, what have I done? What have I done?"

"What *have* you done?" the Empress asked, yanking her hands free of Old One's grasp. Although she had demanded an apology, she hadn't expected anything on this scale. She still looked worried, not so much for Old One's sake as for her own safety in the presence of a demented creature.

"The shock, my lady! The shock that I have inadvertently caused you. Do you not know how dreadfully bad it is for the unborn when the mother suffers any sort of emotional upheaval? I have lived long; I could tell you stories. My great-aunt's neighbor's brother's third wife was frightened by a wild monkey, and her son was born with the longest arms you ever saw. Then *her* father's nephew's sister-in-law was startled by a rampaging stork, and so her son was born with the longest legs you ever saw. And *her* sister's husband's cousin's bride was surprised by a runaway rooster, so her son was born with the longest— Well, they're not all tragedies, but still, can any woman take a chance when it is the very body of her child that may be unalterably altered?"

The Empress' eyes grew wide and wider as Old One's words played upon her fears. The aged seer contained her glee. Although she still could scarcely believe Jingo's tale of her amazingly extended pregnancy was real, the younger woman certainly was behaving like other first-time mothers: She was crossing unfamiliar territory and she was afraid.

"The gods—" Jingo faltered. "The gods would not allow any harm to come to my son."

Old One pressed her palms together. "What do the gods consider to be 'harm'? Health is one thing, appearance another. Do they view matters of mortal beauty as we do? Are all of them pleasing to the human eye?"

"Raiden . . . Raiden, the god of thunder, has fangs," the Empress admitted. "And Fujin, lord of the winds, has a most . . . astonishing aspect. His skin is the color of pitch, his feet and hands are taloned, and his face—his face is— Ah!" She covered her eyes and moaned. "Oh, my child, my child!"

Slowly Old One got to her feet and patted the Empress' back. "Do not fear, my lady. It has been proven that the unborn is only marked according to the nature of the thing that frightened its mother. It's not as if you were scared by the wind-god; just by me."

Jingo's head jerked up. "What do you mean?"

"I mean that if any change has befallen your child, he will enter the world looking no worse than this." Old One spread her arms wide and gave the Empress her broadest smile. Every wrinkle, every missing tooth, every bald patch, every brown spot and gnarled knucklebone and sag of slackened flesh on her body stood out in dreadful relief. Jingo gaped, then groaned.

Hmph! Thank you so much, Old One thought. *Think* you'll *look like a little plum blossom if you live to be my age?* Keeping her resentment to herself, she reassured the Empress, saying: "Gracious lady, never fear! Your case is not hopeless. I can help you."

The Empress looked suspicious. "Why should I trust you or your remedies?"

"Think I'd poison you? Leave your troops without the one leader willing and able to fight a bloodless war? They'd run wild, burning crops, destroying villages, taking indiscriminate vengeance for your death on men, women, and children. Am I fool enough to make such a bad bargain for my people? The choice is plain: Trust me or trust to luck for your child's fate, O Empress."

Jingo rubbed her chin in thought for awhile, then said, "Tell me what you need."

The clay bowl nested amid the glowing charcoal cakes, smoking and sputtering. Old One knelt beside it, stirring it with an iron spoon. Seated on a low stool, attended by her captains and once again wearing full armor for its imposing effect, the Empress Jingo watched.

Her men watched too, but with more hostility than interest. Their Empress had explained the cause of these uncanny doings. Some muttered that Old One ought to forfeit her life for having frightened the Empress and perhaps imperiled her unborn son, but Jingo quickly silenced them.

"Perhaps no harm has been done to him," she told them. "That is what Old One seeks to learn first, by summoning a vision of the child. If all is well, why kill her? And if he has been affected, she will create a potion to set things right. To kill her for that would be ungrateful."

"No killing, no killing, that's her answer to everything,"

one of the captains grumbled. He glowered ferociously at the seething clay bowl and demanded: "What have you got stewing in there?"

"A measure of vinegar, another of water, the skull of a fieldmouse, powdered fine, fishbones and scales, a pinch of red earth, a dribble of pine sap, and a sliver of dragon's toenail: Nothing fancy." Old One grinned.

"And *that* mess will let us see our Emperor-to-be?"

"That mess—" Old One sniffed the steam rising from the bowl, then let her long sleeves slide forward to cover her hands as she removed it from the tripod and set it at Jingo's feet. "—and you." She bowed, then said, "O Empress, my lore can summon my gods, but your unborn babe is the descendant of your own divinities. To invoke a vision of the child, both companies of deities must aid us."

"But I've told you: This is the Month Without Gods! The *kami* are in faraway Izumo—"

"Then you'll have to call upon them *loudly*, won't you?" Old One said. "You and all your troops together. When I give the sign, shattering the clay bowl, raise your voices and shout: *O great* kami *Amatasa— Amarusa—*"

"Amaterasu."

"That's the one. Thank you. So it must go: *O great* kami *Amaterasu, with your blessing we beg to behold this unborn child as he truly is.* Have you got that? It is vital that you speak these words *exactly*—you know how it is with magic—otherwise I couldn't be held responsible for the consequences."

The Empress repeated the seer's invocation several times, to make sure she had it down pat, then directed her captains to relay the words and instructions attending them to her troops. Signalmen were placed as the word ran through the length and breadth of the Japanese encampment. Old One watched it all, and while the commotion was at it's height she managed to steal a word with Snow Moon.

"Beloved child of my grandson's daughter," she murmured. "Very shortly, a small clay bowl will smash into a hundred pieces at the Empress' feet. When that happens—"

"—you want me to clean it up?"

"I want you to run."

Snow Moon was a good girl, biddable, raised to say yes first and to ask why twenty-third. Satisfied, Old One waited for the Japanese encampment to settle down. Then she bowed again to Jingo and simply said, "We begin."

It was a very impressive ceremony, one of Old One's best. She swayed and sang and made all sorts of fascinating gestures. She threw pinches of this and that into the smoldering coals, raising little spits of colored smoke. She chanted words in a tongue so ancient and arcane that even those Japanese fluent in Korean had no idea what she was saying. Neither did she. She let down her hair and used the wooden combs to trace strange patterns in the dirt, then danced over them. She carried on in this manner for a long time, until she saw the glazed stares of the onlookers and knew beyond the shadow of a doubt that when she gave the signal, they would all cry out the words her plan demanded without hesitation, simply because they would shout *anything* just to get this over with.

So she snatched up the bowl and smashed it at the Empress' feet; shards went flying. And from the uncounted multitude of troops, from the throats of the imperial captains, from the mouth of the Empress Jingo herself, there arose an obedient roar aimed for the ears of Amaterasu, demanding that the great *kami* of the sun reveal the child as he truly was.

Izumo was very far away, but they were *very* loud. Someone heard; someone who thought that so importunate a prayer was very like a direct order; someone who thought that after all She had done for Chuai's widow, it was highly impolite of the lady to come demanding things, especially during the Month Without Gods; someone who was just annoyed enough to change Her mind about the whole Korean expedition as quickly as a sunbeam darts from the Plains of Heaven to the fields of Earth.

Someone who thought that if She answered Jingo's prayer just as it was phrased, it would serve her right.

The gilded rivets holding the plates of the Empress' *tankô* exploded from their seatings with a sound like the crack of summer thunder. They whizzed in all directions, faster than an arrow's flight, pinging off the captains' *tankôs* and helmets. The iron plates of the burst imperial cuirass hit the ground with an emphatic clang, soon followed by the reluctant rending of sturdy cloth. Yet all this uproar was no more than the whisper of petals falling on water when compared to the Empress' scream. It was not a scream of agony, but of shock, and betrayal, and red-eyed rage. And it was *loud*.

Old One heard it only as a very faint and distant sound at her back. She had taken to her heels the instant after she'd smashed the clay pot to pieces. She was remarkably speedy for a woman of her age and she didn't stop running until she was in the midst of the Korean forces.

She had already called for an audience with the ruler of the kingdom of Silla by the time Snow Moon caught up with her, accompanied by a familiar third party.

"Who invited *you*?" Old One snarled when she saw a breathless Matsumoto Yoshi clinging to Snow Moon's arm.

"As an honorable warrior, I still consider myself to be this beautiful maiden's prisoner," he replied, panting. "Besides, I'm not stupid enough to face the Empress now. Not after what you did to her. Not until she forgets that I was the one who introduced her to you."

"That might take some time," Old One said. "I left her with rather a large memento of my visit." She shrugged. "I don't know why she's so angry. She's the one who wanted to know how her unborn child was doing."

"She thought she was asking Amaterasu for a *vision*

of the child," Matsumoto Yoshi said. "The child itself has had three whole years' growth in the womb!"

"Still in there, too. And her unable to give birth to it until the war is over," said Old One. "Tsk. You know, for a woman, and an Empress, and a general, she really ought to pay closer attention to how she words her commands."

The king of Silla emerged from his tent just then; Old One and the others bowed before him. "O great ruler," she said. "I am a seer and I bring you news: The war is ending. I promise you that shortly, word will come from the Japanese Empress herself, suing for peace."

The king had the haggard look of a man brought to the end of his rope by frustration. Such men mistrust good news, having been disappointed many times in the past. "Just like that?" he asked. "After all this time, all that water, *now* she quits? Why? Has she suddenly lost her stomach for war?"

"I wouldn't say *that,*" said Old One. "In fact, I *couldn't* say that at all."

Empire

William Sanders

"History," the Emperor often said, "is a lie agreed upon."

"And who'd know better?" Captain Houston said, when I quoted the line to him. "About history, and about lies. Having been responsible for such a hell of a lot of both, in his day."

He did not say it loudly, though; his usual alligator-bellow voice was for once a discreet murmur, though no one was nearby. Houston was a bold young man, even by the standards of his kind; but mocking the Emperor was a dangerous business, especially during that final year.

In any case I did not reply, and after a moment he chuckled and glanced at me. We were walking down the swept gravel walk toward the front drive-way of the palace, the Emperor having told me to see Captain Houston to his carriage. Captain Houston had just returned from a secret mission deep in Spanish territory, and had found his way back from Florida to New Orleans through hundreds of miles of wilderness known only to his Indian friends, so presumably he was capable of finding his own way out; but the Emperor was always one for the courtesies.

"You ought to write a history book yourself," Houston said, grinning. "The things you've seen and heard, it'd be worth reading."

"Slaves do not write histories," I pointed out.

"I heard somewhere that there were slaves who wrote books," Houston said. "Back in Roman times."

"This is not the Roman Empire," I answered, and bit off the irreverent addendum, "However much His Majesty likes to think so." I had no wish to match him for riskiness of wit; for myself I have always found bravery a vulgar quality, and those who possess it generally tiresome—though I did like Sam Houston, who had a keen sense of irony, no doubt acquired from living with the Cherokees.

"Well," he said, "there's my carriage, Albert," giving my name the English pronunciation rather than the proper one. "Good night."

Three days later the British arrived.

I was there when the Emperor got the word; in fact I was the one who brought it to him, though only in the sense of taking the sealed message from the dispatch rider—who was sweating, even though it was a December day and quite cool for New Orleans—and carrying it on a silver tray into the Emperor's private study. I did not, of course, know the contents, but I had my suspicions.

The Emperor read the message, smiled slightly, and tossed it onto his desk. "Well, Albert," he said, "the ball would seem about to begin. His Britannic Majesty's forces have put in their long-awaited appearance off our shores."

It was not, you understand, any great surprise. It was common knowledge, even in the streets of the city, that a large Royal Navy squadron, with a convoy of troop transports, had been working its ponderous way across the Gulf, shadowed at a discreet distance by Lafitte's people.

The Emperor got to his feet, slowly and clumsily, breathing loudly with the effort. I made no move to assist him; His Majesty's increasing corpulence and deteriorating health were among the many things one was required not to notice.

He walked over to the great windows that overlooked the palace grounds. "Ah, Albert," he said, his back to me. "Do you know, at times I wish myself back in France."

I said nothing, merely stood in respectful silence. I knew what was coming, having heard it so many times before.

"I have not seen France since the year 1793," he mused, his back to me. "Yet in some sense it will always be my second home. Strange; I have no such feelings, now, for Corsica."

He turned slightly, placing his face in profile. The morning light sharply silhouetted the famous features; the body might have grown corrupted, but that incredible head was still as beautiful as ever.

"Perhaps," he said wistfully, "I should have stayed. That was my intention, after all, when the traitor Paoli drove the Buonapartes from Corsica. I had no thought but to return to France and resume my military career. It was sheer chance that that American ship happened to be in the harbor, while I was seeking passage to Marseilles to rejoin the family, and that I fell to talking with the captain—and made a sudden impulsive decision, and the rest, as they say, is history."

He turned and smiled at me. "Who knows? Had I followed my original plan, surely I would by now be an officer of rank in the forces of the Republic. Not that that would be such an enviable fate, now," he added, "after the drubbing the British and their allies have given the Republic's armies. But perhaps I could have changed all that, eh? That fellow Wellington might have found General Buonaparte a harder adversary."

"As indeed he soon shall, sire," I murmured.

"What? Oh, yes, of course. Excellent, Albert!" He

laughed. "Yes, it would seem the Duke and I are destined to do battle, in one possible world or another."

His mouth twisted. "If, if. If not for Paoli's treachery, I could have been the liberator of my homeland, and spent the rest of my days as ruler of Corsica. Treachery is a terrible thing, Albert, to be execrated above all other human sins."

I kept my mouth shut and my face blank, and tried to suppress the picture in my mind—of the late Colonel Burr, or rather his ghost, listening to that last little homily. The exquisite treachery by which the Emperor had disposed of his old partner would for sheer seamless detail have impressed a Borgia.

History, by the way, still seems silent on the question of just when and how the former Captain Buonaparte, now a newly commissioned lieutenant in the tiny United States army, chanced to meet then-Senator Burr. I have an impression it was at some sort of social function in New York, but I may be mistaken; at the time, after all, I was still a half-grown servant boy in a wealthy New Orleans household, being educated above my station by a capricious and indulgent owner. (Interestingly, it is possible that the Emperor and I were learning English at the same time.)

Whenever and wherever it happened, it was certainly one of the most fateful encounters of all time. I wonder if they recognized each other, in that first moment, as two of the same breed? Much as two sharks in the lightless depths of the ocean must apprehend their common species. . . .

"But then," the Emperor said with sudden joviality, "in that case who would now reign over the interior of North America? Perhaps your famous and talented relative Tecumseh, eh?"

"Tecumseh is Shawnee, sire," I said very diffidently. "My father's people were Choctaw." Not that it mattered; my mother having been quadroon, I was unequivocally "black" under the laws of the Empire.

"Albert, Albert." He laughed softly and gave me a fond look. "I tease you, but you know how highly I esteem you. See here." He adopted the manner of one who has just made an important decision. "You have been a good and faithful servant for many years. When this business with the English is concluded, I intend to free you."

I bowed my head, as if overcome. "Sire," I said most humbly.

He did this, on the average, two or three times a year. It meant nothing. As many men—and women—had learned, the Emperor was too great a man to be bound by a trivial thing like a promise. But one had to pretend.

The next day they had a big council in the palace war-room. Standing beside the door, awaiting requests for drinks or whatever else the military leaders of the Empire might require, I witnessed the whole thing.

"So," the Emperor said, looking down at the map that covered most of the great conference table, "our guests have arrived, and we must make ready to welcome them. The question is, where?"

"No sign of any landings yet," Colonel Crockett observed. "They're just sort of hanging around offshore. Last message I got from Sam, he said he could just make out their sails, out in Chandeleur Sound."

He scratched absently beneath his fringed buckskin jacket; a gross discourtesy in the royal presence, but the Emperor tolerated much from the eccentric and extremely able chief of scouting operations. Half the alligators in the swamps were in Crockett's pay and the other half his blood relatives—or so it was said.

General Jackson snorted loudly. "By the Eternal, I don't suppose your 'boys' could trouble themselves to give us a more detailed report?" He and Crockett hated each other; it was one of those deadly personal enmities at which the Tennesseeans excel. "At least an estimate of the enemy's numbers?"

"No need," the Emperor said mildly. "We have, after all, a full roster of the enemy's forces, and have had for some time."

This was true. The Emperor's secret agents were everywhere, on both sides of the Atlantic, and very good at their work. If he had wanted to look it up, he could probably have learned the name of the trooper who watered Wellington's horse.

The Emperor was studying the map. "I confess," he said, "I am having trouble envisioning how they plan to do this."

Even with my own utter lack of military knowledge, I could see the problem. New Orleans is an oddly situated port; below the city, the river runs a hundred miles or so before reaching the sea—but it does not flow through solid land, but down the middle of a strange narrow alluvial peninsula that sticks out far into the Gulf, a kind of penis of the continent. The whole shoreline is a perfect mess of lakes, bays, bayous, and cypress swamps, with hardly any firm ground. How the Duke of Wellington proposed to get past all that was more than I could understand.

"Can he come straight up the river, do you think?" the Emperor suggested dubiously.

"It would be difficult." General Latour, the chief of engineers, gestured at the map. "The passage is not an easy one, after all. They would need local pilots—"

"Not impossible to get," Captain Lafitte put in. "Many of the people along the river and the coast are Spanish, and none too loyal to the Empire."

"But they would still have to get past our shore batteries," Latour went on. "Especially here, at Fort St. Philippe."

"Yes." The Emperor nodded. "But how else? Land on the shores of Lake Borgne, or the Ponchartrain?"

Lafitte stepped forward. "Not so simple as that, my Emperor. Lake Borgne is not deep enough for big ships. They could cross it in shallow-draft boats, if they have them, and work their way up the bayous, but it would be a difficult and risky business." He tapped the map with a fingertip. "And the Ponchartrain would be even harder."

He grinned. "Now me, I know half a dozen ways to get at this city through the bayous above Barataria Bay. But Wellington could never do it, not without my people to guide him."

Neatly done, I had to admit; a diplomatic reminder of the service the Barataria pirates had done the Emperor, by refusing British attempts to buy their aid, and later by doing sterling work in keeping track of the movements of Lord Nelson's ships.

Of course it could have been pointed out that Lafitte and his brigands were at least partly to blame for the whole situation, since the official *casus belli*, according to the British, lay in their constant and heavy depredations against British and Spanish shipping—under perfectly legal letters of marque from the government of Republican France—but that would have been specious; the British had long had designs on the Mississippi, control of which would make them once again masters in North America. Lafitte had merely supplied a handy pretext.

"By the great Jehovah!" General Jackson was given to such bombastic oaths; it was one of his many annoying traits. "I still can't believe they plan to attack New Orleans at all. This Wellington must be a fool. He could land at Mobile—a bunch of Creek squaws could overwhelm our defenses there—and march overland, raising the Indian tribes against us. The red devils would be glad enough to join them—"

"They would," Colonel Crockett assented grimly. "Thanks to the treatment they've had from people like you."

The two men exchanged glares. The Emperor said pointedly, "The savages are not our present problem. The Duke of Wellington is. And, General Jackson, I assure you he is no fool."

It was hardly a secret that he detested Jackson as an ill-bred lout—most civilized people did—and distrusted him for his arrogant ambition. But however troublesome and even dangerous Jackson might be, he was the one man who could control the fractious backwoodsmen who populated the interior of the Empire and made up much of its army. The Tennesseeans and Kentuckians and Indianans and the rest had been happy to break away from the United States—the fledgling republic east of the mountains had never meant much to them—and join in the "liberation" of the Spanish province of Louisiana; but their allegiances were personal rather than national, and the Emperor, for all his charm, had never captured their hearts as had Colonel Burr.

Now Burr was gone, and only Jackson still held their childish loyalties. And so the Emperor dared not eliminate him; and so Andrew Jackson, alone among the Emperor's original co-conspirators, remained obnoxiously alive. There was no doubt, though, that he was a competent officer in his way.

Now he gave Crockett a final withering look and turned back to the map. His neck, above the high gold-braided collar of his uniform coat, was even redder than usual. "So what do we do, then?" he asked, as always omitting even the most basic forms of respectful address.

The Emperor rubbed his face with one hand. "There is not a great deal we *can* do, until we have a clearer idea of the direction of the attack. We must not spread ourselves thin, trying to cover all the possible approaches. No," he said, "much as it goes against my instincts, for now we wait."

So we waited; everyone waited, while the life of the city underwent dramatic changes. Troops marched through the streets, volunteer units drilled in parks and fields, women made bandages against the anticipated carnage; and the warehouses along the river-front began to fill up with cotton and sugar, there being no way to ship anything out now that the Royal Navy waited at the river's mouth.

Then one of Crockett's men brought word that a force of warships had been seen on the river, working their way upstream. A few days later a message arrived from Fort St. Philippe that the place was under bombardment.

"Well, now we know," the Emperor said. "Wellington and Nelson have chosen the direct approach. I had expected something less obvious."

"Begging the Emperor's pardon," General Latour said, "but do we in fact know?"

"That's right," General Jackson agreed. "Could be a feint."

"Quite true. We will wait a bit longer before fully committing ourselves. However," the Emperor said, "we can make a beginning. Latour, I want the defensive works along the river strengthened—requisition slaves from the plantations hereabouts, you have my authority. Jackson, bring me a report on what artillery we have available. If they are coming up the river, we will need every gun we can lay hands on."

He glanced out the windows and sighed. "The greatest city on the North American continent," he said, "the beautiful, sophisticated capital of a country of inexhaustible riches. Parks, opera houses, institutions of learning, fine homes . . . and," he slammed his fist suddenly down on the table, "not one God-damned cannon foundry! No one can be bothered with manufacture here, they are all determined to get rich from cotton and sugarcane. *Merde!* Right now I would trade half of this city for a few batteries of heavy field guns."

He fell silent. No one ventured to speak. Even Jackson for once had sense enough to keep quiet.

Certainly no one offered to point out that the Imperial army had at one time possessed a superb corps of artillery, with modern weapons purchased from France and brought in despite the British blockade—and had lost most of it, first in Mexico and then, two winters ago, in the dreadful retreat from Canada. Especially Canada. One definitely did not talk about Canada.

Really, there were so *many* things one did not talk about nowadays.

Over the next two weeks all eyes, so to speak, were turned south, as the British bombardment of Fort St. Philippe continued. Messages from the scene spoke of constant heavy fire from bomb-ships—whatever they might be—while a relief party, sent overland, was ambushed by British marines and all but wiped out.

The atmosphere in the city grew tense and strange, as news of these events trickled down to the populace. The most absurd rumors began to circulate, and here and there citizens were attacked—a couple fatally—on suspicion of being British spies.

Indeed the times seemed to bring out the demented. One day not long before Christmas, while I was in the city on a minor errand, I was suddenly accosted on the street by the Mad Marquis. "Hey, boy," he cried, and put his face close to mine. "Haven't seen you in a long time. Come," he said, hooking my arm in his, "walk a little with an old man. I have no one to talk with, these days."

I glanced nervously about; I had no wish to be seen in the company of the Marquis, who managed to cut a notorious figure even in hard-to-shock New Orleans.

He was not a native of Louisiana, but of France, where he had once been famous—or infamous—for his scandalous writings and equally scandalous personal life. He had been repeatedly imprisoned, first by the royal government and then by the revolutionaries; but then the family contrived to have him shipped off to America, where he could no longer embarrass them. The Emperor tolerated his presence—a favor to certain friends with influence in Paris; anything to maintain the all-important French alliance—

on the condition that he refrain from publishing his outrageous writings within the Empire. (They were, however, widely though illegally circulated in the United States; former President Jefferson was said to be quite a devotee.)

He and I had met at a certain establishment, where he was a regular customer—too old for active participation, he still paid to watch whippings—and where I occasionally made a bit of pocket-money, without the Emperor's knowledge, playing the pianoforte. The proprietress had known my mother.

"Albert, Albert," he said now, "how does His Majesty? Well, one hopes?"

I said that His Majesty did quite well. "Good," he said. "I so admire the Emperor, you know. In a world of canting hypocrites, a man who knows how to take what he desires!"

He dug an elbow into my ribs. "The affair of Colonel Burr, for example. Magnificent! I am dazed with admiration!"

Again I looked about, this time in real fear. No one was anywhere near, but still I tried to pull away. His grip, however, was amazingly strong.

"Oh, not to worry," he added. "No one has been talking. Merely a cynical old man's speculation—but I see by your face that I was right. Ha! Never fear, the secret is safe with me."

He leered conspiratorially at me. "The public all believe the story they have so often been told, and why not? It is, after all, a masterpiece of fiction—I say this as an author in my own right—and the corroborative evidence! The incriminating letters in Spanish, the drawings of the defenses of New Orleans and Mobile, the bag of Spanish gold pieces, the final heart-rending note confessing all—my friend, if I were not such an experienced creator of imaginative tales I would believe it too."

By now I was fairly gibbering with horror, yet he kept his hold and continued: "But the crowning gem, ah! That the smoking pistol clutched in his lifeless hand should be the very weapon with which he had killed Monsieur Hamilton! Sheer poetry!"

I managed to wrench myself free, finally, and I am not ashamed to admit I took to my heels. I had not realized how dangerous the old maniac was. Or what a shrewd intelligence functioned within that deranged head.

(All the same, he was wrong about the pistol. In fact, as I once heard Colonel Burr tell the Emperor, it was Hamilton who furnished the weapons for the famous duel. That detail was not part of the original package, as it were; the story simply arose somehow—possibly from some journalist of the popular press—and was repeated until it became widely accepted. Mr. Irving even put it in his history book.)

Reaching the corner, still at a run, I almost collided with a couple of buckskin-clad figures. A hand grabbed my jacket and pulled me to a stop, and I started to protest, but then I recognized the laughing faces of Colonel Crockett and Captain Houston. "Here, now," Houston said, "what's the hurry?"

"Been talking to the old Mar-kee?" Crockett asked, grinning. "Boy, he's a piss-cutter, ain't he?"

I was too breathless to speak. "Come on," Houston said. "We were just on our way to get us a drink."

They pulled me into a dark and dingy little tavern, where a few idlers sat talking and playing cards. A burly man in homespun clothing looked at me and said loudly, "No niggers allowed in here!"—and in less than a second found himself on his back on the floor, with Crockett's foot on his chest and Houston's knife at his throat.

"You got something to say," Crockett inquired gently, "about who we choose to drink with?"

A few minutes later we were seated in the rear of the room with a jug on the table before us. The people at the nearby tables had considerately moved away and given us our privacy. The one who had spoken first was nowhere to be seen.

"Drink up," Houston advised me. "You look like you could use it."

The raw corn whiskey was quite the worst drink I had ever tasted, but I managed to get a little down, and my nerves did settle a bit. Crockett and Houston applied themselves to the jug with gusto. "Damn good booze," Crockett said approvingly. "Here's to Andy Jackson, the son of a bitch."

"Better drink to crazy old King George," Houston suggested. "Could be we ought to get in practice."

"Is it that bad?" I asked.

"Half a dozen years ago," Crockett said, "I would have said we'll kick their asses back into the Gulf. Now—" He shrugged. "This army ain't what it used to be."

"Oh, shit," Houston said dolefully. "Here he goes again, playing the old soldier."

"Playing hell. I been in this from the start, son. I was toting a rifle under Old Hickorynuts back when we were just a bunch of raggedy-assed rebels, didn't know what we were getting into except that Burr made it sound good and his little French pard was the fightingest one human we'd ever saw. I was there when we marched into this town for the first time and kicked the Dons out, when you were still just a brat."

He paused to lubricate his throat. "And I was there when we fought Mister President Jefferson's pitiful little army—the ones that didn't run away or change sides—when the States tried to take Tennessee and Kentucky back. I was there when we took West Florida from the Dons, too. By then we had the best damn army, for its size, in the world. Hell, the Prussians used to send officers over here to study old Nap's methods. But then—"

He spat on the dirt floor. "Then we couldn't quit. Spent a year putting that fool Joseph on the throne of Mexico and another two years trying to keep him there—quit looking at me like that, Albert, I don't give a coon's ass whose brother he was, he was a God-damned fool and ending up in front of a 'dobe wall was no more than he deserved."

I grabbed the jug and took another drink. This time it went down almost easily.

"Used up a big piece of the army in Mexico," Crockett continued, "specially the cavalry. Lost Pike there, too, best damn officer we had, Jackson ain't a scratch on Zeb Pike's ass as a general. Then before we'd even started to recover—"

"Canada," Houston said. "He's going to tell about Canada."

"What for? Ever'body in the whole world knows what happened. Shit." He made a face. "Oh, it was gonna be so easy. All them Catholic Frenchmen in Canada were so eager to rise up agin the King and jine us. And France was gonna send ships and troops to invade up the St. Lawrence at the same time. Only," he said, "turned out the French Canucks didn't like us no better than they did the redcoats, and Nelson caught the invasion fleet leaving France and made fishbait of the poor bastards, and the weather turned against us—Jesus H. *Christ*, you wouldn't believe it could get that cold!"

"And Tecumseh picking that time," Houston said, "while you were all off up north, to set the tribes on the war path. I remember that."

"Yep. So we had to fight our way through the Indians just to get back home. What there was left of us," Crockett said bitterly.

Houston said, "But that was eighteen-twelve, Davy. They got the army built back up now, nearly to strength."

"They got a bunch of men carrying weepons. Takes more than that to make an army. Them white-trash boys jine up to get away from home, soljering looks easier than plowing and the uniform's good to impress the girls, but they never seen no real fighting. 'Cept now and then marching off with Andy Jackson to burn out some village of peaceful Creeks, sure as hell never faced British reg'lars. Neither have you, either of you."

"True," I said. "The Emperor never takes me on campaign." For which God, if He exists, be thanked on bended knee.

"It ain't like nothing you ever seen." Crockett shuddered. "The way they come on, all in step, not making a sound, it's *skeery* is what it is. And that was just Packenham's men in Canada, not even top regiments. Wellington's boys are supposed to be even better. Can we stop 'em? Damn if I know."

He fell silent, his face morose. Houston reached for the jug. "Don't pay Davy any mind," he said. "It'll be all right."

A few days later Fort St. Philippe fell.

"Never seen nothing like it," Colonel Crockett told the Emperor and the others, at the hastily-convened council that followed. "They bombarded that place steady, all night and all day and all the next night too. Must of throwed in every mortar shell in the Royal Navy. Then, the second morning they stopped shelling, and here come the marines out of the woods and rushed the fort. Didn't take long, there weren't no real defense left. Me and Sam watched the whole thing from across the river."

"Thank you for the report, Colonel." The Emperor's shoulders sagged. "This is terrible. The river is now open, almost all the way to the city. Latour, can we put in more batteries downstream?

"No time, my Emperor. Moving and emplacing guns in that terrain—" General Latour shook his head. "Besides, we have concentrated all our available artillery at English Turn, on your Majesty's orders. We would have to take away—"

"No, no, you are right. We must not weaken the

defenses there. Well." The Emperor sighed. "At least now there is no doubt where they will come."

"Beg the Emperor's pardon, I'm not so sure." Crockett was looking thoughtful. "They're on the river, all right, but not all of them. Not nigh as many ships as we seen when they first showed up. And no telling where the others are, now they got Lafitte's boys bottled up in the Barataria."

"Holding back a reserve," Jackson said, snorting. "Any fool can see that, by the Almighty!"

"Maybe," Crockett said. "Guess we'll know the answers soon enough."

But the British were slow in coming. Not an easy business, of course, working their way against that current and negotiating the tricky channel; apparently there were several groundings. Still, it did seem they were taking their time.

Christmas came, and was duly celebrated by the French and Spanish Catholics of the city, though ignored or scorned by the Protestant Americans. The Emperor attended mass at the great church, as usual concealing his personal agnosticism beneath a cloak of public piety.

All other days, he rode down to the site of the defensive works at the great river bend called English Turn. There was a fairly good road along the levee, so he went by carriage; and, for unclear reasons, I was required to go along. There was nothing much to see but a lot of earthworks along the river, and black and white men laboring alike to reinforce them with sandbags, while others wrestled guns into position. I stood by and shivered in the chilly wind—it was a cold winter for New Orleans—while the Emperor bustled about, talking with officers and men, now and then personally supervising the placement of a cannon. The years seemed to drop from him at such times; he was in his element. For myself I was happier when we returned to the palace, where I could be in mine.

Thus it was that I was with the Emperor the day it all came down.

It was a dank and chilly morning, three days before year's end. A heavy gray fog had moved in off Lake Borgne during the previous evening, and now hung above the river and the eastern swamps, and the plantation fields between, as we rolled southward along the river road. Sitting up on the seat next to the driver, I wrapped a blanket about myself and cursed through my chattering teeth. What a ghastly day to go out, but the Emperor was quite insistent. Nelson's ships had been sighted on the river the previous afternoon, only a few miles south of English Turn; clearly the time was almost at hand.

Suddenly a horseman appeared through the fog up ahead, riding hard toward us. Seeing us, he took off his hat and began waving it frantically up and down.

The driver and I looked at each other. I shrugged and, after a moment, the driver pulled the horses to a stop.

Almost immediately a window opened beneath us and the Emperor's voice came up to us, demanding to know why we were stopping. But by that time the rider was upon us; a slender handsome young man, dressed, I saw now, in the bright uniform of an ensign in the Louisiana Hussars.

"Please," he gasped, "sir—uh, y'r Majesty—"

"Never mind," the Emperor said impatiently. "What do you want, lad?"

The boy—he really was not much more—took a deep breath and gathered himself visibly. "I have to report, your Majesty," he said with strained formality, "that the enemy are attacking our position in strength."

The Emperor's head appeared through the carriage window. "What?" he cried, and then paused, hearing, now that the horses' hooves were silent, the distant rattle and pop of musket fire from somewhere on down the river.

"But the guns," he said then, staring at the horseman. "I hear neither our artillery nor the ships' guns!"

The lad shook his head. "Not the ships, sir. They came in from the east—looks like they crossed Lake Borgne yesterday, in the fog, and moved up through the bayous, and then early this morning they came up out of the swamp and across the plantation fields—one of Colonel Crockett's scouts spotted them, but, uh, well, General Jackson didn't believe him at first—" He stopped, looking appalled at his own indiscretion. "Uh, that is to say—"

The Emperor said, "Name of God! They attacked from the landward side?"

"Yes, sir." The ensign nodded. "Where our defenses were weakest, and of course all the big guns are emplaced to cover the river—"

"The English," the Emperor said, "do they have artillery?"

"Don't know, your Majesty. Haven't brought them into play yet, if they do. Plenty of infantry, though. Must be a thousand, maybe two thousand, hard to tell in this fog. They just keep coming." The ensign's eyes were blinking rapidly. "General Jackson sent me to warn you—"

"Yes, yes." The carriage door opened; the Emperor began clambering down, not waiting for me to attend him. Before I could get down from the seat, he was already standing in the road, snapping his fingers at the young officer. "Your horse," he said. "Give me your horse."

"Sir? Your Majesty?" The ensign looked blank, but then he must have seen the Emperor's expression more clearly. "Yes, sir," he said hastily, and swung down. "Uh, shall I—"

"You shall get out of my way." The Emperor was already hauling himself into the saddle, clumsily and with obvious pain. "Driver, follow me. Let the ensign ride with you."

Swinging the horse about, digging his dress boot heels

into its flanks, the Emperor disappeared at a gallop into the fog, toward the growing noise of battle. After a moment the driver raised his eyebrows and put the team in motion again, while the young ensign scrambled aboard and pulled himself up beside us.

Already we could see the flashes of gunfire through the mist ahead, and now louder explosions came rolling up the road to meet us: cannon getting into the action at last. I looked inquiringly at the young hussar, but he shook his head. "No idea," he said hoarsely. "No telling whose—"

Then there was a blast like all the thunder in the world, and another right on its heels, and his face went even paler. "Oh, my God," he whispered. "Warships firing broadsides. The bastards are hitting us from the river too."

It hardly required a formal military education to see the implications: the defenders caught between advancing British infantry in one direction and the fire of the ships' guns raking them from the other.

The ensign was climbing down now. "You better wait here," he called up to the driver.

The driver pulled the carriage to a stop, while the ensign dropped to the ground, just as the first soldiers appeared through the fog coming the other way. Infantry, wearing the blue uniforms of the Empire, and running very hard. . . .

Perched up on top of the carriage, I had a fine view of the rout. They ran past us on either side, hardly a man even seeming to notice us except as an obstacle; their eyes were enormous in their smoke-blackened faces and their mouths mostly hung open. A few clutched at bloody wounds.

Horsemen appeared now, most of them in flight as well, a few—officers, I supposed—evidently trying, without success, to stop the retreat. Horse and foot, the hurrying tide jammed the road and spread out over the open fields to our left, without order or discipline but with a splendid unity of direction: away from the British, toward the city and safety, while behind them the guns still bellowed and muskets and rifles cracked.

Our hussar ensign stood in the middle of the road, waving his sword, shouting at the fleeing men, ordering them to turn back, till he tripped—or was tripped—and went down and disappeared under all those running feet. I closed my eyes for a moment in revulsion.

When I opened them I saw that the driver was pointing. "Look," he said, and after a moment I saw them, the Emperor and General Jackson, charging their horses this way and that amid the hurrying throng, slowly being forced back along the road by weight of numbers. Jackson was slashing this way and that with his sword, without apparent effect; the Emperor, who rarely wore side arms, was in any case having to use both hands to control the hussar's frightened horse.

And quite soon they went past us too, Jackson on the left—he turned and gave me a furious look as he passed, God knows why—and the Emperor on the right. The Emperor did not even glance our way. His face was terrible to see.

Finally they were all past, leaving us alone on the levee-top road, though off across the open ground a few stragglers still picked their way through the sugar-cane trash. And, a few minutes later, a fresh batch of men came out of the fog, moving less hurriedly and in a far more orderly manner. Even in the misty light, their red coats looked very fine.

The driver's nerve broke, then; without a word he scrambled down from the seat and took off up the road, after the departing Imperial troops. Left alone, I took the reins and quieted the restive horses, and a few minutes later found myself surrounded by grinning red-coated infantrymen. "Wot's the matter, then, Uncle?" one called up to me. "Run off and leave you, did they?"

Another cried, "Look, boys! Burn my arse if this ain't Boney's carriage! Look here, on the doors!"

They all gathered around, staring and chattering; then all fell silent as an elegantly uniformed man came riding up on a horse. "You men!" he called. "Who gave the order to break formation?" Then, seeing the carriage, "Damme!"

He looked at me. "Emperor's driver, are you?"

"Merely a manservant," I told him. "Sir."

"Major Grigsby, 7th Fusiliers." He gave a mocking little half-salute. "Can you drive this thing, then, my man?"

"After a fashion."

"Then," he said, "be so good as to do so, until you reach a point where you can turn off this road, which you are now blocking, and which we need for the guns." He turned. "Sergeant, detail four men to escort this vehicle, and guard it against the light-fingered. The commander will enjoy this, I should think."

A beefy-faced man said, "Sir, what about the nigger?"

"Guard him, too. The commander may want to question him." He turned his horse. "The rest of you, back in formation and resume your advance. Keep the damned rascals on the run."

When they were gone one of my guards gave me a gap-toothed grin. "You 'eard the Major," he told me. "No tricks, now, and look smart. You're going to meet the Dook."

Sir Arthur Wellesley, First Duke of Wellington, was a tall, lean, imposing man with a long-nosed aristocratic face that would not have looked out of place on a Roman statue. By the time he got around to me it was late in the evening, and he must have put in a very long hard day indeed, yet he showed no signs of fatigue. Or much else; I had the impression of a man who, in Sam Houston's phrase, played his cards close to his vest.

Our interview was quite short; it did not take long for him to realize that I was merely a household servant, who knew nothing of the Emperor's military plans and had never overheard anything of possible value—or who, at any rate, was never going to admit otherwise.

"I have no idea," he said at last, "whether you are as stupid as you pretend, or very clever indeed. Some officers, in my position, would issue instructions to see if a sound whipping would improve your memory. But no fear." He allowed himself a very slight smile. "It hardly matters. The lines of battle, from this point forward, are inevitable."

He paced back and forth a bit, looking at me. It was dark outside and the interior of the tent was lit by a single candle.

"So," he said, "what shall I do with you? Strictly speaking, you are not a prisoner of war, since you are not a soldier or even a free man . . . would you like to be?" He raised an eyebrow. "My orders are to free any slaves who wish to join our forces."

"I would like to be free," I told him. "I have, however, no wish to join your forces or any others."

"Ah. Want to be your own man, eh? A worthy ambition, by God." He actually chuckled, very softly and very briefly. "Well, for the moment, I think you had best remain with us. You have seen quite a lot, I'm sure, whilst waiting about."

That was true; I had had nothing to but watch, while men and guns came ashore from the transports and were formed up in order and sent marching northward along the river road. It had been an impressive sight, and not an encouraging one from the Imperial viewpoint.

"You might," Wellington added, "be tempted to run back to your master. I'm sure he'd be interested in what you could tell him. Better to keep you out of temptation's way."

And so I spent the next two days as a prisoner who was not quite a prisoner. The distinction was largely ignored by the soldiers, who made me do various menial tasks about the camp, and occasionally kicked me for no particular reason.

It was from the British side, then, that I watched the final Battle of New Orleans. Not being a soldier, I could make little sense of what I saw—not that I could see much anyway, from where I stood near a battery of unreasonably loud cannon.

But I could see that the outcome was not much in doubt. The British obviously had an overpowering superiority in artillery—the defenders having lost so many guns at English Turn, and the invaders having brought plenty of their own; a child could have seen the discrepancy at a glance, once the battle was joined. Wellington's gunners—joined by Nelson's seamen, who had brought heavy ships' cannon ashore to reinforce the army—turned a devastating storm of shot on the Imperial lines, answered only by weak and scattered fire. Even standing to the rear, I was deafened and well-nigh blinded by the steady and excruciating roar, and my bowels felt very loose; I cannot imagine what it must have been like for those who were its targets. I had had no idea that war was such a noisy and messy business. It looked so much neater in the paintings and engravings.

Then Wellington's infantry advanced in their implacable ranks, and after that I lost any real grasp of what was going on. I could see the battle only as a distant indistinct dark line—one that soon began to grow even more distant, moving first raggedly and slowly, then with much greater speed, to the north, in the direction of the city.

"Buggers are running again," one of my guards observed. "That's it, then. Be a jolly old time tonight in Noo Orleens."

At some point, late in the afternoon, my guards simply disappeared. Heading for the city, no doubt, not wanting to miss out on the looting and general sport.

After an irresolute pause, I set off in that direction myself, walking along the river road. No one paid me any mind; everyone was hurrying toward the city. Already plumes of smoke had begun to appear above the rooftops, indicating that this was going to be a long night.

Then suddenly there was a stir of activity up ahead and I saw the Duke of Wellington sitting on his horse by the roadside, taking reports from dispatch riders and conferring with some officers. I started to detour around the scene, only to be stopped short by Wellington's voice: "You there! The Emperor's servant!"

I turned and walked back and looked up at the Duke. "Well," he said, "your master has lost the hand. And, I believe, the game."

"Yes, sir," I said, blank-faced.

"He seems to have given us the slip," Wellington said. "Would you know anything about that? Ever hear anything to suggest what plans your Emperor might have made, for a contingency such as this?"

"No, sir. I do not believe," I said truthfully, "he ever seriously envisioned such an event."

"Ah, yes. Quite." A quick nod. "Well, well, no matter." To an officer at his side he added, "Boney's done for, no matter where he's gone. Now we hold New Orleans, the Empire can be strangled at our pleasure."

"And then," the officer said, "perhaps we shall see about the damned Yankees and their so-called United States of America."

"Very possibly." The Duke shook his head. "Please God, not until after I have relinquished command to some younger man. I grow tired. I wish to go home."

To me, then: "Go your way, then. You are free—at least insofar as His Britannic Majesty's forces are concerned. If you ever do see your master again, thank him for the carriage. I intend to ride in it, when I enter his city tomorrow."

"On New Year's Day," another officer murmured.

"Why, yes. So it will be," the Duke said, sounding surprised. "Do you know, I had forgotten."

It was dark by the time I made my way into the city. It was a dangerous time to walk the streets; British soldiers were everywhere, helping themselves to whatever struck their fancy—including any women so foolish, or adventurous, as to be caught out-of-doors. From every direction came the sounds of breaking glass, male shouts and female screams, and the odd gunshot.

A hand grabbed my arm and jerked me into the mouth of a dark alley; another hand clamped itself over my mouth. A familiar voice hissed in my ear, "Quiet, now, Albert!"

Released, I turned and said, "It's all right. There's no one nearby."

"Good," Houston said, and Crockett grunted agreement. "Where you been?"

"You wouldn't believe me," I said, "What happened? Today, I mean?"

"Just like I was afeared," Crockett said. "Our boys broke. Stood their ground pretty good at first, but then they seen them redcoats coming on and on, never missing a step, never making a sound, sun shining off them bayonets, it was too much."

"The Tennessee militia broke first," Houston added. "And then the Kentuckians, on the left. But then everybody was taking off. Nearly, anyway. The ones who didn't mostly got bayonetted or captured, I guess."

"Jackson's dead," Crockett said with a certain satisfaction. "Tried to stop the rout, started hitting out with that God-damned sword of his, and somebody shot him right out of his saddle."

I said, "They say the Emperor has disappeared."

"He commandeered the St. Louis steamboat," Houston told me. "Guess that's where he's bound."

"Will you be joining him?" I asked. "If you can escape from the city?"

"No." Crockett spat. "Had enough of soljering. Me and Sam figure to head out west. Trap furs or something."

"Want to come along?" Houston grinned. "See the wild frontier."

"Thank you," I said, "but I think not. I believe I know where I can find employment. Once order has been restored, Madame Letitia's establishment should find itself doing a great deal of business. I'm sure she will need a good pianoforte player."

"Then so long." Crockett slapped me on the back. "And good luck."

"To you as well," I said, meaning it; though I had full faith in their ability to survive and escape, if any men alive could do it. "*Bonne chance,*" I added, as they moved away down the alley.

"Yeah," Houston's voice drifted back through the darkness; and then, with a sardonic chuckle: "*Vive l'Empereur. . . .*"